THE

LAST

GOOD

WAR

A Novel

Paul Wonnacott

For

Andrew
Abby
Eli
Joey
Charlie

May they live in a world without war
— good or bad

In September 1945, as bejeweled dancers swirled at one of London's first postwar high society balls, a gentleman murmured contentedly,

"This is what we fought the war for."

A droll lady, gesturing to the dancers, responded,

"Oh, do you mean they are all Poles?"

George F. Will

THE LAST GOOD WAR

1

Enigma

26 January, 1929. 17:47. Post Office Central, Warsaw.

Maczek had never considered himself anything but a simple postal clerk. He had never met a senior military officer. Certainly never a senior German officer, and certainly never one so flustered and out of breath.

"I'm the military attaché of the German Republic," said Streicher, sucking in his stomach, standing on his toes and stretching to make himself look taller than his pudgy five foot, five inches. "I'm here for a package which came in today, addressed to the embassy. This wide." He held out his hands, about two feet apart.

Strange. Most diplomatic mail, Maczek knew, was carried by courier; it never got near a post office. What could possibly be so important? He looked impassively at the portly but authoritarian figure dressed in the impeccable uniform of — what was he, a major or colonel? This, he thought, is the time to play strictly by the book.

"Sorry, sir, but deliveries must be made directly to the address on the label, or picked up by authorized personnel."

Col. Streicher slid his identification card through the wicket.

"Sorry, sir," said Maczek, checking his list. "Only two people are authorized to pick up mail from the embassy's postal box — Schultz and Nagel."

"But *they're* only *clerks*," Streicher huffed. "*I'm* their *boss.*"

"I'm certain you are, sir. But you can understand. We can't release mail without the signature of one of them." Maczek continued deferentially; the German's temper was rising, and Maczek wanted to avoid an outburst. "We can't allow even a very senior person, such as you, sir, to pick up mail that may be intended for the ambassador."

"I insist on seeing your supervisor.... And I need to use a phone."

"Of course, sir," said Maczek, pointing to a phone in the corner and disappearing into the back room. Maczek and his supervisor, Klimecki, soon found the package. With it were a few letters.

The package was heavy, wrapped in brown paper, sealed with glue and twine. Klimecki shook it gingerly; it didn't rattle. Carrying it carefully, he retreated to his office. Through the open door, Maczek saw him cross the room to his phone and turn the crank.

As Maczek trailed his boss back into the main lobby, Streicher was berating a young man. Maczek recognized him as one of the two clerks authorized to pick up the mail. Maczek knew enough German to understand the clerk's meek reply: he had already been on his way to the post office, for the regular, final pickup of the day, just before closing.

As he spotted the two Poles, Streicher quickly faded into the background, nodding to his clerk, who approached the wicket. Maczek handed over the letters, asking the German to sign.

When he saw only the thin letters, Streicher was suddenly back at the wicket, loudly insisting that the Poles produce the package.

Klimecki took over from Maczek. "I'm sorry sir, but it's not here."

"It *must* be. It was on the train that arrived in Warsaw at 2:00 p.m."

"That's possible sir, but it still isn't here. Sometimes packages are handled separately from letters; they're sorted later."

"You mean it may be in your back room, among the unsorted mail?"

"Perhaps, sir, or it could still be at the train station."

"Then I insist you look for it among your unsorted mail."

"Sorry sir, but we can't do that. It's already past closing time."

"But I insist." The pink in Streicher's face was turning to red; he was clearly struggling, with only partial success, not to shout at the cool, unhelpful clerk. "You want a diplomatic incident? I'll give it to you. *I'm* a friend of the postmaster general."

"Very well, sir, we'll see if we can find it." Klimecki tried to suppress a grin; the postmaster general had died eight months ago, and his replacement had not yet been chosen. As Streicher's anger rose, Klimecki became more certain that he had made the right decision, to hold the package and call Polish military intelligence. He and Maczek retreated to the back room, where they broke out a new deck of cards and Maczek dealt. Klimecki sat impassively, hiding his joy at the three aces in the corner of his hand. Perhaps this would indeed be his lucky day.

The two began to speculate casually on what might be inside the wrapper. Secret war plans? Unlikely. New electronic equipment to intercept Polish radio communications? A new set of burglar tools, to break into government offices? Anything like that, and intelligence should know.

After thirty minutes, Klimecki returned to inform the Germans: After a diligent search, they could assure the Colonel that they simply did not have the package. Undoubtedly it would arrive Monday. Would the Colonel like to have it sent by special messenger to his embassy?

As Streicher stormed out the front door, intelligence officers were already coming in through the rear. The package was indeed important. In it was a coding machine, with ENIGMA stenciled on its cover. Working nonstop from Saturday evening until the early hours of Monday, they carefully disassembled it, taking numerous pictures of the three rotors at the top, and making detailed notes. Then they meticulously reassembled and resealed it, exactly the way it had come. A pristine package, ready for delivery on Monday.

8 November, 1931. The *Grand Hotel*. Verviers, Belgium.
Hans Thilo Schmidt sat on the side of his bed. Beads of sweat were forming on his brow, in spite of the chill in the room. He snuggled his briefcase close to his hip, occasionally reaching inside to reassure himself that the manuals were still there.

He could still go back. But it would have to be within the next fifteen minutes. Then it would be too late. He would be in the clutches of the Deuxième Bureau for life. Or death.

His panic gave way to anger. That stupid woman. He was hopelessly in love with her. But it wasn't just her; he simply loved women. Why couldn't she realize, even a married man must have his flirtations, his little games? He could understand her shock, the first time she stumbled across him with the maid. But why did she insist on such a quick succession of maids, each uglier than the last? He had patiently tried to explain. Her little scheme wouldn't work; the uglier the maids, the more eagerly they fell into his arms.

Finally, her nagging had driven him to look elsewhere, to his cozy little nest in Berlin. But that was expensive. How was he supposed to afford it on his paltry salary at the Cipher Office? If only his father had been something more than that dull, pathetic professor of history. If only his father had restored the family fortune. If only....

It came. Three knocks on his door; then four. He rose, shuffled into the bathroom, and splashed water on his face. He was dismayed by his bloodshot eyes. If only he hadn't had quite so much to drink last night. But they wouldn't get the better of him. He'd drive a hard bargain. What he was offering—pure gold.

He quickly dried his face, slapping it three times—hard—and stepped purposefully from his room. He was quickly up the stairs to the third floor, cautiously opening the door and glancing into the hall. Nobody. Good. Two doors down to Room 34. He gently knocked three times. The door slowly opened.

Gustave Bertrand was ecstatic. Rudolphe Lemoine of the Deuxième Bureau had a promising contact. A mid-level manager in the Cipher Office, no less. Perhaps he would enable them to listen in on communications between Berlin and the German armed forces.

But, said Lemoine, they had to be careful. Schmidt could possibly be an *agent provocateur*, sent by Berlin to lead them into a trap. More likely, he was puffing up his importance; he might have very little to offer. But it was a risk worth taking.

As Schmidt entered the room, he was obviously nervous. He stumbled over the edge of the carpet; he fidgeted with his collar; he kept clearing his throat. Bertrand tried hard not to stare. He had never seen a real, flesh-and-blood traitor before; his work with French intelligence had been confined to a detailed study of foreign codes. Lemoine, in contrast, was an old hand, and tried two small jokes to put Schmidt at ease. No success. Schmidt sat down, all business.

"I offer these samples to overcome your skepticism, to prove that I have access to information of the utmost importance," he said, drawing three manuals from the briefcase. "As agreed, you will make an offer as to what they are worth."

Schmidt placed the manuals on the coffee table. Bertrand could scarcely believe his eyes. They gave the detailed operating procedures for the new Enigma machine. He struggled not to show his pleasure; he didn't want the price to go through the roof.

"This, I should emphasize, is just a sample," Schmidt continued. "I also have access to the current settings of the Enigma—our coding machine. And I will be able to obtain future settings. Provided, of course, that we can come to a satisfactory financial arrangement."

There was a hush, broken only by the faint sounds of Bertrand turning the pages. Schmidt seemed scarcely to be breathing. After ten minutes, Lemoine began to put on his show of *sangfroid*. He leaned over the coffee table, glancing through a magazine to find the newest fashions in bathing suits. He stared out the window at the tennis game below. Shortly thereafter, Bertrand looked up.

"Yes, these may be of interest to us. Perhaps M. Lemoine and I could have a moment or two together." He nodded toward the bathroom door.

The two Frenchmen retreated to the bathroom, leaving the door open so they could block Schmidt's escape if he suddenly changed his mind and tried to bolt. They turned on the taps to hide the sound of their voices.

"This is beyond my wildest dreams," Bertrand began. "If he can provide the settings, we may have an open window on German plans."

"How much should we offer?"

"Something big. Perhaps as much as 5,000 marks."

Bertrand was concerned that he might have trouble with such a large figure; it was coming out of Lemoine's budget. Lemoine surprised him, dropping his pretense that he had not a care in the world. "We've got this fish on the line. Let's reel him in. How about 10,000?" More than a year's salary.

"Fine. Excellent."

"The question is, do we give it to him outright, or do we let him have the satisfaction of bargaining us up?"

"That's your department."

They returned, smiling.

Lemoine got right to the point. "We are willing to make a very generous offer for your material, say 5,000 marks... with more to come for future information."

Schmidt paused. Bertrand was uncertain whether he was dissatisfied with the 5,000 marks, or whether he was thinking how he might provide a continuing flow of information. Schmidt scowled. Bertrand could feel the tension rise; he blurted out:

"We might do even better. We might get authorization for 10,000 marks."

"*Might* get authorization?" Schmidt retorted. "You were supposed to come with a serious, firm offer." He leaned forward, pressing his hands down on the armrests; he was about to rise.

"I can authorize that figure," Lemoine said smoothly. "In fact, I can pay that amount now, in cash. With another 10,000 when you provide the current settings."

Schmidt smiled and held out his hand to Lemoine. They shook; they had a deal. Lemoine thereupon reached in his briefcase, pulled out a stack of bills, and began to count out 10,000 marks. Bertrand retired to the bedroom to photograph the manuals.

He was glad that Lemoine had sealed the deal. If it had been him, he might have detoured to the bathroom to wash his hand. Lemoine was less squeamish; it was all in a day's work.

A very good day's work. Now they had their hooks into Schmidt. They would play him like a puppet.

Bertrand was overjoyed. Then came months of frustration.

French cryptographers saw little value in the manuals, which explained how to encipher a message, not how to read one. British intelligence gave a similar negative response. Even with the manuals, the Enigma machine simply couldn't be broken.

He came back for another round with his French superiors. Lemoine drew him aside with a word of caution. Schmidt was indeed a gold mine. But in more ways than one. The Deuxième Bureau wanted to exploit his other contacts; his brother was a general with access to German military plans. This source was too valuable to risk; codebreaking was a sideshow.

In frustration, Bertrand turned to his last hope. He got permission to share Schmidt's information with Poland.

He was off to Warsaw, to offer his wares to young mathematicians at the Cipher Bureau — Marian Rejewski and Henryk Zygalski. They were delighted.

The trouble was, they were missing a critical piece of the puzzle. They had the manuals, telling how Enigma was used to encode a message. Schmidt also had provided the rotor settings for several months. They had their own extensive library of intercepted, undeciphered German messages. They knew the general design of the Enigma, from the package opened at the Warsaw Post Office. Indeed, they had a complete early version of the machine, which they had had the foresight to buy when it was still available on the commercial market. But in the German military version, the internal wiring of the rotors was different.

Rejewski had been working on a mathematical model of the Enigma. He retired to his office with the undeciphered messages, the wheel settings, and the manuals. Within a brief span of three months, he figured out the internal wiring of the Enigma's three wheels.

With the settings provided by Schmidt, they could now read some German communications. Most were deadly dull — instructions on troop movements, quartermaster complaints, bookkeeping details, and seemingly endless propaganda screeds for the motivation of the troops. But they nevertheless provided a picture of the stirring, rising giant of the German military under the aggressive and determined new Führer.

They were fascinated by one intercept — a very short one:

FROM: HIMMLER, SS HEADQUARTERS
TO: ALL AIRPORTS
30 JUNE, 1934
SECRET

ERNST RÖHM ABLIEFERN TOT ODER LEBEND.

(ERNST RÖHM TO BE DELIVERED DEAD OR ALIVE.)

The brief message gave only a faint hint of the bloody act to follow—the "Night of the Long Knives." The leader of the Brownshirts—street brawlers who had terrorized Hitler's opponents during his rise to power—was about to be eliminated. Röhm wanted a second revolution, aimed at putting "socialism" into National Socialism and crushing the power of right-wing industrialists and generals. He wanted his Brownshirts to become a "People's Army," replacing the regular army. But, for his coming wars, Hitler needed a hardened, disciplined army, not a rabble. Röhm—the only associate close enough for Hitler to call by the familiar du—was dragged from his bed and shot, together with dozens of his comrades.

As the Deuxième Bureau milked Schmidt for other, unrelated secrets, information on Enigma dried up. Decryptions of messages became sporadic. But then, in 1936, Hitler's troops marched into the Rhineland, showing just how eager the Führer was to upset the order established by the Treaty of Versailles. The Polish codebreaking operation moved into high gear; they would need more people.

2

Already Surrounded

May you live
in interesting times.
Chinese Curse

1 September, 1939. 05:20. With the Seventh Cavalry, west of Poznan, Poland.

It began on a Friday morning, as the warmth of summer was giving way to the first frost of fall.

Lieutenant Kazimierz Jankowski touched his spur to the flank of Tiber, enough to make the stallion break into a gallop toward the mist hanging over the lowest, lushest patch of meadow. The mist was unusual, now that the sharp chill of autumn was in the air. As the glow in the east became brighter, Tiber's head shaded from black to charcoal to chestnut. Jankowski loved to ride at dawn. He loved this time of year; the cold, crisp air urged him and his horse onward. He tried not to think of the harsh Polish winter to come. He tried even harder not to think of the grim events of the past week, with Poland feverishly mobilizing in the face of German threats. Better to think of the pleasant things in life. Anna. The soft touch of his new bride.

Tiber was now in his favorite spot, and Kaz began to lead his horse through the new steps being prepared for President Moscicki's visit. First a few prancing steps to the left, then to the right. Another touch of the spur, and Tiber reared up. He held that awkward position for four long seconds, and then, responding to quick jabs of the spur, hopped twice on his hind legs before coming down with four hooves on the turf. Not bad, but it still needed work. The Colonel had observed this unusual maneuver in his recent visit to the Spanish Riding School in Vienna and was eager to show it off to the President. It would have to be done just right. Kaz began the sidestep again. Good. His stallion was getting just the right spring in his step.

Then, as he began a slow prancing turn, the stallion abruptly reared. Startled, Kaz slipped back over the saddle; he instinctively slid his toes out of the stirrups as he fell heavily to earth. His back stabbed with pain... or maybe that was just humiliation. For a cavalry officer to lose his mount was unthinkable. As he lay there, momentarily stunned, he glanced over his brow to see Tiber galloping toward the stables.

Then he realized why. First came a slight whine, scarcely audible over the twittering songbirds, then quickly becoming louder. Between the billowing clouds, a dark, gull-winged plane was in a steep dive. Just as its scream became unbearable, it dropped a large bomb, flanked by four much smaller bombs. The large bomb struck the center of the main barracks; a jumble of splinters and smoke erupted.

As the dawn's sun glinted on the side of the plane, Jankowski could see the dark cross and swastika of Hitler's air force.

World War II had begun.

Kaz headed toward the burning buildings, alternately hopping and limping, occasionally pausing to rub his left leg, trying to work out the numbness. Soon, he was inside the camp. Soldiers were wandering about, dazed. Half a dozen men lay near the flagpole. A medic bent over one, cutting away the bloodstained clothing to expose a massive abdominal wound. Slightly beyond, Lt. Tomczak was applying a tourniquet, struggling to stem the gush of blood from the leg of an ashen-faced sergeant. Still further on, another man was obviously in pain; he kept raising his left leg, then letting it flop to the ground, perhaps a signal that he was still alive.

Kaz was about to go to the medic's aid when he stood up; his man was gone. He didn't wait to fold the dead man's guts back into his body; he quickly moved on to the man with the flopping leg. Kaz went over to Lt. Janusz Tomczak.

"There are more wounded?"

"A few, over by the mess hall." Jan nodded in the general direction. "But you can't be of much assistance. Several medics are already there."

Kaz surveyed the compound, and was astonished how few men he saw. "This is all?... It's *all*? The others were all killed?"

"No, no." Jan was struggling with the tourniquet. "We were lucky." He half smiled—it was so out of place to talk of good fortune as blood oozed between his fingers. "We were forming up for morning exercises when we got the news: Germans were invading. Almost everybody pulled out before the bomber attack."

A second medic arrived, relieving Jan, and soon stopped the sergeant's bleeding. He retrieved a curved needle, tweezers, and thread from his medical bag. As he squinted through his glasses to thread the needle, he reminded Kaz of his grandmother. Methodically, and without expression, he began to sew up the sergeant's leg.

"Pulled out?" Kaz asked. "Where?"

Jan was now standing and looking directly at his friend. "The bluff, two kilometers north. With a commanding view of the valley. A likely route for a German advance."

Kaz glanced around. "So we're in charge here?"

"That's right." Jan raised the pitch of his voice and dragged out the word "right," as if to say: we'd better get used to the responsibility, and quickly. "We should get the able-bodied survivors together, to provide reinforcements."

"They took the machine guns?"

"Just the light, hand-held ones."

The heavy machine guns were still in the armory.

They would be needed. Even though they were too heavy for cavalrymen to carry on horseback, that wouldn't matter; there weren't enough surviving horses anyhow, and the reinforcements would have to proceed on foot. While Jan began to round up the able-bodied survivors, Kaz took half a dozen men to the armory.

Its door was locked; they started to beat it with their rifle butts.

"'Ey, you can't do that." Kaz looked around to see the quartermaster sergeant. "That's army property. Major Kulerski has to sign for weapons."

"There's a war on, sergeant. Haven't you noticed? Give me the key."

"Can't without a proper signature, er,... sir." The sergeant pointed his rifle at Kaz and slid the bolt.

Kaz stared him in the eye for five seconds, and then decided he wasn't going to get the key. He turned his back on the sergeant, and ordered his men: "Keep at it. Harder."

The men looked at the sergeant's rifle and paused. Kaz urged them on.

"Knock the door down. We need weapons. Your lives will depend on them."

The sergeant seemed perplexed, and slowly let his rifle sag toward the ground. The men took up their task with enthusiasm, soon breaking through the door.

Within an hour and a half, Kaz, Jan, and two dozen men were overlooking the valley, armed with four heavy machine guns and two mortars drawn by horses over the rocky, uneven terrain.

They had picked the wrong bluff. With his binoculars, Kaz could see the cavalry lined up half way down the next hill, to the east, well hidden from the valley by trees, waiting for an opportunity to charge.

He turned to the west and his heart sank; twenty German tanks were moving swiftly along the valley floor. There wasn't much the cavalry would be able to do about them. It would be up to Kaz and his men to do what little they could. The tank commanders had their heads out the hatches, and infantry were exposed as they rode on the tops of the tanks, behind the turrets.

"The sniper rifles," Kaz snapped his fingers. A private smartly handed one rifle to Kaz and the other to Sergeant Witos; they were the two best shots.

"The closest tank commander is yours," Kaz told Witos. "Fire when ready."

Witos took a deep breath. So did Kaz, aiming for the second commander, whose goggles were shoved up over the top of his head. Through the scope, Kaz could see his face clearly—the picture of a Prussian officer: firm chin, broad forehead, and just a small wisp of blond hair visible below his helmet.

Witos fired. It was a long shot, but lucky; the first German commander collapsed into his tank. Kaz squeezed his trigger. The second commander jerked his hand up to his left cheek. Through his scope, Kaz could see a flash of anger cross his face before he ducked into his tank, slamming the hatch behind him.

Machine-gun bullets were now rattling off the tanks, like heavy, sporadic hail. Infantrymen scrambled off, crouching behind the tanks, which had swung their turrets to the right and were firing at the bluffs. But the gunners were confused, unable to locate Kaz and his company.

Jan called a ceasefire. He had a better target; he nudged Kaz and pointed to the left. A large enemy procession was approaching: trucks, soldiers on motorcycles, and horses drawing light artillery. The column was still some distance away; Kaz and Jan had time to plan an attack.

"This time, let's set things up for our cavalry," Kaz suggested. "Hold our fire until the column is past us, and almost to the hill where the cavalry is hidden."

"We'll start firing, and throw the Germans into confusion just as the cavalry charges?"

Kaz nodded. "Aim first at the vanguard. Then work our way down the column; we don't want to hit our cavalry as they charge."

Jan disappeared with a semaphore signalman; he would contact Maj. Kulerski in command of the cavalry on the next bluff. He was back in a few minutes.

"Fine. Kulerski says we have the best view to plan the attack. Twenty seconds before we open fire, we should signal him; they'll start the cavalry charge."

This time, Kaz suggested he go with the signalman; he would pick the time to attack. He surprised himself. He wanted Jan to stay behind to command the machine gunners. He was quite prepared to shoot German soldiers, but didn't much like the idea of slaughtering horses.

Kaz selected a small rise that gave him a panoramic view of the approaching battle, plus a clear line of sight to the Polish cavalry and to Jan.

He spoke to the signalman. The semaphore flags snapped smartly. Immediately, the cavalry charged down the hill. Kaz slowly counted to twenty, then waved to Jan. The heavy machine guns erupted. Soon, the cavalry were to the edge of the German column, firing with submachine guns, rifles, and, the officers, with pistols. Jan's men were now directing their fire further back, toward the center and rear of the column. They were indeed creating confusion. A truck blew up; then two others.

With his sixth sense, Kaz felt something was wrong. He looked to the left, back along the German line of advance. A second group of German tanks was approaching, only a few minutes away. Kaz had to warn the cavalry.

But how? Nobody had a flare gun. They might try to fire the mortars into the melee of German infantry and Polish cavalry, risking casualties to their comrades to get their attention. But the range was too great. One of the men began swearing; in their haste, they had brought practice smoke rounds for the mortars—used in training—not live, explosive shells.

All the better, said Kaz; the cavalry might actually see them. The mortars began to lay down wisps of smoke along the valley floor. From the distance, they reminded Kaz of the dark puffs which shot up when, as a child, he and his younger brother made a game of stepping on overripe puffballs. But the signals weren't working. The cavalry were too entangled with the enemy to notice.

Then, someone sensed their peril. The cavalry galloped away. In the rear, several turned in their saddles, spraying submachine-gun fire back at the Germans to keep their heads down.

With dismay, Kaz noticed that three of the lead tanks had doubled back to help their infantry. They moved along the bottom of a hill, hidden from the retreating cavalry, which had now separated into two groups. As the tanks came around the base of the hill and broke into the open, they blocked the retreat of the second, smaller group of cavalry. They opened fire.

For the small group, the situation was hopeless. They lowered their pennant, and one of the officers hoisted a white cloth. The tanks paid no attention. Kaz watched in horror as they machine gunned his surrendering comrades.

By now, the main group of enemy soldiers had detached several artillery pieces from their horses and were setting them up, pointing toward the hill occupied by Kaz and Jan. The time had come to retreat.

With all possible speed, they dismantled their machine guns and began to descend the back side of the hill.

There, Kaz knew, a stream meandered through the valley; the sweating horses needed water. As their soft muzzles slurped from a crystal pool, he was awed by the tranquility of the secluded spot, ringed by towering cedars. In a few short hours, he had gone from an exhilarating ride on the meadow, to the horror of their ravaged camp, to the violent clash with the enemy, and now, full circle, back to a peaceful, pastoral scene.

As he listened to the wind whispering through the treetops, his thoughts drifted back to the dinner with Anna and her family. Could that really have been just the day before yesterday? In hindsight, their table talk was ominous. Kaz hoped that his in-laws at the Foreign Office were wrong. Surely Britain and France would come to Poland's aid in their hour of peril. His thoughts were jarred back to the present as a horse snorted and shook its harness.

When Kaz and his men got back to the camp, most of the surviving cavalry had already arrived. They were a bedraggled lot, missing almost half their original number, with many others suffering the wounds of battle. They were camped outside the compound, not wanting to go in for fear of another attack from the air. Major Kulerski had, however, sent men in to get stragglers, plus medical supplies and a field radio.

The news was not good. Terrible, in fact. Enemy spearheads already were thirty kilometers inside Poland. The Luftwaffe had destroyed most of the Polish air force on the ground. Troops would get no air support. On the contrary, they would face nothing but peril from the skies.

As Kulerski switched the radio off, he issued new orders. His remaining forces would be divided in two. Half would move toward Poznan, to help set up a defensive perimeter. The other half would retire towards Warsaw. Kaz was assigned to Poznan; Jan to Warsaw.

"Would anyone like to go with the other group?" Major Kulerski asked his officers.

They shuffled uncomfortably, glancing at one another. Then Kaz spoke up: "Yes, sir. I would prefer Warsaw."

"Request granted. But why?"

"The reasons are personal, sir.... Could we speak in private, sir?"

Kulerski dismissed the others.

"You wanted to explain?"

"I'm willing to give my life for my country, sir, but I don't want to throw it away."

"Pardon? I don't understand."

"We can make a stand in Warsaw. But from what I've heard, sir, Poznan will soon be surrounded."

Kulerski looked at him sadly. "Lieutenant, this is Poland. We're already surrounded. We were surrounded before the fighting started. Germans to the West. Germans to the North, in East Prussia. Germans to the South, in Czechoslovakia. And to the East, God knows what the Russians have in store for us."

3

Anna

18 December, 1936. Poznan University.

"We're struggling with a complex problem." Prof. Henryk Zygalski looked through his steel-rimmed glasses at the precocious sophomore who had so impressed him in his advanced calculus class. Up close, she was even more attractive than he remembered, with her high Slavic cheekbones, her blond hair tumbling down over her shoulders. Perhaps she wasn't a good candidate. She undoubtedly had an active social life—the girl he wished he'd met ten years ago, when he was an undergraduate. But it was worth a try.

"We need good people. People with mathematical skills and imagination. People like you."

"Sounds intriguing. But you haven't said what the project is."

"Ah, there's the problem. Can't give details until you make a commitment. I realize it's unfair, asking you to take a job without knowing what it is. But it's sensitive, with huge stakes for national security. This chap Hitler. He's stared down the French over the Rhineland. He's begun to rebuild his air force. We don't know what he'll be up to next. Just pray he doesn't have designs on this part of Europe—Poland or Czechoslovakia."

"So you can't give me any more information?"

"Well, perhaps just one bit. Professor Marian Rejewski is working with us. You did outstanding work in his course. He speaks highly of you—he was the one who first recommended you."

"You said it would just be part-time. I'd still be able to continue with my studies?" The job sounded interesting, although she really couldn't tell. And she was delighting in her life as an undergraduate.

"For the present, we're asking for 10 to 15 hours a week. But after a while, you might become a full-fledged member of our research team.

In that case, the job would become full-time, pushing out your university studies."

Anna was bothered by Zygalski's nervous—impatient?—drumming of his slender fingers on his desk.

"I'll have to give it some thought.... When would you like me to start?"

"Right away. That is, as soon as you can. Perhaps early in the New Year? We've already done a security check. A bit of a liberty, but justified under the circumstances. You passed. Not the least blemish on your record."

Zygalski flopped a folder with Anna's name on the desk. She started to lean forward to open it, then caught herself. Curiosity might not be such a good recommendation for the job—whatever it was.

"Can I talk this over with anyone?"

"Your parents, of course. But if you want to talk with anyone else, please ask us first. With the very dangerous international situation, we're not sure we can, ah... trust each and every one of your fellow students.... If you're asked what you'll be doing, say a weather forecasting project. You may have seen our dull gray building on the western edge of campus."

She had indeed. Now, she realized that it was not accurately described by the simple sign above the front door:

SPECIAL METEOROLOGY PROJECT
POLISH AIR FORCE

"Perhaps I should be more explicit. Particularly after you take the job, if someone asks you what you're doing, just say, weather forecasting. For goodness sake, don't say 'I can't tell you.' That just makes them curious. They'll consider it a challenge to pry details out of you. If they ask more questions, just say that you work for the Air Force, on a classified project. People won't find that the least bit odd. You can mention that you work at the SMP building. But that's it. Period. Even when talking to your family."

The interview was over.

The bitter north wind swirled across campus. As Anna headed back toward her dorm, she found herself leaning first forward, then to one side, to maintain her balance, repeatedly tucking her scarf tighter to keep snow from sifting down her neck.

She was torn. She was enjoying her courses. But doing something original; that was appealing. Not to speak of the service she might offer her country. But how was she supposed to know if the job was important? She should have asked Zygalski if she could talk to someone already at the project.

No she shouldn't. The answer would have been obvious: no.

She would have to guess. It wasn't weather forecasting; that was clear. Perhaps it had something to do with intelligence? Rejewski was participating. He had studied at Göttingen before returning to Poznan. He was undoubtedly fluent in German, and his brilliant, intense, orderly mind was obvious to all. He would be a natural for any intelligence operation.

But what sort of intelligence? Göttingen was a center not only for advanced mathematics, but physics, too. The great Heisenberg had spent time there in the 1920s. Anna had heard vaguely of research — there might be a military use for a peculiar phenomenon: close-by aircraft disrupt short-wave radio transmissions. But if Physics espionage was Rejewski's game, it didn't make sense to recruit Anna; she didn't know much Physics. On the other hand, she did know English. Was the intelligence operation directed at the British, too? Anna wouldn't want to participate in that.

Then there's that ten to fifteen hour bit. Her best guess: ten to fifteen hours if the job was dull and dead-end. If she caught on, the demands on her time might escalate. So there it was. Did she want to take on a ten-hour commitment to a dull job, which she would presumably quit after a few months? Did she want to take on an interesting, important job that might push out her studies?

And, she suspected, most of her social life.

As she opened the door to her room, Kirsten met her with a confession.

"I'm sorry. I took Napoleon out of his cage to show Maria, the new girl upstairs."

Anna went over to Napoleon's cage. He seemed perfectly normal, though he was still in his round wire ball as well as his larger cage. She reached in, flipped open the wire ball, and cuddled the hamster to her cheek.

"She was amused to see him navigate around the room, running in his ball." Kirsten still seemed apologetic; Anna wasn't sure why. "I explained that he was *mapping*—finding all the nooks and crannies in case he escaped. Maria corrected me: 'Looking for Josephine, you mean.'

"Before I could stop her," Kirsten continued, "Maria had the door open. Napoleon was out in a flash, making his way merrily down the hall—much to the amusement of the other girls. Before we could catch him, he was at the top of the stairs. Then it was boing, boing, boing, boing. We picked him up at the bottom.... Sorry."

"We need an itsy-bitsy parachute?" asked Anna in baby-talk, holding the hamster close to her nose. She turned back to Kirsten. "No harm, it seems. Except that we'll have to keep our door locked from now on. And keep Maria out. I don't want Napoleon to become the mascot. Some day, he may run into a cat."

She had met Zbig during a mixer, the Saturday before classes started. He came from a good enough family. He was intelligent and handsome, and, as far as she could tell, he had inherited his family's knack for business. But somehow, there wasn't much spark. Maybe her parents were right. They made no secret of their views: Zbig wasn't "suitable." To tell the truth, they had a point; he did have rough edges.

Zbig suggested *The Graven Image*, the fanciest restaurant in town. Anna was surprised; not the sort of place frequented by students. Perhaps he, too, felt that the time had come for their relationship to go one way or the other.

They hadn't seen one another for three days; Zbig was eager to catch up. She mentioned Napoleon's tumble down the stairs, then her Medieval European course. She'd taken it to fulfill her history requirement, but was glad she had.

"Thanks for recommending it. I'm surprised; it's fascinating. The symbolism—Pope Leo deferentially bowing to Charlemagne after crowning him Holy Roman Emperor on Christmas Day, 800. Tensions between the church and temporal authorities—ideas that were never even whispered in high school history."

"More interesting than the endless wars and the mind-numbing memorization of kings. That's for sure."

She was about to mention that she might take a part-time job, but stopped short. "...*not sure we can trust every one of your fellow students.*" Anna wondered if Zygalski had given a hidden warning about Zbig. His mother was German. God, Anna hated politics. Hitler's occupation of the Rhineland had already led to one tense exchange between Zbig and Anna. It ended with a truce: they agreed not to talk politics. But was that any basis for a lasting romance—swearing off important topics, ruling them completely out of bounds?

"I enjoyed meeting your parents, Anna; I'd like you to meet mine. Perhaps you could join us over the Christmas vacation? Maybe Christmas week itself, or, if you prefer, the week after."

"Thanks. But I can't cut into Christmas week, Zbig; it's the only time my whole family has a chance to get together. And that's just next week; we've already made plans."

Anna was slightly irked. If he wanted to invite her all the way down to Lvov, in the southeast corner of Poland, why wait until the last minute? She thought about the week between Christmas and New Year's; she already had a crowded schedule of parties. And her father had arranged an evening in Warsaw; he wanted to have dinner with her and with some of his young friends at the Foreign Office. Perhaps looking for a competitor to Zbig? But if Zbig were going to be in her future, it really was time to meet his family.

Zbig was irked, too, and disappointed. Anna was leaving the week after Christmas hanging.

"Turn about does seem fair play. I met your family."

Not exactly the same thing as an exhausting, seven hundred kilometer train trip, thought Anna. Her parents had visited her in Poznan; that's when they met Zbig. And why should he worry about fairness, anyway?

"I'd like to think about it," she replied. "And check with my family first."

"Your family? Shouldn't my family be given some consideration, too?"

There it was. Fairness. Again.

The small band struck up a Viennese waltz. Zbig knew how much Anna loved to waltz, but seemed preoccupied. When Anna gazed toward the dance floor, he finally took the cue. Would she like to dance?

As they returned to the table, she wanted to avoid a squabble about Christmas, and changed the subject. "Your courses—anything interesting?"

"Not really. Well, yes. Yesterday, in psychology, we were talking about pets. How they take on the personality of their owners."

"Like Hitler and his German shepherd?" asked Anna. "They both love to wolf down tasty morsels. Countries, in Hitler's case." She wished she hadn't said that; she wasn't supposed to mention politics.

"Or perhaps Napoleon."

"Hunh? He had a German shepherd, too?"

"No, no. I mean your hamster. You let him roam around in his ball, rather than keeping him in a cage. The psych prof would have fun with that. You're expressing yourself. You don't want to be trapped in a cage either."

Unlike other people? Anna thought to herself.

But Zbig was dead right. She didn't want to feel trapped. At least, not in a romance with him.

The first Monday of the New Year, as Anna entered the Special Meteorology Project, she glanced around the building which, she guessed, might become her home for the next few months. The reception area was Spartan, with a secretary seated in a tiny cubicle in front of a telephone switchboard.

Glancing down the halls, Anna saw that all the walls were the same dingy, insipid air force blue. She wondered when they had last felt the stroke of a paintbrush. Not since it was built, she was willing to bet. The building was standard military—not the least imagination in its design, with everything perfectly rectangular and straight. Except for the floor, which was already beginning to sag in spots, even though she guessed the building was less than twenty years old. Suddenly, she felt uneasy, even more out of place than when she first arrived at the university.

It was too late for second thoughts.

She introduced herself. The secretary fumbled with a cable, finally managing to plug it in. She buzzed twice. Zygalski appeared almost immediately.

"Delighted to see you.... Well?"

"I'm inclined to accept. But I need to know something first."

"Of course. Hope I'll be able to help." He led her around to his office, a spacious room at the corner of the building. A large window looked out toward the Gothic tower of the Arts building. The newly-fallen snow was still crisp; Anna imagined the crunch, crunch as students trudged to class.

"You wanted to find out about something?" Zygalski asked.

"I was wondering if you offered me a job because I understand English. My first loyalty is to Poland. But, as you know, my mother is English. I won't spy on Britain."

Zygalski laughed. "No need to worry. Your job will have nothing to do with the English language."

"Then yes, I'm happy to accept."

"Marvelous. Just a few formalities, in the administrative offices in A3. Then you can join us in B8. Just around the corner," Zygalski said, leading her down the hall and stopping in front of A3.

Most of the paperwork was routine. But there were a few added features: mug shots and fingerprints. There were security forms to sign, threatening dire consequences, up to death, for violation of the Secrets Act. Anna paused, then signed. In for a penny, in for a pound.

4
The Inscrutable Six

Things are seldom as they seem.
Skim milk masquerades as cream.

Gilbert   and
Sullivan,   HMS
Pinafore

When Anna got around to B8, she knocked, heard a shout inside, and entered. Three men were huddled around a typewriter. She knew Marian Rejewski from the University. Zygalski introduced her to Jerzy Rozycki.

Rozycki was thirtyish. His solid frame suggested that he might have been athletic in his youth, but his expanding waistline told another story: his main exercise now was raising a fork to his mouth. Rejewski was perhaps five years older, his sharp features accented by a pointed beard, prematurely flecked with gray. He wore a rumpled tweed jacket with elbow patches—the same jacket he had worn every day in class the previous year. Surprising; he should be able to afford better, even on his slim salary. He was something of a legend from his undergraduate days. A professional gambler had spent a weekend hanging around his dormitory, looking for easy pickings. In a marathon encounter, Rejewski relieved him of a stupendous sum, equivalent to $8,000.

"Here we use only first names: Marian and Jerzy, and I'm Henryk. Of course, I will still be Professor Zygalski when you see me at the university, and Marian will likewise be Professor Rejewski."

He stepped aside and motioned her to sit down by the machine. It wasn't a standard typewriter: The keyboard was smaller, with only the 26 letters of the alphabet, no numbers or punctuation marks. Behind the keys were three wheels with letters and teeth; apparently the wheels could be rotated. At the top was a panel on which the letters of the keyboard were repeated in a set of recessed glass circles.

"Let's try an experiment," said Henryk, rotating the three wheels. The teeth clicked slightly as he set them so that the letter "A" was at the top of each. "Why don't you type in a message. Let's make it short, not more than ten or fifteen letters."

Anna thought of her favorite operetta, *The Merry Widow*. She pressed the letter "M."

The right-hand wheel clicked, rotating one notch, from "A" to "B." On the lampboard at the top, the circle "V" lit up.

"V," she announced, and Henryk, who was then at the other machine, pressed a key.

And so it went. As she typed in her short phrase, she announced the letters one by one:

VSOBP TXVHE.

"Merry Widow," said Henryk immediately, with a smile.

"Impressive." Anna leaned back in her seat. "A cipher machine. And not a simple one. The two R's in merry came out differently — O, then B."

To check, Anna pressed Z four times. "WHFI" she announced.

"ZZZZ" came the immediate response.

Anna decided to cheat. The first two wheels were still at A. The third wheel had by now rotated to Q. As inconspicuously as possible, she rotated this wheel until it was again at its initial setting, A. No one noticed; the slight clicking noise of the wheel was hidden by the banging of the pipes as the heating system warmed up.

Merry, she typed in again, announcing the results: VSOBP.

"QIJJC," Henryk replied, with a puzzled look. "Oh, he said," you're testing me. "MERRY. You reset the third wheel back to A."

"Marvelous," replied Anna. "The letters are scrambled. But if you start with the same wheel setting — in this case AAA — a word, such as merry, always comes out with the same encoded result."

She thought for a few moments.

"I think I see how it works. Every time you push a key, a wheel rotates one notch, giving a different encoding. But how can the other machine decode so quickly? It must be a mirror image of the first one. Sounds complicated."

"Not really. The two aren't mirror images; they're identical. They work on an electric current. Pins on the three wheels stick out and make an electrical connection with the next wheel; the wheels have internal wiring to translate each letter into a different one. If all three wheels are set at A, you won't get an A if you press the A key; you'll get any other letter, say, T. Next to the third wheel is a reflector. It means that the machine also works the other way round: if you pressed T, you would get A. Thus, the same machine is used either for coding or decoding."

"Great. So we've been developing it for the Polish Air Force?"

"Not exactly. It's a copy of a German machine."

Anna wondered where they had gotten it but didn't want to seem too curious.

Henryk read her mind. "It was invented in 1919 and manufactured by a German company, who sold it commercially to railroads and other businesses who wanted to keep their communications secret. We bought one, but the Germans stopped selling them when the machine was adopted by their army in 1926. Our technical services are in the process of making additional copies."

Henryk didn't want to give the least hint that they had a spy in Germany. Accordingly, he hadn't told the whole truth—that the Germans were using a modified version, with different rotors, and that Marian had worked out the wiring of the new ones, using information supplied by Schmidt.

"I suppose our task is to decipher the German messages by figuring out the setting of the wheels."

"Right you are."

"Let's see. The right-hand wheel can be set with any letter at the top? That's 26 positions. The same is true of the other two?" Henryk nodded. "That's 26 x 26 x 26 possible settings... over 15 thousand."

"17,576, to be exact. If you pushed the keys 17,576 times, your setting would come back to where it started."

"Like an odometer on a car? Once it reaches 99999, it turns back to 00000—provided the car hasn't fallen apart by that time."

"Exactly.... Or maybe not exactly," added Henryk. "A new car starts at 00000. But with the Enigma, the Germans don't start at AAA. They can start anywhere. And, as far as we can tell, they use a different setting for every message."

"So what's left is brute force—trying each setting for every message?" Anna wondered.

"Yes and no. That's one place to begin. But our game will be to figure out some pattern—so we don't have to run through all 17,000."

"We've got a good place to start," said Jerzy, "a long, clear intercepted message." He slid several papers across to Anna. She was distracted by the cloud of cigar smoke when he leaned across the table, but tried to ignore it as she looked down at the papers. She could read the first few lines, but they were followed by a jumble of letters:

Discriminant: Blue

Seventy-two

One hundred and twenty eight

Then came a line with six apparently random letters, in two groups of three:

DSI FDR

The next line was a series of 50 or 60 letters.

Next came groups of five letters each, filling a number of lines.

"First," explained Marian, "is the so-called discriminant—Blue. It appears in about 40 percent of the messages. It indicates the army; anyone with a blue codebook will be able to look up the initial settings of the rotors for army messages. There are different settings for different organizations—red, green, orange, and so on—so they can't read one another's mail.

"The next line, 72, is the number of letters giving the address—from so and so to such and such—and the date. Then comes 128, the number of letters in the main message. They're divided into groups of five to help the recipient keep track; if he only has four letters in a group, he knows he's dropped one letter and he knows where. If he doesn't keep track, the wheels won't click the right number of times, and he won't get anything but gibberish.

"Our best guess is that the six letters—two groups of three each—have something to do with the resetting of the rotors. We're not sure;

the Germans have changed their procedures since we were able to break some messages several years ago. What we do know is that, once we figure out the wheel settings for the address, the settings don't change again, at least not for that particular message; we can read through the rest of it."

There was a knock on the door. Henryk opened it, letting the security officer in.

"Yes, Liwicki?"

"Sorry to interrupt, sir, but there's a problem with Miss Raczynska's forms."

Anna was astonished; what could the trouble be? According to Henryk, her security check hadn't turned up any problem.

"She gave her mother's birth date as 1896. Her older brother was born in 1904. That means her mother was only eight when her brother was born."

"That's right," said Anna, deadpan. "Only eight."

"But...." Liwicki was perplexed.

Henryk looked at her sharply. She hadn't learned the first rule of military security: *no jokes, please.*

"He's only a half brother. My father's first wife — Stefan's mother — died in 1914."

Liwicki retreated, apologizing profusely.

"Coming back to the subject," said Henryk, a hint of exasperation in his voice, "we're in the process of decoding a set of blue messages by trial and error. When we've got several dozen, we'll see if we have enough to work backward to figure out the previous six letters — the two sets of three letters.

"We'd like you to work on the message Jerzy gave you. We've found that the Germans tend to avoid settings near the beginning of the alphabet, so why don't you start by setting the wheels in the middle, say, at MMM. See if you get anything in German in the first few letters of the address line. If it's garbage, start over with the next setting, MMN. If you get a German word, keep going to see if you can read the whole message. Sooner or later, you should find the right setting.

"Unless there are questions, you might as well get your feet wet," continued Henryk. "If you can start this evening," Anna nodded, "you can see how it goes. Be sure to keep a record of what the settings were when you stopped; that will tell you where to start when you come back.

"Tonight, as you leave, stop by the security office and let Sergeant Liwicki know your schedule, when you'll be available. When you do, please try not to give him a hard time."

Anna felt properly admonished. Later, when she got around to seeing Liwicki, she would make a point of apologizing.

"And remember," concluded Henryk. "We're not here just to decode any single message. Most of all, we're trying to figure out the German system. Even when you're doing this sort of drudge job, ask yourself: are there clues, how their system works?"

The third afternoon, Anna hit the jackpot. When she came to the setting QRT, she could read the message:

FROMGENHEINRICHSCHIMITZTOALLDIVISIONCOMMA
NDERSTWENTYTWODECEMBERTHIRTYSIX
ALLIN FANTR YDIVI SIONS SHOUL DBEGI NTOPR
EPARE FORTH EINTE GRATI ONOFT ENADD ITION
ALANT ITANK GUNSP ERREG IMENT....

When she put the spaces in the right places, the message was clear: ALL INFANTRY DIVISIONS SHOULD BEGIN...

In her excitement, she was about to rush in to tell Henryk, but decided to try another puzzle. Could she do anything with the beginning of the message: those six first letters, in two groups of three? Let's see. Suppose that they were also part of the same setting. That would mean that the setting was not initially QRT, but became QRT only after six letters had been sent. She went back six letters and tried the setting QRN. No luck; the first six letters produced gibberish.

She went to Henryk with the news. Almost immediately, Marian and Jerzy appeared. Anna quickly explained what she had done.

"Very good. Very good." Henryk responded. "A bit of beginner's luck — you only had to go from MMM to QRT."

"Indeed," said Anna. "Suppose the setting had been MML. You wouldn't have seen me for a month. Unless I'd found a shortcut."

"We're in the process of bringing together several dozen messages which the staff has been able to decode," said Marian, "to see what we can make of them. But you said something about a shortcut. Did you have something in mind?"

"Well, yes. You said that the first line was probably the address. That means it would start with "From," or VON in German—as my message in fact did. I was playing with the idea of doing a quick run, to look for settings where the first letter was V."

"Very good. Very good," Henryk repeated.

"Just think how easy it would be," Anna continued. "In the encoded message, the first letter of the address was K. Starting with a setting of MMM, I could just hit the one letter K. If it showed up as a V, then I would go on, to see if I got VON. But if I got any other letter but V, then I could simply hit K again. The right-hand wheel would already have turned one notch, giving a setting of MMN, and that's the one I would want to try next.

"In other words, we can cut way down on the brute force," Anna concluded. "Simply push the first letter—K in this case—over and over again until it comes out V. Whenever we get a V—one time in twenty-five—we can go on to the second letter. If it's an O, we keep right on going."

"Very good. Very good," Henryk said once more. "Brilliant."

In fact, as Anna would soon discover, the "brute force" exercise had been a test, to see if she would pick up the V clue. The staff were already using this approach, with impressive results. Looking just for the first letter V worked in about half the cases, giving a quick decryption. As for the other half, many started with the date, not the address, so the V test didn't work.

"We now come to the main event," said Marian, thoughtfully stroking his beard. "How do we tackle the first six letters—the inscrutable six?"

He looked around the room. Silence.

Finally, Henryk cleared his throat and spoke: "Can everybody get back together at 8:00 a.m. tomorrow?" The professors nodded. He looked at Anna.

She nodded too. She was delighted to be included with the big boys. There goes the topology class, she thought.

Henryk wound up the meeting: "Let's focus on our next big puzzle: that irksome group of six. Let's sleep on it."

Anna had trouble sleeping on it. In fact, she had trouble getting to sleep at all; she was too excited. She had successfully decoded the German message. More important, she had figured out how to shortcut the process by using the V test. She had been accepted as one of the core group struggling with the Enigma. True, she had hit one pothole in the road during her first day. That bit about her eight year old mother was childish. But it was out of character, she reassured herself; it could be written off to her initial nervousness. There was no reason to fear a repeat.

As she began to drift off, she had a warm, satisfied feeling. She had broken a long-standing, unwanted habit. When she was younger, she realized that it might not be such a good idea to answer the toughest math questions in class; her classmates resented it. And, with a few well chosen errors, she could keep her exam scores to a respectably mediocre B+, a practice she discarded—spectacularly—when it came time to take the university entrance examinations. Now, she noticed, she was giving direct answers to direct questions. After just a few days, she felt comfortable with her colleagues. There wasn't the slightest risk that she would make brilliant men like Henryk or Marian or Jerzy look bad.

Henryk resumed the meeting at 8:00 a.m. sharp. In front of each of their places was a pile of about a dozen messages, in both the original and decrypted versions. Across the top of each decrypted message, three letters were printed in colored ink; they gave the rotor settings that had been used to encode that particular message.

"You'll observe," said Jerzy, "that the rotor settings are different for each of the messages, even though they're all Blue, and they were all sent within a few days. That indicates that, as we suspected, the settings are changed for every message—not just once a month or even once a day. Well, we can't expect the Germans to make life easy for us."

"And again, we were probably right in our guess," responded Henryk. "The inscrutable six tell recipients the correct setting for that specific message.

"You mean," asked Jerzy, "they not only send the three-letter settings for the wheels, but then repeat them?"

"Exactly," replied Henryk. "They send them twice so the recipients can be sure they've gotten them right. Otherwise, if they made a mistake, the message would be gibberish."

Jerzy puffed at the stub of his cigar, with a skeptical frown. "But the three letters *aren't* repeated. He glanced down at the messages. "DSI FDR, in Anna's message, for example. And there seem to be no repeats in the other messages, either." He leafed through the papers in front of him.

Anna spoke. "The Germans have a cipher machine. Why should they send the wheel settings in the clear? If they did, then anyone who captured one of their machines, or anyone who already has one," she smiled as she glanced across at the machine, "could read the message. Just as Henryk read my 'Merry Widow' the other day. Instead, why not use the machine to encrypt them?"

"In other words," said Henryk, "there are two settings. The first we might call the basic setting, indicated by the discriminant—Blue in this case. Anyone with access to the Blue codebook can look up the basic wheel setting currently in use. Using this setting, the signalman receiving the message reads the inscrutable six. That gives him the three letters to reset the wheels, to read the body of the message—what we might call the message setting."

"Now we can see why they call it an Enigma machine," observed Jerzy. "A puzzle within a puzzle."

"And so," said Henryk with finality, tapping his pencil on the table, *"we can't really break the enigma machine.* That's impossible. *All* we can do is read specific messages, or, at the best, figure out the basic wheel setting—for Blue messages, for example. It will be good only for a fraction of the Enigma traffic, and only until they change the setting."

All eyes turned to Marian. He had been sitting silently stroking his beard, deep in thought.

5

Anna's Idiots:
The Opposite of Genius

Gentlemen do not read each other's mail.

Secretary of State Henry Stimson, expressing shock when shown deciphered Japanese communications in 1929.

(Stimson had the "unethical" decoding shut down, but it was soon revived.)

"Things aren't quite so bad." Marian broke his silence, lightening the gloom. "I think we're just about there. If Henryk's right—if the inscrutable six represent a repeat of the message setting—we've got the key to unlock the basic setting, the one which all Blue operators start with. We can find it by working backward, through trial and error. Let's use brute to find the wheel setting that translates the inscrutable six—DSI FDR in Anna's message—into the setting for her message, QRT QRT. When we do, we should have the basic Blue setting. Then we should be able to decode all the Blue traffic. I'll have the staff work on this. Any questions?"

As they broke up, Henryk glanced toward Anna and raised his index finger, a sign that he wanted to talk to her. When they got to his office, her eyes were again drawn out the wide window. The earlier cold, crisp snow had been softened by warming air; the moist snowflakes were now ideal for packing. Young boys were engaged in a glorious snowball fight. Off to the north, a young couple, surrounded by their entranced children, were leaning against a snowman, struggling to raise the head to its rightful place. For a fleeting moment, Anna wondered if she would pay too high a price for her challenging new job.

34

"Now that you've proven yourself—even faster than I expected—I want to talk about your role. We're dividing our operation into two groups. One will look at ways to deal with brute force problems: how to go through the multitude of possibilities quickly. Marian Rejewski will be working with me in this group. He has some very promising ideas for a machine to speed up the process.

"The other group—which I'd like you to join—will be headed by Jerzy. Your job will be to find patterns or other ways of reducing the number of iterations we have to wade through to read a message, so we don't have to slog through all 17,000. We've already got a start. As you discovered, messages often start with V; that makes trial and error much easier.

"In brief," concluded Henryk, "your job will be to rule out some of the 17,000 possibilities—to cut it down to a few thousand. Or even less, if we're lucky."

"Rule out things that *seem* possible but are in fact impossible," mused Anna. "The opposite of genius. Geniuses find out how to do the impossible; they show that things that seem impossible are in fact possible."

In the coming weeks, Anna wished that she had kept that little comment to herself. It leaked out, and the junior members of their team quickly began to call themselves "Jerzy's Idiots," using a signature logo of what was, apparently, a cross-eyed imbecile. A few— perhaps those who had a crush on their pretty new boss—went so far as to call themselves "Anna's idiots," using a drawing of an imbecile of uncertain gender.

Of course, the other group were not to be outdone. They began to use a picture of a gorilla dragging its hands on the ground, with "Brute Force" written below.

Even more than Anna, Henryk wished he hadn't passed her quip along to his secretary. He wondered if the names could cause a security breach; jokes could lead to blabbering at the local bistro. He finally issued a written order:

> Personnel may joke about "idiots" and "gorillas" inside this building, but the two terms *and their logos* are to be kept strictly inside; they are not to be mentioned outside *under any*

circumstances. And please, no scrawling of idiots or gorillas on bathroom walls. From time to time we have visitors. Some of them, at least, should leave with the illusion that we're doing serious work on weather forecasting.

Indeed, thought Anna one day, looking out to the quadrangle. There was Jerzy, playfully releasing several balloons, measuring their rise with a stopwatch and sextant. Henryk was delighted to humor him in his hobby as an amateur meteorologist; those outside the building would see the rising balloons and conclude that the Special Meteorology Project was, as advertised, working on weather forecasting. Jerzy also had another talent: he could talk knowledgeably to outsiders about forecasting.

The job was enough to make the researchers into manic depressives. There were the early inspirations — particularly the decoding of the first inscrutable six, which gave them the basic settings and led to a rapid deciphering of a whole set of Blue intercepts from December. But when they tried January's intercepts, nothing. The old Blue settings didn't work for the new Blue messages; the Germans had apparently changed the settings at the beginning of the year.

Also, the V clue — which had made the process so much quicker — became useless. The Germans were putting a set of between five and a dozen random letters right after the inscrutable six, to prevent codebreakers from working backward. It was only after three weeks of dreary work that the codebreakers figured that out, and started the decoding effort with the twentieth letter rather than first. But the process was now tedious. When they started in the middle, there was no point in looking for V. In fact, the twentieth letter was likely to be in the middle of a word, which made it much more difficult to figure out when they were actually reading a German passage, not just gibberish.

Then, disaster struck. At the beginning of April 1937, they found that even the Blue messages were indecipherable. That wasn't such a surprise. The Germans had apparently changed the basic settings again; they could now presumably be counted on to do so every three months or so. But, as the months passed into May, June, July, and August, with no deciphering of any message after March, it was clear that something more fundamental was wrong. They couldn't even get to the first step, of reading a single message with brute force, no matter where they started. Henryk asked the core group of four to set aside everything for a brainstorming meeting the first Monday of September, after everyone was back from vacation.

He started the meeting with a broad statement, what everyone already knew: they'd been unable to crack anything for five months. The General Staff in Warsaw was impatient, wondering if they had hit a stone wall. But that wasn't the worst of it. Over the weekend, Jerzy had run into a problem with the Enigma machines.

"Suppose we look at this methodically," Henryk suggested. "Let's look first at the puzzle we've had for the past five months, then turn to Jerzy's problem. But, before we begin, I think the time has come to start keeping detailed records of what we've done, what's worked and what hasn't."

All eyes turned toward Anna. "There goes not only topology, but my whole university program," she thought. But she nodded. In spite of the drudgery of note-taking and record-keeping, the project would be just as interesting as university work. Also, it could be a whole lot more important: the security of the nation might depend on it.

"Thank you, Anna. Now, let's come back to our first problem: What could the Germans have done five months ago to make their messages indecipherable?"

"One," responded Jerzy, "they may have scrapped the old machine, and are now working with a completely different design."

"Well," said Henryk, taken aback, "that certainly puts it on the line. If so, it seems that we have only two ways out. We might be able to steal one of their new machines. I wonder what kind of talent we have in our jails?" he mused, only half joking. "The second option—try to reconstruct the new machine from the messages we've intercepted. What do you think, Marian?"

"That would be tough—much tougher than the first time I did it back in 1932, because then I had both messages and wheel settings. If it's the same machine, with different wheels, I could calculate how many intercepts of the same type—Blue, say—we would need to reconstruct the wheels. I bet it will be a pile, but I may be able to have some rough calculations by the end of the week.

"If they've done something other than introduce new wheels—for example, if they're now using a bigger keyboard and larger wheels to accommodate numbers as well as letters, all bets are off. In that case, I don't know what to suggest."

Jerzy picked up his line of thought. "Another possibility: The Germans may be using double encryption. That is, once a message goes through the Enigma scrambler, they may send it through a second encryption—for example, with a codebook, or by somehow modifying the Enigma machine."

"In other words," responded Henryk, "we're not sure if we just want to steal a new machine, or whether we want our burglars to pick up codebooks while they're at it.... Any other thoughts?"

There was no response. "Let's come back to this later," said Henryk. "It's time for Jerzy's problem."

Jerzy puffed on his cigar, laying a pall of smoke over one end of the conference table. "When I got back from vacation, I dropped by the office late Saturday evening and found something peculiar. The staff were all confused. The two machines were no longer giving the same results. I called Henryk about it yesterday. "

There was thunderstruck silence.

"Are they *sure*?" asked Marian.

"Yes, they're sure, and, what's more, *they're right*. I checked. When the wheels are all set to AAA, one machine gives T when you press the A key, as always. The other gives R."

"How long this has been going on?" Marian asked. He seemed indignant. But at the misbehaving machine, or at the delay in letting him know?

"Just since Saturday.... Late last week, one of the machines was balking. The wheels weren't clicking cleanly from one letter to another, and sometimes no letter at all would show up when they pressed a key. They thought maybe a tooth on one of the wheels was broken. Saturday morning, they removed the wheels. There was nothing broken, or even severely worn, as far as they could tell. But the pins were dirty, perhaps breaking the electrical connection. They cleaned the wheels and reinstalled them. They get a result now, but it's wrong. That is, it disagrees with the first machine."

"Then we'd better call in technical services, to go over the machine to see what's wrong." Henryk was usually calm and businesslike, but now he became forceful. "Just be *certain* they don't touch the first machine. If it misbehaves, too, we won't know what were doing."

That week, there were two major developments. The first was Marian's quick calculation. Based on his earlier work, it would take at least two months to reconstruct wheels from intercepted messages, perhaps longer. It would depend on the volume of intercepted traffic.

The second was more encouraging. After several hours of swearing and tinkering, technical services figured out what had happened to the misbehaving machine. When the staff had put it back together, they had accidentally changed the order of the wheels. When technical services switched them back to the right order, the machine again duplicated the results of the first one.

"And that," announced Henryk when the group of four met again, "means we face a far more complicated situation. The wheels can be installed in any order—six different ways. Instead of 17,000 possible encodings, we may have to slog through six times as many—over 100,000.

"But the misbehaving machine may have been simple, blind luck— one of those well disguised blessings. It's possible that our problem of the past five months began when the Germans reordered the wheels. And we have a place to start. We can go back over the intercepts to see if, with brute force, we can decipher a message by putting the wheels in different order. That means we'll need bigger and stronger gorillas; they'll have to go through all possible orderings of the wheels until they find the one the Germans used."

It worked. Unfortunately, it wasn't until the sixth and last try that they got the right ordering of wheels for April. After all that work, they felt they were back on track.

But Henryk was furious. "How could we have been such idiots— such cretin idiots—not to think of something so simple as a reordering of the wheels?"

Their success was not to last. In January of 1938, they faced an indecipherable mess, no matter how the wheels were ordered. They struggled for several months. Then Henryk, in a stage whisper, asked if anyone had a burglar in the family. A few days later, he disappeared.

While he was gone, Jerzy went over to the gorillas, to help with the machine Rejewski was working on. Anna was left behind as the only idiot, struggling without success to make sense of the pile of indecipherable messages. She found herself leafing through them again and again, hoping for an inspiration.

But it didn't come. Day after day, she pored over the intercepts, looking for some sort of pattern where none existed. She was becoming demoralized. At the weekly staff meetings, she found herself saying less and less.

After one of the meetings, Marian invited her to drop by his office. When she did, she noticed, in the uneven lighting of his room, just how worn his face had become in the past several months. But he wanted to talk about her, not himself.

"I'm concerned. We may be demanding too much of you."

"Not at all. But I'll admit, it's tough." Anna didn't want to let him know how tired she really was.

"It's not the hard work; it's the frustration," Marian commiserated. He suspected she wasn't being honest, that she was nearing exhaustion. "The others have been working very hard too, but work on the new machine is coming along splendidly. I'm afraid that we've left you alone with the most frustrating job."

"Somebody's got to do it. Sooner or later, we'll make a breakthrough. It may be something very simple. It makes sense for someone to sift through the rubbish for clues. It makes sense for me to do it. I don't have the skills to help with the machine. I've been trying a new system—start off each morning with a list of possible tricks the Germans may be using. It gives my day some structure. It also gives me an illusion of progress." Anna smiled wryly—"most evenings I've succeeded in my task for the day, working through the whole list. Unfortunately, everything on it is crossed out."

"I think the time has come for us to take a long-run view."

Anna was surprised. They needed results. Hitler had seized Austria; the threat to Poland was growing. Marian paused. Anna waited for him to finish. After a few moments, he continued.

"I think — we think — that it might be a good idea for you to take an extended vacation, say six weeks."

"Six weeks?" Anna was astonished.

"You've been slaving away, almost nonstop, for more than a year." True, thought Anna; she had taken only the one vacation, over Christmas. "Anybody can get overtired and stale. Spend two weeks relaxing, sleeping 'til noon. Then have fun for a month; you're young. When you come back, you'll be refreshed. That's when you get new ideas."

Anna couldn't help but smile. It was good advice, but, from what she had heard, Marian was careless in following it himself. Just before he left on his last vacation, one of his historian friends had given him an encoded letter written in 1904 by Pilsudski, who was trying to rally support for an independent Poland. The letter was addressed to the Japanese, who were at the time embroiled in a conflict with Russia — one of the powers occupying Poland. Marian said he was too busy, but made the mistake of taking the letter with him. It wasn't much of a vacation. He behaved oddly, pacing back and forth in an upstairs bedroom. When he got home, he presented his friend with the deciphered message. He also gave his friend gentle, but firm, instructions: *no more encoded letters.*

Marian continued. "Keep a note pad with you; you never know when your subconscious may throw up an inspiration. But make your notes obscure — if anyone sees the notebook, they shouldn't be able to figure out that you're working on a decoding project. Throw in a few distracters — equations on the velocity of weather balloons, and stuff like that, which makes it look as though you really are working on meteorology."

It was an offer Anna couldn't refuse. She realized just how exhausted she was — and how marvelous it would be to have a social life again. In retrospect, even Zbig seemed attractive. But that was an illusion. Whenever she had begun to feel the least bit serious about him, she couldn't help but think back to her earlier boyfriend, Ryk. He was so much more fun—that secret plane ride and all. She wondered what he was doing. Odd. She was sure that they'd both been in love, but never at the same time. Perhaps she should get in touch with him during her six weeks off. Some day, their timing might be right.

Now that Marian offered her a holiday, she couldn't wait to escape the social wasteland known as the "Meteorology Project." Social gatherings were rare; people were completely consumed by the Enigma puzzle. The few eligible men seemed to shy away because of her senior position. And the demands of her job had cut her off from her college friends. Oh, well, she sighed. She didn't have many illusions when she took the job. Or did she?

She spent the first week at her family home, west of Warsaw. Marian was right; she did sleep in every day 'til noon. Then she was ready for the fun part. She was off to visit her first cousin, Krystyna, who was also in her late teens and attended the University of Warsaw, where the fall term was just beginning.

After a few days, Anna began to realize what the last years of the Roman Empire must have been like. A frantic round of parties had begun, each vying to be the best of the year, on the assumption— obvious, but under no circumstances to be uttered—that it might be the last.

The tempo intensified at the end of September, after the Munich conference ceded Czechoslovakia's heavily defended borderlands to Hitler. The sense of impending doom was heightened by the growing number of uniforms around the university; the undergraduate men were increasingly distracted by the demands of the army reserve training program.

In keeping up with the parties, Anna had an advantage. She wasn't taking any classes. She was staying with Krystyna's parents, who had a comfortable apartment only a few blocks from the university. She still had the luxury of sleeping until noon.

One evening—the third evening in a row of partying—Anna went alone; Krystyna would join her at the party with her boyfriend, Pawel, and one of his friends. Quite early, only a little after 10, Anna felt drowsy, and slipped away to an alcove to rest for a few moments on a sofa. Soon she drifted off into a soft, untroubled sleep.

Vaguely, she felt someone sit down on the sofa beside her, and heard Krystyna in the distance, "... my cousin, Anna."

"Ah, a real sleeping beauty," responded a voice on the sofa beside her.

She opened her eyes the slightest crack, barely enough to see the hazy outline of a young man in uniform. She could see him just well enough to realize that he was staring at her face. She stirred, fluttering her eyes as she opened them.

They were not the ice blue that he had expected, to match her blond hair. Rather, he was gazing into warm hazel eyes.

He abruptly looked away, toward Krystyna and Pawel on the sofa opposite. He rose quickly to his feet as Krystyna repeated the introduction.

"Anna, this is Kaz Jankowski. As I mentioned, he's an old friend of Pawel."

Anna held out her hand. Kaz took it, and bowed with the slightest click of his heels. She motioned for him to sit down again. Handsome, she thought. She asked what unit he was in; the Seventh Cavalry, he answered.

"So you love horses, too?"

"Particularly Tiber, my stallion. We all look after our own horses ourselves; it builds a bond. You ride?"

"When I was younger."

She paused, but then continued; he seemed interested.

"Quite a bit younger. My father put me up on a pony when I was only 18 months old.... I'm afraid I screamed and cried when they took me down."

"What's the matter with that?" he asked, grinning.

"They almost had to pry me off; I made quite a scene."

"As I said, *what's* the matter with that?" Kaz repeated, with an even broader grin. "So you've been riding ever since?"

"Mostly when I was young. I guess you've got a point—there was nothing wrong. In fact, I was rewarded. On my fourth birthday, they gave me a pony. 'Lightning' I called her. Not very appropriate. She was barrel-like—as wide as she was tall. With small legs that stuck down like sticks at the corners. Gave me a bumpy ride. But how I loved her — my best friend when I was growing up."

"Sounds idyllic." Kaz imagined a slim young figure on her pony, the sun flashing through the highlights of her windblown, flaxen hair.

"It was." Anna suddenly looked sad. "But then it came to an end. One day, when I was 12, my father took me for a walk in the woods. Slowly and softly, he got me to recognize the truth: the pony was so old, and in so much pain that the only humane thing was to have her put down. The vet would be coming the next morning, after I left for school. I spent rest of the afternoon and evening brushing and hugging my four-legged friend. It was a bittersweet parting."

After all these years, it still brought tears to Anna's eyes.

Kaz responded with tales of how he was training Tiber. Anna thought it was sad, to train horses for the battlefield. Because of their size, they would be the first to be killed. Kaz wanted to agree, but thought it might be unsoldierly to do so. He offered a consolation: within the coming decade, most horses would be replaced by tanks as the main weapon for thrusts through the enemy's lines.

Anna was surprised to find herself asking about tanks, a topic in which she had absolutely no interest. The Germans and French had the best new ones, Kaz said. The difficulty was that Poland did not have the heavy industry to produce tanks, and were unable to buy new models from the French or even the British. Those two countries had begun a feverish buildup of their own. He then turned the conversation to a more interesting subject, Anna.

"I understand you're a student at Poznan University."

"Well, yes and no."

Kaz raised an eyebrow.

"I *was* a student. I gave up my course work when I became involved in a research project — on weather forecasting."

"Ah, then that would explain how you could get away to Warsaw at this time of the year."

"Yes, we've had a very intense summer. I needed a break."

"Intense? Weather forecasting? I would have thought it was a timeless topic — to be approached in a methodical, unhurried way."

Kaz wanted to bite his tongue. He wished it hadn't come out quite that way; he hoped she wouldn't be offended.

"Actually, it is urgent. The Air Force needs better forecasts. Short-range planes can get stuck up in the air, unable to land because of thunderstorms. Running out of gas."

"I see your point. That would be dangerous."

"Not to speak of embarrassing." Anna smirked.

"And you've been working on...?"

"Studying weather balloons. We fill them with hydrogen so they rise rapidly. Above 4,000 meters, they often change direction as they encounter upper-atmosphere winds. Those currents help us predict the movements of weather fronts."

"You've been...?"

Anna took a deep breath; she normally hid her interest in calculus when talking to young men. Or men of any age, for that matter.

"I've been working on a mathematical model of upper-atmosphere air currents."

"Really?"

Anna was even more surprised; he seemed interested in the details. Now, she appreciated Jerzy's enthusiasm for his hobby. She also was grateful for the equations she had scribbled in her notebook, following Marian's recent instructions to disguise any notes she might make on Enigma.

She reached over the coffee table for a napkin, and scratched down an equation of the vertical velocity of balloons, how they slowed down as the air got thinner, and how the upward velocity depended on the elasticity of the balloon.

He still seemed interested. Apparently, he had at least a smattering of calculus. She wrote down a second equation—the horizontal acceleration of balloons as they hit upper-air currents.

"Impressive. You're really comfortable with calculus."

"And I'm pleased—a cavalry officer is interested."

He put his hand on the sofa. Near Anna's, but not quite touching.

"Well, actually, my interest doesn't come from the cavalry."

Anna waited, hoping he would elaborate.

"When I was in high school, I loved math. In fact, I wanted to go to university to study engineering.... But things didn't work out."

Again she was curious, hoping he would provide details. He did.

"My family—my father—wouldn't hear of it. I come from a line of military officers. My grandfather was a general, my father a colonel. His heart was set on my continuing the family tradition.... I'm afraid we had a few, ah, mmm... disagreements. But then we compromised...." His voice trailed off.

"Compromised?" Anna didn't want to state the obvious: some compromise, off to the military academy. But then, of course, the father did have a hold over his son. He was the one who would pay for university.

"I would go to the academy for one year. If my heart were still set on math, I could transfer to the university. He would no longer object."

"So you liked the academy when you got there?"

"Well, yes and no. I started out with a concentration on artillery; that seemed the closest to mathematics. In a sense, it was. But if you have a knack for math, you quickly get bored with parabolic trajectories of shells. And in combat, the artillery works from tables; they don't do their own calculations."

"Sounds as though you were disappointed. Why didn't you switch to the university after the first year?"

"I had a lot of friends. In the military, the sense of comradeship is remarkable. You know that some day your life may depend on your friends. And I became very interested in the cavalry; I've always loved horses."

"So we have the same two interests—mathematics and horses. You picked horses; I picked math."

"Put that way, horses seem pretty trivial." Kaz spoke gently, without the hint of offense.

"Not at all. Not at all. With the grim international situation, it's obvious, how important our armed forces are." Anna waved her hand in front of her face, attempting to shoo away a fly. She put her hand back on the sofa. Close once more, but not quite touching.

"You found your niche; you seem unusually good at mathematics."

"It's in the genes.... My grandfather was a cousin of Marie Curie."
Again, he seemed impressed.... "I'm also radioactive," she added with
a smile. "I glow in the dark."

"My little glowworm."

Anna suddenly realized that she and Kaz were alone. She hadn't
noticed; twenty minutes earlier, Krystyna and Pawel had slipped
away. She felt a warm glow. Kaz was different—so unlike the boys she
dated in high school, who were so... so *shallow*. Even Ryk, the fun-
loving Ryk, always seemed to be skating along the surface. She'd
known him since she was fourteen, but somehow she wondered if she
really knew him at all. She was so much more comfortable with Kaz.
Now, after only one evening, she felt as though she had known him
for years.

6
Steckered

When you have eliminated the impossible, whatever remains, however improbable, must be the truth.

Sherlock Holmes,
The Sign of Four

The next afternoon, Anna curled up in a well stuffed chair and began to read *Anna Karenina*. This was, she realized, the first time in several years she had enjoyed the luxury of sitting down with a novel. When Krystyna dropped by to pick her up for the evening's festivities, Anna demurred; enough parties for the time being. Krystyna smiled quizzically. Anna responded: I'll be going out with Kaz on Saturday. That's the first time he can get away.

For the next three weeks, Krystyna got the same answer: Anna would be seeing Kaz. Then, on Tuesday of the following week, Anna received a message: a telegram from the "Special Meteorology Project" for her to return—at once. At this time of day, she couldn't contact Kaz by phone to break their date. She wrote, and then rewrote, a telegram to him; and rewrote a follow-up letter at least half a dozen times, saying how much she hoped to get back to Warsaw.

There was no need to be concerned. Three days earlier, Kaz had put in for a transfer to a base near Poznan. It would come through quickly; many officers were eager to transfer the other way, from Poznan to Warsaw.

When Anna got back to the "Special Meteorology Project," she was surprised at the upbeat mood. Substantial progress had been made with Rejewski's machine, although undeciphered messages were still piling up. The following day, Henryk reappeared, carrying a large case. He called the group of four together and opened the case with a flourish. Inside was an Enigma machine with an attachment—something like a small telephone switchboard, dotted with round holes or sockets, each labeled with a letter. A tangle of cables connected the sockets in no apparent order.

"That," announced Henryk, pointing to the switchboard, "is a plugboard, or, as the Germans call it, a Steckerboard. It comes to us, compliments of Army intelligence.

"Its purpose is just what Jerzy suggested—a second encoding. It's an integral part of the machine, and that makes it easy to use. Each of the short cables can be plugged into two sockets connecting any two letters—say C and K; then C and K are steckered together. When a key is pushed, and C comes out of the three-wheeled scrambler, the current is routed through the steckerboard, changing the C to a K; the K appears in the lighted board at the top. As the connections run both ways, the steckerboard will also switch every K to the letter C. So the machine works like the original: at any initial setting, it can be used either to code or decode a message."

Jerzy was leaning over the machine, obviously fascinated—like an eight-year old preparing to take a watch apart.

"Yes, Jerzy, you may play with it; the present settings don't mean anything in particular."

Jerzy began to unplug the cables, resetting them in a different order. Each time, he set the wheels to AAA and pushed one of the keys, scribbling the results on a pad.

"The steckerboard seems like a very simple second coding," Henryk continued, "and it is. C always becomes K, and K always becomes C, as long as the cable settings remain unchanged. If that were the only coding, it would be child's play to decipher it. But it's not. We have two codings in tandem: first the scrambling from the three wheels, with the results then passed through the steckerboard.

"Unfortunately, this simple system has spectacular results. Consider. The first letter, A, may be steckered to any of the other 25 letters, obviously giving 25 possibilities."

Marian squirmed in his seat; he had been suffering most acutely from the frustration of preceding months. His mind was now racing ahead; he interrupted Henryk.

"Once A is steckered, there are 24 remaining unsteckered letters. The next one, B, can be steckered to any of the other 23 open plugs, and so on. Thus, the number of possible combinations is 25 x 23 x 21.... That comes to a total of..."

Henryk paused to let Marian demonstrate his impressive ability to do calculations in his head. He waited expectantly, head slightly forward, brows raised, his ten long fingers pressed against the table.

"What? Almost 10 trillion?" Marian reported after a few seconds.

"Actually, *only* 8 trillion." Henryk paused to let the number sink in. "For each of these possibilities, there are the 100,000-plus combinations coming through the three-wheeled scrambler. In very rough terms, that makes almost a quintillion possibilities — or, if you like it straight and simple, a billion billion."

Without realizing it, Anna sighed.

"I think," Henryk said in a record understatement, "that this will require the best from both our gorillas and idiots. Indeed, the next round goes to the idiots. Brute force, by itself, *simply won't work any more.* We're to the end of the line with that approach. We expect a lot from Marian's brute of a machine, but not magic."

The responses of his small audience varied. Marian smiled slightly; it was the first time that Henryk had allowed himself to use the terms gorillas and idiots. Jerzy and Anna, as the chief idiots, were now on the spot; they looked decidedly glum at the huge odds against them. In the past two years, the possible encodings had escalated from a "mere" 17 thousand to a billion billion. To read a message by brute force would take many trillion times as long. They should live so long.

"I also think," concluded Henryk, "that we might all turn the problem over in our minds before meeting again — next Wednesday morning, I would suggest."

They didn't get anywhere the next Wednesday. Nor the following Wednesday, nor the next, nor any of the Wednesdays until mid November.

Then they collectively found the key that would be used, not only by the Poles, but also by the French and especially the British all the way up to the time of the invasion of France in May 1940, when the Germans would have another particularly nasty surprise.

When they sat down for the regular Wednesday meeting, Henryk asked Anna, as the raporteur, to sum up the current situation as she saw it; this would give them a starting point.

Unconsciously, Anna sat a bit straighter in her chair, giving a formality to her report. "There are obviously two parts of the puzzle: the wheels from the original Enigma — the scrambler, in other words — plus the steckerboard. Our basic problem is: how can we solve the scrambler settings without first knowing the steckerboard settings, and vice versa? In other words, we have to solve both sets of settings — the wheels and the steckerboard — *simultaneously*."

Anna noticed that Marian was stroking his beard. She continued.

"What do we know that might be helpful?

"First, some of the messages start with 'From,' or VON in German. It's not clear how much help that is. After it goes through the steckerboard, VON may be transmogrified into *any* three other letters. In spite of it all, there might be something here," she said, trying to be upbeat. "We've also collected a list of other similar cribs."

Marian was now stroking his beard even more slowly, more thoughtfully. Anna hoped he was still listening. She took up her story.

"Second, the pattern of messages has remained the same: a preamble followed by two sets of three letters, followed by a string, followed by groups of five letters. Thus, it is reasonable to assume that the two sets of three letters — the inscrutable six — still give the wheel settings. But how can we use that information? Again, it will go through the steckerboard, which will change all the letters from the scrambler. Again, we're driven back to our fundamental problem: it's hard to see how we can crack any corner of the problem without figuring out everything — wheels and steckerboard — at once. We will have to..."

Her voice trailed off because it looked as if Marian was ready to say something.

"I'm not so sure," he began. "If we do what we did before, it's true that we would have to decode a message to figure out the inscrutable six. That brings us to our little problem of a billion billion possible settings.... But suppose we attack the inscrutable six directly, *without* a decoded message. Would that be possible?"

Henryk was about to say "How?" but caught himself; Marian was already continuing, slowly and thoughtfully.

"The way to start, it seems to me, would be to look for some clue in the six letters themselves. What would that be?"

He swallowed a sip of water and continued:

"What are the inscrutable six? Instructions on how the recipient should set the wheels to decode the incoming message. The instructions are repeated, giving two sets of three letters. For example:

PQR PQR

"But of course, this information is encrypted; any six letters may show up. Suppose we find an intercept that happens to give the same letter for the first and fourth position, for example:

ABC AFG

"Then we would know that we're at an interesting place in the wheels. If we first push a P, it comes out A after encryption. Three letters latter, when we push P again, it once more comes out A. We might use that to pry open the problem."

He paused for about a minute; everybody at the table was deep in thought.

"But I'm not sure that will help. There's still the steckerboard problem...."

"But is there?" responded Jerzy, his words tumbling out. "Isn't the steckerboard beside the point? Suppose, for example, that the A is steckered to K. Then, looking at the first and fourth positions of your example, the scrambler part of the machine would be kicking out

Kxx Kxx.

"In other words, *the steckerboard is irrelevant for your basic conclusion.* The initial setting of the wheels gives the same letter in positions 1 and 4 — although we don't have any idea of what that letter might be."

Now Henryk was smiling. The billion billion, he though, has just been cut down to something like a "mere" billion.

An excited conversation — interspersed with long, thoughtful silences — ensued. After an hour, Henryk brought this part of the meeting to a close.

"So we need to figure out some way of using messages in which the first and fourth letters of the inscrutable six are the same—or the second and fifth letters, or third and sixth.

"I think it might be better if we broke into two groups. We might think along different lines; we won't all chase down the same dead-end path. I suggest Marian and me in one group, and Jerzy and Anna in the other.

"Let's take a two-hour break, to recharge our batteries and have lunch," Henryk suggested, "and come back at two o'clock. I'd like Marian to report on the impressive progress with his new machine. If we all know what it will do, our problem may not seem quite so formidable. Also, some of us may be able to make suggestions for his next model."

After lunch, Marian gave a detailed account of his machine; it would quickly run through the results from possible wheel settings. This first version worked, spitting out answers several hundred times as fast as a skilled operator entering letters in an Enigma machine by hand.

Marian was already hard at work on a version at least ten times as fast, and explained in detail the modifications he had in mind. There was an intense discussion of the new model—Mark II—and how it might be improved even more.

"With the new model, a thousand times faster than hand, the billion has been cut down to a million," observed Henryk. "We may win after all."

Anna had never studied the inner workings of machines—the penalties of being a college dropout, she thought—and felt left out of the conversation. Afterward, she saw that her notes were garbled, but Jerzy was most helpful in explaining patiently and in detail what Marian was doing.

She certainly appreciated Jerzy's help.

But, as she and Jerzy worked closely together in his tiny office, his cigar smoke began to bother her. When Henryk asked to see her on an administrative matter, she cautiously raised the subject. To soften her complaint, she began on a positive note:

"Jerzy's brilliant. And he's exceptionally helpful, patiently explaining stuff I don't understand. In many ways, he's a joy to work with.... But there's one problem. Normally, I don't mind cigars, but his office is so small and his cigars so cheap. I'm finding them hard to take."

"Sorry. We try to put up with eccentricities."

Anna was concerned that Henryk might dismiss her problem. "Maybe vee should take up a Kollekshun, and buy him deszendt Zigars," she said, flippantly, in a mock German accent.

"Wouldn't recommend it. He might smoke more. You've noticed how often he has an unlighted cigar in his mouth? And a collection? He might take it as an insult."

Anna hadn't meant her suggestion—for a collection—to be taken seriously; she just wanted to keep the conversation focused on smoking. In future, she'd have to be more careful with offhand little jokes. She and Henryk usually communicated so well. But when it came to humor, they were on a different wavelength.

Now, she wasn't sure exactly what she wanted. But she continued. "He puzzles me. So often, he seems like a perfect gentleman, even a patrician. Impeccable manners, a light sense of humor, and thoughtful. At other times...."

"Ah, I'm afraid he's had a rather, um, uneven upbringing."

Anna gazed attentively in order to encourage Henryk to continue.

"He comes from an aristocratic, land-owning family in the Ukraine. But his father...."

Henryk's voice trailed off. Shifting uncomfortably in her chair, Anna thought that perhaps the time had come to leave. Just as she leaned forward, about to get up, Henryk continued.

"A jolly type. But not much of an example. Heavy drinking. Gambling. More than the usual eye for the ladies."

Again there was a pause, again Anna shifted in her chair, and again Henryk continued.

"To compensate, Jerzy's mother expected a lot from him. One day, when he was only four, she caught him signaling under the table, helping his older brother with a math problem. After scolding him— gently, because she was so proud of his precocious abilities—she

54

expressed her greatest hope: 'One day, you'll be a great man. I'll be proud of you.' Nice, in some ways. But quite a burden to lay on a four-year old."

Again Henryk stopped. This time, Anna sat tight. Henryk had his chin resting on his loosely clenched fist, the other arm across his chest to support his elbow. Apparently, he was trying to think something through.

"There is one way out of our problem. With the expansion, we're about to get new offices. I can find an office for Jerzy next to a conference room. As the construction is not yet complete, I think I can arrange both an upgrade in the air circulation system and a connecting door from his room. I'll arrange to keep the conference room as free as possible; your meetings are likely to migrate there naturally. If they don't, please let me know. I'll suggest to him — as tactfully as I can — that the two of you meet there, rather than in his small office.

"We need Jerzy. We need you — we're delighted, how quickly you proved you belonged in the senior group. And we need the two of you to work together. If you find you can't stand the smoke, we might ask him to stay in his office while he's puffing away. But let me think about it."

Anna expressed her thanks. She had been embarrassed to raise the subject of smoking. Now she was glad she had.

The Wednesday meetings were canceled until further notice. Henryk really did want the two groups to work independently, not simply follow the same approach. A good idea, perhaps. But Anna and Jerzy — in their new conference room — sweated away, day after day, which stretched into week after week. They weren't getting anywhere, and Anna took Marian's earlier advice. She decided she would be more productive if she took more time off. Whenever Kaz could get away.

Then, one afternoon in March 1939, Henryk's secretary called. The core group of four was to meet right away. There were some ideas to consider.

"Let's look at the machine and its settings," Henryk began. "Rather than trying to work directly toward a solution, we propose to go at the problem from the opposite direction — to rule out impossible settings. Settings that could *not* give a repeat. Then we can focus our work on what remains — the ones that *are* possible."

"Ah," said Jerzy, "you've intruded into the idiot's territory. We welcome you."

Henryk ignored the interruption. "What information do we have? We're going to pick out German messages where there's a repeat in the inscrutable six. But there are thousands of possible wheel settings. How can we keep track of the absolute blizzard of detail? What we propose is to use square sheets — 26 spaces across, labeled from A to Z for each setting of the second wheel, and 26 spaces down for each setting of the third wheel. We will need 26 such sheets, one for each setting of the first wheel.

"Consider an example, where the three wheels are set at the letters BDH. This will show up on the second — B — sheet, in the D column and the H row. If it is possible for that setting to give a repeat on the third press of the key, our staff will mark that box.

"It will be tedious to make the sheets. But whenever there's a repeat within the inscrutable six, the sheets will tell us which settings are worth testing with our new machine. We can ignore the unmarked boxes; they're not possible."

"Mention the six sets," interjected Marian. "Mention the six sets."

"Oh yes," said Henryk, trying to add a light touch to a difficult topic. "I left out one little detail. As we know, the three wheels can be set in six different orders. We will have to have one set of sheets for each ordering — that is, 6 sets of 26 sheets each."

Anna lowered her head. She was very much afraid that she was going to start rolling her eyes; that wouldn't be very good form.

"But we'll have help," said Marian. "We'll be producing six of the new machines as soon as possible, one to test each of the possible wheel orderings."

Henryk wound up the meeting. "Finally — and this must remain secret, just among the four of us — I've asked the General Staff for permission to inform the British and French of our progress. With the barbaric behavior of Germany, we need to give our allies as much help as possible."

This was the first time that Anna could remember Henryk speaking harshly of the Germans; thus far, their work had seemed like a dispassionate, intricate academic puzzle. But they were all aware, in the backs of their minds, just how much might be at stake. The events of the past week had driven home the dangers facing Poland. Hitler's legions had goose-stepped into the remnants of Czechoslovakia. The Czech government, shorn of its Sudetenland defenses by the British-French capitulation at Munich, chose not to resist. If they did, Hitler threatened, he would bomb Prague flat. This, after promising the umbrella-toting British Prime Minister that Sudetenland was his "last territorial demand," and that "peace in our time" could be gained by selling out the Czechs.

Hitler already had his eyes on his next victim; he was threatening Poland. In response, France and Britain declared that they would guarantee Poland's independence. The Poles were going out of their way not to provoke the ranting Führer; they did not want to give him the slimmest pretext to invade. But the prospects were grim.

Marian asked Anna to come to his office.

"I notice from your file that your mother was British."

"That's right."

"You speak English?"

"Some."

"Let's not be coy. This is important. Didn't you spend your first eight years in Britain, when your father was at the Embassy?"

"Yes."

"So English was your first language. You speak it comfortably?"

"So-so. When I was young, I spoke English to my mother. I spoke Polish to my father. When we came to Poland, my father insisted that I speak only Polish. I confess, mom and I cheated from time to time. I can think in English, but still speak it like an eight year old. More or less. I don't know many technical terms."

"Can you translate this?"

Anna took the book—a Polish treatise on the physics of radio—and translated a paragraph, stumbling over a number of technical terms, but otherwise speaking fluently. Marian was satisfied; as far as he could tell, she had a perfect Oxford accent.

"Our number one priority is a meeting with the French and British. To let you in on a secret," he lowered his voice, "I met with French and British intelligence officers in Paris in January. Our government instructed me to listen, not pass on information. But, from what I can tell, we're substantially ahead of them. Can't be sure, of course; they may have held back when I said so little. But now the time has come for everybody to get serious."

Anna's face must have shown surprise; she had always thought of the British and French as being serious. It seemed ungracious to suggest that they were not, when Rejewski apparently hadn't offered any information in return.

"I'm particularly eager to work with the French." Rejewski gave Anna a brief summary of the early codebreaking effort. "I haven't mentioned this before, but I got one of the first big breaks on the Enigma from Bertrand — now the head of French intelligence — way back in 1932, before Hitler came to power. He was just a captain then, but was their specialist in foreign ciphers. He came into contact with a German official who gave him Enigma settings for October and December of the previous year.

"Bertrand thought they were priceless," continued Marian, "but the French Intelligence Bureau wasn't interested; they wanted to milk their spy for other information, on German rearmament plans. Then Bertrand went to the British. They weren't interested either; they thought the Enigma simply couldn't be broken. In frustration, he turned to me. I was ecstatic. I already had good relations with him, and they've been even better since."

"So the French and British did drop the ball," Anna conceded. "But what motivated the German? Treason is so hard to understand."

"Really? There are three great reasons: divided loyalties, sex, and money, in no particular order." Marian's tone was slightly patronizing; he was explaining the wicked world to a naive twenty-year old. "In this case, it was sex and money; he needed money to afford his love affairs.

"But let's get back to the point. If you think your English needs work, you could go back to the University for an hour or two each day, to study English intensively. Concentrate on technical terms. If the meeting with the Brits does work out, I'd like you to take the lead in presentations to them. With a bit of work, I think you'd be up to it. We — the old guard — chose French as our main foreign language.

"We could get translators from the Foreign Office," Marian continued. "But we'd rather not. The fewer people present, the smaller the risk of a security breach. Also, things will move much faster if one of us can explain things directly to the English — not go through a tedious translation. Of course, none of the Brits speaks Polish. They don't much believe in learning other languages. The farther East they go, the less interested they seem to be."

With her English studies, Anna's next few months were hectic, but she made a point of getting away whenever Kaz had a free day.

At the first Enigma meeting in June, Anna asked if she might say something. Henryk guessed what it was.

"Is it related to Enigma?"

"No," said Anna softly.

"To the security of the realm?"

She realized she was going to be teased; she might as well take it in good humor. She answered in dramatic style:

"No, no, my liege. I humbly do confess."

Henryk played along; they now really were on the same wavelength.

"And what can claim the time of these great knights?"

He waved his hand expansively around the table, ignoring the inconvenient fact that there were only two other people present. Anna responded:

"Great knights? But is the table round, my lord?

My senses do betray me."

Conspicuously placing one hand over a corner of the table and raising the other to her brow, she feigned a half swoon.

Henryk insisted:

"The table round, I swear.

The corner square — 'tis but a mere mirage."

Anna got to the point:

"I beg your leave to wed my noble knight.

The month of Caesar, prime, the full moon's time."

Jerzy smiled. "The Seventh Cavalry, no doubt."

Anna ignored him. The game was now afoot; she had no wish to end it. She spoke again to Henryk:

"One boon, my liege, one single boon, I pray."

"O what, young wench?"

"Forsake *ius noctis primae*, lord, my liege.

Thereby shalt thou make virtue doubly safe."

Marian snickered; not such a naive twenty-year old, after all. Jerzy broke into a belly laugh; Anna feared he might hurt himself. Henryk — the cool, rational Henryk — was he actually blushing?

As Henryk sat silent, she followed up, pretending to beg:

"I prithee, lord."

He was now trying hard to hold up his end without seeming stiff.

"I deign to grant the blushing maiden's wish."

Turning to Jerzy, Anna continued the game:

"And thou, bold knight, hast thou a gift for me?"

Dramatically twisting out his stogie in the ashtray, Jerzy replied:

"The greatest gift that man can e'er bestow."

Anna pressed her luck:

"Till dread and darkest death between us come?"

Jerzy responded immediately:

"Less fast, dear lass, for death t'would be

The weed, you see, has pow'r of life o're me."

Henryk ended the game with a rhyming couplet:

"Then heart's enigma fast unraveled be,

With happiness and joy for all to see."

"Joking aside," he said in his normal businesslike voice, "we all congratulate you, Anna, and wish you and Kaz the greatest happiness. But it's time to get back to unraveling the real Enigma.

"With our new sheets, we've been able to decipher some of the messages from last October, November, and early December. But we've hit a stone wall since mid-December. We've been able to decode only a few messages, and only when the German operator did something stupid — like sending part of a message in code and part in the clear. But those few messages have been enough to tell us that the Germans introduced two new wheels in December."

The group looked glum. Except Anna, who had been floating on a cloud since Kaz proposed.

"Marian and I have concluded that the Germans use only three wheels at any one time, even though they now have five available. If we're correct, our problems have multiplied tenfold. Now there are 5 possible wheels in the first position, 4 in the second, and 3 in the third — 60 positions altogether. We'll need 60 sets of sheets, not just six, and we'll be able to make the 60 only if we get our hands on those last two wheels."

Everybody — again except Anna — looked even glummer.

"Nevertheless, I do have some good news. We have permission to tell the British and French everything we know, and even give them copies of the Enigma machine. The meeting is scheduled for July 11 and 12. For security reasons, it won't be here. You should all be prepared to travel with your overnight bags on the previous evening, the 10th."

When the 10th came, they were taken in several army staff cars, along a circuitous route, to a hunting lodge deep in Pyry Forest. It was a rustic building, surrounded by towering fir trees, swaying and sighing in the gentle breezes. Even in summer, a huge stone fireplace in the middle of the Great Hall provided a coziness to the lodge, taking the creeping chill off the late-evening air. The high, open ceilings of the hall were supported by roughhewn timbers. Corridors ran off the hall in all directions, some to meeting rooms, some to the bedroom wings.

The French and British were now very serious indeed; the prospect that they might all be destroyed by the Nazis had marvelously focused their minds. The French were headed by Gustave Bertrand, who was warmly welcomed by Marian Rejewski. The two old friends quickly disappeared into one of the meeting rooms, accompanied by several other French officers and Jerzy.

As planned, Anna and Henryk retired to another room with Dilly Knox and Alastair Denniston. In spite of Henryk's limited knowledge of English, he would be able to follow Anna's main points, and suggest additional ideas from time to time.

He was lugging a heavy case, which he placed on the table in front of Denniston. Henryk snapped the cover back.

"This, Mr. Denniston, is the German Enigma machine," Anna began dramatically. "More precisely, it is our copy of the machine. Please accept it as a gift of the Polish Government."

Denniston mumbled his thanks, and began to examine the machine. "Please call me Alastair," he added. "I notice that you all call one another by your first names."

So he did, apparently, have at least a smattering of Polish, or perhaps Russian.

Anna explained how they figured out the basic Blue code for the early machine, then went through the complications that had arisen, especially the steckerboard. She emphasized the importance of repeats in the inscrutable six. They might be exploited with Rejewski's machine—details to come this afternoon—and the Zygalski sheets. Henryk appeared slightly embarrassed when she used that term.

The British seemed duly impressed, but then she got to the disappointing bit. Although they had sporadically deciphered messages for 1938 and earlier, they had run into a major problem. The Germans were now using five wheels, although only three at a time. The codes might still be broken, if they could ever reconstruct or steal the other two wheels and produce a complete set of Zygalski sheets. Marian was working intensely, trying to figure out the internal wiring of the two new wheels.

Alastair and Dilly followed the presentation intently, asking penetrating questions; it quickly became clear that they were familiar with many of the issues. But apparently, this meeting was to be the reverse of January's. The Poles were the ones providing information; the British were listening.

During the luncheon break, Anna made a brief, and, she hoped, discrete, visit to the office of the hunting lodge.

The afternoon was dedicated to Marian's description of his machine; detailed plans would be provided to the British and French, along with ideas for the upcoming Mark II. Through the mishmash of languages, it became clear that that the British were working on a similar decoding machine.

At the end, Dilly Knox observed that Marian had simply spoken of "Mark I and Mark II." But Mark I of what? What was the machine called? A "bomba" or bombe, he was told.

"Why in the world a 'bomba'?" he asked.

"Because," replied Marian, "it keeps on ticking until something happens."

Thereafter, whenever Anna was asked why it was called a bomba, she repeated Marian's explanation. Even after she discovered the truth. Marian had been too embarrassed to give an honest answer. When he first thought of the machine, he, Henryk, and Jerzy were eating a popular ice cream called bomba. So bomba it was.

As the meeting broke up, Anna was asked to accompany Denniston and Knox back to the British embassy. As the two visitors settled in the back seat, they began to rehash the events of the previous 24 hours. The meeting was a tremendous success; Denniston was delighted with the Enigma machine and information provided by the Poles.

"It was bloody-well time," retorted Knox, apparently forgetting that Anna was in the front seat. "Bertrand is livid."

There were a few moments of silence; Anna could feel anger simmering in the back seat. Knox exploded.

"The bastards told Bertrand that they would inform him at once if they succeeded in breaking Enigma. It was their solemn promise when Bertrand passed Schmidt's information on to them way back in 1932."

So Schmidt, thought Anna, was the German traitor. Not much of a security breach — there must be thousands of people named Schmidt in Germany. But she hoped that the driver didn't understand English.

She wondered if she should try to defend Rejewski. He had been eager to talk to the British and French, but had been unable, until recently, to get permission. She decided to let it pass.

Denniston apparently remembered that Anna was in the front seat, and switched the conversation to the recent games at Wimbledon.

The next day, the British and French headed home with a mixture of gratitude and resentment, the gift machines following in diplomatic pouches.

For the Poles remaining behind, those troublesome fourth and fifth rotors presented a roadblock. But in a remarkable mathematical feat,

Marian succeeded in figuring out their internal wiring from radio intercepts. He was helped by a German blunder. The final piece of his puzzle fell into place when the Poles intercepted a long message, with plain text and coded passages interspersed.

A month later, as Denniston was working methodically through a sample of Zygalski sheets, his secretary buzzed. A messenger from the Polish embassy was in the outer office. He had come with a package. But they were having trouble with him; he flatly refused to give it to anyone but Denniston himself. Denniston had him sent in. Denniston slit open the plain brown cardboard box and saw a note at the top.

> 22 August, 1939
> Dear Alastair,
> Thought that numbers four and five might be of
> some interest to you.
> Regards,
> Anna.

Rummaging through the packing material, Denniston extracted two Enigma wheels.

Anna, he thought, has certainly inherited the British tendency toward understatement.

7
Dinner Party

If Poland is attacked, Anglo-French military plans to come to her aid are ready for immediate operation.
The Sunday Times (London), August 20, 1939

...just for a scrap of paper – Great Britain is going to make war!
Theobald von Bethmann-Hollweg, to Sir Edward Goschen, August 4, 1914

Wednesday, 30 August, 1939. Raczynski Family Estate.

Anna's parents had invited the newlyweds to the traditional end-of-summer family reunion at their estate 60 kilometers west of Warsaw. Also invited were Anna's two brothers, together with an assortment of aunts, uncles, and cousins. Anna and Kaz quickly accepted; Kaz would have a chance to get to know the family during the long, four-day weekend.

A few days later, she had been deeply disappointed when Kaz said that his visit would have to be cut short. Poland was mobilizing in the face of German threats; only a few officers would be given time off. Kaz's four-day leave had been cut down to 24 hours, but he couldn't be sure that he would be able to get away at all. He hoped to join the family some time Wednesday evening.

Zambrowski, the family chauffeur, met her at the station early in the evening in the old black Mercedes. Anna couldn't help but notice that the small dent in the rear fender was still there; it hadn't been fixed yet, but otherwise the car was immaculate. During the leisurely twenty-minute drive to the estate, Zambrowski brought her up to date

65

on the family. Stefan, her half-brother from her father's first marriage, had just arrived from his foreign office post, but, with the crisis atmosphere in Warsaw, he would have to catch the noon train back to the capital the next day. So would Uncle Michal, who likewise worked at the foreign office, although Aunt Maria expected to stay until early the next week. Josef, Anna's younger brother, was on leave from his regiment, but he would have to depart mid-morning on Friday. Sisi, her twelve-year-old sister, would of course be there for the whole weekend and beyond; her school year did not begin until Sept. 12.

Unfortunately, several of the cousins had sent their last-minute regrets; they couldn't come because of the tense international situation. Other cousins, aunts, and uncles would be arriving throughout the day on Saturday. Naturally, Anna's parents were disappointed that attendance would be so light, and, for some of the guests, brief. But it couldn't be helped; they would try to make the most of it.

As the Mercedes turned into the circular drive, Anna heard the familiar crunch of gravel. Her mother was standing in front of the mansion to greet her; her younger sister came bouncing down the marble steps to throw her arms around Anna as she stepped out of the car.

Dinner was later than normal; they waited an extra hour and a half in the hope that Kaz would arrive. Around the table, the mood was somber and subdued, in keeping with the dark oak paneling of the room. Sisi entertained herself by making faces at the portrait of great grandpapa; she carefully leaned back between Josef and Stefan so her parents couldn't see her. Across the table, Uncle Michal and Aunt Maria looked on with amusement; they had raised children of their own.

According to an unstated family rule, proper topics at the evening meal included music, the theater, books, or family matters. Politics were not to be mentioned, although exceptions were permitted if anyone wanted to introduce the subject with a discussion of Plato's *Republic*, Machiavelli's *Prince*, or Gibbon's *Fall of the Roman Empire*. Religion was likewise out of bounds, although, in this case, there was just one exception: C.S. Lewis's forthcoming *Screwtape Letters*. Anna's mother had recently received a manuscript copy from the author, and was interested in her family's reactions.

Just nicely into the main course, younger brother Josef broke the rule.

"All the officers seem to think we're in for it, that the Germans will attack." He was addressing his comment to Uncle Michal. Michal looked for guidance to his hostess. Anna's mother, the daughter of an English Duke, was the social arbiter of the family. She had married Anna's father when he was with the informal Polish liaison office in London, back during the Great War, when the Poles were hoping to have an independent nation once again.

Josef tried to redeem himself. "I mean, a book's coming out, that says our officers are afraid the Germans will attack."

The hostess smiled indulgently at her son's verbal contortion, and nodded to Michal. He had her permission to reply.

But the irrepressible Sisi cut in, with her usual optimism. "Won't the Russians restrain the Germans? They keep saying that they're the ones who can save the world from Fascism."

"I thought it was the other way round—Hitler says he's going to save Western Civilization from Stalin and Bolshevism." Anna still liked to tease her little sister.

"No, no. We need somebody to save us from both of those tyrants. That brings me back to my question. What do you think, Uncle Michal? Will the Germans attack us?"

"We can always hope. But the pact between Russia and Germany...." He shook his head. "Hitler despises the Bolsheviks, and vice versa. On that, Sisi and Anna were both right. But Ribbentrop and Molotov have signed this nonaggression pact. What's its purpose, other than to clear the way for German aggression against us?"

"But surely," said Sisi, half-cheerfully, "Hitler won't attack us. Britain and France guaranteed Poland's independence when the Nazis marched into Prague last March."

"Also, Britain reacted to the Ribbentrop-Molotov Pact by signing a formal alliance with Poland last weekend," added Aunt Maria, trying to sound equally upbeat but not quite succeeding.

Stefan entered the discussion rather pompously, making it clear that he considered himself an expert on the Western powers. "From my experience with the French and British, I doubt that we can count on either. After all, the British said last year they'd fight if the Germans invaded Czechoslovakia, but a lot of good that did the Czechs. The Brits turned right around and sold them out at Munich. To be frank, the Czechs—with their solid fortifications facing Germany—would have been in a stronger position to fight than we are. I may be wrong—why would the French and British sign the formal alliance if they were going to do nothing? But then, they don't have much to lose by bluffing, given the huge stakes. So I still come down on the pessimistic side. When the crunch comes, they probably won't help." He leaned forward, his elbows on the table—a social no-no that seemed out of place with his exquisitely tailored suit. But he wanted to emphasize his point.

Anna noticed the elbows. So did her mother. At an earlier time, she would have asked him if he were staking out a land claim. But now she seemed caught up in the conversation, and, at any rate, it was already out of her control. She simply winked at Anna.

Josef was about to come to the defense of the Polish armed forces, but decided to let the insult pass.

Anna joined the optimists. "I'd rely on both the French and British to help us. When I talk to them, they both seem to be much more committed this time."

"Weather forecasters of the world, unite," retorted Stefan sarcastically.

Sisi quickly took Anna's side: "And jackasses of the world, unite."

This time, their mother did exert her authority, giving Sisi a searing glance. Sisi lapsed into silence. In fact, everyone around the table was silent for some minutes.

Josef decided to press the topic again. As a young boy, he had been in awe of his uncle, who had been an officer during the last great European cavalry battle in 1920. The Poles cut off Tukhachevsky's Soviet army that was threatening to encircle Warsaw, taking 100,000 Russian prisoners and saving the eastern third of Poland from Soviet occupation. Josef naturally directed his question to his boyhood hero. "What do you think, Uncle Michal?"

"I think we can count on the British and French to stand by us, and declare war on Hitler. But it's not clear that they can or will do much to give us real help. I'm not optimistic that Hitler will be restrained."

He paused. This time, Aunt Maria encouraged him to continue. "Why not, Michal?"

"Hitler's hell-bent on war. He's not just interested in the Danzig corridor. It's like Czechoslovakia—he was interested in the whole country, not just the Sudetenland. He's interested in *Lebensraum*— living room for the expanding German population. That means seizing lands in Poland, and even more in Russia."

"But what about his nonaggression pact with Stalin?" Sisi was again trying to be optimistic.

"Hitler will tear it up the moment it's convenient, just as he tore up his nonaggression pact with us. He's determined to attack us, the British and French be damned. I doubt they will do much to help us. I doubt they can. I think they'll follow us right over the cliff into war, but they'll be ineffectual. Nevertheless, we'll fight, no matter what the odds." Michal's stern words were reinforced with a firmly set jaw. He was graying at the temples, but had kept himself trim; Anna could easily envision him on his horse, charging into battle, even at his age.

A subdued silence settled over the table once more. It was broken when the dog barked. Zambrowski, who doubled as the butler, entered and announced that Mr. Ryk—or more precisely, Flying Officer Ryk—was calling. Should he ask Mr. Ryk to wait in the drawing room until after dinner?

"Not at all, not at all," replied Anna's father. "Show him in, and set another place. I'm sure that the young man will be happy to have something to eat. With the last-minute cancellations, we have more than enough." Anna's mother was about to say something, but stopped short.

Stanislaw Ryk—a neighbor, longtime family friend, and sometime beau of Anna—entered the room.

"Oh, Ryk, Ryk, you look so dashing in your uniform," Sisi said excitedly, standing on her tiptoes to give him a big hug. "And you already have your wings. Now that I'm twelve, will you take me up in your flying machine?"

"I do apologize. Thought dinner would be over by now. I'm home on leave, but have to report back on Friday. I'll be away from some time; my squadron's moving to a new base, further south. Didn't want to leave without saying goodbye."

He went down the table, greeting the various members of the family. When he got to Anna, she rose and rather antiseptically offered her cheek, which he softly kissed.

"Anna's just been married," Sisi announced. "To a cavalry officer." Anna wondered: was that a flicker of disappointment on Ryk's face?

"But when are you going to take me up?" Sisi pressed her question.

"Not sure I'll have a chance," mumbled Ryk.

"Bet you still have the old plane." Ryk had originally learned to fly when he was fifteen, taught by his barnstorming uncle who had an ancient German triplane that dated from the Great War. His uncle had jerry-rigged a back seat, so he could take paying customers up for flights. "Come on, Ryk. After all, you took Anna up three years ago."

She realized she had said the wrong thing. Anna looked daggers at her. That was supposed to be a secret; their father had explicitly forbidden Anna to go up in the plane with her teen-aged, daredevil friend. Fortunately, Anna's father didn't pick up Sisi's enthusiastic query; he was losing his hearing. Anna's mother heard perfectly, but pretended not to. She had known about the flights for years. That was scarcely surprising, as Ryk had showed off by buzzing the local convent school for teenaged girls. Anna decided she had better change the subject. Quickly.

"We were just talking about the war scare. We had a difference of opinion within the Foreign Office. Uncle Michal thinks the western powers are willing to go to war if Hitler attacks us. Stefan doesn't. Why don't we hear the two sides in more detail? Stefan?" She hoped to put her half-brother on the spot.

"I agree with Uncle Michal on the critical point, that Britain and France can't or won't do much to help us, at least not unless we can hold out for six months or more — until the spring weather makes operations in the West possible. So let's put ourselves in their shoes.

Why blunder into a war with Hitler, if they can't actually help us? Not clear."

Zambrowski arrived with an extra table setting, but paused; Anna's mother seemed uncomfortable. Ryk took the hint. "Thanks, but I've already eaten. Must be off. Sorry to interrupt." He closed the thick, paneled door behind him.

Anna picked up the conversation, again looking on the bright side. "Won't the prospect of war with Britain and France discourage other countries from joining Hitler's war — Italy, Hungary, or Lithuania?"

"Point well taken," replied Stefan, managing to sound patronizing towards Anna even when he was agreeing. "They could also have other reasons — their honor, and to make sure that Hitler doesn't pick them off one by one. It's particularly important for France to get the British committed. If the British don't come through this time — after all their huffing and puffing — the French may feel that they won't be able to count on Britain if Hitler moves West.

"But this point isn't very strong. If Hitler defeats us and then does have a go at France, Britain will have to fight or give up any hope of stopping Hitler. They will be in a much better position to help France than to help us.

"Now let's look at the British-French case for bluffing, without actually coming to our aid. What's the very best they can hope for? That Hitler will be restrained by their threats. Not very likely, I'm sorry to say. Here again, I agree with Uncle Michal." Stefan was showing that, surprisingly, he did have some diplomatic skills, something Anna had always doubted.

"What's the next best, from their point of view, if Hitler does attack us?" he continued. "The British, in particular, don't much like either the Nazis or Communists. If they can't really help us, what's the point of declaring war?"

Stefan paused, allowing the question to sink in. No one ventured an answer, so he continued.

"Why not just take a pass, and hope that Hitler keeps right on going east, trying to seize *Lebensraum* in Russia? The Germans and Russians might bleed one another white, fighting it out. The two great tyrannies might collapse without Britain and France having to fight at all. Even if Hitler does turn west once he's finished with us" — Anna was appalled by Stefan's coldbloodedness — "Britain and France will have gained another six months or so to rearm."

Again the dog barked. There were muffled voices in the hall. Anna jumped up and rushed from the room. After a few minutes, she reappeared, hand in hand with Kaz, and introduced him to Uncle Michal, Aunt Maria, and Stefan, who had not been able to make the wedding. The family made light conversation for several minutes, talking of the weather, crops, and the new floral arrangement encircled by the driveway. Then Josef dragged the conversation back to the threat of war.

"Mother's allowed us to break the house rules — to talk politics," he explained to Kaz. "If Hitler attacks, nobody thinks the French or British will be willing or able to help us much. You're a military man; what's your opinion?"

"Willing to help? That's a political question. As you said, I'm a military man. Able to help? I'm uncertain. The French have more tanks than the Germans, and they're just as good. But tanks are made for offense; they're made to be used in concentrated spearheads, to cut through enemy lines. Victory goes to the bold and the aggressive. Will the French be bold and aggressive? I simply don't know."

"And the Molotov-Ribbentrop Pact. What do you make of it?"

"For goodness sake, Josef, do let Kaz have a bite to eat," Anna pleaded.

"Thanks, darling, but I really don't mind. The Russians mystify me. I can see Hitler's objective — keep the Russians out of the game while he attacks Poland. But the Russians? Why did they sign the Pact, giving Hitler a free hand? I can see only one answer. Stalin may hope that the Germans and French will bleed each other white. If that happens, the stage may be set for Communist revolutions throughout Europe."

"Bleed each other white. Strange. That's exactly what Stefan said," Josef observed. "But he was referring to the other side of Europe. The French and British may renege on their commitment to us, hoping that Hitler and Stalin will exhaust each other, fighting it out."

"And what would happen to us while the two elephants were fighting?" Kaz asked. "Let's hope that there's some shred of honor left, that the French and British help us."

"Uncle Michal?" Josef was now acting as chairman.

"Stefan has a point," he replied. "France and Britain do have a reason to abandon us. Hitler's occupied Austria and Czechoslovakia and cut a deal with Stalin; it may already be too late for the Western Allies to influence events in this part of Europe. Nevertheless, I think the British Parliament will force Chamberlain's hand—make him declare war to avoid utter humiliation. The ones who really worry me are the French. Last spring, they promised to invade Germany from the West within two weeks if Hitler attacked us. At the time, I had no confidence that they would honor that commitment. As we'll soon be approaching winter, I have even less confidence now."

"But what about the British?" asked Sisi. The gravity of the crisis was beginning to sink in.

"Their pledges are ludicrous. The Chief of the Imperial General Staff, Ironside, promises to match any air raids on us—one for one—with similar raids on Germany. Just a few weeks ago, when diplomats were trying to put together a broad Soviet-Western alliance to stop Hitler, Stalin lost interest when he came to the conclusion that the Western countries weren't serious. The feckless French and the bumbling Brits."

Once again, everybody looked distinctly uncomfortable.

"There is, however, a glimmer of hope," Uncle Michal added. "If we can get through the next three or four weeks without an invasion, we may make it. It will be too late for Hitler; he'll have little hope of defeating us before the bad weather."

Uncle Michal didn't add his main worry. If Hitler really was after *Lebensraum*—if he wanted somewhere for the expanding German population to live—he might drive Poles out of their country. He might even start killing civilians to encourage the survivors to flee eastward. A fight with Germany would be bloody, but surrender might be even bloodier.

Anna felt a rising terror, taking with it any lingering doubts about the value of her codebreaking exercise. And she felt panic for Kaz. She needed the reassurance of holding him; she had had quite enough of the depressing conversation. As soon as Kaz was through his main course, Anna made her excuses and the newlyweds retired.

The next morning, she was floating in a dreamy, semiconscious state, cuddling in Kaz's arms, when she became vaguely aware of Sisi practicing the piano in the distance. First it was one of Chopin's etudes; then Beethoven's *Für Elise*. She wasn't satisfied with her treatment of the opening bars; she repeated them over and over again. Suddenly, Anna was wide awake. "That's it!" She said, sitting up abruptly in bed. "Repeats. Repeats. That's the secret."

"Secret? Repeats?" said Kaz groggily, only half awake.

"Repeats, darling, repeats," she said, leaning over and kissing him. Somehow, Kaz didn't care what "repeats" meant. There was no temptation for Anna to break her vow of secrecy.

What the codebreakers needed was a message that the Germans had repeated, using two different encryptions. Then they might be able to figure out the wheel settings.

The next evening, with Kaz gone, Anna thought she might have difficulty sleeping. But as she threw open the window, the smell of new-mown hay produced a wave of nostalgia. Its soporific, relaxing effect lulled her into a deep, dreamless sleep.

Once again, she was wakened by sounds in the distance — this time, much further away. There was a strange, intermittent sound of sirens, and what seemed like explosions. She was about to go to the window, to see what was causing the noise, but just as her feet touched the floor, Sisi burst through the bedroom door.

"The Germans are attacking. All military personnel have to report at once. Josef is leaving for the station. If you hurry, you'll have time to say goodbye."

Anna threw a dressing gown over her shoulders and followed her sister down to the front steps. Josef was hugging his mother; tears were flowing freely down her cheeks. They were also flowing, not quite so freely, down Josef's cheeks. Then he turned to Anna with a big hug.

"Until we meet again," he said softly in her ear. "But I'm afraid, Anna, I'm afraid. I hope that we were wrong the other night, when we said all those unkind things about Britain and France. We need help. I'll be praying for Kaz." He gave Anna a big squeeze, stepped into the Mercedes, and was gone. He didn't look back.

8

Last Stand

Give no quarter! Take no prisoners!
Just as, a thousand years ago, the
Huns under Attila gained a name
that still resounds in terror, so may
the name of Germany resound!
    Kaiser Wilhelm II, addressing
    troops leaving for China, 1900

As ordered, Kaz and Jan left their comrades to the defense of Poznan and headed eastward toward Warsaw. With them were about 65 men, 40 horses, two heavy machine guns, several mortars, one mobile field radio, and miscellaneous light weapons and carts. They could only hope that heavier weapons — most of all, artillery — would be available when they got to the defensive positions west of Warsaw.

As long as they rode along back roads, their trip was uneventful, although, on occasion, they did have to scurry into the woods as German planes flew overhead. When they got to the main highway, however, progress became much more difficult. The road and shoulders were crowded with swarms of refugees. The confusion periodically degenerated into panicked chaos, as low-flying German fighters attacked. Because of the crowds, soldiers had trouble finding cover, and horses reared in terror as the planes flew over, their machine guns chattering.

By evening, a new pattern was developing: the Germans were strafing the sides of the roads rather than the road itself. As a result, civilians were crowding even more tightly onto the road, obstructing the military units and forcing them to leave the road in an effort to move more rapidly. It made no sense to go on this way, with the cavalry being held up by the chaos on the road. The time had come to divide the small force once again. One group would take most of the horses and head across country, while the other group, with the machine guns, other equipment, and wounded would continue down the crowded road, traveling mainly at night.

Jan and Kaz drew straws; Kaz got the group that would break away across the open country. Before parting, they warmed up the radio. The news was depressing, but not hopeless. A major defensive force was gathering around Poznan, and the fortifications around Warsaw were being strengthened as many army units retreated in a more-or-less orderly way toward the capital. Britain and France had declared war on Germany. The time had come to pray for a French thrust into Germany, to force Hitler to shift army and Luftwaffe units to the west.

Kaz and his group of 35 set out immediately; there was still enough daylight to travel rapidly, and German air activity had almost ceased with the oncoming dusk. They made remarkably good time for the first hour, but then had to slow down because of the gathering darkness. Kaz set out his plan for the most rapid movement eastward: they would travel at top speed, and as directly across country as possible, during the periods when there was enough light for horsemen, but not enough for German aircraft—for almost an hour at dusk, and a briefer period each morning, beginning with the first glimmer of light. Where they had the protection of forests, they would continue to move during the day. Otherwise, they would rest and let their horses graze, and move during the night instead.

After two days and nights, they reached and crossed the Bzura River—about 50 kilometers west of Warsaw—and were greeted by a group of Polish infantrymen. This, they were told, was where they would make a stand.

As the German tanks approached, the Polish plan was to direct artillery fire over the river at the Panzers, and to use all available weapons to disrupt any attempt by the Germans to cross. On the flanks, infantry and cavalry would probe. The infantry would seek out and destroy German infantry units unprotected by tanks or heavy artillery; the cavalry's objective would be to disrupt and destroy German supply lines, while avoiding German armored units.

The Polish attack began on Sept. 9. Kaz and Jan — who had survived a five-day ordeal along the main road — would each lead a marauding band of about 30 men; they had picked up reinforcements from other cavalry units. Kaz and his men crossed the river before dawn, and galloped west-northwest about ten kilometers. They then began to proceed, more slowly, in a leftward arc, searching for Germans.

They were in luck. As they proceeded along the edge of a hardwood forest — for protection against air attack — they spotted a convoy of a dozen German trucks, accompanied by half a dozen soldiers on motorcycles. Moving up behind two low hills, the Poles set up their light machine guns and small mortars. They would fire at the Germans as they came around a bend in the road.

Their attack could not have worked better. The machine gunners made quick work of the motorcyclists, and mortars soon had the first and last of the trucks on fire, making it impossible for any of the others to move. As troops dismounted from trucks, they were attacked with machine-gun fire. Then the third truck erupted in a spectacular explosion; apparently it had been filled with ammunition. Another truck exploded, less spectacularly, but continued to burn with the dark, greasy smoke of diesel fuel.

The Poles continued to fire for another five minutes; by then, there was little left of the German column. A number of survivors had escaped into the woods on the far side of the road, but it would be foolish to pursue them. Kaz ordered his men to pack their weapons and retreat towards the woods on their side of the road.

It was none too soon. Just as they had mounted and begun to move, they heard the terrifying sound of a Stuka's siren as it began its dive. The riders scattered; an explosion erupted on the side of the hill as a German bomb hit the ground. Kaz's men were far enough separated that there were only two fatalities, with the men and their horses being thrown into the air. After leveling out, the plane began a sharp turn; it was going to return and attack the fleeing Poles with machine guns. Fortunately, Kaz and his men reached the safety of the woods before the Stuka could complete its turn.

The surviving cavalrymen reassembled in the protection of the woods. Other than the two dead men, they had escaped unscathed, but had lost one of their machine guns. They waited in the woods for about half an hour, fearful of a follow-up air attack, but then continued along the side of the woods, looking for additional victims.

That day, they found none. Early the next morning, as they were passing a small village, a horseback rider galloped up.

"Germans are in the village," he said breathlessly. "You're our only hope."

Kaz was torn. But he had his orders. "I'm sorry, friend, but we have a specific mission. We can't go into villages the Germans have already occupied."

"But the Germans have taken hostages. They may shoot them. They're just young boys."

Helmut Krueger joined the SS at eighteen. He wanted to show those high-school snobs that he really was better than any of them. His few friends considered the SS the best, the most elite unit, a military force directly answerable to the National Socialist Party. He felt a secret thrill every time he looked at his solid black uniform. The skull on his cap—indicating he was a member of a *Totenkopf* or Death's Head Regiment—signified Hitler's will: this elite unit was the arbiter of life and death. After rigorous training, both military and political, he recommitted himself to the Nazi Party and received his commission. Within a few months, he was promoted to *Obersturmführer*, the SS equivalent of the regular army rank of *Oberleutnant* (First Lieutenant).

As war clouds gathered, he was indoctrinated with the ideas of the Führer. Hitler would crush the Bolsheviks in Russia and save Western civilization. Just how the murder of civilians would save "civilization," Hitler did not say; and the young officers, mesmerized by their Führer, had no inclination to ask.

Hitler blamed Jews for Germany's humiliating defeat in the First World War, for stabbing the armed forces in the back. In his crude view of history, Jewish-led revolts caused a collapse on the home front. To the men in the trenches—including Corporal Adolf Hitler—the shock of defeat was particularly painful, coming, as it did, so soon after the glorious victories of early 1918. They needed a scapegoat.

Shortly after the invasion of Poland, SS Chief Reinhard Heydrich met with his officers to underline their duty:

"As the army advances, you will move in to pacify the population. Any act of resistance must be dealt with ruthlessly, without mercy. You have authority to execute civilians summarily, without trial. The regular army is forbidden to interfere. Jews, gypsies, priests, bishops, and the Polish nobility are your first targets."

Krueger steeled himself for the test ahead. It soon came.

His men entered a small town about 70 kilometers west of Warsaw, just as the regular army was moving out. Two quick shots were fired from the church steeple; one of the soldiers fell to the ground, blood spurting from the side of his head. The army commander could not stop to find the sniper; his orders were to move eastward as quickly as possible. It was up to Krueger to deal with the assassin.

Krueger ordered two of his men to circle around to the back of the church and climb the stairs to the steeple. They were soon back, with a pimple-faced 15-year old and an ancient rifle. Krueger then ordered another four of his men to search the church. Within five minutes, two dozen boy scouts emerged with their hands in the air. Behind them was a priest with hands folded in front of his body. Behind were the SS troopers, bayonets fixed. They had interrupted a scout meeting in the basement; the Poles were trying to carry on with their normal lives.

Krueger ordered the two dozen scouts and the priest lined up along the side of the church. A private bound the hands of the young sniper and held him on the ground, off to one side, a pistol to the back of his head. A few villagers were beginning to assemble in the street. Krueger instructed his Polish-speaking sergeant to shout a proclamation:

> People of Poland. You are now under the rule of the German Reich. Any resistance will be crushed. A German's life is worth twenty Poles. Those attacking German soldiers will be shot. To even the score, so will their friends and relatives. In this case, the lives of the boy scouts are forfeit. The boy who killed our soldier will be shot last. He will live just long enough to see the consequences of his act. Anyone attempting to interfere will be shot.

Thereupon, five of Krueger's men turned toward the villagers on the street, lowering their rifles, bayonets fixed. In a panic, one of the boy scouts tried to escape. He rushed to get around the corner of the church, but was shot before he could take more than a dozen steps. Six other soldiers opened fire immediately, killing first the boys at the ends of the line, then working their way toward the middle.

A woman screamed and rushed toward the soldiers. One of them knocked her to the ground with the butt of his rifle.

Within a few seconds, the scouts lay dead. The priest alone remained standing, quietly, motionless, arms clasped at his waist, staring coldly at the Germans.

"Finish!" shouted Krueger.

Several soldiers fired and the priest fell to the ground. Krueger turned to the private holding the young sniper, struggling in vain to get loose. Krueger nodded. The private fired a single shot.

Krueger marched quickly to the back of the church and turned the corner. He stepped behind a bush and vomited. He didn't want his men to see his weakness. He had passed his first test as a member of Hitler's Totenkopf.

And his last.

Kaz and his men rode cautiously toward the village. When they were still short of the first house, they dismounted, leaving four men to guard the horses, with the rest approaching the village on foot. Just as they were about to reach the first house, rifle fire broke out and continued sporadically for about a minute. Kaz and his men quickly left the side of the road and raced along the edge of the woods behind the houses and sheds.

A little way into the village, they heard a commotion across the street. Half a dozen German soldiers were amusing themselves by chasing chickens around a pen, apparently trying to catch their dinner. Kaz left five men hidden.

"Hold your fire until the shooting starts," he instructed them. "Then kill the chicken thieves and any other Germans you can find."

A little farther on, Kaz and his remaining men came to the village church, and were sickened by the sight—bodies of two dozen teenagers. Half a dozen German soldiers were guarding a group of villagers who had been forced to lie down at the edge of the street. Another six or eight soldiers were guarding a group of Poles chosen to dig new graves in the church graveyard.

Kaz told Sub-Lieut. Jaroszewicz to take eight men further along the edge of the village, looking for additional German soldiers. They, too, were ordered to hold their fire until the shooting started.

Whispering, Kaz gave each of his men a specific German target. Those assigned to the guards at the edge of the street were to aim high, for the upper chests of the Germans, to avoid casualties among the civilians lying on the ground. After a tense wait of several minutes, Kaz ordered his men to fire. Many of the Germans fell at once. Kaz could hear firing break out at the edges of the village.

Soon the shooting stopped. About a dozen Germans lay dead near the church, and another six or eight were wounded—some so seriously that they could offer no resistance, and others were holding their hands in the air. Within a few minutes, the chicken-coop gang arrived. They reported having killed the six chicken thieves, and had five prisoners with them. The prisoners had been in one of the houses, and had come out with their hands up when they heard the firing.

In all, the German casualties were 18 dead, 11 wounded, and seven unwounded prisoners. One of the wounded prisoners was a lieutenant, apparently the commander of the group. The Poles had suffered only one dead and four slightly wounded.

Kaz called for Sgt. Kowalski, who spoke German fluently, and asked him to interrogate the German lieutenant. Kowalski took the lieutenant's Luger and escorted him to the back garden of the next house, where there were several chairs and a table. On the way, the lieutenant was awkwardly trying to bandage his wounded right arm.

Kaz ordered six men to take up strategic points in the village in case more Germans appeared. Another six were to go back down the road and bring up the horses. The rest of the men were to look after the prisoners, gather up the weapons, and prepare to move on to their next objective. Kaz and Jaroszewicz retired into the back of the church to plan their next move.

Kowalski took the chair facing Obersturmführer Krueger, offering him a cigarette. Krueger lit it, and made a sour face; apparently it did not meet German standards. Kowalski decided not to smoke, to keep his hands free. He held the Luger loosely in his right hand.

"OK, lieutenant, what's your unit?"

"As you can see from my uniform, I belong to the SS." Krueger pointed to his collar, which had two stylized S's, each looking like a lightning bolt.

"Yeah? What's the SS?"

"The Schutzstaffel. We're Hitler's praetorian guard. We were set up to protect the Nazi Party. We're not part of the regular army. We answer directly to Himmler and Hitler."

"Bully for you. Your job is to kill young boys?"

"Krueger, Helmut. Obersturmführer. 253776."

Kowalski almost lost hold of the Luger as it recoiled; the bullet whistled about 6 inches from Krueger's ear. "My, your Luger does seem to have a hair trigger."

The German turned slightly pale but otherwise showed no emotion.

"OK. Let's start again. What other German formations are in the area?"

Krueger was now looking directly down the barrel of the pistol. He saw no harm in telling the truth; it would scare the Pole. "The fourth infantry division is to the east, and the seventeenth is coming up rapidly from the west. There are two Panzer divisions already along the Bzura River—the second and ninth, if you must know. So if you want to get back across the river, you'll have to fight your way through infantry and tanks. Lots of luck. You'll need it."

"Now we're making progress." Kowalski was resting his elbow on the rough, unpainted table; now he had a firm grip on the Luger. "What were your orders? If we hadn't come along, what were you supposed to do?"

"Krueger, Helmut. Obersturmführer. 253776."

This time, the bullet nicked his left ear.

Krueger glanced around at the ripening corn, browning at the edges where the early frost had nipped the leaves. It reminded him of his boyhood home in Bavaria. Was he about to die in this beautiful, Godforsaken place? He decided to answer.

"Our job was to stay here for 24 hours, to pacify the village. Then we were to await new orders."

"Pacify the village? What the hell does that mean?"

"To make sure that you Poles cause no trouble. That you recognize who's in charge, that you respect our rule."

"You shoot young boys to gain respect?"

"That was a necessary lesson. One of the boys shot a German soldier." He then repeated his incantation: "Twenty Poles are worth no more than one German."

The third bullet went through Krueger's heart.

Meanwhile, Kaz and Jaroszewicz had made their decision. They would ride back toward the river and their lines, hoping to get back by the morning of the next day. They would follow their orders, attacking targets of opportunity and avoiding armored German forces.

As they emerged from the church, a corporal came up and saluted. "The horses are here, sir, and we're prepared to leave at once."

"Good," replied Kaz. "Where are the prisoners?"

"The prisoners? We asked a dozen civilians to bury them in the church graveyard. They refused to put them in hallowed ground, but agreed to bury them in a field."

"Bury them? But they weren't dead."

"They are now. You said to get ready to move on. Obviously, we can't take them with us."

"Ah, yes." Kaz wasn't sure whether it had turned out the way he really wanted. It would be difficult to move with the SS men, and the prisoners could scarcely claim the protection of the Geneva Convention. He realized that, in the very unlikely event of an inquiry, it would be unclear who was responsible.

Kaz also made a point of leaving the dead Polish soldier behind. If the Germans showed up again in the next day or two, the dead body, still in uniform, would verify that the German soldiers were killed by Polish soldiers, not by the villagers. There would be less risk of another brutal reprisal.

As before, the cavalrymen kept toward the edges of forests where possible, but had to gallop over open countryside whenever there were no trees. They were also trying to keep close to roads, in order to ambush German trucks. They destroyed a lone German truck, then a group of three others; the German trucks had no protection, and the Poles suffered no casualties.

As they were crossing an open field, however, they were attacked by a low-flying Messerschmitt 109 fighter, which machine gunned their group and then circled back for a second attack just before the cavalrymen reached the cover of the nearest woods. Even though they had scattered, they suffered heavy casualties, along with the loss of most of the horses. They now had only 15 unwounded men and ten horses left.

Because of the wounded, Kaz decided that his major task was to get his men back to safety across the Bzura River. Their best chance would be to wait in the woods until dusk, and then move as rapidly as possible during the last hour of fading daylight and through the night. Their medic had been killed; Kaz sent three parties of two men each out in different directions, to see if they could locate a town or village with a doctor. The scouts must get back before 5:00 p.m.; otherwise, they would be left behind.

They all got back, but empty-handed; they could not get a doctor. Jaroszewicz and his companion were badly shaken. As they cautiously approached a town, they had observed smoke rising. They slowed down even more. When they got to the edge of town, they were met by civilians who told a grisly tale. German troops entered the town that morning, and went directly to the Jewish sector. They forced several hundred Jews into the synagogue, which they then sealed and set on fire.

The two remaining doctors in town were overwhelmed with work, ministering to burned and wounded civilians, plus a dozen or so severely wounded Polish soldiers in hiding. Neither doctor would be able to come to help the wounded cavalrymen in the woods. Fortunately, the Germans had finally left town. Jaroszewicz asked the townsmen about the German uniforms. The officers had skulls in their caps. The SS.

With the shortage of horses, the cavalrymen were now as many as three to a single horse, although each of the wounded was carried, as gently as possible, on a horse with only one other rider. The small force was no longer fit for combat; they left their mortars and last machine gun behind. Kaz made some quick calculations of the distance back to the river, estimating their current position as best he could. If there were no interruptions, and if the horses held up under the strain, they might make it back to the Bzura River by daybreak.

They did. Just as the first glimmer of dawn lit the eastern sky, they arrived back across the River. Kaz had sent several men ahead, shouting in Polish through the dark, to avoid being mistakenly attacked by their countrymen.

The defenders were in an increasingly desperate situation. In concert with the pocket of troops around Poznan, they had surprised the Germans with their counterattacks; an estimated four thousand Germans had been killed. But it had not taken long for the Germans to respond. Kaz's experience had been typical: German planes had strafed many of the intruding Polish groups. German artillery on the western side of the Bzura was now retaliating fiercely to the fire from the Polish guns. Even more devastating were the attacks from Stuka dive-bombers.

By now, however, many of the Poles had seen the ruthless hand of the German invaders, and were determined to hold out. When would help come from the West? When would the French distract the Germans by launching an assault?

On Sept. 17, just two and a half weeks after the start of the German invasion, the Poles had an answer—of sorts. The French were doing nothing. The Poles, not the Germans, would have to fight on two fronts. Hitler's new ally, Joseph Stalin, played his part as the jackal, attacking the dying Polish state from the rear. Four columns of Soviet troops thrust rapidly through the light defenses into Eastern Poland. The position of Kaz and the other defenders along the Bzura River now became untenable; the order came to withdraw to Warsaw, to strengthen its defenses.

When Kaz got back to the Polish lines after his incursion around the German flank, he was relieved to find Jan still alive; many officers had been killed. Kaz was promoted to captain because of his successful raid. Together with Jan and two young infantry lieutenants, Karol Kwiatkowski and Edward Szymczak, Kaz was to command a group of about 120 men during the retreat.

When they reached Warsaw, many buildings had been destroyed by bombing and artillery. Fires raged out of control in several sectors of the city; the fire department was overwhelmed.

Kaz, Jan, Karol, and Edward took up defensive positions with their men in a group of buildings and newly dug trenches. In their exposed position, Kaz expected the worst, but he was lucky: the Germans apparently wanted to avoid the casualties that would come with house-to-house fighting, and intended to bombard Warsaw from the air and with artillery until it surrendered.

Several days later, as the bombardment continued, Kaz and Jan were summoned to headquarters several kilometers to the southeast, to report to Army Intelligence. When they arrived, they were met by Maj. Zagorski, a middle-aged officer with a droopy mustache and sad eyes:

"I wanted to ask you about your recent forays around the German flanks."

Jan responded first. "We ran into a German patrol almost immediately, sir. In the ensuing fire fight, four of our men were wounded. I sent them back across the river, escorted by three uninjured men. Although we were left shorthanded, we succeeded in ambushing three supply columns, destroying ten trucks, two of which exploded.

"Any evidence of German atrocities?" Major Zagorski wanted to know. "We want information to pass on to the French and British. They might actually bestir themselves."

"Yes indeed, sir," Kaz reported. "One of my patrols came back with a report of the SS locking two hundred Jews in a synagogue, then lighting it on fire. We also entered a town where two dozen boy scouts and a priest had been murdered by the SS; I personally counted the twenty-five bodies."

Maj. Zagorski carefully wrote down the details, repeatedly licking the end of his pencil to keep it writing on the grimy paper. Kaz also mentioned the military units identified by Krueger. He did not report what had happened to Krueger. The Major did not ask.

Kaz was interested not only in giving information, but also in finding out what was going on. "I understand that German atrocities are common. Is this correct, sir?"

"Yes, there have been many, most carried out by the SS. They add up to a barbaric, dreary picture. There are also some very strange events."

"Really?"

"Yes. The oddest—Heinrich Himmler has begun to travel around Poland in his special train, which he has modestly labeled the *Heinrich*. His men have begun to separate the Polish population into groups: those of German ancestry, Jews, and Slavic Poles. It all fits into the Nazi idea of racial superiority.

"But something bizarre has happened. The *Lebensborn*—their 'Fountain of Life' organization, aimed at preserving the purity of the German race—has been kidnapping blue-eyed, blond children from our orphanages. They're being taken to Germany, to be raised as Germans. So much for our racial inferiority."

"Darwinism gone mad," said Kaz, shaking his head.

In fact, it was even odder than they thought. Himmler couldn't help but notice that the kidnapped foundlings were closer to the blond, blue-eyed "Teutonic ideal" than his very own children.

Kaz got back to the war. "The French and British aren't putting much pressure on the Germans, sir?"

"That's an understatement," replied the major bitterly. "The French army did cross the German border. They inched their way forward for ten kilometers, along a twenty-kilometer front, boldly seizing a dozen deserted villages. The conquering heroes thereupon took up defensive positions, preparing to withdraw if the enemy attacked. When the Germans failed to appear, the French withdrew anyhow. As far as I know, that's it.

"The British are almost as hopeless," he continued. "The RAF has attacked naval ships in German harbors. But other RAF planes have been wandering around Germany dropping leaflets, urging the Germans to overthrow the Führer. Apparently they believe that the

Germans are basically civilized; they will get rid of Hitler as soon as they find out what a barbarian he is. The British are under the illusion that this war will be fought according to the Marquis of Queensbury rules. Gentlemen don't bomb cities."

On cue, there was a thunderous explosion as a bomb hit the building next door. Part of the ceiling fell, hitting the table between the major and the two younger officers.

"What are our chances, sir?" Kaz wanted to know. "Frankly."

"Not good," replied the major. "Particularly now that the Russians have attacked from the East. Our government has already withdrawn to Romania; it looks as if they will be going on to Paris to set up a government in exile. I don't see how we can hold out more than a few days. Don't risk unnecessary casualties."

"We'll have to surrender to the Nazis?"

"As the end comes, those who can escape into the countryside should try. We're beginning to work on an underground home defense army. But basically, it will be every man for himself."

"All in all, I think I'll take my chances with the Russians, sir; I've seen what the Germans do. We're quite close to the river, and should be able to slip across into the Russian occupation zone. What do you recommend?"

"Sounds reasonable," replied the major. "But it's a tossup. After all, Stalin shot the leaders of the Polish Communist Party last year, and I suppose he won't mind shooting the rest of us if it suits his fancy. If you do head east, you may have a chance—you may then be able to turn south and get to Romania."

When they got back to their unit, Kaz and Jan found their small command post in a shambles. It had been hit by a shell and their two new comrades—Karol and Edward—killed. Sorrowfully, they removed the dog tags from the dead men. Kaz put Karol's tag around his own neck to avoid losing it, and Jan did the same with Edward's.

The major's pessimism was well founded. Within a few days, organized resistance collapsed. Kaz, Jan, and most of his men made it across the Vistula River. Then they broke into small groups, to make them less conspicuous as they headed southeast toward the safety of Romania.

The major had also been right on another score. The Russians, too, could be barbarians.

9
Goodbye

A s soon as the Mercedes disappeared around the corner, Anna realized her mistake. She should have dressed quickly and gone to the station with Josef. She urgently needed to get back to Poznan and her colleagues.

She rushed up to her room, threw a few possessions into a small suitcase, and went back down to the front steps to wait for the chauffeur to return. Her mother was still there, waving weakly and tearfully to a car that had long since disappeared. Anna sat down on the top step. Her mother sank slowly down beside her. Anna drew her mother's tearful head toward her until it was resting on her shoulder.

"Oh Josef, Josef, my beloved Josef. May God be with you," her mother repeated, over and over.

Then she noticed her daughter's suitcase. "Surely you're not leaving too, Anna?"

"I'm sorry. I have to."

"But what will become of us?" Her mother caught herself; she still hadn't gotten used to the idea that her daughter was a married woman. "Are you going to meet Kaz somewhere?"

"I only wish. But I have to get back to my job in Poznan."

"But why? With the invasion, research will be in chaos—or will be abandoned altogether."

"I haven't told you before, mother, but we're working on a special project for the Air Force. With the German attack, it will have even higher priority."

"But what can be so important about weather forecasting, at a time like this?"

Anna found herself repeating the story she had told Kaz on their first meeting. Forecasting was particularly important during wartime. Air Force planes had to fight in poor weather—but not such bad weather that they were unable to land. The line was a fine one: when would the weather be barely good enough to operate? Anna was following the security rules. But, even more, she didn't want her parents to know what she really was doing. It would protect them — and her — in case they were interrogated by the Germans.

"Please don't worry, even if you don't hear from me. We may flee to a neutral country or to England. I may be unable to contact you."

"But what about Kaz? You'll leave him behind?"

Suddenly, Anna's tears were flowing even more freely than her mother's. The two women, hugging and weeping as they sat on the top step, were interrupted by the crunch of the Mercedes on the driveway, returning from the station.

Anna pulled herself away. "May God be with you. We'll come through it somehow. Poland has survived disasters before." She gently loosened the grip of her mother's arms around her neck. She was afraid that, if she didn't leave quickly, she might not be able. As she closed the door of the Mercedes, she waved to her mother. Unlike Josef, she continued to wave through the car window until her mother and her home were hidden behind the trees.

When she got to the station — a small, red, wooden structure, with only one ticket agent — she found it jammed with a mixture of civilians and men in uniform. She went directly to the ticket counter; surprisingly, there was no line. The agent looked up, and, without a word, pointed to a crudely printed sign beside the window:

MILITARY PERSONNEL ONLY

"I'm with the Air Force," Anna protested, an edge of desperation in her voice. She slid her identification card across the counter. The agent studied it; he obviously was puzzled.

"But aren't you still a civilian?"

"Yes." She immediately regretted her answer; she should have lied.

"Sorry. Rules are rules. Next." The agent nodded to an army lieutenant who was now directly behind Anna. The lieutenant seemed more than willing to wait. But the agent insisted.

Anna wandered to the middle of the room, perplexed; what should she do now? The lieutenant was soon beside her. "I have a pass to Kolo. I'll try to get you on the train with me. As my wife."

"Good. That's on the way to Poznan, where I'm headed."

"Things are chaotic. You should be able to stay on the train as it goes on to Poznan, even after I get off. I suppose, if we're supposed to be married, we should at least know one another's names. I'm..."

He was interrupted by an announcement.

"The train that left 15 minutes ago was attacked by a German airplane about 5 km to the east. It's disabled. Some of the passengers are wounded. Those with friends and relatives on the train: wait for further information."

Anna didn't wait. She was immediately out the door, even forgetting her suitcase. There was Zambrowski, standing beside the Mercedes. He had been patiently waiting, to make sure she actually got on a train.

She hopped into the back seat.

"The last train's been attacked. Joseph may be on it. We've got to get there. Five kilometers east."

She had barely slammed the door when Zambrowski gunned the engine; Anna had never seen him drive so fast. She was terrified as the tires screeched around corners, but nevertheless found herself urging him on.

"Faster, Zambrowski, faster." She closed her eyes, tightening her grip on the ceiling strap.

The train was a wreck. The attackers had concentrated on the locomotive. One of the engineers was dead, his body slumped over the side of the cab. The other was lying on a patch of bloodstained ground.

The German plane had also made one pass along the length of the train, firing its machine guns. Broken glass and splinters of wood were strewn along the side of the track. Luckily, most of the passengers had survived. They had left the train and were sprinkled along the embankment, the uninjured aiding the wounded as best they could.

Anna and Zambrowski passed along the line. They quickly found Josef. He had been cut by flying glass, and was still in the process of bandaging himself with strips of his undershirt; one of his boots was off, and he had a bulky bandage around his left foot. Anna cried out in joy to see him. She and Zambrowski put his arms around their shoulders and began to help him back toward the car.

"Others need help more than I do. Ryk is here somewhere."

Soon, the Mercedes was crowded with six wounded, including Josef and Ryk. One, with only superficial cuts, lay in the trunk, with the lid propped open.

The most severely wounded soldier had a bullet through his left shoulder. He was in obvious pain and danger; his comrades took turns applying pressure to stem the flow of blood. Zambrowski headed for the nearest hospital. It was crowded, and would accept only the one most severely wounded soldier. At any rate, all the others wanted to get back to their homes.

Zambrowski dropped Anna, Josef, and Ryk off at the Raczynski Estate—Ryk because his parents had left their home that morning. The chauffeur then headed out into the countryside to deliver the other casualties to their families.

Now that the others had gone, Anna could see that Ryk was more seriously wounded than she had realized. A splinter had been driven deeply into his right calf. Anna's mother began helping the maid, setting up an informal operating room in the parlor. They retrieved four wooden boxes from the wine cellar; they placed one below each leg of the table, raising it to a comfortable height for surgery. They then softened the oak table with two blankets, covered with clean sheets. Anna quickly had knives, needles, and a few carpentry tools—mainly pliers—boiling in a pot on the stove, with a sheet, torn into strips, bubbling in a second pot.

Anna and her father acted as surgeons. Even with pliers, they couldn't extract the splinter; it seemed to be barbed, like a fishhook. As they tugged and twisted, tears welled in Ryk's eyes. The muscles on his cheek stood out as his jaws clamped on a thumb-sized oak stick. Anna's father probed with his fingers, but still couldn't find the obstruction. Reluctantly, he picked up a carving knife to enlarge the wound. Anna held Ryk's head up, turning it slightly to the side so she could pour more vodka past the stick and between his lips. She kissed him lightly on the forehead, murmuring words of encouragement.

Finally, Anna's father proclaimed success, holding up a jagged splinter, dripping with blood. Unprofessionally, he took a large swig from the vodka bottle, and then turned back to the wound, probing with his fingers and drawing out half a dozen smaller splinters. Anna poured the all-purpose vodka into the wound and began to sew it up.

The operation was over. Anna wiped the sweat from Ryk's forehead while her father removed the oak stick from his mouth. He had bitten most of the way through it, and her father snapped it easily, with a flourish. Anna offered Ryk another drink of vodka. He shook his head, and mouthed the word "water." Within a few minutes, he was sound asleep.

They were afraid the wound might not heal. Ryk was feverish, and by the next morning, the whole of his lower leg was inflamed. They finally prevailed upon the local doctor to come by to see him. The doctor made an incision, and a stream of yellow-green pus oozed out into a basin. The doctor left some pills, and explained how they would be able to tell if pus was building up again, requiring another incision to drain it. If so, they would have to manage by themselves. He could not promise to return; he was overwhelmed by the large number of wounded.

Within a few days, Ryk began to improve. His fever disappeared and he began to limp around unsteadily. One morning at breakfast, he looked across the table at Anna, and announced that the time had come for him to try to get out of the country.

"But you're scarcely able to walk."

"I wasn't planning to walk," he joked. "I can't stay. The Germans may be here within a few days. I don't fancy a prisoner-of-war camp."

"There are rumors that a resistance army is being organized. You might join them."

"That's fine for soldiers, but I'm a pilot. Our air force has been wiped out. The best thing I can do for our cause is to get out, to fly and fight with the French or British."

"But how?"

"The Mercedes would be a possibility." He saw the surprise on Anna's face. "I know it's nervy to bring up the subject, but the car won't be much use to you. The Germans will seize it the moment they arrive."

Anna was about to object, but decided to keep quiet. She needed to get out too, and it was much too late to think of joining her colleagues; they would have long since left Poznan. Anna knew that their security people had drawn up emergency plans. If Germany invaded, the codebreakers were to move to the southeastern corner of Poland, taking their precious equipment and records. In the event of an imminent German victory, they would destroy their equipment and burn their records, then cross into Romania. From there, they would attempt to get out to London or Paris, and put themselves at the service of the allies. She wondered where they were now.

"Anyhow," Ryk retreated, "that's probably not a good idea. I don't know how much gas you have, and Romania's a long way to go."

"You can forget Romania," said Anna's mother. "The Russians have invaded from the east."

"Then I'll have to move to Plan B. The time has come for the Red Baron to make one last flight." The Red Baron was Ryk's nickname for his old German Fokker triplane, which had been repainted red—complete with black German crosses—to make it look like the famous World War I fighter of Baron Manfred von Richthofen. "If I hadn't been wounded, I would have asked Josef to help me with repairs, and offered him the back seat. But it's obviously too late, now he's left to help in the defense of Warsaw." Ryk gazed at Anna.

"I might be able to help. Provided I could have that back seat."

"No you don't," interrupted her mother. "The skies are full of German fighters. It would be suicide."

"I think it might just be done," Ryk responded to Anna. "With luck. We need three things. To get the engine running. I think that's possible. Second problem: we need gas. A hundred and fifty liters, at the very least. Third, and biggest problem. Your mother is right. Normally the skies would be too dangerous, with enemy fighters on the prowl. But if we could get our hands on an artificial horizon, we could fly at night or through clouds. You could use your weather forecasting skills to figure out when the cloud cover was thickest."

Anna looked distinctly uncomfortable.

"Where, pray tell, would you get such an instrument?" asked Anna's mother frostily.

"The most likely source would be a plane—Polish or German—that has crashed."

"I hear that a Messerschmitt crashed somewhere to the North," Anna reported. "Perhaps Zambrowski could find out where." Zambrowski was part of the chauffeur's fraternity. They kept in touch, and were great sources of information and gossip.

Ryk warmed to his subject. "That would be great, if you could check with him. Find out if he knows about any downed plane—one that has a horizon. It's an instrument mounted on the panel, with a horizontal line across it—that's the artificial horizon—and a wing that tilts whenever the plane does. There's a ball attached to the back of the instrument's face. It's essential; it makes the thing work. In most planes, the apparatus can be taken out by unscrewing the facing on the instrument panel and then pulling out the assembly from the back. It's important not to cut the electrical leads too short; we'll need them when we reinstall the horizon."

Meanwhile, Ryk would busy himself trying to get the engine running and seeing if he could scrounge up enough gas.

An hour later, after talking to Zambrowski, Anna returned to the mansion. Her mother was in the kitchen, preparing lunch. Except for Zambrowski, the servants had returned to their families, to help meet the wartime disruptions and crises.

Anna picked up a knife and began to peel potatoes. Her mother said nothing; the air was electric. Anna broke the silence.

"I know you don't want me to fly out, mother, but I don't have any choice. I just have to get out."

"What good will it do, if you just get yourself killed? Then you won't be of any use to anybody—to Poland, Britain, or anyone else. Just think of Kaz." The knife flashed as Mme. Raczynski sped up her task of slicing carrots.

"You don't need to remind me of Kaz," said Anna, tears welling in her eyes.

"You'll never make it. If the Germans don't shoot you down— which they probably will—that old rattletrap will fall apart. It's made of rotting wood, rusting wire, and torn cloth. How can it stand up to a long flight?"

"It's remarkable what wood and wire can hold together."

"Well I don't like it. The risks. And you a married woman. Running off with another man." Her mother's knife slashed even more rapidly; she was setting a speed record for slicing carrots.

Anna was taken by surprise. The danger of getting killed was all too obvious. But this other bit. Was her mother serious? Not likely. In her terror over a flight in an ancient airplane, she was probably clutching at any argument she could make.

"Do you really think I don't care about Kaz? I've tried to find out where he is. All I know: he survived the early battles, but he's no longer near Poznan. Don't you realize, mother, that the army is collapsing? Any survivors that don't head for the hills will be taken prisoner. Visitors not permitted. Whatever happens, I won't see Kaz till the war is over.

"Mother, we have to face it. The Germans will be here within a week. At the most. If we don't get out in the next few days, it will be impossible. Also, to put it bluntly, the Germans may torture me."

"Going off with Ryk. Don't you know what a daredevil he is? Don't you realize that he's been in love with you ever since you were fifteen? That he's quite prepared to risk *your* life as well as his own, just to be with you."

"Oh, mother." Anna spoke softly, with pain in her voice. Her mother *was* grasping at straws.

"You mean you really don't know that he's still in love with you? Ask Sisi. She can see what's obvious."

Anna paused, thinking back two weeks to the dinner party, and to earlier years. Her mother was right on one thing; Ryk certainly was a daredevil. But in love? Maybe—just maybe, at one time. But mostly, wasn't that just fun? And yet....

Anna suppressed the thought. She would try to get out. The sooner the better.

Ryk was anxious to get started and asked Zambrowski to take him home. As they were starting out the drive, Anna hailed the chauffeur. As he stopped, she jumped in the back seat beside Ryk.

The old Fokker triplane was in a shed and was in surprisingly good condition; it had been used regularly by Ryk's uncle until shortly before his death the year before. Rummaging around among the tools, Ryk found an extra set of spark plugs, and within a few hours, he and Anna had the engine running. A bit roughly, but it was running.

As instructed, Zambrowski returned at 8:00 p.m. to pick up Anna, and brought her home for the night. She would return early the next morning, when work would begin on the difficult problem of fuel storage. The gas tank in the old Fokker would hold only 90 liters, enough for its designed task—an hour and a half of violent combat—and probably enough for three hours' cruising. They would have to find some way of storing another 60 or 70 liters to give them a sporting chance to reach Sweden. As she left, Ryk asked her to start making weather forecasts; they would need them before they took off.

Anna wondered how she had gotten herself in this box; she knew nothing about forecasting. But she quickly figured out the next best thing. She listened to the German-language short-wave broadcasts from Sweden, which included detailed forecasts for the Baltic. Much of the weather came from that direction at this time of year, giving her the beginnings of a forecast. Before leaving for Ryk's, she checked by with Gwido, the supervisor of farming operations. He had a knack for forecasting, developed over the years—he was the one who decided when it was time to make hay. She combined the forecasts for a report to Ryk; he was duly impressed by its accuracy.

Within two days, Ryk had solved the fuel storage problem—or, at least, so he hoped. When the machine guns were removed from the triplane right after the Great War, the ammunition boxes were left. He welded these shut and ran a short copper tube down to the main fuel tank; gravity would drain these two supplementary tanks before the main tank. But this was not enough. Each of the boxes would hold less than 15 liters; they would still be at least forty liters short.

To make up the deficit, they briefly considered mounting a 50-litre can on top of the fuselage where the machine guns were originally located. But that would be too risky. If they were intercepted by a German plane, the pilot would immediately be suspicious; a supplementary tank could have only one purpose, to increase the range so the Fokker could flee the country. They rigged the can inside the fuselage, directly behind the passenger's seat.

In that location, it was too low for the gasoline to be fed to the engine by gravity. Ryk solved this problem by inserting the stem from a bicycle tire in the top of the can. Anna's job—at least during the early part of the flight—would be to pump air into the tank, forcing the gasoline up into the main tank as fuel was consumed. When the tank was empty, Ryk would close a valve to prevent gas from running back into the can.

Zambrowski did his magic, obtaining an artificial horizon. After installing it, Ryk flew one quick circle around the pasture to make sure that it worked. A longer flight was out of the question; German forces were already in the area.

The time had come. They would leave as soon as weather permitted.

"I'm afraid I haven't exactly told the whole truth." Anna realized that Ryk needed to know. "I really know nothing about weather forecasting; I just work on theoretical models. I got my forecasts from Swedish short-wave broadcasts and the farm foreman."

"But that's great. It means we'll have information on the weather over the Baltic. What's your best forecast for cloud cover tonight?"

"Scattered clouds. Small risk of storms. I can check the radio again this evening when I'm home."

"Too late. We have to make a decision now."

"It's up to you; you're the pilot."

"Tonight it is. At night, German fighters will be on the ground. With the artificial horizon, altimeter, and compass, I'm reasonably confident I can make my way to the Baltic. Even if we have trouble with the horizon, there probably will be enough lights on the ground to help me keep my wings level."

"I trust you, Ryk." Anna felt she had little choice.

"The big trouble starts when we get to the Baltic. Night flying over water can be tricky. If there are clouds—or even a light fog—you're in the pitch dark. You have no idea which way is up. Even on a clear night you can run into difficulty. The stars are out, but they also glitter off the water."

"You really can't tell which way is up? But you know even in a completely dark room."

"Ah, but a plane's different. It's treacherous. When you're in a turn, the lift from the wings keeps you pressed straight down in the seat. If it's dark, you'd swear you were still flying level, even if you're banking quite sharply." Ryk illustrated by holding his hand out flat, palm down, and then gradually tilting it. "Without realizing it, you can continue to bank, and slide into a spin." When his palm became vertical, he ended with a circling, sinking motion. "That's why the artificial horizon is so important. In the dark—or in the clouds—your normal senses betray you. You've got to trust your instruments, even when the readings seem preposterous. *Particularly* when the readings seem preposterous."

"So what happens when we get to the Baltic?"

"German fighters may be out. We could risk crossing the sea at night, hoping our instruments are still working. We'll need daylight to land, but we could aim for Sweden at dawn."

"Or?"

"Or we can try to arrive at the southern coast of the Baltic about dawn, so that we won't be flying over the water at night."

"And you suggest?"

"I suggest we leave tomorrow morning around 3.00. According to my calculation, that should take us over the coast right at dawn."

"Fine by me. I'll be back by 2:00."

"Dress warmly. Especially around your head. It'll feel like the North Pole when we're up in the air. No luggage. We'll have trouble enough getting off the ground with the extra fuel."

That evening, her mother was in an especially grumpy mood, complaining about her daughter's plan to fly off. With "that swashbuckler." Anna was torn; she felt she couldn't tell her mother that this was the night, that she would be gone long before dawn. She was already half sick, worried about Kaz, and, when she was honest with herself, about the dangers of the flight. She just couldn't stand a scene.

She turned to her father, asking him to join her for a walk in the cold, clear evening air.

Just one-on-one, he could hear her, at least when she spoke slowly and directly to him.

"Tonight's the night. We'll be leaving shortly after 1:00."

"I know."

"You know?"

"I may be hard of hearing, but I can still sense how you feel. Those sixteen years at home count for something. I guessed you would be leaving tonight. And I noticed that Zambrowski left the Mercedes out at the end of the drive. Why would he do that, unless he wanted to be able to start the car without waking your mother? I asked him straight out; he admitted he would be taking you tonight."

"Oh, Daddy," Anna threw her arms around him. "I love you so. And Mother."

"No matter what happens, remember how much we love you. How much joy you brought into our lives. How proud we were when you got that scholarship to the University. How happy we were when you married Kaz."

"Mommy. She's in such a mood."

"I think she suspects that tonight's the night, too."

"You told her?"

"No. But when you've been married as many years as we have...."

"I don't know if I can tell her."

"You don't have to. I'll do it tomorrow morning. Just be sure you give her a big hug and kiss before you go to bed. A warm last memory."

Anna hugged her father. As they stood there, she could feel him silently crying.

10

In Honor of the Red Baron

There are old pilots. There are bold pilots. There are no old, bold pilots.

An American pilot, World War I

The old Mercedes left the narrow gravel road and crossed the soft turf to the edge of the pasture; Ryk and the old triplane were waiting. As usual, Zambrowski quickly opened the rear door and stood at attention as Anna stepped out. In the moonlight, she could see a tear in the corner of his eye.

"May God be with you, ma'am."

It was no time for formalities. Anna gently put her hands on Zambrowski's arms, stood on her toes, and kissed him softly on the cheek.

"I'll miss you, Pawel. And may God be with you, too. Look after mother; she'll need your help."

Ryk had by now approached; he had brought his father's hunting jacket for Anna to put on over her other clothes, to protect her from the cold. He helped her buckle into the back seat, then jumped down for a few words with Zambrowski, who took his position with his hand on the propeller.

Ryk quickly climbed up into the pilot's seat and tested the primitive intercom, explaining the final details to Anna.

"I'll need to warm up the engine for two minutes. Then, as we move forward, I'll keep the nose down, to prevent a premature takeoff. Don't be worried. Even though the nose is low, the three wings will provide plenty of lift to clear the trees."

"You're the doctor."

Ryk signaled to Zambrowski, who pulled smartly on the propeller. The engine sputtered, then caught.

Anna was concerned; the engine was running roughly. The warmup period dragged on—perhaps four minutes, but it seemed like fifty. Then, abruptly, Ryk applied full power. By now, Zambrowski had driven to the far end of the pasture, just in front of the scrub pines. He turned the car to illuminate the makeshift runway. The plane rolled forward.

Anna had forgotten just how bumpy a pasture could be. But suddenly, the plane was steady; its wheels had lifted off the ground. As promised, the plane rose rapidly, gaining altitude even though its nose was almost horizontal. By the time they passed over the Mercedes, they were 20 or 30 meters in the air. Anna waved to Zambrowski—a useless gesture in the dark, but it seemed like the thing to do.

The air was freezing cold, and clear as crystal. Ahead and to the right—just below the middle wing—the big dipper twinkled brightly, pointing to the North Star. Below, lights from a few farm windows began to appear. The farmers were making an early start on their morning chores; the cows had to be milked. Sadly, Anna also observed occasional fires—some real infernos—as buildings and equipment burned.

After an hour, she heard Ryk's reassuring voice. "So far, so good. You're giving the bicycle pump two or three strokes every five minutes?"

"Yes indeed. And congratulations on your navigation. I've been watching the North Star. You're keeping it in exactly the same place, just off the right wing tip.... Strange. I've never noticed before how the big dipper rotates. I've been imagining water spilling out over the handle."

Other than the fires, the ground seemed strangely tranquil. There were practically no signs of lights from cars or trucks, but activity would undoubtedly start again after dawn. Anna was glad that they were flying in the dark, that she did not have to witness the chaos from recent battles. Gradually, she began to relax. Not such a bad way to travel. No hassle with customs officers.

Ryk interrupted her reverie. According to his calculations, the back tank was almost empty. He was shutting the valve; she could stop pumping.

"Sorry, but I've got bad news. Those two winding sets of lights.... I think they're along the banks of the Drweca River."

"Yes?"

"If so, we're bucking a strong headwind. Keep your fingers crossed. It may be a close thing, whether we'll have enough fuel to make it to Sweden."

There was a tense silence. Then Ryk was back on the intercom.

"We've got a big decision. We can increase our range by slowing down. But that will mean a fifteen or twenty minute flight over German territory after dawn. Which do you prefer — the risk of getting shot down by the Germans, or ending up out of gas, swimming the last lap in the frigid Baltic?"

"All in all, I'd choose a quick death to a slow one in freezing water. If we slow down, perhaps we can count on the incompetence or chivalry of the Luftwaffe."

"Don't bet on either. But I vote for a slowdown, too. We can always hope for cloud cover."

Anna surprised herself. For fifteen or twenty minutes, she remained very worried and tense: would they make it? But then she became serene. There was absolutely nothing she could do; it was in Ryk's hands.

An hour later, the Eastern sky began to lighten. She looked down. In the faint light, land stretched as far as the eye could see; the Baltic was nowhere in sight. She looked even more eagerly for clouds. White streaks were faintly visible in the distant sky, somewhat higher than their present altitude.

Apparently Ryk saw the wisps of cloud at the same time. The power in the engine increased, and they began to climb, very gradually, toward their distant goal.

As the light increased, Anna once again felt apprehensive. She could now do something, and she did. She began to scan the sky, particularly behind the Fokker, searching for German airplanes.

"The Sea, ho!" came Ryk's excited voice over the intercom.

But Anna didn't look ahead. Her eyes were focused on a small, dark, ominous dot in the sky, which was rapidly becoming larger.

"A German fighter. Almost directly behind," she shouted.

Ryk responded with a surge of power; the triplane accelerated toward its top speed of 165 km per hour.

With Ryk warned, Anna glanced forward anxiously, toward the water. They wouldn't make the coast before they were intercepted. But there were scattered clouds ahead. Involuntarily, she grasped the bicycle pump more tightly.

Suddenly, the German fighter was very large indeed. Anna was relieved; it was going to pass on the left side rather than attack. It streaked by; Anna had the odd sensation that their triplane was going backward. Then the Fokker rocked in the wake from the heavier plane.

The German pilot began a sharp turn; he was going to circle back. Anna looked longingly toward the clouds; they were still in the distance.

There was something more she could do. She pulled back the hood of her jacket and removed her goggles, heavy scarf, and cloth helmet with earphones. Her long blond hair began to flow backward in the airstream, dancing lightly in the turbulence from the propeller.

Fortunately, the German showed no signs of attacking this time, either. He was going to pass once more to the left. Now, he was flying much more slowly; his flaps and leading-edge slats were down. As he approached, he slowed even more, gradually drawing closer and then holding his position directly beside the Fokker. The pilot had pushed his goggles up over his forehead. He was obviously puzzled. Anna waved, and tried hard to smile. He smiled and waved back. She blew him a kiss.

Anna was much prettier than Ryk, and the German pilot gazed at her for some time. Anna mouthed a few words in German, hoping that the fighter pilot would waste precious minutes trying to make out what she was saying. She dared not glance ahead, to see how close the clouds were. Then the German moved up a few meters, and waved — in a decidedly less friendly manner — to Ryk. The fighter pilot pointed downward, and mouthed the words "Follow me" distinctly in

German. Obviously, he was ordering Ryk to land. But Ryk pretended not to understand. He held his hand to his ear; he could not hear.

The German wagged his wings and lowered his wheels; Anna guessed this must be a signal to land. Ryk still played dumb. But the games were over; the German, still beside the Fokker, fired a burst into the open sky. Ryk waved, to indicate that he now understood, that he would accompany the Messerschmitt. The German began a slow turn to the left; Ryk turned left, staying side-by-side.

Anna felt a surge of panic. She couldn't stand the thought of a German interrogation. She had no parachute. Still, she had the urge to jump. She faced death, one way or another. Why not skip the torture?

Suddenly, Ryk reduced power and veered to the right, toward his original course. The German turned right too, and also cut his power. But he was now in front of the slowly moving triplane; he would stall if he tried to slow down further, to get back even with the Fokker. For a moment, Ryk was directly behind the German, and lined up the Messerschmitt in his gun sight. If only the Fokker still had its two machine guns!

The German broke off, turning sharply to the left as he raised his landing gear and flaps. He was going to go around again, and this time there would be a hail of bullets. Ryk applied full power and pointed toward the nearest cloud.

Anna closed her eyes, held her breath, and began to count. She half expected her life to flash before her, but all she could think of was the German circling for an attack. Ninety five, ninety six.... She reached one hundred and opened her eyes. She was surrounded by light, fluffy, pure white clouds. She began to breathe freely again.

She put her helmet back on; she was back in communication with Ryk. Their plan was obvious. Ryk would try to keep in the clouds, while heading in a generally northwesterly direction toward Sweden. Whenever there was a break in the clouds, Anna should scan the skies for Germans; Ryk would head for the nearest cloud cover. What was Anna's weather forecast again?

"Clouds all the way."

A little white lie.

They broke out of the clouds ten minutes later. In front, there was another bank of clouds, perhaps a kilometer away. Ryk headed straight for it, lowering his nose and adding power for maximum speed. He hoped this contraption would take the strain.

Anna scanned the skies. Two German fighters were circling, off to the right. She guessed they were several kilometers away, and perhaps a thousand meters higher. Suddenly one of them broke into a dive, headed directly toward them. Anna cried a warning to Ryk, who turned slightly to the left and steepened his dive.

This was going to be close. Anna apprehensively glanced forward, trying to estimate the distance to the cloud; then back toward the diving Messerschmitt. It looked as if they were going to make it. Anna wondered: what's the range of a machine gun? The clouds were closer, closer; now they were in them. Ryk banked sharply to the left, pulling back on the stick and the throttle. Anna was horrified as machine-gun bullets ripped out a jagged line in the lowest right wing.

Ryk was now well into the clouds, going much slower, and obviously testing his controls. He was soon on the intercom; the German had gotten off one burst at extreme range, just as they were disappearing into the cloud. There was no problem with controls; the ailerons were on the top wing. But the damaged wing would cost them lift and speed.

For a moment, Anna was indignant. They had certainly been beyond German territorial waters when they were attacked. But then she relaxed: what were a few technicalities between enemies?

Another 15 minutes, and Ryk announced that the fuel situation was becoming critical. He would slowly descend and fly just below the clouds, looking for somewhere to land. If German fighters appeared, he would climb back up into the clouds.

When they broke out of the clouds, they were still over the sea. The plane was bouncing; apparently the air was turbulent just below the clouds. Anna began to feel queasy.

Ryk pointed back over his right shoulder. Anna looked back, scanning the sky. Nothing. Then she looked down. In the distance, she could see a large ship; she couldn't be sure, but she thought there were two huge guns in each of its forward turrets.

"A German battleship," was Ryk's guess. "Looks big."

"We've been living right," he added. "Look ahead and to the left."

From the back seat, Anna's vision was blocked. Ryk explained: he could see land.

The approach was painfully slow; they were still fighting a headwind. Soon it became apparent that it was not the Swedish mainland, but a large island.

"Swedish, I can only hope," said Anna.

"Can't really tell. I'll take one low pass along the coast, to make sure we can't see Nazi flags. If we don't, I'll land as soon as possible. Have your pump ready. If I wave my hand, start pumping as hard as you can. If the engine starts to sputter, I want to be able to use whatever's left in the back tank."

As they flew along the coast, it was a tranquil sight. A few villages were tucked into small inlets and, on the right, out to sea, fishing trawlers dotted the water. Ryk could find no sign that the island was German. He chose a field, pointed into the wind, and gradually descended. The instant he flew over the last line of trees, he dipped the nose sharply; Anna felt as though she had left her stomach behind. Then, just as abruptly, the nose came up again; she got her stomach back. But Ryk was an expert; they touched down softly. Then came the bumpy part, as they bounced across the rough, freshly plowed field. Ryk cut the engine and they scrambled out of the plane.

A number of people, apparently farmers and their families, came running across the field. "Sweden?" Ryk asked in German. "Sweden?" Anna added, in English.

"Danemark," came the answer. Ryk was puzzled. How could they get that lost, to land in Denmark? And how could they possibly have gotten there so quickly?

The Danes made it clear, through a mixture of languages, that they were to go to a nearby village, to see the Prefect of Police. One of the teenagers would accompany them on bicycles.

The police station was a Spartan wooden building, unpainted, and obviously beaten by the weather whipping in off the Baltic Sea. The Prefect was a slim man in a heavy woolen uniform which was

surprisingly crisp; apparently it had recently been ironed. His pipe—
Joe Stalin style—seemed oddly out of place.

"Sprechen Sie Deutsch? Or you speak English?" he asked
hesitatingly, in a heavily accented voice, puffing rapidly on the pipe.

"Oh English, please," Anna implored. "I'm English. We want to get
to England."

"Slowly, please."

She repeated herself, pausing between each word.

"If English, what for in German plane? And what for here?"

"I've been visiting Poland," she replied slowly, shaving the truth.
She nodded toward Ryk, and shaved the other side of the truth. "He's
a Polish businessman. His family have owned the plane for twenty
years."

The Prefect waited.

"We would like to get to the Danish mainland as soon as possible,
and fly from Copenhagen to London."

"Bad idea."

"But why?"

"Better... go to Sweden. Closer. This Bornholm Island, near Sweden.
Also, Germans stop Denmark boats. Sometimes. But not Sweden boats.
Keep Sweden happy. Need Sweden steel. You lucky. Sweden mail
boat leaves... two hours. I take you on bicycle."

The phone rang. The Prefect picked it up and listened. Anna tried
to make out his reply, in Danish of course. As far as she could tell, he
was being asked a series of questions, and didn't have whatever
information the caller wanted. Ominously, he said goodbye in
German.

"We leave... five minutes. I telephone first."

Anna couldn't follow the conversations. Unfortunate, because she
would have been delighted with what she heard.

The earlier call had been from the German consul. He had heard
that a pirate plane from Poland had landed on Bornholm. The prefect
replied that he knew nothing. The plane had been stolen from the
Germans, said the consul; he insisted that the plane and the miscreants
be turned over to Germany. The prefect didn't see how, as he knew

nothing of the plane. Then the Danes had better search the island from the air, or the Luftwaffe would.

Now, the prefect made three calls. The first was to his deputy. He was to rush out to Ryk's landing field and burn the Fokker. At once. They should pile brush and small logs on the fire, to obliterate the shape of the plane and make it look as if the farmers had been celebrating the end of the harvest with a bonfire.

The second call was to the tiny airport in the center of the island. Did they have a small plane available? Good. They should get a pilot to take off—sometime within the next hour or two—and search the island for a plane with German markings. He should be methodical, starting at the west end of the island, and flying north and south in narrow swaths until he had completed his job. Thoroughness, not speed, was important; he should take whatever time was necessary to make sure he didn't miss anything.

Needless to say, Ryk had landed near the eastern tip of the island.

The third call was back to the German consul. The prefect had checked with the other police stations and there was no report of any unauthorized landing. But, in the interest of harmonious relations with Germany, he was having a small plane scour the island for any sight of a downed German plane.

Anna had no way of understanding the three telephone calls, but she still had ample reason to be grateful. As she was about to get on her bicycle, she pressed several Reichsmark notes into the Prefect's hand.

She could scarcely avoid the unhappy truth. She could have offered him pound notes, but there was no doubt: marks would be more useful.

11

Katyn:
The Dark Forest

War would end if the dead could return.

Stanley Baldwin

K az and Jan headed southeast from Warsaw—the most direct route toward Romania and freedom. Midway through the first day, they had an unpleasant surprise: they saw German tanks and trucks moving eastward, and the planes overhead were definitely German, not Russian. Somehow, without thinking, Kaz and Jan had simply assumed that the Russians would occupy all the area east of Warsaw and the Vistula River. But they were obviously mistaken. They readjusted their plans. They would head eastward until they got to the Russian zone—wherever that was—and then turn south.

After crossing one more wide river—the Bug—they were, at last, in the Soviet sector. Goodbye to the German army; an especially fervent farewell to the SS. The first part of their journey was over. It had been uneventful, although distinctly unpleasant.

Most uncomfortable was the biting nighttime cold. They were still wearing their heavy military jackets, but these were inadequate for the increasingly frigid weather. They took to staying in the warmth of stables, and, along the way, found several heavy blankets in a partially burned-out farmhouse. They were subsisting mainly on handfuls of grain that they found in the stables, meager rations indeed. In his hunger, Kaz thought back to the story of the Prodigal Son: "he would fain have filled his belly with the husks that the swine did eat." For a moment, he felt nostalgia for his childhood Sunday School, and smiled at the way he used to squirm and fidget as the priest tried so earnestly, but vainly, to hold their interest.

The third night into the Russian zone, they approached a small stable cautiously; they came up from the side opposite the farmhouse to avoid being seen by the inhabitants.

The stable was a ramshackle affair, obviously built in stages, over a period of decades, by farmers unskilled in carpentry. But it had a loft, whose very smallness would trap the heat rising from the animals below. Kaz and Jan were exhausted. They each munched on a handful of oats that they found in the loft. Kaz was getting sick of the restricted diet, but it eased the hunger pains. Although the evening was still early—about 7:00 p.m.—they each pulled a few inches of hay over their single blankets and were soon dead asleep.

Kaz was awakened several hours later by voices; from the sound, two teenagers. He shook Jan to waken him. The young people were climbing up to the loft. Kaz didn't want Jan's light snoring to betray their hiding place, particularly as the teenagers were not speaking Polish. Kaz was, however, relieved that their language was Slavic, not German. Probably Russian; he thought he could make out some of the words, but wasn't sure.

Kaz pressed closer to Jan as the two teenagers flopped on the hay, less than a meter away. Now, he was scarcely breathing. The boy said a few soft words in an importunate tone; the girl giggled; they kissed. They broke for air; the girl was again giggling, while the boy was making a soft purring sound. The teenagers began to roll slowly toward Kaz. He couldn't move; he was already pressing hard against Jan, who was unaware of the imminent danger. The girl bumped into Kaz; she squealed. At once, all four figures were sitting upright. They could barely see one another in the pale moonlight filtering through the cracks between the boards.

"Please be quiet," whispered Jan, apparently in Russian, a language that he spoke with ease. "We're only here for the evening." Kaz didn't understand every word, but guessed what Jan was saying.

"Don't worry," said the boy. The girl now had her arms around his neck; she was clearly frightened by the two unkempt interlopers, with their scruffy week-old beards. "We don't want to be given away either. We'll be quiet if you will." The two teenagers were now withdrawing toward the ladder leading down to the stable.

As the young couple got several meters away, the immediate danger receded, and the girl became curious. "Who are you? How long have you been here?"

The truth, thought Jan, is as good as any story I can concoct on the spot.

"Polish soldiers. We just got here. We'll be gone tomorrow. We're trying to get to Romania.... We've escaped from the Germans," he added, thinking that it might help if he suggested that Germans, not the Russians, were their enemies.

"You'll be gone tomorrow?" the boy wanted to be sure.

"Guaranteed. Before dawn."

The girl disappeared down the ladder and the boy slid down behind her.

"We've got to go," urged Kaz. "Right now. They may betray us to the Soviet army."

"Oh, no," Jan moaned. "I'm aching all over. We may have to search for hours for another stable. It's freezing out there, with driving snow. It's already beginning to sift in through the cracks between the boards."

"You've got a point. And the kid was right; it's unlikely he or his girl want her parents to know where they were."

"I wonder what they are doing here. They didn't come with the Red Army."

"My guess — they live in this area, settlers from the period when the Russians occupied Poland. If their parents are living here, you're right. They're not likely to tell anybody."

Kaz and Jan would stay.

It was the wrong decision.

The next morning, shortly before dawn, as Kaz was beginning to stir, he heard a motorcycle drive into the yard between the stable and house. Peering out, he could see its headlight and a smaller light on the sidecar. A man — perhaps the girl's father? — was coming out of the house, pointing toward the stable; the two Russian soldiers leaped off the motorcycle and headed towards the stable, their rifles at the ready.

Kaz shook Jan, and was appalled by how hot he felt; he must be running a fever. He shook harder. "Jan. Jan. We've got to get out. *Right now*. The Russians are coming."

Suddenly, Jan was wide awake. The two Polish officers slid down into the stable, looking for a back door. They couldn't find one. Kaz helped Jan out a window, and followed headfirst.

A rifle shot whined, ricocheting off the stable siding just above Jan's head. One of the soldiers was about 25 meters away, approaching rapidly, pointing his rifle in their direction. They raised their hands; they were prisoners of the Red Army.

They were in a boxcar, together with thirty Polish officers captured while resisting the Russian advance. Kaz and Jan were the only two regular army officers; the rest were reservists recently called to active duty. In spite of their dirty, unkempt appearance, they were an impressive lot—some of the leaders of Polish society: businessmen, sons of aristocratic families, middle-to-senior level civil servants, teachers and professors, and, fortunately, a few doctors.

Jan was diagnosed with the flu. The doctors insisted that he be put off to one end of the boxcar so that others wouldn't catch his disease. They also insisted that only Kaz and one of the doctors attend to him; they had already been exposed.

Kaz had two main concerns—to keep Jan from getting a severe chill, and to provide him enough water. Kaz gave Jan his sweater; he would do with just his jacket. One of the hardier officers offered his great coat; he wouldn't need it in the relative warmth of the boxcar. The prisoners also provided some water from their already depleted canteens. Fortunately, the looming water crisis was eased when they reached the Soviet border. Because the Russian rails were further apart than those of Poland, the prisoners had to transfer to a Soviet train; in the process, they were allowed to fill their canteens.

Their new home was Prisoner Camp #043, near Smolensk. It was already crowded—over 6,000 prisoners, mostly reserve officers—when Kaz and his group arrived.

Although it was only October, a scattered frosting of snow already formed white splotches on the ground. The task for the next five or six months was clear—simply to stay alive through the severe Russian winter. For Jan, the test would come early; he still had a high fever. Again, the doctors insisted that he be put off separately at one end of the barracks to reduce the risk to other prisoners. The end of the barracks was already getting very cold at nights. There was only one small stove for the entire building, and the other prisoners had crowded their bunks around it. Even for them, the nights were frigid. The Russians provided no fuel, although they did allow the prisoners to bring pieces of wood back from the forest when they were out on work details. Kaz vaguely recalled that, according to the Geneva Convention, officers could not be required to do physical labor. But it would be idiotic to make a fuss; the Russians had the guns.

Each prisoner was provided with one thin blanket; they therefore slept with their clothes on. Kaz thought of giving Jan his blanket, but decided not to; if he were going to look after his friend, he would have to remain healthy himself. Both men—and most of the other prisoners—learned to sleep in a curled position, folding the blanket in two while still remaining covered. Kaz found three large stones outside, near the corner of the barracks, and realized they could help to keep Jan warm. Kaz rotated them from a perch on top of the stove to Jan's bunk. His reward was the weak smile that came over Jan's face as he felt the warmth of the stone on his feet or back. Fortunately, Jan was his old self within ten days.

As the weeks stretched into months, Kaz began to feel like a dog. It wasn't just the harsh treatment by the guards. With the prisoners buttoned up for the winter, he discovered that he could recognize his fellow inmates from their smell. There was one slight compensation. Because each prisoner involuntarily announced his approach, there were fewer nighttime thefts of the inmates' meager possessions.

In the lonely, crowded camp, Kaz's thoughts drifted back to Anna. He worried; what had happened to her? She had some sort of classified job—he wasn't sure he believed the bit about weather forecasting. But he feared it was important enough to qualify her for a class-A interrogation by the Gestapo. He suppressed the thought. Particularly what the Gestapo might do to a young woman.

He found himself daydreaming of his time with her, from that very first evening when he saw her softly slumbering on the sofa. Of his urge to take her in his arms. He tried to order his thoughts, to relive their time together. He dreamt of the wedding, and of their two days and three nights at the lodge in the forest. He once again imagined the fresh fragrance of balsam trees drifting on the soft breeze through their window.

He began to embellish his dreams, imagining what might have been if only Europe had remained at peace. The joy of coming home to Anna after a hard day's work. Legs crossed, bouncing his son on his ankle, thrilling to the tot's joyful squeals. He wondered: is it healthy, to live in dreams? Yes. In a mad world, daydreams are a blessed island of sanity.

Occasionally, he dreamt of Anna at night. He could control his waking dreams, but, sadly, not those in his sleep; his recurring nighttime dream was scarcely the fulfillment of his wishes. He and Anna were on an ice floe. A jagged crack began to split the floe; he tried and tried and struggled to jump to her side, but his legs refused his urgent command. Their fingers parted; the two islands of ice drifted apart. He would wake up shivering.

He struggled back to reality. He and Jan began what every prisoner of war is supposed to do: plan an escape. Winter was not the time to try; it might be even harder to survive outside the camp than inside. But escape at any time would be difficult; it was none too soon to start planning for the coming spring.

Trying to get out through—or over, or under—the two barbed wire fences seemed hopeless, even if the rumor was wrong, that mines dotted the strip between the rows of barbed wire. When the prisoners were sent out on work detail, cutting lumber in the nearby forest—that would be the best chance. True, the work details were guarded by soldiers and dogs, but the guards were obviously bored. An opportunity might arise; they might find a hiding place while they were working. But the chances were not good; the guards always counted the prisoners as they returned to the camp.

They therefore began planning a larger escape, with some prisoners creating a diversion while others got away. It might be bloody, requiring some prisoners — the ones creating the diversion — to sacrifice themselves. Undoubtedly the Russians would retaliate. Perhaps, if they got a group of twenty or so to join, they might draw straws. The lucky ones would try to escape; the unlucky few would create the diversion.

Their plans were disrupted when the Russians began to rotate prisoners randomly among the barracks; their obvious goal was to make it much more difficult to plan and execute an escape. In February, three prisoners in the next barracks disappeared completely; the rumor quickly spread that they had tried to escape. Several inmates — the optimists — thought that they had succeeded. Others reached a darker conclusion.

Kaz and Jan were aiming for an escape in April; the warmer weather would give them a sporting chance of surviving on the outside. Working backward, they decided to bring others into their plan about two weeks before the escape; this way, there might be some hope of keeping a group together long enough to actually carry out the plan.

At the beginning of April, however, their plans were derailed. As the first mild breezes of spring sifted through the trees, baring patches of dark, muddy earth, the work details into the forest came to an end. Apparently, logging went on only during winter months, when the snow, ice, and frozen ground made it possible for horses to slide heavy logs out of the woods.

The most alarming development came several days later. One evening as the sun was setting, eight trucks rumbled in through the gates. The inhabitants of three of the barracks — two hundred men — were prodded in. They were not even permitted to take their meager personal belongings. Two soldiers jumped into the back of each truck, and another guard was posted in each cab with the driver. The tailgates slammed; the trucks quickly left the compound.

The next night, the trucks returned. Rumors began to spread among those who remained. The Russians were sending them off to mines in Siberia. They were sending them north, as forced labor on the canal system between Moscow and Leningrad. They were being taken off to "indoctrination centers," to see which of them might be persuaded — and trusted? — to join the Soviet army. They were being sent to a new camp, further to the east. Nobody knew.

Early the third evening, Jan drew Kaz aside.

"I've got an awful feeling about this."

"Me too. The rumors... they don't make sense. Why shouldn't the camp commandant let us know — unless he's sending us to one of the forced labor camps? I hear that people don't come out of them alive."

"Maybe worse than that. I overheard a couple of guards. One said that they should keep us all as calm as possible, to avoid a riot. The other guy asked, why should we riot, when they had all the guns? The first one suggested that his companion really didn't want to know."

Jan let his information sink in. After a pause, he added:

"*I think they're killing us. Nobody's going to survive.* Stalin wants to control Poland. The people here are nothing but trouble. They're leaders. If they're allowed to live, they'll challenge Stalin's stooges when the war's over."

"But if they're killing us, why not all at once? Why only two hundred a night?"

"Think of the mechanics. How do you kill six thousand people, without some escaping, and without everyone in the area knowing about it? My guess — they're trying to do it as inconspicuously as possible; that's why prisoners are taken away at night. All I can say is, if we're asked to dig ditches, everybody should use their shovels to attack the Russian soldiers. At least somebody might escape."

Kaz stood scratching his beard, thinking, for what must have been three or four minutes. Then he responded. "I think you're right. They're killing us. If they were just moving us, why not let us take our paltry possessions?

"That means," he continued, "we've got to make plans right away. Something quick and dirty; we don't know when our turn will come. If we have time, we can work out the fancy stuff later."

The inmates had jammed straw into the corners of the building to cut down on drafts. The two men pulled some out of the chinks, and stuffed as much into their jackets and pants as they could without being conspicuous. Kaz already had half a dozen matches. A month earlier, one of the Russian soldiers dropped a handful when he was relighting the stove. Kaz happened to be shuffling by at the time. As casually as he could, he nudged some of the matches under a bunk, and came back later to recover them. The two had also managed to accumulate bits of newspaper.

The two conspirators cautiously approached a dozen other prisoners in their barracks to join in their plan, but most simply couldn't believe Kaz and Jan's fears. Only two joined their pathetic plan—Piotr and Wincenty.

Their barracks' number came up four nights later. As the prisoners were herded into the trucks, Kaz, Jan, Piotr and Wincenty managed to maneuver their way to the end of the line, and all got into the last of the eight trucks. Piotr took his spot at the back of the truck, near the guards. The other three went to the front, Kaz sitting in the very corner, with Jan and Wincenty to either side to hide their comrade. As the truck bounced along the washboard road, the three made a small pile under Kaz's seat—crumpled paper and damp straw. Kaz gripped his half dozen matches, hoping that they would be enough.

There was a rip in the canvas cover, and Kaz could faintly see the road ahead in the moonlight. As they rounded a curve, he could make out a sign. The first three letters were K-A-T; he was unsure of the last two—perhaps AN or YN, in Cyrillic letters, of course. The winding road was beginning to narrow, and Kaz thought he could see a hill ahead. Good. The truck would be slowing down.

He nodded to Piotr. That didn't work. It was too dark for Piotr to see him. Kaz coughed loudly.

Thereupon Piotr broke into a fit of coughing. He collapsed to the floor. One of the guards kicked his ribs. A prisoner near the back of the truck shouted angrily; he was about to jump up, but was restrained by the two men at his sides. The second guard cocked his rifle and pointed it straight between his eyes. Piotr continued to cough, but managed to get to his knees. The first guard was now shouting at him, jabbing him in the ribs with the muzzle of his rifle.

Smoke began to fill the front of the truck. The other prisoners began coughing and surging towards the back. One of the guards fired a warning shot, but the smoke was now too thick for the men to stop.

Prisoners began to tumble out the back of the truck, along with the two guards. A prisoner began to struggle with one of the guards, trying to get his rifle. The other guard smashed his rifle butt into the side of the prisoner's head; he collapsed, blood trickling from his ears.

By now, Kaz and Jan were over the edge of the road, alternatively slipping and tumbling down the hill toward a narrow river; behind were Piotr and Wincenty. The truck had stopped, and the guard sprang out of the cab, shouting. Piotr and Wincenty fell to the ground, hiding behind some low bushes; Kaz and Jan were further down, and dove over an embankment to the edge of the river. They ran along the gravel beside the river for about fifty yards, keeping their heads down. They could hear shots and shouting from above.

Kaz stopped to peek over the embankment. One of the guards had gone a quarter of the way down the hill and was approaching the place where Piotr and Wincenty were hiding. Suddenly, the two prisoners stood up, their hands in the air. The guard fired two quick shots; Piotr and Wincenty fell to the ground. Apparently satisfied that he had gotten all the escapees, the guard clambered back up the hill. Kaz and Jan did not wait to see the prisoners herded back into the truck.

In the pale moonlight, Kaz could see the pain on Jan's face.

Kaz and Jan each felt a surge of guilt. They needn't have. As they would soon learn, their suspicions were right. Katyn Forest was a killing ground. Every night for a month, executioners of the NKVD — the Soviet Secret Police — shot over 200 Polish officers in the back of the head with German Walther 2 revolvers. Soviet guns were not considered sufficiently reliable for such continuous, demanding use.

On Stalin's orders, similar executions were taking place at two other camps, near Kalinin and Starobelsk. The Soviets shot a total of 15,000 officers — the core of what might have become a noncommunist Polish government after the war.

12
Bletchley Park

*... a riddle, an enigma, an
inexplicable mystery*
David Hume

The morning after arriving in London, Anna went around to the British Admiralty, Intelligence Branch. At the hunting lodge in Pyry Forest just three months earlier, Alastair Denniston had mentioned that the British codebreakers grew out of the naval intelligence office of World War I. Anna told the receptionist that she wanted to contact Mr. Denniston of British Intelligence. Why, the receptionist wanted to know. Because she had some important information for him. What information? She couldn't say; she needed to talk to Mr. Denniston personally. Anna was asked to wait in a small library to one side of the reception hall. She began to peruse the shelves. She found a moldy volume on codebreaking since Roman times and started to leaf through it.

After half an hour, a young sub-lieutenant appeared.

"You wanted to see Mr. Denniston?"

"Yes, please."

"Might I ask why?"

"I have important information for him."

"And what would that be?"

"I'm sorry, but I can't say."

"Why not?"

"It's important. And secret. That means, I can't tell just anybody."

That didn't come out at all the way Anna intended. Not surprisingly, the young officer was insulted; he was not used to being referred to as "just anybody."

"Right. Let's go at this another way. Who are you?"

"Anna Jankowska. I've just arrived from Poland."

"You had a job with the government there?"

"Yes."

"With...?"

"With the Special Meteorology Project of the Polish Air Force."

"What was your rank?"

"I didn't have a rank. I was a civilian employee."

"Right. But there's a difficulty. Mr. Denniston doesn't work on meteorology."

Now, thought Anna, we're getting somewhere. He actually knows something about Denniston.

"I know. But I don't work on meteorology, either."

"But I thought you just said that you were with...."

"I know. But I still didn't work on meteorology."

"Right. Then what did you do?"

"Surely you've heard of a cover story. My cover story is, I worked on weather forecasting."

"But you really didn't?"

Now it was Anna's turn. "Right."

"But you really work on...?"

"As I said, I can't say. If I could say, it wouldn't be much of a cover story, would it?"

Both·of them were now struggling, with only limited success, to conceal their irritation.

"But you were sufficiently senior, that you have important information you can only give to Denniston?" The sub-lieutenant was obviously skeptical; Anna looked much too young to have a senior position.

"That's correct. Please contact him. He'll know who I am."

"I'm sorry. That was Anna...?"

"JANKOWSKA," said Anna, spelling her name slowly as the sub-lieutenant wrote it down.

"One last question. You said you just arrived from Poland. How did you get out? In an Air Force plane?"

"No. In an old Fokker triplane."

The sub-lieutenant half expected her to add, "with the Red Baron."

"Would you please wait," he said, and disappeared.

Anna waited. And waited. For well over two hours. She was famished. Finally, the sub-lieut. reappeared.

"I'm sorry, but Denniston says he doesn't know who you are."

"Oh damn," said Anna. "I forgot. I've just gotten married. He would know me by my previous name, Anna Raczynska."

"You forgot that you've just been married? I'm afraid I'll have to ask you to leave."

"No. I insist on seeing your superior."

The sub-lieutenant left, stopping at the desk to ask the receptionist to call security and have them send up a non-uniformed guard. He should stay just outside the library, in case the visitor became violent. This was, by rough count, the seventh mental case to come walking in off the street in the past month.

The young officer then went upstairs and knocked on his boss's door. The lieutenant called for him to enter.

"We've got a real live one down there. Says she wants to see Denniston. Says she worked for a Special Meteorology Project of the Polish Air Force, but didn't do weather. 'I can't say,' is her response to most questions. Says she forgot that she was recently married. Says she arrived on a magic carp..., I mean, in a Fokker triplane. She insists on seeing you. She's apparently sane enough to figure out that I'm not going to be helpful."

"Oh, good grief. Should we have security throw her out, or is it serious enough to call the mental hospital?"

"Hard to say. There's just one thing. I just thought you might actually like to see this one."

"What?"

"She's rather interesting. Might give you an amusing interlude. Even though she's nutty, she seems perfectly rational—even intelligent. And, oh yes, just one other thing. She's *remarkably* pretty. I might even say, stunning."

The lieutenant was on his way downstairs, picking up his hat on the way. The receptionist was astonished to see him, but he ignored her, brushing by her and the newly arrived security guard on his way into the library.

Anna had been counting to ten, over and over, trying to regain her composure. When the lieutenant entered, she smiled slightly, and he motioned her to sit down.

"I understand you want to see Mr. Denniston."

"Yes." Then, to smooth things, Anna added, "sir."

"Might I ask how you got his name?" That wasn't quite the way the lieutenant wanted it to come out. "I mean, have you ever met him?"

Anna paused. The meeting in Pyry Forest was supposed to be a deep secret. Finally, she responded simply: "Yes, sir."

"When was that?"

Anna paused again. Damn, thought the lieutenant, that wasn't what I should have asked, either. What's so intriguing about her?

"I meant," he corrected himself, "if you could describe him."

She could, and did. In considerable detail. He was a short man—perhaps 5'6" or 5'7", said Anna, translating meters into feet. He spoke with a Scottish bur. His features were sharp, but pleasant. His dark hair was graying not only at the temples, but along the sides of his head. He had an unusual way of walking—not a limp, but an odd gait. She surprised herself, even remembering the color of his eyes. Correct on all counts, thought the lieutenant. And not the sorts of things she would get out of a newspaper or magazine article—even if there were one about Denniston, which he very much doubted. This certainly is a fascinating one.

"Would you please excuse me," he said. "I would like to contact Denniston again. What name did you say he might know you by?"

"Anna Raczynska."

The lieutenant got up to go.

"Oh yes," said Anna. "I'm sure he's very busy, and perhaps even a bit absent minded." Correct again, thought the lieutenant. "Ask him," she added, "if he liked my little gift."

"Your little gift?"

"Surely you know by now. I can't say." Again, she smiled slightly.

"Ah, right," he said, about to leave the room. He had meant to be clinical and expressionless, but he smiled back.

This time, she didn't have to wait two hours. Not even fifteen minutes. The lieutenant was back, and full of apologies.

"Mr. Denniston sends his sincere regrets. He didn't know your married name. He's eager to talk to you. They'll be sending around a car for you in half an hour. Would you like to come up to my office while you wait?"

Anna paused. She was famished. She looked at her watch: 2:37. The lieutenant looked at his watch too.

"I'm sorry. I wasn't thinking. I don't suppose you've had anything to eat. I could have my secretary go to the pub around the corner and pick up something for you."

When they got back to his office, the sub-lieut. noticed that his boss carefully closed the door behind him. An unusual case, indeed.

After the frustrations of the morning, Anna was delighted to be on her way to see Denniston. She was traveling in a small, olive drab staff car with worn seats and threadbare carpets; she guessed it dated from the mid thirties. The side curtains were drawn and there was another curtain behind the driver that blocked her view to the front. She wanted to peek out, to see what she could of London and wherever it was they were headed, but she decided not to. The curtains were drawn for a reason. Someone didn't want her to know where she was going.

About 5:00 p.m., the car stopped. The driver opened the door and snapped a salute as Anna stepped out. Apparently, anyone who rated a staff car also rated a salute. "I'd better not get used to this," she thought as she nodded back to the corporal. "On the other hand, I hope I don't have to get used to this morning, either."

She was in front of a lovely, large Victorian mansion that apparently had been built in sections. It looked like a set of fashionable London townhouses — partly Tudor and partly Gothic, with a series of bay windows on the second floor, some overhanging and some resting on first-floor bays. Later, Anna would learn that it reflected the eclectic tastes of Sir Herbert Leon, a stockbroker who built it as his country house in the late 19th century.

When she was ushered in to Denniston's office, he was most apologetic.

"So sorry about the cock-up in London. They were treating you as something of a joke. Seemed to think that they had a mental case on their hands." Denniston was trying not to smirk, but felt more relaxed when Anna laughed good-naturedly. "They get quite a few wandering in. When they said Anna Jankowska, they emphasized your last name, and I didn't recognize it. They also seemed to have gotten the amusing idea that you arrived in a World War I triplane."

"Actually, that's how I got out of Poland. To Denmark. But let's not get into *that*."

"At any rate, welcome to Bletchley Park. When they mentioned your 'little gift,' I knew at once it was you. We can't thank you too much. We're finding the wheels invaluable, although our success in breaking the basic codes has so far been very limited. What we're picking up are mostly training exercises—full of nursery rhymes and chitchat. The Boche are sharpening their skills, but they're also giving us practice. For example, we found out that they're now changing their basic settings every night at midnight. So we face a huge task. But they said that you had some information for me?"

"An idea, really. My mind was going back over the earlier messages. The one I remember most clearly was the first one we decoded—a message telling the army that they would be getting antitank guns in their infantry regiments."

"And?"

"The message itself wasn't important. What is important—it was repeated several times the next day. It occurred to me that this may be a standard practice when they send orders to a large number of divisions. We could get a good idea of when repeats were occurring. They would have the same number of letters in the main message—76, or whatever. If we've deciphered one message, and it's repeated after the basic settings are changed, that would give us an enormous leg up in figuring out the new settings. It might be especially helpful, now that the Germans are changing the settings every 24 hours."

"Indeed. We're hard at work, collecting a set of such clues. We're also identifying some individuals by the style of their transmissions; we hope that some will have idiosyncrasies that we can use.

"But before we get to that, I wonder if you would join Sandra and me for dinner?"

"I'd be delighted."

"And we'd like you to stay with us for at least a few days."

"Again, I'd be delighted. But I'm afraid I've left my things in a London Hotel. Perhaps I could ring them and have them move the stuff out of my room—I don't like to sit on an unused room when they're so terribly hard to get."

"Of course. It's getting a bit late. But, most days, we have a courier come up from London, either by train or car. He could bring up your suitcases tomorrow. Can you do without for this evening? Sandra might be able to give you a few things you need."

"My suitcase," she corrected. "I've been traveling very light."

"Done. I'd also like you to join us here at BP—I mean, Bletchley Park. However, I'm afraid that might be difficult. Our security people are tough—understandably—and they may balk at us hiring a foreign national. And we still have to answer to Naval Intelligence, and, through them, to the Admiralty. That may take some time, but I'll see if I can move things along—if you want."

"Of course. I can't imagine any place I'd rather be."

At dinner that evening, Anna started to mention something about Pyry Forest, but Alastair quickly changed the subject. He clearly didn't want to talk shop in front of his wife. It wasn't that he didn't trust her, Anna guessed. But, for her sake, he didn't want her to know things she didn't need to know. If she knew secrets, she might be under continuous stress not to let them slip out. She might not know when some detail was important.

Alastair wanted to know about the flight out of Poland in the old Fokker. Anna obliged. Even with her understatements, the drama and danger of their escape shone through.

Sandra asked about the wedding. They had been married, Anna said, on the last weekend of July. She described the wedding ceremony, and the general delight of the two families; the darkening international clouds were pushed to the back of everyone's mind. Anna then came back to the subject of Pyry Forest, but in a way to which Alastair could scarcely object.

"Kaz and I spent our honeymoon night at the hunting lodge in a forest near Warsaw. We'd intended to go to Sweden to visit some of his cousins, but, with the tense international situation, the Army wouldn't let him travel outside the country. Fortunately, I was able to get a reservation at the lodge at the last minute. We thought that we handled the day very calmly; we didn't think we were the least bit nervous. But when we came to open the champagne, we rummaged around, looking for a corkscrew. We couldn't find one. Kaz called the front desk, and a bellhop appeared, corkscrew in hand. Kaz told him what he wanted. The bellhop folded the corkscrew and put it in his pocket. He then crossed the room with an absolutely expressionless face, undid the foil on the bottle, and worked the cork loose with his thumbs. When it popped, he retreated back across the room, but we could tell he was having trouble maintaining his composure. As he disappeared out of the room, we could see his shoulders jiggling with laughter."

The evening was capped off by Sandra telling stories of their early years of marriage. How delightful, relaxed, and carefree those days now seemed. Neither of Anna's hosts had the bad taste to ask about Kaz. She obviously didn't want to talk about him; it hurt too much.

Alastair had trouble getting Anna's security clearance—as predicted, only more so. After two weeks, he got her name past the internal security people at BP. They were finally convinced when he pointed out that, if Anna really were a German spy, they were all wasting their time anyway. The Huns would know about their work in detail, and simply play games with their deciphering operations. It wouldn't take much imagination to make the machine much, much more complicated.

But that was just the internal people; he then had to go to Naval Intelligence. Anna was becoming embarrassed, staying with the Denniston's for such a long time, but didn't feel she could commit herself to lodgings until she knew if she really had a job.

In frustration, Alastair finally decided to bypass Naval Intelligence and take the case directly to the office of the First Lord of the Admiralty. The senior officers were equally uncooperative. But then, finally, he announced success. Anna was to report to his office the next morning at 10:00 for work.

When she got there, Alastair let her know what had happened.

"I finally got a call from the First Lord himself. Winston's intensely interested in our work; he's almost boyish, the way he delights in the intrigue. He wanted to push us along, to know if there was anything he could do to help us move faster. I took the opportunity to ask about your clearance. When I mentioned your English mother, it turned out that he knows her family. I described how helpful you and your colleagues were at Pyry Forest, and he agreed at once.

"We're just now getting up to speed. As you've been studying the Enigma for the past few years, I'd like you to take an office next to mine, so I can bounce ideas off you, to see if you've run into them before. I should mention right at the outset that this arrangement will be temporary. Once our people get more experience, I'll want one of them as my right-hand assistant. But I think you can count on a job with us for as long as the war lasts — or as long as you can put up with our peculiar ways."

Anna responded that this was more than satisfactory. She was thereupon sent down to the administrative offices for the normal paperwork, and for a very abnormal — even spectacular — security briefing. After she signed the Official Secrets Act, she was informed of the special rules applying at Bletchley Park. Anyone intentionally passing on information about BP could expect a firing squad; even careless breaches of security could lead to the death penalty. It sounded like an operation run by Ghengis Khan. But carelessness could not be tolerated: countless lives might be endangered. It might seem that they were playing an incredibly complicated chess game. But it was deadly serious, with huge stakes.

Anna's position would be special, with her office next to Mr. Denniston. He would come through the door as he pleased, but Anna was not to use it. If she wanted to see Mr. Denniston, she would go out into the hall and enter through the office of Mr. Denniston's secretary, asking her if Mr. Denniston were free.

When she got back to the office, Alastair immediately came in.

"Until further notice, I'd like you to work on clues or cribs that might be useful." He flopped a large pile of undeciphered messages on her desk, and a much thinner file of decoded ones; at least some of these were the decodings previously given to Denniston by the Poles. "Take your time—don't feel pressured, although I'll probably check by with you once or twice a day. I'd like you to take an independent look, but I might first mention of some of the things we're exploring.

"First of all, we've broken a few Luftwaffe messages. One of our keys is a variation on the VON theme. The address is a longer string of letters: AN DIE GRUPPE (TO THE GROUP). We're hopeful that, when our new bombe comes along, we'll be able to break these messages—with that great big, lovely clue—very quickly, even though the Germans throw in as many as ten meaningless, random letters at the beginning, before they get to AN DIE GRUPPE, just to make our job more difficult.

"Then there's the very interesting idiosyncrasy of the Enigma. When you push in any letter—say G—it can come out any *other* letter, that is, any letter *except* G. I don't believe you mentioned this at Pyry Lodge."

Anna was surprised. How could they have forgotten to pass on this important detail? The surprise showed on her face. Alastair apparently misinterpreted her expression, thinking she was unaware of this peculiarity of the Enigma.

"The reason is quite simple. If, at a randomly chosen setting of the wheels, G comes out T, then it's reversible. T will come out G. To make the machine reversible—so it can be used for both coding and decoding—the designers not only used the three rotors, but also a reflector at the end. Without getting into the mechanics, the reflector not only ensures reversibility, but also ensures that a letter must come out as some other letter. This is so even with the steckerboard, which is an integral part of the wiring."

Anna thought it would be impolite to interrupt his explanation; she saw no gracious way of saying that she already knew. Also, with Alastair's explanation, she might actually learn something new.

"This idiosyncrasy turns out to be surprisingly useful. For example, suppose we suspect that a German message is addressed:

ANDIEGRUPPE. We line these eleven letters up directly below the beginning of the encoded German message. If any one of the letters corresponds — for example, if the second letter of the encoded message is also N — then we know the encoded message *doesn't* have ANDIEGRUPPE at the very beginning. We slide ANDIEGRUPPE along one space, to find if we now have possible solution, with the Germans having put one random, dummy letter at the beginning. As long as we find a matching letter in the top and bottom lines, we know we're not in the right place, and can continue to slide ANDIEGRUPPE along, one letter at a time, until we get a possible solution. If we move a dozen spaces to the right, with a matching letter each time, we can be pretty sure the message isn't addressed ANDIEGRUPPE, and can turn to a different message.

"There's also a whole set of additional clues that Welchman and others in Hut 6 have been working on. They occur when the German operators do something stupid. In fact, you may know about this type of clue because Rejewski was working on them."

"Yes, of course. But I'd also be interested in the specific ones you've found."

"The most obvious cribs come from operators who use their girlfriends' names. One of the first was a girl named Cilli. Her boyfriend often uses CIL and other parts of her name for the wheel settings.

"Not surprisingly, our decoders quickly corrupted 'Cilli' into 'silly.' But it's just one example of a whole series of sillies. Come on into my office, and I'll show you what I mean." Alastair led her to what was apparently a closet, but now concealed an Enigma machine. He pointed to the keyboard:

QWERTZUIO
ASDFGHJK
PYXCVBNML

"We occasionally find a really stunned operator who just works his way along the top row. He picks QWE as the setting for the first message, and RTZ for the second. The chances are pretty good that the next one will be UIO. Or, if he starts diagonally with QAY and then WSX, the next ones are likely to be EDC and RFV.

"Then, there's the Herivel Tip, named after John Herivel, whom you'll undoubtedly meet. John noticed that the enigma operators may be just plain lazy. When picking a setting, they sometimes just move each wheel one or two notches. Thus, for example, if the initial settings is GNU, the new setting for the first wheel is likely to be within one or two letters of G, and so on. Occasionally, we're really lucky. An operator will set the wheels at AAA for the first message, BBB for the second, and so on.

"Finally—and I've got to go. I mentioned we have a new version of the bombe coming along. Alan Turing was already designing the machine before our Pyry Forest meeting. He recently went to see Marian Rejewski and Henryk Zygalski; they got out of Poland and are working with Bertrand near Paris. Marian and Henryk were a great help, proving once again that three heads are better than one.

"Oh, by the way, don't even *dream* of contacting Marian or Henryk. Just so there are no misunderstandings: you are flatly forbidden to leave the country, and you're also forbidden to contact Poles outside Britain—or *anyone* outside Britain, for that matter. Also, you should check with security before you have contacts with Poles even within Britain."

"So those two, at least, got away," said Anna, obviously relieved.

"So did Jerzy Rozycki and some of the others."

Anna was delighted, but also puzzled. Alastair seemed almost embarrassed as he gave her the good news. She waited to see if she would get more information. It came.

"It's shameful, what happened in Romania. When your colleagues got out of Poland, they headed straight for the British embassy in Bucharest. The imbeciles there didn't realize what they were being offered. Brushed off your colleagues, suggesting they come back in a few days."

Anna couldn't help but think of her experience at Naval Intelligence, the first day she arrived.

"But, of course, they couldn't wait around. They had entered Romania illegally, without papers, and were afraid that the police might pick them up and put them in an internment camp. Naturally, they went to the French embassy and were greeted with open arms. In fact, Bertrand was there waiting for them; he made a special trip to Romania in the hope that they would show up. So they immediately got French visas. It worked out all right for the allies, I suppose. But we were fools."

During the next few weeks, Anna worked away methodically, spending the mornings with a "tabula rasa," so to speak—starting with a clean sheet of paper and jotting down ideas when they came to her, whether they seemed good, bad, or indifferent. During the afternoons, she would work through the pile of unbroken messages, not quite sure what she was looking for.

Then, one afternoon, she thought she found something. Two messages, both from the same source, and both with exactly the same number of letters—92. Could this be what she was after? A repeat of a message, on different days, using different basic settings? Her reason—or excuse?—for contacting Alastair in the first place? She looked at the messages themselves; the letters did not correspond at all. Then she looked at the times of transmission: 11:31 Dec. 29, 1939 and 12:14 Dec. 29, 1939. Damn. They weren't sent on different days. Was it possible that the Huns were picking new settings twice a day, once at midnight and once at noon? Unlikely. Changing a code in the middle of the day and in the middle of action would cause too much confusion. Probably just a coincidence. After all, if messages are generally less than 100 letters, it would be surprising if she *didn't* occasionally find two different messages with the same number of letters. And yet....

She sat there, staring at the wall. More precisely, at the place where water had seeped in from a leak in the roof, leaving a stain on the wallpaper. An informal Rorschach test. She wondered: did it look more like a frog or a butterfly?

She then started leafing slowly back through the unbroken messages of Dec. 29. She found what she was looking for. A very brief return message to the original sender, at 11:47. She got up thoughtfully, and walked toward Alastair's door. She was about to turn the knob absentmindedly when she caught herself. She detoured through the secretary's office. Yes, Mr. Denniston would see her.

"Suppose," she said, laying the three messages before him, "that the operator was having a bad morning. He forgot to enter new wheel settings for the day, and simply transmitted, using the basic settings from the previous day. Then comes the abrupt response: 'We can't read your message. Please transmit again.' Or whatever. Then the original chap does retransmit, this time using the current day's settings."

It was now Alastair's turn to sit and think. After a few minutes, he said simply, "Sounds promising—an idea worth pursuing. I'll try it out on Alan Turing and Gordon Welchman over in Hut 6; they may find it useful.

"You know, Anna, it brings back one of our most notable successes in the Great War, when I was a junior member of the codebreaking unit. One Christmas eve, a German commander in the Middle East had much too much to drink. In a mellow, inebriated haze, he decided to send season's greetings to all his stations. Apparently his wireless operators had quite a bit to drink, too. They should have sent the greetings in the clear, but instead sent exactly the same message in six different ciphers. We could scarcely believe our good luck. It was a time when there was practically no other traffic, and it was obvious what had happened. We had already broken one of the ciphers, and the drunken commander gave us a key to break the other five. Quite a Christmas gift. At the time, we called him the Snookered Santa. Maybe we could revive that name."

"That reminds me, Alastair. I think that we might be a bit more obscure and nondescript in our code names. I overheard a discussion in the cafeteria the other day. These two young chaps were talking about FUN clues, and sillies. They wondered if there was an office game going on, and if so, how they could join it. As they were leaving, I walked up beside them and said: For your information, FUN doesn't have anything to do with fun. That's just how the German word V-O-N—meaning from—is pronounced. So it's all business, not fun. Just keep your mouths shut.

"Perhaps, Alastair, we should use some other shorthand besides VON. As far as I can see, the words 'sillies' and 'snookered santa' don't convey any hints. But VON may."

She had a point. Thereafter, the denizens of BP would refer to VON and other standard introductions simply as one of the "sillies."

And so it was. They had a number of cribs and clues that might lead to the Enigma settings—sillies, snookered santas, Herivel tips, and others that were yet to come. Soon, however, santa was retired. When two identical messages with different keys were matched up, the match came to be known simply as a "kiss."

13
Lady Luck

You do your worst — we will do our best.
Churchill, pretending to address
Hitler

12 February, 1940. Aboard minesweeper, *HMS Gleaner.*

It was a typical February day. A blanket of fog covered the waters near the Firth of Clyde, off the western coast of Scotland. As Lt.-Commander Hugh Price strained to see past the bow of his minesweeper, his ship abruptly came out of the fog bank. There, about 100 yards, almost dead ahead, was a faint, sinister gray form — a German submarine, lying low in the water.

Price immediately sounded Battle Stations, thoughts racing through his head. "Now we're in for it. They've got a bigger gun than we do. They're a smaller target, and they're more solidly built. There's nothing for it but to have a go at them. With luck, we may put them off their stroke." He ordered the wheel turned slightly to port, heading straight for the U-boat, and signaled full power. If they could only get up to 12 knots!

He did have luck. The dozen men on the sub's deck quickly sprang to action, but were confused. Some headed for the conning tower, hoping to submerge before the minesweeper was upon them. Others rushed toward the deck gun. As they prepared for action, an invisible stopwatch clicked in Price's head. 75 yards; 15 seconds to collision. 60 yards, 12 seconds; 50 yards, 10 seconds. His deck gun fired, but the shot was high. There went the gunner's only chance; they wouldn't be able to lower their gun enough to get a second shot.

25 yards, 5 seconds. The sub's gun had now swung around, and Price felt the peculiar sensation of looking straight down the barrel. It fired; Price was surprised to be alive. As the front of his ship pitched

137

upward, the German shell struck the very top of the bow, sending shrapnel across the deck and wounding two gunners.

One of U-boat gunners was apparently thinking of reloading, but for them, also, it was too late; they too had taken their one and only shot. The minesweeper would soon be upon them. Price ordered the wheel adjusted slightly to starboard, aiming directly for the conning tower. He braced for a collision. The German gunners dove for safety over the far side of the sub.

A crunch was followed by a grinding sound as the minesweeper came to rest, partially supported by the sub. Price called to his Number One, asking him to send a Tommy gunner up to the deck. On the double. He then proceeded to the right side of the bow and looked down at the sub. The front of its conning tower had a five-foot gash; it was in no condition to submerge.

Several minutes passed while Price—and presumably the sub commander, too—pondered the situation. Neither ship was in a position to move. With the larger ship draped over its deck, the only direction the sub could go was down. And it couldn't do that because of damage to the conning tower; it would sink. On the other hand, if Price backed off—assuming he could—the sub might slip away on the surface; the fog was beginning to close in again.

By now, two—not one—Tommy gunners had appeared on deck, along with another half dozen of the crew. Price decided that the time had come for action; he didn't want to give the U-boat commander more time to think. Able Seaman Skinner was on deck; he spoke some German. Price quickly gave him instructions and sent him over the side on a rope, carrying a hammer and several grenades.

Skinner got to the top of the conning tower and banged on the hatch with the hammer. As it slowly opened, he slid around behind the hatch to avoid presenting a target for anyone inside with a firearm. He shouted an ultimatum: the Germans had two minutes to abandon ship and surrender. They would be taken aboard *HMS Gleaner* as prisoners. They had just two minutes, he repeated; then the submarine would be sunk. Meanwhile, the *Gleaner's* crew had brought forward a rope ladder, which was being lowered toward the conning tower.

Price hoped the bluff would work; he wasn't sure what he would do after two minutes if it didn't. After 30 seconds, nothing had happened, and Price nodded to Skinner, who thereupon inched his hand over the top of the hatch. In it was a hand grenade, with the pin pulled.

There was panicked shouting in German, and the crew began to emerge, hands spread to their sides. Skinner threw the grenade over the side; it sank about five feet, then exploded like a miniature depth charge, sending a spray over the sub's deck. He scampered up the rope ladder.

The U-boat crew followed, under the careful watch of the two seamen with Tommy guns. After five minutes, the whole crew of the sub was up on the deck of the minesweeper, so far as Price could tell; the gun crew had been only too eager to swim up and join their comrades, thus escaping the frigid waters.

Price ordered his men to take the Germans to the mess in the middle of the ship, providing blankets for the shivering gun crew. The mess was a small, windowless room, but submariners were supposed to like cramped, windowless quarters.

Price asked his second-in-command, Sub-Lt. Hempsted, to join him on the bridge.

"What would you do now?" he queried the Sub-Lieutenant.

"Back off, sir, and sink the sub with our deck gun."

"Doesn't that run the risk of further damage to our ship—perhaps enough that we'll never make it back to port? And isn't there a risk that the Germans might have left a skeleton crew aboard, and the sub might slip away in the fog? It's also possible our deck gun was damaged by their shell."

"Granted. But what alternative do we have, sir?"

"We could send someone down into the sub to open the sea cocks, and sink her. We might pick up codebooks on the way."

"I'm not wild about that, sir. The Germans may have set demolition charges, following their standing orders. They'll go off within ten or, at the most, fifteen minutes. Anyone in the sub would be killed."

"Suppose, Hempsted, that you were the U-boat captain. Would you have set the charges?"

"Yes.... Well, maybe. On second thought, I guess not. If we were to back off, the sub might get away on the surface, if it hadn't set the charges—as you've already pointed out, sir."

"Suppose we don't try to back off. We just sit here, talking?"

"Then when the damn charges go off, we'll all be killed—both British and German." Hempsted's voice was rising. "If I might, sir, I think the time has come to stop talking and do something."

"Ah, but what? That's the problem. I don't think you've answered my question. What would you do if you were the German captain, and you thought we might just sit here?"

Hempsted was now sweating, but realized he would have to answer. "I suppose," he said, calming himself, "that I wouldn't set the charges. It would just mean that everyone would be killed."

"So that, regardless, you wouldn't set the charges?"

"With great respect, captain, I've a feeling you've tricked me somehow."

"I think," said Price, "the time has come for a little social visit with the German captain. Let's see how nervous he is—whether he's expecting explosions at any moment. Go below and ask him to join us. On the way, you might have the cook bring up a bottle of rum and some glasses. And, just for form, we should have an armed guard posted outside the door."

The rum, glasses, guard, and German captain all arrived within a few moments.

"We seem to be in an interesting situation," began Price, hoping that the German spoke English. He did.

"The fortunes of war," replied the German with a shrug. "But it's your move. What do you intend to do?"

"Nice question," said Price, pouring three drinks—a large one for the German. "But before we get to it, I've never met a U-boat captain before. Why did you choose this line of work? Seems a trifle dangerous."

Price was observing the captain closely, looking for any signs of nervousness.

"Because..." replied the captain, somewhat stiffly, "because this was the best way to contribute to a German victory. Our cause is important. I am not."

"You expect to win the war?"

"*Natürlich*. We crushed the Poles in short order. You decadent Western democracies will soon experience the full force of German arms. Certainly *you* don't expect to win."

"Well, actually, we do."

"Then we'll just have to agree to disagree," replied the German. "But get used to being hungry. With our U-boats, we'll cut off your supplies." He then proceeded with a detailed and surrealistic tale of what the Germans were about to do to British shipping.

"If you do win, what sort of a Europe will you have, with Hitler in control?"

"A disciplined, civilized Europe. Our historic mission is to save Western Civilization from the Bolsheviks."

Price had been periodically glancing at his watch. The German had not. If he was nervously expecting a series of explosions, he was keeping his concern well hidden. They had now been talking almost 20 minutes.

"As you said, we'll just have to disagree," replied Price, signaling for the guard to come and take the captain back down below. The cocktail hour was over.

Price turned to Hempsted. "The twenty minutes are up. The time has come for a boarding party."

"Who is to lead it, sir?"

"I was rather thinking of you, Hempsted. The boarding party will have two objectives—to get any codebooks and other communications equipment we can salvage. We need an officer who has a good idea of what to look for. That's you.

"The second objective, once all the intelligence has been collected, will be to open two sea cocks—one toward the bow and one near the stern, so that the sub will settle evenly. Don't look so worried, Hempsted. It will take you 10 minutes to get the boarding party together; there isn't much chance of a boom after that. In the unlikely event that charges do go off, we'll all be dead anyhow, so you don't really have much to worry about."

Price was exaggerating. Even if the U-boat's charges were powerful enough to sink the minesweeper — which was by no means clear — the crew would be able to take to lifeboats. Even then, however, their chances of survival would be uncertain, and the little exaggeration was a way to spur Hempsted to action.

"Four men should be enough for the boarding party," Price continued. "They should be able to find the radio room quickly. Bring anything that looks the least bit interesting. Oh, by the way, you might like to know. We don't have much choice. I've received a damage report. The engineer thinks our ship is still seaworthy. However, he's doubtful that it will be if we back off, inflicting more damage."

The boarding party must have set a record. They completed their job in 15 minutes, bringing back what was apparently some sort of coding machine, with a keyboard and miscellaneous wiring, together with several codebooks and arms full of papers.

The U-33 settled slowly and evenly below the waves, and *HMS Gleaner* headed back to port. Shortly after it arrived, Lt.-Cmdr. Price was awarded the Distinguished Service Order for sinking the U-boat. In private, he was warmly congratulated, not only for getting German code materials, but for doing so without the prisoners knowing. They were all locked in the mess.

Within a few months, Turing's new bombe, "Victory," came on line. With it, and with the wheels and other materials recovered from U-33, Turing and his associates were able to break Dolphin — the Enigma key used by U-boats — for several days in April, although there was a delay of several weeks in doing so. They were also able to break other German messages, including some German diplomatic traffic.

They were beginning to succeed, and their triumphs continued even after the German Navy introduced three more wheels. With the new ones — numbers 6, 7, and 8 — they added a nasty twist. These three wheels moved the next wheel two notches after each revolution, not just one.

For the wizards of Bletchley Park, a nagging worry accompanied their successes. The Germans could be counted on to complicate Enigma even more.

They had an even more immediate concern. A decrypted diplomatic message, from Germany's ambassador in Rome back to Berlin, contained a shock—verbatim quotations from Churchill's communications with Roosevelt. How could transatlantic traffic be so vulnerable? The hunt for the leak was on. The German message itself contained a clue. Since it originated in Rome, an Italian was somehow privy to the most secret of communications.

The culprit, it turned out, was a cipher clerk in the U.S. Embassy in London. Concerned that Roosevelt was eagerly and treacherously drawing the United States into war, he was collecting messages between the two leaders; he intended to expose FDR's duplicity by leaking them to Congress. But he made the mistake of showing them to sympathetic friends in Britain. One gave them to an official in the Italian embassy in London; they were transmitted to Rome.

In tracking down the clerk, the British searched his apartment—a violation of diplomatic norms. But the evidence they discovered was damning: not only stolen documents, but a duplicate key to the embassy's code room. The British police thereupon escorted him to Ambassador Joe Kennedy's residence. Kennedy had some sympathy with the clerk's views; he, too, resented the way Roosevelt was conniving to draw America into the war. But he could not abide the clerk's treacherous act. He waived diplomatic immunity and the clerk was on his way to Brixton Prison.

Hitler's invasion of Denmark and Norway, in April 1940, marked the end of the *Sitzkrieg*—the Phony War. Although the Germans quickly occupied those two countries, the mood at BP reflected a degree of grim satisfaction. As the enemy moved north, they introduced a new Enigma key. Within five days, the gnomes of BP had broken it. Winston Churchill, First Lord of the Admiralty, eagerly devoured the intercepts. He had already made one intelligence blunder, disregarding the warning of his naval attaché in Copenhagen that German warships were headed for Norway. As a result, he had been taken by surprise when the Germans struck. He had no intention of repeating his mistake.

He used the flood of information to raise the price paid by Hitler for his northern victory. British warships intercepted a German landing force near Narvik. Ten German destroyers, carrying a large fraction of the landing troops, were trapped and sunk in the Narvik fjords. In other actions near Norway, Hitler lost three cruisers, and the battleships Scharnhorst and Gneisenau were put out of action, at least temporarily, by British torpedoes.

What BP did not know was that the German intelligence service — the *Beobachtungs Dienst* or *B-Dienst* — had even more reason for satisfaction. They had broken British naval codes. Their intercepts had eased Hitler's concerns over the risky thrust across the North Sea, and had thus opened the door for the successful invasion of Norway.

With the end of the Norwegian campaign, Alastair, Anna, and others at BP had been half expecting the German radio traffic to ease off. But nothing of the sort happened. On the contrary, it intensified rapidly.

With the heavy new traffic came a shock. In most traffic, the inscrutable six were cut down to three letters. German operators were no longer repeating the wheel settings; BP had lost the cornerstone of its operations. From now on, codebreakers would be dependent on the incompetence of the German operators — on the sillies and other cribs — and on powerful new machines.

The following days were packed with history, particularly May 10, 1940. At dawn, German armor thrust westward through Belgium toward France. That evening, a troubled House of Commons replaced the ineffectual Prime Minister Neville Chamberlain with Winston Churchill. Although Churchill gave up his position as First Lord of the Admiralty, he signaled his intention to remain deeply involved in the daily details of the war. He retained the position of Defence Minister for himself.

Alastair decided that the time had come for Anna to move; he wanted a British national in the office next to him. Yvonne Snow, an equally youthful math graduate of Cambridge, was his choice; she had been working with Welchman and others in Hut 6, poring over sillies and other cribs. The two young women switched jobs; Anna would now be in Hut 6.

Although there was some gossip that this was a demotion for Anna, she took it in good grace, particularly as Alastair had warned her ahead of time that her position was temporary. She had no reason to be jealous of Yvonne; in fact the two became close friends, and had lunch together at least once a week.

At their first lunch, just three days after the job switch, Yvonne seemed insecure; the flood of information was overwhelming. "How in the world were you able to keep your head above water?"

Anna was reassuring. "The first week's always the worst; hang in there. Two main things. Try at least to glance at every paper that comes your way; don't let anything critical slip through your fingers. But then focus on the few issues that seem most important. Don't spread yourself too thin. Selectivity, selectivity. That will come with time; don't worry about it for the first few weeks. For the immediate future: try not to appear flustered, regardless of how you feel."

A few days later, Yvonne was already feeling more confident. "Great advice. Alastair has already referred to 'the cool Miss Snow.' Gave me something of a thrill, although I do hope he won't beat that phrase into the ground.... He seems like a great person to work for. Generous—willing to give others credit."

"An uncommon virtue, but the golden rule for any administrator. In return, people give their best."

Yvonne seemed eager for more information about her new boss; Anna obliged. "He's more than a bit absent-minded, but that's true of almost everyone here.... It's a natural result, thinking hard on a difficult, engrossing problem. You block out everything else."

"So I have to be careful. I can't assume he's heard, just because I've told him something?"

"Exactly. It helps to make eye contact, to see if he's actually receiving. Really important things should be mentioned again, several hours later, to make sure he heard. He doesn't mind, even if he did hear the first time, but it does take a bit of tact."

"He has a lot of experience in codebreaking?"

"Right back to the First World War. He worked with 'Blinker' Hall at the Admiralty's cryptography office. Alastair could see how important the work was, and kept the codebreaking operation alive during the lean years between the wars."

"*Blinker* Hall?"

"Admiral Sir Reginald Hall, for the likes of us. 'Blinker' because he had a twitch that made one eye blink like a ship's signal lamp. His huge contributions in the First War are not well recognized. I only hope we can do as much this time."

"I'm embarrassed. I don't know hardly anything about codebreaking during the First War."

"It just got the Yanks in on our side, that's all."

Yvonne wanted details.

"The Zimmerman telegram. In early 1917, Zimmerman—the German foreign minister—sent a telegram to his ambassador in Washington, Count von Bernstorff, asking that it be forwarded to the German ambassador in Mexico. Hall's group decoded it. It urged Mexico to enter the war on Germany's side. Mexico was offered a huge reward. They would get back their lost territories of Texas, Arizona, and New Mexico."

"Really?"

"Yes, really. Hall immediately recognized that he had a marvelous windfall—but one that would have to be handled with utmost care. The British couldn't let the secret out, that they had broken the German code. Also, they might have trouble convincing President Wilson it was genuine."

"Of course." Yvonne was encouraging Anna to continue.

"As luck would have it, Britain had an agent in the telegraph office in Mexico. He was able to get a copy of the incoming message from Bernstorff. Hall decided to use this one; it would look as if the message had fallen into American hands either in Washington or Mexico City.

"He thereupon sent one of his agents over to the American embassy with a copy of the telegram and a codebook, and decoded the message in front of the American Ambassador. Incidentally, that allowed Wilson to assure Congress that the message had been decoded on

American soil — a more-or-less true statement, at least by wartime standards. Anyhow, Wilson was cautious at first, not wanting to be suckered by a fake. His administration leaked the telegram to the *New York Times*.

"But that, of course, was not the end of it. The German ambassador to Mexico flatly denied that he had received the message; so did the Mexican Government. Then came another enormous break. For reasons nobody will ever understand, Zimmerman admitted he had sent the telegram.

"The Americans, of course, were enraged. Together with unrestricted submarine warfare, that brought them into the war."

"You're not making this up, are you?

"Oh, no. Never," replied Anna. "On my honor."

Several weeks later, Yvonne's face was ashen white when they met for lunch. Her hand shook; she dropped her fork. "Not quite the cool Miss Snow," thought Anna. Some minutes passed before Yvonne regained her composure enough to speak.

"Sorry. But I just got a ride back to BP with Dilly Knox."

"And?"

"You haven't driven with him?... All I can say is, *don't*. When he gets to an intersection, he speeds up."

"*What?*"

"He has this crazy idea, the faster he goes, the less chance someone will hit him from the side."

"Sounds logical to me," said Anna with a smirk.... "Provided he's more interested in his car than his life."

"*My* life, you mean."

Anna took the opening to mention something that had been bothering her.

"Talking of strange behavior, I didn't meet Alan Turing 'til last week. *Weird.* I spoke, but he wouldn't even look at me; he stared away and edged his way sideways down the hall. When I saw him on the lawn a few days later, he looked away toward the duck pond. Yesterday, I was going down the hall. He came around a corner. The moment he saw me, he abruptly turned and disappeared around the corner again. Guess I'm losing my touch with men."

"No need to be concerned." Yvonne laughed. "They're looking for brilliant people around here, regardless of how odd."

The two young women thereupon exchanged stories of the bizarre goings-on at Bletchley Park.

Somebody got the bright idea to set up a local unit of the Home Guard. The so-called parades were a joke—people shuffling around, not even walking in a straight line, much less keeping in step. They didn't understand the first rule of the military: always march smartly, acting as if you know exactly where you're going, even when you don't—*particularly* when you don't. Turing almost brought the farce to an abrupt end when he told the officer that, now he'd learned how to fire a rifle, he was quitting. Learning to shoot was the only reason he joined in the first place.

The officer naturally objected. Turing had signed up and was committed. "Oh, no I'm not," replied Alan. "I made out the form, but if you check, you'll find I didn't sign it." Thereupon, the officer put in for a transfer.

Turing also had bizarre, and famous, eccentricities. He kept his coffee mug chained to his radiator. He wore a gas mask when he bicycled to work. He wasn't afraid the Germans would use gas; he did it to filter out the pollen and prevent hay fever.

He also had the idea—perhaps not so strange—that the war would destroy the value of the pound. To protect himself, he buried bars of silver. He had elaborate, encoded instructions, how to find them after the war.

He had briefly been engaged. Then he had a dream. In it, he introduced his fiancée, Joan, to his mother. She didn't like Joan. End of engagement.

And Dilly Knox—reckless driving was not his only oddity. He was notoriously absent-minded; couldn't tell the two doors in his office apart. He often walked into the closet when he meant to enter the hall. Occasionally, he would become so preoccupied during lunch that he would tamp pieces of bread into his pipe.

Then there was the strange case of Alan Ross, taking his young son on the train. He was worried that the boy would cause trouble, so he gave him laudanum—a derivative of opium. When his son passed out, Ross casually stretched him out on the luggage rack.

But, in spite of the stiff competition, Anna and Yvonne agreed: the odd bawd prize went to Josh Cooper.

Cooper's most famous faux pas came when he participated in the interrogation of a captured German pilot. The pilot marched in smartly, clicked his heels, and snapped a sharp Nazi salute, shouting "Heil Hitler." Apparently Josh had picked up the idea that when someone salutes you, you *must* return the salute. He jumped up as smartly as he could—which wasn't very smartly under the circumstances, as he kicked over his chair. He stuck out his hand in a Nazi salute, and loudly repeated "Heil Hitler." Of course, he was immediately overcome with embarrassment and abruptly tried to sit down. But his chair wasn't there any more. He fell to the floor and disappeared under the table. The German looked down disdainfully, not even cracking a smile. Maybe he thought this was a normal event—what could be expected from the decadent Western democracies.

Turing's new machine was a marvel. It not only led to the sporadic breaking of Dolphin, but also to continuous success in reading Luftwaffe traffic. In this, the codebreakers were much assisted by the sloppiness of Luftwaffe operators. Perhaps they were less well trained than their Army and Navy counterparts. Perhaps their minds were less focused. Their lives were not on the line; they were unlikely to find themselves in combat.

The Enigma decryptions were useful in the Battle of Britain, but perhaps less than expected. True, the Enigma did provide some hints regarding targets. But usually the targets were simply numbered, or referred to by code names. Korn, for example, stood for Coventry. But BP didn't figure that out until after that city suffered a devastating bombing.

Rather, it was in the naval war that Enigma decrypts made their most important early contributions.

Anna felt as though she had a ringside seat on the struggle. As a worker in Hut 6, she had practically unlimited access to decryptions. Security had been persuaded to acquiesce. It was good for morale for people to be able to read the decoded messages, and, if any of the senior people at Bletchley Park decided to tip the Germans off, the game was over, anyhow.

Anna had made a standing request for decrypts regarding Poland, but she could scarcely resist the deadly drama unfolding on the high seas.

The opening act came when the new German battleship *Bismarck,* accompanied by the heavy cruiser *Prinz Eugen,* broke through the Iceland Strait into the Atlantic, sinking the showpiece and pride of the British navy, *HMS Hood.* The thought of the two formidable German warships in the midst of a convoy was too terrible to contemplate. The order came directly from the Prime Minister: *Sink the Bismarck!*

The trouble was, just where was *Bismarck?* Harry Hinsley was monitoring German Naval traffic at Bletchley Park. He became convinced that the battleship was heading for the safety of a French port, even though there were no naval decryptions to back him up. His reasoning was straightforward: radio control of the *Bismarck* had been switched from Germany to Paris. He telephoned the Admiralty's Operational Intelligence Centre. OIC was skeptical; they hadn't figured this out on their own and therefore dismissed it—the "not invented here" syndrome.

Hinsley was furious. It was not the first time that OIC had spurned his ideas, including his conclusion, prior to the attack on Norway, that the unusual buildup of undeciphered naval messages foreshadowed German action. His advice ignored, Hinsley visited the Admiralty and the Home Fleet at Scapa Flow—in the Orkney Islands, all the way up at the Northern tip of Scotland—in an effort to mend fences, even acquiring something more presentable than his worn corduroys for the occasion. But his efforts apparently had gone for naught.

"The pigheadedness of OIC," he fumed. Anna wasn't so sure. The transfer of radio control to Paris didn't necessarily mean the *Bismarck* was headed for France; it might simply be a way of moving communications closer to the ship. And OIC had a great big ocean to worry about. *Bismarck* might materialize out of any fog bank to wreak havoc in shipping channels. But Anna kept her mouth shut. It really was none of her business, and Hinsley was in such a foul mood that she didn't want to raise any questions.

Then, the vulnerability of the Luftwaffe's Enigma saved the day. Two decoded messages came into Hut 6, and Anna huddled around a table with the others to read them. The first was from Luftwaffe Chief of Staff, Jeschonnek, who was worried about a relative serving on the *Bismarck*. The response was reassuring: the battleship was steaming toward the safety of the French port, Brest. It needed refueling. In the rush to leave its Norwegian fjord, it had not taken time to top off its tanks. And, since the encounter with the *Hood* and *Prince of Wales*, it was trailing oil; one of its tanks had been ruptured by an incoming shell.

The word "Brest" was all the Royal Navy needed. A Coastal Command Catalina flying boat—provided by the United States and piloted by an American officer "on loan" to the British—soon located the German battleship. Ancient Swordfish biplanes took off from the *Ark Royal*, their fabric wings fluttering in the breeze and their baling-wire struts straining under the load of single torpedoes. Although obsolete, they had an unforeseen advantage: they flew too slowly for the *Bismarck's* modern, automated fire control system to lock on. One scored a lucky hit, clipping the very end of *Bismarck*, jamming its rudder and sending it in circles. The crew struggled to control the ship, using only one propeller in an attempt to straighten its path. But to no avail. Then night fell—sleepless hours of hopeless terror. Quietly, in small groups, men talked, passing pictures of their families and reminiscing of their time as school boys, then lapsing into pensive silence. Too soon the dawn, and the nervous scanning of the horizon for British battleships.

Anna and Yvonne were off in a corner of the dining room having lunch when a Navy Commander clinked his glass and called for quiet: "Ladies and Gentlemen, I have an announcement. Shortly after daybreak this morning, the Royal Navy engaged the *Bismarck*. As a result of heavy fire from *HMS Rodney* and *King George V*, plus torpedoes from the *Dorsetshire"*... he paused for effect... *"the Bismarck has been SUNK!"* A cheer went up.

"I only hope," murmured Anna, "that Jeschonnek never finds out."

14
Fire in the Sky

You might think that it would take a lot of courage to jump out of an airplane with only a parachute. Actually, if the plane is on fire, it doesn't take any guts at all.

A veteran of the Battle of Britain

For Ryk, it was no easy matter to get out of Sweden. Unlike Anna, he didn't have the remotest claim to British citizenship. The Swedish authorities met his story—that he was a simple Polish businessman—with amused and well-justified skepticism, particularly when he was unable to provide the name of even one of his Swedish clients. Somehow, they suspected that he might be a member of the Polish armed forces! As neutrals, they would have an obligation to prevent him from passing through Sweden to a belligerent country. He finally solved the impasse by making the rounds of the waterfront bars in Stockholm, where he arranged passage on a tramp steamer to Ireland. Thence, it was on to England.

As a result of the delays, he didn't arrive in England until June of 1940. But, all in all, his timing could have been worse. France had just fallen, and the British in their lonely solitude now faced the full force of the Nazi war machine. Ryk was accepted with enthusiasm into the Royal Air Force—with qualified enthusiasm, to be sure. He was assigned the rank of sergeant. Naturally, he was disappointed. In the Polish Air Force, he had been the equivalent of a Flying Officer.

Perhaps his low rank was understandable. There were British pilots with months of combat experience who were still sergeants, and many of the refugee pilots from other countries—not only Poles, but also Czechs and Frenchmen—were made sergeants in the RAF, regardless of their earlier ranks. Maybe this was a hangover from the First World

War, when many British pilots had been sergeants. Especially in the early days of 1914 and 1915, pilots were not like captains of ships, but rather chauffeurs to the gentlemen officers in the rear seats, who were doing the "important" task of observing German troop movements.

Furthermore, there was a huge hole in Ryk's training: he had never flown one of the fast, new, single-wing fighters. He was immediately assigned to the Polish 303 squadron, where he spent two weeks in intensive training. Only one day was devoted to flying in close formation—the sort of flying he had done in Poland, which looked so impressive in air shows. But the fighting in France had quickly taught the British that this was no way to fly in combat. It was too easy for German fighters to pick off one wingman, then the other, and then attack the leader in quick succession.

Perhaps because of their experience in the Spanish Civil War, the Germans had developed a much looser formation, with the wingman several hundred yards off to the side, usually the sunny side, a thousand feet higher, and somewhat to the rear. There, he would be visible to his comrades, providing reassurance. He would be in an excellent position to protect them from any attack out of the sun, and any attack on the wingman would provide timely warning to the others. As the wingman's job was to provide protection, not initiate an attack on the British, his first responsibility would be to continuously scan the sky; he would be hard to surprise in the first place.

For Ryk, his Hurricane was pure joy. Its ability to accelerate while climbing was a new and exhilarating experience. But he was warned: although the Hurricane could exceed 300 miles per hour in level flight, the Messerschmitt 109 was even faster. Furthermore, its advantage increased in a dive. There was one compensation, however: the Hurricane could dive more steeply and to a lower level than the Me 109, whose wings were weak; a sudden pullout from a steep dive could rip its wings off.

Because of the Hurricanes' slow speed, their primary task would be to attack bombers. Faster, more maneuverable Spitfires would take on the Me 109's. But of course, Hurricane pilots would have to be prepared to fight Messerschmitts when necessary. Most of all, a simple message was drilled into the pilots: watch out for German fighters attacking out of the sun. A bold warning, "BEWARE THE HUN IN THE SUN," was stenciled above Ryk's instrument panel, in both English and Polish.

The third day, he was called in to see Squadron Leader Rozek, commanding officer of the 303. They would soon enter combat. The time had come for them to form pairs—leader and wingman. Was there anyone with whom Ryk would particularly like to fly? No; he really didn't know the other pilots very well.

"Then let me suggest a wingman for you." Ryk was pleased that he would be the leader; he wouldn't be the lowest man on the totem pole. "Sergeant Josef Frantisek. He will be arriving tomorrow morning."

"Frantisek? Doesn't sound Polish."

"He's not. He's Czech. When the Germans marched into his country, he jumped in his fighter and flew to Poland. Joined our air force and fought bravely. Survived three weeks of combat—quite an accomplishment. Fled again, to Romania, when our war effort collapsed. Then escaped from a Romanian internment camp."

"Sounds like a enterprising chap."

"Superb pilot. He shot down a Jerry last week." Ryk wondered why Joe would be under his command; Ryk hadn't even had combat experience in Poland. Rozek shifted uncomfortably in his seat, apparently searching for the right word. "Just one... ah, problem. The Brits won't have him in their squadrons—say he's completely undisciplined. He doesn't want to join the Czech squadron—reasons unclear."

Ryk didn't know how to respond. Flying in combat would be dangerous enough with a disciplined wingman. Rozek could see his hesitation.

"I don't need an answer right away. Why don't you see how the two of you hit it off?"

They hit if off just fine. Instead of practicing loose formation flying, Ryk thought that the best way to spend the first few days was to take turns chasing one another around the sky. He could probably learn a thing or two from someone who had survived combat.

He did. They started by choosing a place to meet—12,000 feet over a small town about 20 miles west of the airfield. They would play a game—see who could get on the other's tail, and how long he could stay there.

Of the first five tries, Ryk managed to get on Joe's tail only once, and managed to stay there less then ten seconds—until Joe began a tighter and tighter turn. If he had been an enemy, Ryk wouldn't have been able to get a clean shot, once the circling began. In contrast, when Joe got on his tail, Ryk found it was almost impossible to shake him, no matter how sharply and erratically he turned.

That evening, over beers, he quizzed Joe, looking for tips.

"I cheat," replied Joe. "I knew where you were going to be, because we'd already agreed to that. I came late to the rendezvous, and the first three times I came out of the sun. Then, when I thought you would be looking toward the sun, I snuck up through a cloud and was able to get into your blind spot, just below your tail. That time, it was luck. Well, mostly luck. You flew straight and level for almost half a minute—not a good way to survive."

"And the turns. How did you stick with me?"

"You're right handed?"

"Of course. But so what?"

"When you're trying to get away, you always turn left; I guessed which way you were going to turn. I noticed the tendency for right-handers to turn left back in Czechoslovakia, when I was in training. I'm left handed. In some ways, that's a problem. Whenever I need to keep my left hand on the throttle—particularly in takeoffs and landings—I use my right hand on the stick. But in combat, I'm more comfortable with my left hand on the stick. It's awkward to switch back and forth, but I rarely have to. In combat, I'm going full bore. I just leave the throttle alone—all the way open.

"Being left handed has an unexpected plus. In combat, it's natural for me to turn to the right, which generally throws off the right-handers. If Jerry's on your tail, try turning sharply to the right instead."

"The circling.... How do you make it so tight?"

"Start the turn sharply. Then, as you get into the turn, pull the stick back hard, until you gray out—until you can't see anything in color. Hold it there, in the gray twilight. The guy on your tail won't be able to turn any tighter, inside you. If he does, he'll black out completely. Use your rudder and power to maintain height. You've got to be careful, especially if you're not very high to begin with. In a tight turn, you can lose altitude very quickly. Fortunately, this is one place where you have an advantage over the Messerschmitt. He's more likely to lose altitude fast and hit the ground. In fact, once you get the hang of it, tight turns close to the ground are a good way to get rid of the Jerry; he may focus so much on you that he packs it in. But this ain't exactly a stunt for beginners.

"There's one big danger. If you start your turn too abruptly, you can do a high-speed stall. Perhaps tomorrow we can go up to 15,000 feet — where there's plenty of time to recover — and see what a high-speed stall feels like. That's also a pretty safe altitude to practice tight turns."

The next morning — before experimenting with high-speed stalls and tight turns — Ryk went to see Sq. Ldr. Rozek. He'd be delighted to have Joe as his wingman. He'd never met such a skilled pilot.

"Good luck," was Rozek's only response — somewhat disconcerting, the way he said it.

Ryk had his first encounter with the Germans ten days later, when Stukas were dive-bombing a convoy in the English Channel. Above, at 15 thousand feet, the contrails showed Spitfires and Messerschmitts engaged in a deadly dance.

Ryk and Joe came in low; there was scattered cloud cover, and they darted from one cloud to another to hide from the German fighters above. Stukas would be most vulnerable just as they were pulling out of their bombing dive; they had automatic controls to pull out several hundred feet above the ground. They leveled out so sharply that the pilots blacked out.

The game would be to catch the Stukas at this vulnerable moment. As the two Hurricanes broke from their cloud cover, Ryk could see several Stukas beginning their dive. He picked one, and calculated how wide his sweeping turn should be. He cut back on the throttle, so that he would not simply whiz past the slow German plane. Beginner's luck. He caught the Stuka just as it leveled out. Two bursts from his eight machine guns, and the Stuka began to trail smoke; it fell off toward the sea.

Automatically, he glanced up toward the sun and was in for a shock. Two Messerschmitts were diving towards him, closing fast. He pushed the throttle to full power and headed for the nearest cloud. It was his lucky day; he made it.

Flying through the clouds, he seemed to have lost Joe. He decided that, with his ammunition partly gone, it was best to return to base. He radioed to Joe: he was going home. No reply. Strange.

Joe didn't turn up until 20 minutes after Ryk landed. As his plane taxied up, Ryk could see bullet holes in Joe's wing.

"A spot of trouble," was all that Joe would offer.

That wasn't good enough for Ryk. "Where the hell were you? You damn near got me killed."

"Target of opportunity. Didn't want to miss it."

"But that made me a target for the Jerries. I don't like the trade."

Joe looked embarrassed. But it was the only satisfaction Ryk would get.

Joe was more forthcoming with the operations officer. He had taken a wider circle than Ryk, allowing him to close on a second Stuka. He had time first to climb, then to make a diving attack on the Stuka just as it was about to drop its bomb. The results were spectacular—a huge explosion as both the plane and bomb blew up. But then he was jumped by a couple of Messerschmitts and just barely managed to escape into the cloud cover.

Wasn't he supposed to be covering Ryk, not flitting around the sky? A sheepish grin was the only response the operations officer got.

That evening, Rozek summoned Ryk; he wanted a full report. The commanding officer was annoyed that Joe had left Ryk unprotected. Ryk wasn't exactly happy. But he had had time to calm down; he was surprised to find himself defending Joe. After all, Joe got a Stuka too. Ryk repeated his earlier statement: Joe was the best damn pilot he had ever met.

Rozek was torn. The story was even more complicated than Joe had reported to the operations officer. From Joe's gun camera—which had been specially mounted on his plane so that the Squadron Leader could keep track of what he was doing—Rozek got a good view of the exploding Stuka; it really was spectacular. But Joe hadn't simply tried to escape from the Messerschmitts. He had taken the two of them on, damaging one before running out of ammunition. Ryk smiled; somehow, he wasn't surprised. Rozek summed up his problem. Good pilots were scarce. They couldn't be casually discarded. But they couldn't be permitted to do anything they wanted; it would needlessly imperil others.

"I'm not so sure," was Ryk's reply. He'd spent the last two hours thinking: What should be done about Joe? The problem on which the British had given up.

"Not sure? Really? You were lucky to get out alive."

"Anytime he sees a German plane, he has only one thought. Attack. He's absolutely fearless. No wingman will be able to keep up. Or have the nerve to try. Joe wants his private war with the Germans. Let him have it."

And so it was. Joe ceased to be part of the squadron and simply became a "guest." The squadron would service his plane. But he would fight alone, when he wanted and where he wanted. He would come and go as he pleased; he would at last have his very own private war.

A very successful little war it turned out to be.

Ryk now became the wingman for Pilot Officer Gabriel (Gabe) Polonsky. His new job would provide more than enough excitement.

Strangely, they didn't see action for more than a week. After the British stopped using perilous coastwise convoys to transport coal—which was now sent by rail—there was a brief respite. During the lull, the 303 Squadron had a pleasant surprise: Spitfires began to arrive to replace the Hurricanes. The 303 would be shifted to a more demanding task, taking on German fighters. Their heroism and skill were being rewarded. They were shooting down twice as many enemy planes as the average British fighter squadron.

The Czech "guest" managed to get the first Spit. Somehow, Ryk wasn't surprised. But he was surprised—and pleased—when he and Gabe got the next two.

The timing could not have been better. The next phase of the Battle of Britain was about to begin, moving from the Channel to England itself. Göring assured Hitler that he could sweep the RAF from the skies within a few weeks, setting the stage for *Operation Sea Lion* — the amphibious assault on England.

His strategy was the one used so successfully on the continent: attack the airfields, and destroy planes either on the ground or in combat. One of the first assaults was on the fields southeast of London, including the home base of the Polish 303. Fortunately, Ryk, Gabe, and most of the others were already in the air.

In attacking the airfields, the Germans relied on the twin-engine Junkers 88 dive bomber, which, unlike the abysmally slow Stuka, came in very, very rapidly, gaining speed in its shallow dive. Luckily, Gabe, Ryk and half a dozen other Polish pilots were almost directly overhead when four of the Nazi bombers approached their field. The Poles dove quickly at the attackers, but had seen the bombers too late; even the Spitfires were not fast enough to catch the Germans until they had dropped their bombs.

If they could not prevent the attack, they could at least exact retribution. Just as the bombers cleared the trees at the far end of the field, Gabe closed on one of them. He fired two bursts from his machine guns. The German kept climbing. A third burst, and smoke began to trail from one engine. The plane slowly lost altitude and crashed. There were no parachutes; the plane had been too low.

Ryk had been covering the action from above, on the sunny side. Seeing no German fighters, he directed Gabe toward a second Junkers, which was now fleeing at low level toward the southern coast. Gabe was soon on its tail, closing rapidly and firing several short bursts before the telltale spew of tracers warned that he was running out of ammunition.

There was no apparent effect on the German. Gabe shouted to Ryk, who assured him there were no German fighters to be seen. Gabe suggested that Ryk have a go at the fleeing German; Gabe would move to the wingman position and keep a lookout.

Ryk dove toward the German. Gabe's bullets had been ineffective; Ryk would get closer. Two bursts, and still the German refused to go

down. Ryk closed up further. 200 yards. 150. He fired a long burst—
too long; two of his guns jammed. Still the German flew on; Ryk's fire
had been too widely scattered to bring the bomber down. He closed
up even more, and fired another burst. Again, he seemed to be
spraying bullets all over the sky. Then he, too, came to the tracers that
signaled the end of his ammunition. He shouted in frustration to Gabe,
and the two returned to base.

In their debriefing, they complained bitterly to Rozek; the fire of the
eight machine guns was too dispersed to be effective. Rozek was
aware of the problem, but had had the armorers check. The guns were
set according to specification. They converged 650 yards in front of the
fighter.

"*Six hundred and fifty yards*. That's damn near half a mile." Gabe was
incredulous. And furious.

"I know. But those are the specs."

"What jackass set the specs?" Gabe wanted to know. Well, actually,
he didn't want to know. But, in his anger, he was ready to settle the
issue, one on one. The damn fool could have his guns set for 650 yards,
and Gabe would set his much shorter. Then they would see who
survived. Perhaps that was unfair; the fool had probably never seen
the inside of a cockpit. "You've got to have the bullets converge to rip
a plane apart. You can't shoot at a target half a mile away. It wasn't so
bad with the Hurricanes; their guns are clustered close together just
outside the prop. But for a Spit, it's critical: the guns are spread along
the leading edge of the wing. Stupid specs are ruining a great plane."

"I wonder," said Ryk, trying to smooth over Gabe's fury. "We don't
have much leverage with the RAF. But the Brits need us. I bet if you
told the Armaments Officer to set the guns for a shorter convergence,
he'd do what you want, no questions asked."

"What do you suggest?" Rozek wondered. "Say, 500 yards?"

"Closer, closer," replied Ryk. "That's still a third of a mile. I'd say
350 yards."

"Still not close enough. 250 yards, and not an inch more," insisted
Gabe. "At least, not if you want me up in the air again."

The hint of mutiny surprised Ryk; he suddenly realized how tired
Gabe must be. How exhausted they all were getting!

Rozek ignored the threat. He would talk to the Armaments Officer, and get him to have the machine guns reset for a 250 yard convergence for any pilot who asked.

They all did.

There was more good news. They would be getting new, more effective ammunition. Of the four guns on each Spitfire wing, one would be loaded with armor-piercing bullets, and one with incendiaries.

The Spits, the new ammunition, and the decision to reset the guns paid off. During the next two weeks, the 303's toll of German aircraft doubled. Gabe alone had three kills—two Messerschmitts and a straggling bomber that he picked off on his way back to base.

One Saturday morning, when heavy clouds and an intermittent drizzle were conspiring to keep the Luftwaffe at their home bases, Ryk took the opportunity to sleep in; he was exhausted. As he lay half asleep, he heard machine-gun fire in the distance. *Not so distant. It was very close.* He pulled on his clothes and jacket and stumbled, half awake, out toward the hangers.

He saw the source of the commotion. Joe had persuaded his ground crew to hoist the tail of his Spitfire up onto the bed of a truck, and two of them were holding the tailplane in an effort to steady it. Joe was shouting encouragement—in a mixture of Polish, Czech, and English—to his armorers, who were adjusting his guns toward a makeshift target. They signaled that they were ready for another test, and Joe squeezed the fire button. The guns erupted. Spent shell casings danced and bounced off the tarmac like heavy hail. The bullets converged perfectly on the target.

Its distance: 100 yards.

Joe noticed Ryk, waved, and jumped down out of the cockpit. As he approached Ryk, he smiled broadly.

"Now," he said, "you can bring on the whole damn Richthofen squadron. I really am ready for that Hun in the sun."

15
Tomorrow May Never Come

*Life is a preparation for something
that probably will never happen.*
William Butler Yeats

Bomber Briefing. Fliegerkorps II. Amiens, France.
24 August, 1940. 14:00 hrs.

"Gentlemen, we are now about to enter a new stage in the campaign against the RAF. You've been wearing down Fighter Command. Now the time has come for the knockout blow."

Lt. Emil Niehoff listened impassively, hiding his doubts. True, the Luftwaffe must have been inflicting heavy damage on the RAF fighter squadrons, attacking their bases. But as for wearing the RAF down — in spite of repeated statements of senior officers, he hadn't seen any decrease in the number of enemy fighters. On his last mission, as fighters were circling for an attack, his dorsal gunner sarcastically shouted: "Hang on tight. Here they come. The last twenty Spitfires."

The briefing officer was aware that his upbeat statement might be met with a degree of, well, skepticism. "We recognize that the RAF is still a formidable force. Our job is to change that.

"The new campaign will have two new features.

"First, we recognize that our bomber losses have been greater than anticipated." The audience shuffled uncomfortably; they were well aware of the fact. Their friends were being killed. "Consequently, in this new phase, we will use larger, more concentrated bomber formations, so that attacking fighters will have to face the combined fire from many bombers. Even more important: we will provide additional, and tighter, fighter support. They will accompany the bombers more closely." Good news for the audience; there were scattered smiles. The briefing officer had even hoped for cheers, but the crews were too tired—and, not to put too fine a point on it, particularly tired of empty promises.

"Second, we will intensify our attacks on RAF airfields and supporting facilities. Bombing the fighter factories will be an even higher priority. Intelligence indicates that you have already inflicted heavy damage on the Spitfire plant in Birmingham. You will soon be receiving targeting information for this evening's raid on other factories.

"Finally, I repeat your standing orders. You are to attack only military targets. You are to avoid bombing within cities unless military targets have been identified. Most specifically, you are forbidden to bomb residential areas of London.

"You will pick up your fighter escorts over the Channel; their bases are now concentrated in the Pas de Calais, so that they will be able to stay with you more than 100 kilometers into Britain. Be in your bombers, beginning your preflight checks, by 15:00 hrs.

"And good luck."

After the briefing, the fliers clustered around in small groups, discussing the new plans. Niehoff sought out his closest surviving friend, Lt. Ernst Heitz, and they were joined by an older—and well-connected—pilot, Capt. Jurg Kalbfleisch.

"This is crazy," Heitz complained. "This emphasis on avoiding cities. When we're wandering around, above the clouds, how can be sure where we are?"

"We'd better take it seriously," responded Niehoff. "The orders are strict—and they come directly from the *'Heiliger Berg'* (Holy Mountain)." He was using the irreverent slang for the bunker of Feldmarschal Kesselring, commander of the Air Fleet.

"Higher than that, much higher," responded Kalbfleisch, glancing toward the ceiling. Then, to show he was one of the boys, he added, "from the little corporal himself." That reference to Hitler would cause trouble if it ever appeared in his security file. But there was no chance that it would.

"But why?" Heitz wondered. "After all, he threatened to bomb Prague. And we flattened Warsaw. We got orders to bomb Rotterdam. Massively. In all three cases, we got a quick surrender."

"Ah," replied Kalbfleisch, "but those were different."

"Different?"

"Very different, my dear Heitz. None of those three countries had bombers that could reach Berlin."

"Anyone who bombs London will be in deep trouble with Göring, too," added Niehoff. "He doesn't want to provoke the British. He's guaranteed that the RAF will never, ever bomb Berlin. If they do, people can call him 'Meyer.'"

Fighter squadrons throughout Southeast England got the word: scramble, and climb to 16,000 feet. A massive German air armada was forming up near Calais, headed for the Channel.

Ryk had come to hate high-level combat. Messerschmitts had a big advantage at high altitudes—fuel injection. If a Spitfire did manage to get on a Messerschmitt's tail, the German could escape by pushing his stick forward until he began to rise out of his seat. If the Spit tried to follow, its carbeurated engine would be starved of fuel.

As he approached 16,000 feet, he got a puzzling—and welcome—message: there were no German fighters to be found at that level, even by the few Spitfires that ventured out over the Channel. All the German fighters were far below, down with the bombers. Orders were changed. One British squadron was to stay on high-level patrol, to guard against attack. Everybody else: go after the Germans.

Ryk recognized the joyful whoop over the radio. Joe was on the loose.

The 303 Squadron got their orders: they were to take on the eastward section of German formation. The dirty job again. With the sun on their left, they would be in greatest peril from a enemy fighters.

As he accompanied Gabe in a steep dive toward the German formation, Ryk could scarcely believe their good luck. Not only were the Messerschmitts at a low level; they were also going slowly enough to keep in loose formation with the bombers.

Gabe leveled out just below and behind the most exposed Messerschmitt, guarding the corner of the formation, and came up in his blind spot. Gabe held his fire, closing quickly. 400 yards. 250 yards.

Two quick machine-gun bursts, and the German plane belched smoke. Three cheers for the reset guns!

Now came the exciting part. Aware of danger, the Messerschmitts accelerated rapidly, and began to bank sharply to turn on their attackers. Gabe picked the next most exposed enemy, and began his turn in pursuit. Ryk was having trouble following; he couldn't afford to turn so tightly he would gray out; he wouldn't be alert enough to protect Gabe from danger.

Gabe was now firing sporadic bursts every time he got the turning, twisting German in his sights. This one was tough. But finally the Messerschmitt began to trail smoke and slid off into a downward spiral.

Gabe was low on ammunition, and was heading home. Ryk could stay for the fun, if he wanted. Yes, he would.

By now, the sky was cluttered with circling planes, friend and foe— utter chaos. Ryk decided that the best attack was the most direct. He didn't want to stick around this tough neighborhood any longer than necessary. He took a deep breath and, with one eye on his rear view mirror, headed straight down the edge of the German formation at full throttle, firing a burst every time he could line up an enemy.

As he approached the front of the formation, he saw the telltale tracers; he was almost out of ammunition. He began a sharp turning climb—to the right! After climbing a thousand feet, he leveled off, to gain precious airspeed, and headed homeward, abruptly changing direction every few seconds and keeping his head on a swivel, looking for danger.

As he came in for a landing, he noticed that one of his wings had been neatly stitched by a line of machine-gun fire. He had no idea what damage—if any—he had inflicted on the enemy.

When he taxied up to the service bay, his adrenaline was flowing. He wasn't sure that his plane was still airworthy, and, at any rate, he didn't want to wait for it to be refueled and filled with ammunition. Was the extra Spitfire fueled and ready to go? It was. Had Gabe arrived? Did he want it? Yes, he had arrived, but no, he didn't want it. He wouldn't be needing an airplane. Today, or for some time. A machine-gun bullet had passed through his left calf and nicked his right leg; he was on his way to hospital.

Within ten minutes, Ryk was headed down the grass runway, taking off in his new Spitfire.

Somehow, thought Niehoff, things are not working out right. It was very reassuring and all, to have the fighter escorts clearly visible off their wing tips. But, when the RAF attacked, things became decidedly dicey. The Messerschmitts gulped fuel in their dogfights and some were heading home early, while the bombers still had to fly on more than half an hour in daylight. The bomber formation closed up even tighter, for additional protection.

Fortunately, the Spitfires and Hurricanes were disappearing, too; they also had been gulping fuel. The Messerschmitts that had stayed with the bombers still had enough fuel to engage the remaining enemy fighters.

Nevertheless, several Hurricanes were nipping at the edge of the flight. The bomber next to Niehoff began to trail smoke and sank out of the formation. Now Niehoff was on the exposed corner. *"Wunderbar,"* he thought.

Another Hurricane attacked, in a shallow dive. Niehoff's top gunner opened up, and other bombers were also returning fire. The canopy of the Hurricane shattered, and it sank into a slow, smooth decline.

Niehoff's plane had taken hits, too. It would simply not be possible to continue to the target area. But they were in luck; they were close to a cloud formation, and banked sharply right. They would be on their own.

The sun was sinking, and Ryk feared that he might be too late to reenter the fray. As he headed northward alone, he was very much aware of the danger. He constantly scanned the skies.

There, below and headed in the opposite direction, was a lone Heinkel. Ryk turned in an abrupt dive and was soon behind the German. No need to take unnecessary chances. He would approach directly behind the bomber, and slightly higher; he would be too high for the belly gunner, and too low for the top gunner to fire without blowing his own tail off. Ryk squeezed the button.

Damn. Just as he began to fire, the German turned into a cloud.

For the next fifteen minutes, Ryk replayed his escape from Poland, with the roles reversed. He kept above the clouds, weaving and waiting for the Heinkel to emerge. Each time it did, he dove to the attack. But the bomber always seemed to find another cloud. Ryk managed only one short burst before he lost his quarry. It was getting too dark to continue the hunt.

Up ahead, Niehoff now had no idea where he was, with all the twists and turns. He had suffered additional damage with the last machine-gun burst from the Spitfire. To have any chance of getting home, he needed to get rid of his bombs. Quickly. He ordered the bombardier to dump. As the bombs fell through the clouds, Niehoff gratefully felt his plane lighten. With luck, he would make it back to France.

Below the clouds, many Londoners had taken to the subways or basements as the air raid sirens wailed. But some were unperturbed, and were sitting down to dinner. A few would regret it. A string of bombs shattered windows and buildings along a residential street in East London.

Barbaric, said the British. In retaliation, Bomber Command was ordered to attack Berlin the next night. They had long since learned that it was suicide to fly over Germany during the day.

Göring—Meyer—was humiliated. The Führer was enraged. The Luftwaffe received new orders: prepare a full-scale assault on London. Two weeks later, the Blitz began.

For the people of London, the time of testing had come. For the RAF, there was a respite. London, not the airfields and aircraft plants, would now be the targets of Hitler's marauders.

One Saturday evening in the middle of the Blitz, Ryk and his fellow pilots received a welcome message: the weather would be cloudy and stormy for the next 36 hours, with heavy rain. The Luftwaffe would be unlikely to appear. They should take the opportunity to get a good rest.

Ryk—now Pilot Officer Ryk—flopped in his bunk. He was dozing off when a familiar figure loomed over him. Gabe was holding himself unsteadily erect with crutches.

"There's a party at the officer's club this evening, and I've been asked to bring you along."

Ryk didn't want to go; he wanted sleep. But the party was special; Gabe promised he wouldn't regret it. Ryk resisted; most of his friends were still sergeants, excluded from the commissioned officers club. He didn't feel comfortable or even very welcome. Gabe assured him he would feel more than welcome tonight. For a change, there would be women present, from neighboring air bases. Ryk grumbled, but pulled himself out of bed.

As they entered, Ryk was surprised to see that he was one of the guests of honor—those who had recently shot down their fifth German plane. There was a banner, with three English names and Ryk's. As he and Gabe came in the door, there was a cheer, and Group Captain Sutherland came over to congratulate him.

Ryk gravitated to a group of Polish officers who were engaged in an animated discussion of recent action. Ryk wasn't very interested. On the other side of the room, the Brits had a better idea; they were flirting with young women. Ryk detached himself from the Poles and casually made his way across the room. He hoped his English was good enough to hold up his end of a conversation.

As he passed a small group, Sutherland stepped back, inviting him to join.

"I believe you know Pilot Officer Lois Winslow," he said with an enigmatic smile.

Ryk was puzzled. He had met surprisingly few British women at all, and he certainly would have remembered her.

She could see his expression, and quickly solved the puzzle. "303. Climb to 12,000 on a heading of 85."

Hers was the familiar voice that had directed him into battle.

"Ah, my guardian angel," Ryk replied, kissing her on the cheek and hugging her.

She had been at the University of London, but had dropped out to work with the Air Force. Her parents lived in a village close by. They loved to see her wards—she said it with a smile. Ryk wasn't quite sure what the word meant; he would have to look it up. Perhaps Ryk would like to drop by some weekend, if and when things calmed down, and visit her family. They often had her Air Force officers in for parties on weekend afternoons, but only when the weather was bad enough to keep the Germans back where they belonged. He knew how to get in touch with her.

Sutherland scowled slightly; air control was not a dating agency.

"Only when the Boche have disappeared back over the Channel," she quickly added. "When I start giving you overly detailed instructions how to get back to base, you can take that as a special invitation. But you can come any weekend." She gave him, not her own address, but the address of her parents.

Ryk suddenly didn't feel quite so tired.

She wanted to know how he had gotten out of Poland. He provided a brief report of the flight of the Red Baron.

"There's someone I'd like you to meet," she said, taking his hand.

They headed toward a corner, toward a tightly packed group of pilots. They didn't seem to be acting precisely the way officers and gentlemen should. They were jockeying for position; occasionally, there was just a hint of an elbow.

"Ah," said Lois, with a touch of envy, "some girls just have it."

As they approached, Ryk caught the eye of one of the civilians just as she turned. She broke away from her admirers and rushed to Ryk, throwing her arms around his neck.

"Oh, Ryk, Ryk. I was afraid I might never see you again. I'm so glad you got out of Sweden."

"Anna. Anna." For a few moments, that was the only thing he managed to say.

They began an animated conversation in Polish.

At least the other officers were gentlemen enough to fade away and to leave the two alone. One by one, they turned their attention back to Yvonne and a number of other vivacious young ladies who worked for the government. Where was not exactly clear; the pilots were having the worst time trying to get telephone numbers.

Ryk and Anna talked of their adventures; they had so much to catch up on. Anna recounted her difficulties during her first morning in Britain, substituting the Air Force Meteorological Service for Naval Intelligence and not mentioning any names. Ryk was astonished that anyone could be so enthusiastic about weather forecasting, but he was grateful that someone was doing it.

Ryk tried to ignore the way she rubbed her cheek with her left hand, displaying her wedding ring. The message was unmistakable. Only too clearly, Anna was still deeply in love with Kaz. Or, thought Ryk, grasping at straws: she was still deeply in love with his misty, fantasy memory. Unlikely they'll ever see one another again.

Anna rubbed her cheek again. "Message received and understood," said Ryk lightly. Anna blushed, and, to make amends, leaned over and did up the top button of his tunic. As he felt her hand brush against his chest, he briefly grasped and squeezed it. She looked him softly in the eyes for a few seconds, then gently withdrew her hand.

Someone cranked up a gramophone and started to play Glen Miller records. Beer was flowing; the party was warming up.

Would she like to dance? The speaker was a boyish officer with pilot's wings. Anna wondered if he was shaving yet. Yes, she'd love to.

Anna hadn't danced to Glen Miller before. She swung from one pilot to another; she hadn't had so much fun since the war began. A dark thought intruded: what a horrid war. So little fun, so much danger for these marvelous young men. But she suppressed the thought as she went on to the next partner. Each seemed more lively than the last.

The music switched to Vera Lynn. "We'll hang out the washing on the Siegfried Line." Each time they came to that phrase, the dancers joined in the song. Then, "Bless 'em all, bless 'em all...." The dancers stopped, formed lines with arms around their partners' waists, and swayed as they sang along. "There'll be blue birds over, The White Cliffs of Dover...." Then, "Wish me luck as you wave me goodbye."

The music turned sentimental. "We'll meet again, don't know where, don't know when." Anna was in Ryk's arms; he had worked his way back to her side as the dancing resumed. How wonderful to meet again! They talked of their fun as teenagers. The time Ryk and his daredevil friend Radek scaled the church steeple to put a chamber pot on the peak. It could have been even better. They could have used a tin pot; that's what Ryk wanted. Because it was porcelain, the priest quickly solved his problem with a well-aimed rifle shot. Anna had a confession. Radek mentioned the plot ahead of time. She talked him into switching from tin to porcelain. The priest had been a mountain climber thirty years before, when he was a young man. She was afraid he might take a tin pot as a personal challenge; it could have ended badly.

"Oh, Anna, how could you betray me?" said Ryk in mock disappointment.

A Wing Commander tried to cut in, an officer from a neighboring base. Ryk pretended not to understand, responding in Polish: "Don't you realize what a royal hash you're making of the war, sir?" But he spoke with a smile. Anna put her hand to her mouth to hide a giggle. The Wing Commander graciously backed off; perhaps the young lady didn't speak English.

"I've been waiting to say that for months," Ryk whispered in Anna's ear. The Wing Commander—the RAF's answer to Col. Blimp—had dragged his feet on resetting his Spitfires' guns, and relented only when faced with a mutiny.

The music started again.

"Who's taking you home tonight?" Anna and Ryk were now dancing cheek to cheek. "Please let it be me," Ryk sang softly, accompanying Vera Lynn's words. Anna didn't respond, pretending that Ryk was simply continuing the sing-along.

The music stopped. Holding hands and looking into her eyes, Ryk repeated, "Please let it be me."

"Oh Ryk, Ryk, please don't ask," she said, kissing him softly on the cheek.

Music again drifted across the floor. FOR ALL WE KNOW, WE MAY NEVER MEET AGAIN.... TOMORROW WAS MADE FOR SOME. TOMORROW MAY NEVER COME. FOR ALL WE KNOW.

"Tomorrow may never come," Ryk choked as he spoke the words. "Life is so uncertain."

Uncertain.... The fleeting life span of pilots. Anna felt a sudden pang, a surge of soft emotion; she might never see him again.... It wouldn't be immoral. This was wartime.... Or maybe he was hinting that Kaz was gone; there was no point in waiting. Her tenderness toward Ryk was overwhelmed by her longing for Kaz. In the background, she could now hear the words of the Anniversary Waltz: COULD WE BUT RELIVE THAT SWEET MOMENT DIVINE. Oh, Kaz, Kaz. There were tears in her eyes.

They were close. Anna looked first into one of Ryk's eyes, then the other.

He asked: could he see her again?

She paused. Yes, she guessed so. Lois had offered an open invitation. Maybe she could meet him at the Winslow open house some Saturday or Sunday, when the weather was too bad for Germans to be flying.

Ryk sighed.

Nevertheless, he would eagerly take her up on the offer.

On the trip back, Anna couldn't help but notice that the bus was only a third full; it had been packed on the way to the party. Tears began to trickle down her cheeks. Would she ever see Kaz again? Or Ryk?

Perhaps she had been right to throw herself so completely into her work.

Anna was sitting beside Yvonne. As the antique bus bumped and creaked along the back roads, the two women said nothing. Anna didn't notice, but Yvonne, too, had tears in her eyes.

For Ryk, the evening could have turned out worse. Seeing Anna brought all those pleasant memories rushing back. And a week later, he received a very small package in the mail. A button from an RAF officer's uniform. It was Anna's way of saying sorry. Apparently someone had told her. Pilots who had fought through the Battle of Britain were entitled to leave the top button undone.

Ryk took the button as a small sign of encouragement and faithfully carried it into combat as a good luck charm.

A small flight, of only a dozen bombers, was approaching the coast. A British squadron would intercept them. The 303 could stand in readiness, in case additional Germans came.

A single Spitfire taxied out to the end of the grass runway and immediately began its takeoff run. It rapidly climbed away, toward 15,000 feet, in a curving turn to the right until, in the distance, it faded out of sight.

It was the last anyone would see of Joseph Frantisek.

At the beginning of the Luftwaffe's onslaught, a memorial service was scheduled each time a pilot was lost. As the casualties mounted and the pilots approached exhaustion, memorial services for all the losses of the preceding week were held immediately after the Sunday chapel service; or, if the weather was clear and the Germans threatened, it was postponed until the first rainy day.

At first, Ryk attended each of the services, even for the pilots he had not met. But the services became painful, and unnecessary, reminders of their mortality; he stopped going.

Joe's service would be different. As Ryk was the last one to fly with Joe, he was asked to say a few words.

"We are here to pay tribute to one of the best pilots in the Battle of Britain, one who shot down seventeen enemy planes, more than any other man.

"I had the privilege of flying with Joe. In a few short days, he taught me skills that have helped me survive. I owe him my life." Ryk wasn't telling the whole truth. *De mortis nihil nisi bonum:* Of the dead, nothing but good.

"Joe was a joyful and irrepressible individualist. He was happiest alone, chasing Germans out of his sky.

"An individualist. If he had been born at a different time, in a different place, we can only wonder what he might have done. In ancient Rome, he might have been one of Horatio's noble three who held the bridge and saved the city of seven hills. If he had been born a hundred years ago, in America, he might have ridden shotgun, protecting the stagecoach from the James gang.

"To our great good fortune, however, he was born in Prague in 1918. He was here when we needed him most.

"He was a free spirit. He died that the rest of us could be free."

Ryk couldn't go on; he could feel the tears welling up. Tomorrow may never come. He had to sit down.

Strange. He scarcely knew Joe. But it was a warning he had already learned to his great sorrow. Don't make friends. It can cause too much pain.

16

"They Have Run Away"

*[Russia] is a riddle wrapped in a
mystery inside an enigma.*
Winston Churchill

In the months after their escape, Kaz and Jan often wondered if
they had made the right decision. Their rash actions had caused
the deaths of Piotr and Wincenty. Even though the two of them
had escaped, life was little better than that in a prison camp; they faced
a constant struggle to survive.

Their first objective was to get away from Smolensk as far and as
fast as possible. In the excitement immediately after their escape, they
made quick time; they moved about 100 kilometers in the first week.
There were few notable events.

One was a brief ceremony as they crossed a bridge. If they were
caught, they didn't want the Russians to know they had escaped from
Katyn; that might be fatal. Rather, they were Polish soldiers who had
fled east from the German invasion, and didn't know where they were.
They had been disoriented by the German shelling, and were simply
wandering around trying to survive. Kaz Jankowski and Jan Tomczak
would have to disappear. As they got to the middle of the bridge, they
took off their dog tags, kissed them, and dropped them into the water
below. Kaz briefly buffed his new dog tag on his sleeve; from now on,
he would be Lt. Karol Kwiatkowski, his fallen comrade from the
defense of Warsaw. Similarly, Jan became Lt. Edward Szymczak.

They decided to head west, back to the Russian sector of Poland,
and then south toward Romania. With luck, they would get help from
Polish farmers. If they did get caught, their story—that they were
itinerant survivors of the German attack on Poland—would be more
believable once they were back in Poland.

By late summer, they had worked their way to the southeast corner of Poland; they could almost smell the freedom of Romania, less than fifty kilometers away. But then, perhaps lulled into complacency, they entered a small village. They were eager for news of the war, and hoped to find a newspaper posted somewhere in the village. They were particularly anxious to find out if Romania had entered the war; if so, there might be no point in trying to escape to that country. They didn't realize that the newspaper bulletin-board was a favorite spot for NKVD informants; people make careless remarks when they read the news.

Kaz was shocked to see a small story on the German occupation of France: "My God, Jan, the French have collapsed. The Germans are in Paris."

His exclamation drew the attention of a middle-aged woman, who looked almost as scruffy as the two travelers.

"You hadn't heard of the German invasion of France?" she wanted to know.

Kaz mumbled something incomprehensible.

Her eyes narrowed with suspicion. "Where have you been? Who are you?"

She signaled to a Russian soldier fifty meters away. Kaz and Jan were soon back in a prison camp—as Lt. Karol Kwiatkowski and Lt. Edward Szymczak. Fortunately, the NKVD informant had not heard Kaz call Jan by his right name. The two determined never again to be so careless; Karol and Edward it would be, regardless of the circumstances.

The prison camp—just over the border in the Ukraine—was a repeat of the dreary camp of the previous year, except that it was filled with officers of the regular army, not reservists. The routine was harsh, but not as bad as the first camp. Jan had an explanation: most of the guards were Ukrainians, not Russians.

As 1940 passed into the early months of 1941, they noticed another welcome difference. The winter was not nearly so bitter; the camp was further south. Somehow, the one thin blanket seemed much thicker and warmer than the blankets in Smolensk. The struggle to survive was not so desperate; fewer inmates died. And spring arrived early.

Kaz delighted in filling his lungs with the warm, moist spring air, particularly when it carried the soft, sweet fragrance of apple blossoms; he would drift off into memories of springtime on his uncle's farm. Occasionally, his daydreams were jarred when the wind shifted, blowing in quite a different smell from the latrines.

Soon it was June.

Early one morning, Kaz was awakened by an ominous, familiar noise—the drone of German aircraft. He and his comrades were quickly on their feet, pulling on their pants as they tumbled out of the barracks. Above flew a formation of Heinkel bombers, their German crosses clearly visible on their wings.

Operation Barbarossa—Hitler's blitzkrieg aimed at defeating the Soviet Union within a few months—had begun.

In less than a week, the situation in the camp improved. Many of the guards were sent to the front. The flow of supplies into the camp fell sharply, but the remaining guards let some of the prisoners out to forage for food. Hostages were kept behind; they would be shot if the prisoners didn't return.

Then came the news they had been waiting for. They were to be released. Stalin had agreed: the Poles could establish an army in the Soviet Union, under Gen. Wladyslaw Anders. Diplomatic relations were to be resumed between the Soviet Union and the Polish Government in exile in London.

Now they would be soldiers again.

By September, more than 150,000 Polish troops had moved to a training camp. Their spirits were high; Kaz and Jan delighted in every day of freedom.

The word went out from Gen. Anders headquarters: he needed Russian-speaking officers to handle liaison with the Soviets. Jan/Edward volunteered. Soon he arranged for Kaz to join him; he explained to the colonel how closely the two had worked together in the past, and how indispensable "Karol" would be to him.

Kaz wasn't sure that he wanted the job; he was a soldier, not a politician. But he surprised himself; he was soon caught up in the work at headquarters. They were preparing for a December meeting between Stalin and General Sikorski—the Polish Commander-in-Chief and Prime Minister of the Polish Government in London.

The question was: what would Anders' army do? Would they fight the Nazi invader along side the Soviets? Or would they try to get Stalin's permission to leave the Soviet Union and join the British?

The Poles couldn't agree among themselves. To seek a consensus, Sikorski would fly into Moscow to meet with Anders several days before his meeting with Stalin.

"Edward" and "Karol" were invited to join the group going to Moscow, to help with security and administrative matters. They eagerly agreed.

Plans for the Moscow meeting almost unraveled one morning in the middle of November. Karol was in his "office"—actually not an office, but a small area separated from other "offices" by charcoal markings on the barracks floor—when a lieutenant approached, pretending to knock on Kaz's pretend door.

"I'm looking for Karol Kwiatkowski; I was told I might find him at this end of the barracks."

Kaz looked up from the papers on the battered board that was serving as his desk. "That's right. I'm Kwiatkowski."

"But I was looking for Lt. Kwiatkowski from Lvov."

"Yes. That's me."

"No you're not. I went to school with Karol Kwiatkowski."

Kaz wanted to kick himself; he had not prepared for this obvious complication.

"You were friends?"

"Yeah. He's my best friend."

"I'm sorry. He's dead. Killed in the defense of Warsaw."

"And who the hell are you?"

"Let's just say that I needed a new identity, and took his. We were together when he was killed. I'm a regular army officer.... Really."

The lieutenant's eyes narrowed. "Are you a Russian spy?" He, in turn, wanted to kick himself; a stupid question.

"No." Kaz felt equally silly answering. "But take your suspicions to Col. Polonsky. He handles security."

"Why should I trust him? Maybe he's in it with you."

"Maybe our whole army is made up of Russian spies?"

The lieutenant's eyes narrowed even more. He slowly and suspiciously backed away, through the imaginary wall of Kaz's office.

The lieutenant did tell someone. In fact, he went directly to Gen. Anders. He wanted to act as quickly as possible; his life might be in danger if Kaz really were a spy.

That afternoon, Kaz was summoned to Anders' office. It actually *was* an office, more or less—the only one in the camp. Blankets were hung to separate it from the rest of the barracks, and give Anders some semblance of privacy. Col. Polonsky and Jan/Edward were there already.

The General called a corporal and spoke a few quiet words. The corporal disappeared. Almost immediately, a loud chorus of men broke out into barroom songs. Kaz looked puzzled.

The Col. leaned forward and spoke in a barely audible voice. "We really do have to worry about Russian spies. If they're eavesdropping, they won't hear anything but the songsters."

"Now," said the General in a stage whisper, "let's get to the point. Kwiatkowski, I'm told you're an impostor. The real Kwiatkowski was killed near Warsaw."

"That's correct, sir."

"I want an explanation. Better still: Szymczak, you explain. Did you know about Kwiatkowski? What did you mean by bringing an impostor into my inner circle?"

"Yes, sir, I did know. I confess, General, that I'm an impostor too. I'm really Lt. Janusz Tomczak of the Polish Cavalry."

Thereupon, Jan and Kaz described their escape from the prison camp near Smolensk, their fears that the Russians were shooting prisoners, and how two prisoners were killed during the escape. They just happened to have the extra dog tags from the Warsaw battle. They decided to use the false identities; the Russians would be less likely to shoot them if they were recaptured.

Jan was speaking more and more softly. By now, the four men were head to head; it looked like a conspiracy.

"If possible, sir, we'd like to keep our false identities. We're still worried what the Bolshies will do if they find out who we really are."

"Well you might," responded the Colonel. "After the end of June—when the Russians agreed to release Polish prisoners—we expected thousands of officers from the Smolensk camp, and from two others near Kalinin and Starobelsk. But as far as we know, you're the only ones who made it."

"Just from Smolensk?" Kaz wanted to know.

"From any of the three camps. We're very concerned. We're afraid you were right—the Russians murdered the others."

Kaz was surprised by his mixed emotions. He was appalled at the thought of all his fellow prisoners dying. But he was also relieved. He and Jan had not been responsible for the senseless death of the two would-be escapees.

The General continued the Colonel's story. "For your information—and keep this confidential—next month, when Gen. Sikorski meets the Russians in Moscow, he may ask about Katyn—the forest near Smolensk where we suspect our officers were executed. It looks more and more like a brutal massacre. Until further notice, you will maintain your false identities. We don't want to give the Russians any hint that we have two escapees among us.

"Also, we'd like the two of you to keep yourselves apart from the rest of the troops. We don't know who may recognize you. We don't want rumors going around. But it will be helpful if you are in Moscow and can give your story first-hand to Gen. Sikorski."

General Anders reiterated his main point. "Most of all, don't give any hint of your true identities when you're in Moscow. Even at our most optimistic, we think the discussions with Stalin will be difficult."

Not only were the talks with Stalin difficult. So were the preliminary discussions between Sikorski and Anders.

They took place at the British embassy, which provided some chance of a secure conversation. They were in the main conference room on the third floor, but even there, concerns about listening devices were in evidence. A gramophone was kept playing in the corner to disguise the sound of voices. The music was better than the barroom singers at the barracks. Perhaps as a courtesy to any Russian eavesdropper, they played Tchaikovsky's 1812 Symphony. Over and over. Kaz realized how much he preferred church bells to cannon fire.

After more than two years in captivity, Anders was eager to get his troops into action. How would they get out of the Soviet Union?

Sikorski interrupted. "That's not the first question, General. The real issue is: do we want to keep our troops in the Soviet Union, where they can roll back into Poland with the Red Army? Or do we want to get them out to help the British?"

"Let's get out, by all means, sir. We can fight alongside the British as close allies. There's too much suspicion for us to fight beside the Russians."

"But Russia's the critical front. *The Soviets are our only hope.* If they collapse, it's hard to see how Hitler can be defeated. We may *never* have a free Poland."

"Many of our men have had bad experiences with the Russians, sir." Anders made a point of not looking at Kaz and Jan, who sat inconspicuously at the side of the room.

"Granted. But does that make a compelling case for leaving the Soviet Union?"

"I would certainly think so." To Anders, it seemed obvious.

"Not so clear. Why do we have trouble with the Russians? Partly, it's history—centuries of sporadic fighting. But Communism is a big complication. Stalin wants world revolution. That means a Communist government in Poland. If we don't have an army on the ground when the Nazis are driven out of Poland, the Soviets may set up a Communist regime. That means you should stay here. Precisely because we *can't* trust the Russians. It's essential that the Russians beat the Germans. But it's also essential that we have an army on the ground when they do."

"I see your point, sir. But isn't that the job of our underground Home Army?"

"Yes, but they may not be nearly strong enough. If your army joins the Home Army, our forces will be too big for the Russians to ignore.

"There's one more thing," Sikorski continued. "It's important. President Raczkiewicz takes a much harder line on the Soviet Union than I do. When Hitler invaded Russia, the President didn't want to resume diplomatic relations with the Soviets unless they would first agree to restore our 1938 borders after the war. We had a real row. He tried to fire me — too soft with the Russians."

Sikorski anticipated the obvious question: how could he still be Prime Minister? "I only hung on because the British Government intervened on my behalf. They put pressure on Raczkiewicz to keep me, and to restore relations with the Russians. So we need to take the President's hard line into account. He wants you here, to increase our bargaining power."

Anders didn't much like the idea of his troops being used as a bargaining chip. In his anger, he struggled to keep his voice down. "That puts us in an impossible position, sir. Our men are brave; they're willing to face the Nazi enemy, and die if necessary. But they don't want to fight with enemies at their flanks and rear, too. If the Russians see us as a threat to their postwar plans, they'll simply put us in the most dangerous position on the battlefield. We'll be exterminated. That's why our officers here are unanimous. They want out. We can help Britain. We'll just have to trust Britain to protect our postwar interests. If they won't, our situation is hopeless."

"Perhaps not as hopeless as you suggest." Stanislaw Kot, the Polish Ambassador to the Soviet Union, interrupted. He had just returned from a brief absence from the room; he had left when a British secretary came in and handed him a note. "The Americans may be in our corner, too. The British Embassy has informed me that the Japanese have just bombed Pearl Harbor."

Formalities disappeared. Everyone cheered; there were handshakes all around. America was finally in the war.

"Unfortunately, there are also two bits of bad news," continued Kot. "The Japanese sunk most of the American fleet, including almost all their battleships. And according to the British embassy in Washington, the Americans are about to declare war on Japan, but not Germany. So it's not clear how much they'll help us and Britain. They may spend their energies chasing the Japanese all over the Pacific."

"That may also complicate our own plans," added Sikorski. "I was in America last March, and set up a recruiting campaign among Polish Americans. Now those men will be going into the American Army.

"Coming back to the main point," continued Sikorski, "we should also take into account Stalin's views. What does he want? Will he ask us to keep our army here, or does he want us to leave? Ambassador Kot?"

"Unfortunately, I can't help. Everybody in the Soviet government is preoccupied, trying to stop the German advance. Many are trying to get their families out, to the east. Nobody is even willing to guess at what Stalin wants. Particularly on a dangerous topic like this."

Kot summarized: "The Soviets can obviously see one strong argument on each side. Our troops can help in the defense of the Soviet Union. But later, if and when the Soviets roll westward, they may look at our army as a nuisance—a threat to their plans for postwar Poland.

"Incidentally," he added, "the Soviets are preparing a big counteroffensive against the Nazis. Somehow, their intelligence picked up the story that the Japanese were going to move south, against the Americans, British, and Dutch. That gave them an opportunity to bring troops back from the Far East. They're good. They beat the Japanese two years ago. Their new T-34 tank is first-rate—better than anything the Germans have. My guess is, Hitler's in for a nasty surprise."

Again, smiles all around, but the reaction was more subdued this time.

"OK," replied Sikorski. "Let's figure out what we want and how to get it. I'll have to check with the President in London. But I've modified my views; I think the attitude of officers here in the Soviet Union needs to be taken into account. Tentatively, I'm willing to go along—we should try to get our army out. The President and I will make the final decision."

"Assuming you decide that we should leave the Soviet Union, sir, how do we deal with Stalin?" Anders queried. "Do we take the initiative, or do we wait for him to express his views first?"

Sikorski looked toward Kot; he wanted his opinion. Kot obliged. "I'd be inclined to go first. If Stalin says what he wants first, and then we go for the other side, he may dig in his heels. He's pretty insecure.

Otherwise, why would he shoot so many people around him? Looking good in front of his colleagues is very important."

"Fine," replied Sikorski. "Let's work on our opening statement this evening. Regarding Stalin's sensitivities, there's a much touchier issue. I'm under explicit orders from the President to ask about the missing Polish officers from the prison camps near Smolensk, Kalinin, and Starobelsk. Our people in London have prepared a list of 4,000 officers who we know were in one or other of those camps. The President wants an explanation."

There was sober silence. Sikorski passed two copies of the list around the table. Some of the officers passed it quickly on; others leafed through it, looking for familiar names.

"That will give us even more to talk about this evening," Sikorski said, looking first at General Anders and then at the Ambassador. The meeting was over.

As some of the participants milled around the room, Kaz managed to get his hands on the list. As he looked through it, he saw many familiar names. Two particularly caught his attention: Kazimierz Jankowski and Janusz Tomczak.

The meeting with Stalin, which had been scheduled for the next day, was delayed more than a week. Stalin was unavailable. With the Germans at the gates of Moscow, he was struggling with the immediate crisis. He would not see the Poles until his winter counteroffensive had been launched.

For the Poles, the interim was more than worthwhile. They were able to consider their approach to Stalin in great detail, and they joyfully received news that would change the course of the war. Hitler declared war on the United States.

Kaz couldn't understand why. Didn't the Führer learn anything from the First War? Why would he want to fight America again? True, he had a treaty with the Japanese. But he was obliged to help only if Japan were attacked. There was no mystery, who did the attacking at Pearl Harbor.

"If you go looking for enemies," he mused, "there's no counting the number you'll find."

"Maybe it was Hitler's strange sense of honor," Jan suggested wryly. It was the best reason they could dredge up. But they didn't really need an explanation. They could rejoice that they now possessed the time-tested secret of military success—the blunders of their foes.

The interval also gave Sikorski the opportunity for a detailed talk with Kaz and Jan. He wanted to know how they had escaped; if anyone else had escaped; and what made them suspect the Russians were shooting prisoners. Partly, it was the conversation between the two guards that Jan had overheard. Partly it was the peculiar way the Russians were taking 200 prisoners away each night without any explanation. But it also was just a vague, uneasy feeling, perhaps the result of a general suspicion of the Russians.

Sikorski repeated Anders' instructions: they were to maintain their false identities and not give the Russians the least hint of who they really were. Jan wanted to know, should their two names be deleted from the list? No, came the answer. They couldn't be sure that the list had been kept from spying Russian eyes. If their names were omitted now, the Russians might wonder why.

When Stalin did appear, the signs of the crisis were on his face. He looked much older than his sixty-two years. His graying mustache drooped. His face was dotted with pockmarks, in sharp contrast to the airbrushed portraits so prominently displayed around Moscow. His uniform was an odd mixture—baggy trousers covered on the top by a crisp, carefully tailored tunic, and on the bottom by boots polished to a mirror-like shine.

Kaz was surprised, how short he was, and, for that matter, how short his aides were. There was one exception: a tall general who carefully took his place at the end of the table, far from Stalin. Kaz couldn't help noticing. Stalin briefly greeted most of his aides, but carefully stayed away from the general.

Stalin began with a short opening statement of only a few sentences, welcoming the Poles to Moscow.

Sikorski responded by stating how much he appreciated meeting the Soviet leader, and looked forward to fruitful talks. He congratulated Stalin on the success of the counteroffensive, and on the valor of the Soviet troops. He began what promised to be an extended, flowery statement. Stalin brusquely interrupted him. Time was short. Would Sikorski get down to business?

"Our governments have agreed," responded Sikorski, "that the main issue before us is the role of the Polish troops in the Soviet Union. I convey the appreciation of my government, that these troops have been permitted to recommence their training." In expressing his thanks in this way, Sikorski was laying down a marker: the Government in London was the legitimate government of Poland.

Stalin grunted.

"Now that our troops are close to being battle-ready," observed Sikorski, "the question arises as to how they might be most useful in promoting the allied cause.

"Now that we have a new American ally," he continued, "the prospects for invading France in the next year or two now seem much brighter — a second front that will distract Hitler from his attacks on the Soviet Union. Together with the glorious, heroic actions of the Red Army in the East — first on the defensive, and now attacking the invaders — actions in the West can contribute to the eventual defeat of the Nazis. It is the view of my government that our troops can make the greatest contribution by joining our British allies, hastening the time of the second front."

Sikorski was laying it on a bit thick, but he wanted to be as persuasive as possible. Kaz was impressed at the General's skills, particularly as a withdrawal from the Soviet Union was not his own personal preference.

Stalin thoughtfully puffed on his pipe, then took it out of his mouth and began to stoke it. He put on quite a performance, poking away at the tobacco. He put the stem back in his mouth, lit several matches, and half smiled as the puffs became larger and thicker. He turned to Molotov, Commissar for Foreign Affairs, and the two conversed briefly.

"Conditionally agreed," said Stalin. "The details will have to be worked out — when and how you will leave, and payments to be made for the supplies you have used and will use in the future."

"I understand," replied Sikorski. Stalin clearly didn't want to fuss with the details; they would be dealt with later. Sikorski guessed from

Stalin's quick agreement that he wanted to get rid of the Poles. One more reason to be worried about postwar Poland. "We were thinking of a move to the south. The British have asked for reinforcements in their battle for North Africa."

Stalin began to rise, indicating that the meeting was over.

"There is one more matter," Sikorski quickly added. "My Government is concerned about the disappearance of thousands of Polish officers captured by your forces between September of 1939 and this past June. We have a partial list."

He slid a copy of the list, typed in both Cyrillic and Roman letters, across the table. Stalin seemed briefly taken aback. He disdainfully glanced at the list and tossed it aside to Molotov.

Kaz held his breath. He thought Stalin might simply leave, without any response. Then Stalin replied brusquely.

"We're overwhelmed with our own problems. It's impossible to know where they are."

Sikorski looked impassively but directly into Stalin's eyes. Kaz could taste blood. He was biting the inside of his cheek to maintain his expressionless face.

"They've run away," Stalin finally said.

"But where could they have run to?" asked Sikorski, coolly.

"Well, perhaps to Manchuria." Stalin got up, tipping over a chair as he moved toward the door.

The Poles sat in stunned silence.

Later, when they had a chance to compare notes, Kaz found that Jan had also noticed the short height of the Russian leadership.

"We can take some consolation in that," observed Jan.

"Hunh?"

"Hitler may think that the Third Reich will last a thousand years, but the Soviet Union certainly won't."

"What in the world does that have to do with the height of its leaders?"

"Very simple. Apparently, there's an unwritten rule: Soviet leaders must be shorter than their boss. Within a thousand years, the Soviet dictator will be no more than two feet tall. Somebody will step on him before that."

17
ELL of a Problem:
The Strange Case of the Missing L

*B*ismarck was not the last gift of the Luftwaffe. During the North African struggle in 1941-42, Rommel's messages to Hitler went through Field Marshal Kesselring, Commander-in-Chief South. Kesselring was an Air Force officer; the Luftwaffe transmitted Rommel's plans. They were quickly decrypted and forwarded to British headquarters in Egypt.

The greatest assistance to the North African campaign came not from the Luftwaffe, however, but from the Italian Navy, and from a student from London University—Mavis Lever—who had been brought to Bletchley Park at the tender age of eighteen. For the first time in her life, Anna felt old; she was no longer the youngest prodigy. To help Mavis adapt to the new life at Bletchley, Anna and Yvonne invited her to join their regular weekly lunch.

One day, Mavis insisted that they sit in a dark corner, well off by themselves. She wanted to talk about her work.

"I don't know what to make of a signal I was puzzling over this morning. The usual jumble of letters. But one thing was *very* peculiar. There was every letter except L. Not a single L in the whole message."

"Perhaps just a random event," suggested Anna. "How many letters in all?"

"About 200, as I recall."

"That many?" Yvonne was curious. "Perhaps still a chance occurrence. But I wonder. What else could conceivably explain it?"

"I've only thought of one possibility," replied Mavis. "The message was intercepted from an Italian source. They use a lot of L's. *La* this and *il* that. When an L is typed into the machine, it comes back some other letter, never an L."

Yvonne was skeptical. "That should reduce the frequency of L's in an Italian message. But eliminate them entirely? Seems unlikely."

The three young women were stumped. They sat thinking.

"But that's *exactly* it!" Mavis exclaimed, and then quickly lowered her voice to avoid being overheard. "We're dealing with some young idiot in training, who sent out a practice message. He did the same thing I did when I first got my hands on an Enigma. I can remember punching the 'A' key over and over; I was fascinated to see a whole jumble of letters come out. This imbecile pressed the L key over and over. More than a hundred times, it seems."

Mavis was right. With the L-less message, the wizards of BP were able to figure out the internal wiring of the Italian wheels.

Their Navy paid a heavy price. Forewarned of the approaching Italians, the British sank three cruisers and two destroyers at the battle off Cape Matapan in southern Greece.

Even more important, BP now had advanced information on enemy convoys from Italy to North Africa.

Admiral Sir Andrew Cunningham, victor of Cape Matapan, came by Bletchley Park to express his appreciation. The Enigma intercepts, he said, offered him the sword to smite the Fascist enemy. After the Admiral's brief remarks, Alastair led him over to the young women who had been so instrumental in cracking the Italian code, singling out Mavis. The Admiral greeted her warmly; he was delighted to congratulate her in person.

"Thank you, Admiral, but the navy did the dangerous work. You were the ones who got shot at."

Sunlight was streaming through a window into the Admiral's eyes. To escape, he backed toward the wall—the better to see the three attractive, attentive young women. They saw their opportunity.

"That's *such* a dashing uniform," cooed Anna. "What do all those stripes mean?" She knew very well; Kaz had drilled her on military ranks. She moved closer, doing her best to giggle with girlish glee, and brushed her hand on the gold braid on his sleeve.

He began to explain, taking two more steps backward.

Yvonne moved in from the other side. "And what happens when you fire a salvo?" she asked brightly. "Must be deafening."

"It is more blessed to give than to receive," replied Sir Andrew, trying hard not to sound stuffy and taking another step backward.

His mistake; he was now leaning against the wall. When he got back to his quarters and took off his uniform, the back of his jacket was covered with whitewash. He sighed; perhaps his tailor could replace just the back. Fortunately, there was no white on the sleeves or gold braid.

And, he mused, it was worth it. After all those months at sea, he was delighted to be surrounded by admiring, flirtatious young women. So what, if they laughed at his expense? They would, he fancied, remember him. Mavis and Anna.... What was the name of that third girl?

As the months passed, Anna became increasingly concerned about security. The point of information was to exploit it. But the more they used it to attack Africa-bound convoys, the greater the risk that the Axis powers would suspect their codes were being broken.

At her regular weekly luncheon with Yvonne and Mavis — which again gravitated to an isolated corner of the dinning room — Anna expressed her concerns. Yvonne was reassuring.

"You're not the only one to worry. A few months ago, strict orders were sent to all commanders with access to Ultra — the code name for Enigma decrypts. Absolutely no action may be taken against any target unless preceded by air reconnaissance or similar measures.

"As far as I know, this order is being strictly obeyed. It gives our observation planes a bizarre role. Their objective is not to observe, but to be sure that they are *being* observed. When they spot the convoy, they radio back a report in the clear, as much for the benefit of German listeners as for Allied air forces."

Anna felt relieved; reasonable precautions were being taken.

"Under pressing circumstances, however, the rules are broken."

"Really?" Anna was taken aback.

"But those decisions are made only at the highest level."

"The highest level?" Anna was encouraging Yvonne to go on.

"The Prime Minister."

There was a lengthy pause. Anna was finally about to change the subject, when Yvonne decided to provide details.

"The Germans are killing thousands of people, sometimes whole villages, as they advance into Russia. We know from decoded messages."

Anna nodded; she had seen several of the intercepts and had heard of others.

"Churchill became so enraged that he decided to denounce the slaughter. He was very blunt, accusing the SS of 'scores of thousands of executions in cold blood.' To underline Nazi barbarity, he exclaimed, 'Since the Mongol invasions of Europe in the sixteenth century, there has never been methodical, merciless butchery on such a scale!'

"You may have heard about the speech," Yvonne added.

"Better than that," said Mavis, "I just happened to hear it on the BBC. Churchill at his bulldog best. He positively spat out 'Nazi' and 'butchery.'"

Yvonne continued. "It was quite a gamble, because Orange intercepts — SS messages — were the source of much of the information on the slaughter. Fortunately, we've also intercepted German police messages about the killings. They were much less detailed and less securely encrypted, just using a hand cipher unrelated to Enigma. Let's hope we're lucky, and the Germans come to the obvious — incorrect — conclusion: that Churchill's denunciations were based solely on intercepts of police messages."

Out of the corner of her eye, Mavis noticed that Hugh Alexander — one of the wizards of Hut 6 — had entered the dining room and was looking around. When he spotted the three young women, his face brightened and he headed toward their table.

"Don't look now, but wicked uncle at nine o'clock," said Mavis under her breath. Without thinking, Anna began to turn her head, but caught herself as Mavis frowned. An embarrassed smile crossed Anna's face.

The "wicked uncles," as the younger staff knew them, were senior men—Welchman, Turing, Milner-Barry and Alexander—not noted for their patience with mere mortals.

They had created a sensation several months earlier. They became so exasperated with the lack of support that they spurned normal channels and wrote directly to Churchill. Churchill had recently visited Bletchley Park, praising the codebreakers for their brilliance and discretion—"the geese that laid the golden eggs and never cackled." The time had come, decided the uncles, for some cackling. They deputized Milner-Barry to deliver their request—demand?—for more resources directly to the Prime Minister.

The comic scene at No. 10 Downing Street reminded Anna of her own first morning in Britain. Milner-Barry forgot to make an appointment or take any official identification. He managed to get as far as the PM's private secretary, who insisted on knowing what was so urgent. Milner-Barry wouldn't tell him; it was too secret. The secretary finally agreed to pass a sealed envelope on the PM without opening it. The results were spectacular. Churchill ordered his chief of staff to give BP top priority. At once. "Action this day," he scribbled across the letter.

"He's almost here," whispered Mavis, even more softly, "but you can relax. He's actually smiling. No kidding."

"May I join you?" Alexander asked, still smiling. Yes, he might. "I want to congratulate you, Mavis, on you're brilliant work with the missing L's."

"Thank you. We were just talking shop—Yvonne was explaining about observation planes whose main objective is to be observed."

"You might also be reassured by other steps to protect security," Alexander elaborated. "With our successes, the Germans may be wondering if we've broken Enigma. To send them off in another direction, we've invented nonexistent spies. One is supposedly in Naples—tipping us off on the sailing of Rommel's convoys. But we're proudest of 'Boniface,' a fictitious officer close to Hitler.

"I sometimes like to imagine, as I'm in bed falling asleep, the troubles that Boniface must be causing the Germans—the witch hunts within the German high command trying to track him down. I'm also amused by our own intelligence officers who aren't in on the Enigma secret. They think we've been spectacularly successful, penetrating Hitler's innermost circle. 'This chap Boniface must have nerves of steel!' one of them said to me the other day. I replied: 'You wouldn't believe how daring he can be! A real Scarlet Pimpernel.'"

"Ever thought of pointing the finger at someone specific?" Anna wondered. "Himmler would be my first choice. That really would be the god of vengeance at work. Imagine him being shot on Hitler's orders. History would turn out right. For once."

"I nominate Göring," Yvonne volunteered. "A nice fat target for a firing squad."

"We've got a little list. Society offenders who never would be missed," quipped Alexander. He needed only the slightest provocation to quote Gilbert and Sullivan.

"But security is not why I wanted to see you." He got to the point. "I want to pick your brains." Actually, he was supposed to have lunch with a permanent undersecretary, but the senior official canceled at the last minute. But, even though they were his second choice, he did want to talk to the three; they might come up with something.

"Every once in a while it's good to step back and take a broad view of what we're doing. Are we missing anything in the way we collect information, or in the way we try to get the wheel settings?" Alexander paused. That was a pretty broad topic. Yvonne was about to ask if he could be more specific when Anna spoke up.

"I suppose we might look at what we're doing now. Is anything falling through the cracks?

"First is the heavy lifting—Turing's machines and the new ones being developed. That's a very specialized operation; I don't think we have much to offer."

"Other than something that's way above our pay grade," Yvonne interjected.

"And that is?" Alexander asked.

"It looks as if this war will go on for years," Yvonne responded. "As the Germans make Enigma more and more complicated, Turing-type machines will become even more critical to our success. I wonder if

British industry will be able to keep up with the demand. We might look to the Yanks as a source of machines."

"You're right. Above your pay grade." But Alexander grinned as he said it.

The young women paused. They hoped Alexander would say more. He did. "It's been taken up at the highest level. For the time being, the Americans won't be let in on our Enigma secrets. Too much risk that information will leak out."

After waiting briefly for more information, Anna continued. "Second is the hardware and information we get from captured German ships. I suppose we might try harder to damage U-boats rather than sink them, but I doubt there's any way to depth-charge a submarine gently."

"Third is the radio interception program. Maybe there are ways of improving that operation—such as a more methodical search for possible kisses and other German mistakes—but I think Welchman's doing a first-rate job keeping his eye on that part of the operation."

"I'm afraid this isn't much help. But maybe I've missed something."

"That's exactly the question," Alexander added. He paused thoughtfully. The three young women waited. Then he continued:

"You mentioned German mistakes. We look for them all the time. Perhaps it might be possible to *get* the Germans to make mistakes."

"You mean," asked Mavis, "get them to send a message, whose contents we already know?"

Anna responded. "But how—unless we have someone inside the German system? In other words, a spy? We really do need a Boniface."

"Perhaps *we* could do something that they would have to report to their superiors," Mavis replied. "Or to one another."

"That's it. That's exactly it," said Alexander excitedly. "Suppose we lay mines, without being too subtle about it. The Germans observe us. They send out a coded message. What will it say? British mines in the area—then they give specific longitude and latitude. They'll have to spell out the numbers, because the Enigma machine has no number keys, only letters. We laid the mines; we know what the numbers are."

The RAF was thereupon set to work laying mines at very specific points in the North Sea. The aircrews were puzzled. They got their

196

orders. It was essential to lay the mines in *precisely* the right spot. But they also got a not-too-subtle secondary message: it didn't much matter if the Jerries saw them or not.

Gardening it was called. Planting seeds of information that could quickly be harvested.

Within a few months, it was much more than gardening. It became commercial farming. British Intelligence had tracked down every enemy agent in England. They were given the option: work for British Intelligence or face the hangman. Without exception, they picked the first choice. They were handed over to the Committee of Twenty—the XX Committee; the double cross. One agent, code named *Treasure*, was indeed a treasure. Her reports back to Germany—approved and monitored by the XX Committee—were loquacious, to say the least; she never used two words when ten would do. Although her reports were vacuous, they were trumpeted by her German handlers, who repeated them word for word in coded messages. Kisses on command.

Over their regular weekly lunches, the three women occasionally exchanged information on new machines, wheels, and German codebooks that were appearing at BP.

One day, Yvonne was obviously shaken. She had just received a codebook from an enemy plane that had been shot down. She couldn't read the last fifteen pages; they were stuck together with fresh blood that was beginning to coagulate. Somehow, the war was much closer. Real people were getting killed.

The three friends picked at their food; none had much appetite.

In the following weeks, the lunches were much less depressing. Anna eagerly awaited Yvonne's reports of newly captured material. In early 1941, a German ship was seized off Norway, providing the Dolphin key tables. Although they were for previous weeks, they allowed BP to read earlier U-boat traffic; they might provide the secret to unlocking future communications. Success could not come too soon; U-boat attacks were intensifying.

Then the destroyer *Bulldog* rocked the U-110 with a series of depth charges. The sub's main power went out. As it surfaced, its terrified captain, Lemp, saw the *Bulldog* bearing down, about to ram his vessel. "Abandon ship!" he shouted. There was no time to set the charges.

As the sub's crew leaped overboard, the Bulldog's captain recognized his golden opportunity. He swung hard aport, missing the sub. A boat was soon lowered, carrying a boarding party.

Too late, Lemp realized his mistake. He had to get back to scuttle his U-boat. He left his men, and vigorously began to swim back. A burst of machine-gun fire erupted from the Bulldog's deck. Lemp—the captain who had breached instructions to sink the liner *Athenia* on the very first day of the war—now faced his own fate; he slipped below the waves.

The boarding party groped their way down the narrow, gloomy corridors lit only faintly by the sub's emergency system. In the radio room, they found a typewriter-like machine; they passed it along to the bridge. Going through Lemp's desk, a British officer found a sealed envelope. It looked important.

It was. The Bulldog had captured not only an Enigma machine, but also the settings to read Dolphin traffic for the first half of May.

Anna thought that they were close to a continuous real-time breaking of Dolphin—the key to routing convoys around U-boat packs. Yvonne reported that there would be a meeting that afternoon: was there any way to steal Enigma material to order, rather than waiting for lucky windfalls? Yvonne would check to see if Anna might attend.

The meeting started with a suggestion: mount a commando attack on a U-boat base, to seize material. The idea was quickly discarded—too dangerous and too costly. Even if it succeeded, which was very doubtful, it would tip the Germans off: the British were after Enigma secrets.

They then turned to a proposal of a naval intelligence officer, Lt.-Commander Ian Fleming. He had submitted an elaborate, written scheme to refurbish a downed Luftwaffe bomber. With a German-speaking British crew, it would join a flight of enemy planes returning from a raid. As it crossed the channel, it would begin to lose altitude and leave a trail of smoke. It would ditch conveniently near a small German navy boat; the crew would wait to be picked up.

Thereupon, the plan was simple: "Once aboard rescue boat, shoot German crew, dump overboard, bring boat back to English port."

To Anna, the idea seemed far-fetched. She said nothing, but inconspicuously slipped a note to Yvonne:

> Fleming has missed his calling. With his supercharged imagination, he should be writing spy novels.

Others were less skeptical; they would try the idea out on the Navy. Yvonne thereupon passed a note back to Anna:

> Cheer up. It's not the craziest idea the Navy has ever considered.

When Anna looked puzzled, Yvonne scribbled an explanation:

> During the first war, they considered a plan to blind submarines by training seagulls to poop on periscopes.

Throughout the discussion, Harry Hinsley sat silently and impassively, obviously sunk in thought.

"Let's work backward," he said slowly. "What do we want? More naval Enigma machines and material. Where do they exist? On ships. What ships are most vulnerable? Slow surface ships. What are the slowest, most vulnerable ones? Weather ships. They're continuously sending messages. With radio direction finders, they should be easy to find. They also offer another advantage. A big one. They've got no guns. They don't shoot back."

"Brilliant," was Alastair's response. "But how do we attack the ships, so that the Germans don't twig to the fact that we're after their Enigma machines?"

Anna was about to make a suggestion but held back, waiting for someone with naval experience to speak. As she looked around the room, she realized how few people met that criterion. Accordingly, she broke the silence.

"The key to success would be to board the ship quickly, with as little warning as possible. That would mean a small ship, certainly nothing bigger than a destroyer. It could stand off, over the horizon, waiting for fog. Using its radar — do destroyers have radar? — it could appear suddenly out of the fog. Even if the weather ship did get off a quick message, the Germans might simply dismiss it as a chance encounter."

The navy liked Hinsley's suggestion, but not Anna's details. In May 1941, they went after the weather ship München, not with a single destroyer, but with a line of ships—three large cruisers and four of the newest, fastest destroyers, strung out in a line, ten miles apart. The idea was to come on the München as quickly as possible, firing from a distance, trying not to hit the ship but come close enough that the crew would panic and abandon ship without either sending a distress signal or destroying their coding equipment.

The operation was partially successful. The München crew managed to throw their Enigma overboard, but the boarding party seized the Dolphin settings for June. The radio operator was interrupted in the middle of a message and dragged away from his key; presumably he was trying to warn Berlin that they had been boarded.

Toward the end of June, a second weather ship was boarded, with the settings for July. With these keys, BP was able to read Dolphin traffic for those two months.

It would be unwise to press their luck with another ship. The Germans might write off the first two as unlucky accidents. But a third? That would be just too much coincidence—particularly when the weather ships were so isolated.

Furthermore, there was no pressing need. By August, 1941, Turing and his team had their new bombes—the "Jumbos." They also had two months' worth of decryptions, and enough cribs and sillies to decipher Dolphin almost continuously.

18

Shark

Operational analysis showed that its [a U-boat's] chances of survival after the delivery of a sixth close [depth charge] attack rapidly diminished, probably because the U-boat captain lost his capacity to think his way out of danger.

John Keegan, The Price of Admiralty

With the decoded messages, the Admiralty routed convoys away from the wolf packs. The results were striking. Sinkings by U-boats fell by almost two thirds. But just as they were beginning to quietly celebrate their success, Anna got a disturbing call from Yvonne. She had to see her at once.

When Anna got to her old office, Yvonne looked worried.

"You've seen the Enigma machine they've just captured—the one from U-570?"

"Yes. But I didn't inspect it—busy with Army intercepts."

"You should. Carefully. But, before I tell you what to look for, you might like to know how we came by it."

"I'm all ears."

"The sub surfaced south of Iceland to recharge its batteries. Almost directly above was one of our Hudson bombers—more precisely, a Hudson bomber provided by the Yanks. The pilot could scarcely believe his luck. He dropped four depth charges, straddling the sub. It was so badly damaged that it couldn't risk diving. It signaled its surrender to the Hudson, which radioed to a nearby destroyer. It soon appeared and sent a boarding party."

"Interesting. But why, pray tell, should I be concerned with this particular Enigma?"

"Because, my dear Anna, it was designed with room for a fourth wheel. Only three are installed, but there's space for a fourth."

"So when they get around to..."

"When they get around to using the fourth wheel, we may be back to square one. We're winning Round 1 in the U-boat war. But I shudder to think of what will happen when they use that fourth wheel."

Round 2 was indeed coming. It would be tough. But fortunately, the fourth wheel was not operational for almost six months, and before that time, the United States would be drawn, reluctantly, into the war.

1 February, 1942. Bletchley Park.

Each day, the codebreakers faced the task of unraveling the basic keys. It was a struggle, even with all the power of the new bombes, reinforced by cribs, sillies, and the sloppiness of German operators. Soon after midnight, when the first messages of the day would begin to come in, the codebreakers would begin their methodical, intense routine, hoping all the while for inspired guesses. Usually the Luftwaffe settings would be broken first; the first cheer of the early morning would go up, sometimes as early as 2:00 a.m. Success with Dolphin came later.

But on this early February morning, there was no second cheer. Noon came, and the day's Dolphin had not yet been unraveled. The afternoon stretched into evening; still no success.

After a few frustrating days, they knew they faced a fundamental problem. No Dolphin traffic had yet been decoded for February. And on these decodings depended the safety of Atlantic convoys.

Reluctantly, they came to the obvious conclusion: the Kriegsmarine had introduced the fourth wheel for communications with U-boats. Dolphin was now relegated to less important communications with surface ships.

The primary responsibility for breaking Shark—BP's name for the new four-wheel cipher—lay with Turing and others at Hut 8; Anna was not intimately involved. But thorny problems were tackled at occasional meetings. The Shark puzzle was not altogether hopeless. Before the official introduction of the fourth wheel on Feb. 1, some U-boat crews mistakenly used it, and, when their error was pointed out, they retransmitted with just the first three wheels. Such lovely, repeated, teenaged kisses, it might have been hoped, would lead to a quick breaking of Shark.

But that was not to be; the new Enigma was very resistant to attacks. Hut 8 finally did figure out the settings for a few days in February and March, but for each of these days, it took six of Turing's bombes an average of 17 days working around the clock.

Seventeen-day old settings couldn't protect convoys. Fortunately, the Germans didn't know that Dolphin had been broken; they didn't know of their huge new advantage with Shark. Fortunately, also—at least for the British—U-boats were occupied with easy pickings off the coast of the United States. It was a time of painful learning for the New World. Rather than use convoys, the Navy sent single tankers along the east coast. They were interspersed with occasional sub-chasers, little more than a nuisance for the U-boats. They simply lay low in the water until the sub-chasers passed.

Furthermore, to put not too fine a point on it, blackout policy was bizarre. Inhabitants of Washington were encouraged to cover their windows—perhaps to give the fuzzy, warm illusion that they were doing their part in the war effort; perhaps as a precaution against a fancied threat from the Luftwaffe. But lights from cars and arcades were left shining merrily in seaside resorts in New Jersey and Florida. Against the glow, the low, slow silhouettes of loaded American ships made easy targets for the raiders of the deep. Exploding tankers provided spectacular fireworks for partygoers, blissfully unaware of their complicity in the fiery deaths of their countrymen. During the first half of 1942, losses to east-coast shipping ranked with the disaster at Pearl Harbor.

Then, belatedly, the navy instituted coastal convoys, and the U-boats turned their attention back to the mid-Atlantic, beyond the range of patrol planes. Sinkings increased spectacularly. By September, with almost a hundred U-boats prowling in wolf packs, they sank almost half a million tons. U-boat losses: 3.

At Bletchley Park, the pressure was on. They might be successful in breaking other German traffic. But they were not providing critical U-boat information, on which all else depended—preparations for an invasion of France, and conceivably even the survival of Britain itself. They concluded that they were not producing bigger and faster bombes quickly enough; they reluctantly accepted America's offer to develop and build new machines. By now, they had little alternative; American codebreakers intended to work on Enigma, with or without British cooperation.

The Yanks were coming to BP. Their slim vanguard—only two men— had arrived. They were going to have lunch with Yvonne, to bring them up to speed on BP's progress. If Denniston could get away, he would join them. Would Anna like to come? Yes, she would.

"You'll find them interesting," Yvonne added. "I certainly do. But then, I've never met an American before.... They're real patricians— courtly and reserved, not at all the brash, exuberant youth I expected. And they're *very* bright."

Anna and Yvonne took turns, providing a brief history of how messages were decoded. They had permission to be frank with the Americans, who had shared details on how they had broken the Japanese "Purple" code. Furthermore, Bletchley Park—in the person of Jim Rose—had been allowed to interview the Americans and pick the ones who would be allowed to come.

Anna and Yvonne talked of cribs, kisses, and gardening. Of the decision to seek out weather ships, and of the stone wall they now faced with the four-wheeled Shark.

Bill Bundy was interested in weather ships. Could they seize a third?

"Not clear how useful it would be," replied Anna, "even if we could make it look like another 'accident.' Weather ships are still using old, three-wheel machines. It's the subs' four-wheeled Shark that's the problem."

"The weather ships and subs—they communicate with each other?" Lewis Powell wanted to know.

Anna was slow in responding. She had never heard that soft, mellifluous Southern accent before.

Yvonne picked up the slack. "Yes, I think so."

"Two-way traffic? The submarines also send messages back to the weather ships?"

Yvonne paused. "Again, I think so." She obviously wasn't sure.

"I wonder...." Powell stopped.

Denniston had been nibbling at his lunch, apparently lost in another world. Now, he came to life.

"Good question. And the right question's half the game. When U-boats talk to weather ships, they *must* use only three wheels. It can't be all four. The weather ships—with only three wheels—wouldn't be able to understand. Maybe we can use the subs' messages to figure out how those first three are set. Once we do, we'll have a leg up on the fourth."

Denniston passed the idea on to Hut 6. They indeed found sub-to-weather ship traffic. The 17 days needed to read submarine messages was reduced. But not enough. A real-time decoding of Shark would have to await another lucky break.

30 October, 1942. Port of Alexandria, Egypt.
Aboard the Destroyer, *HMS Petard*.

Commander Mark Thornton looked down over the bow of *HMS Petard*. Workmen had been scurrying all night to complete the installation of a new "hedgehog" antisubmarine system—a set of grenades that could be fired forward. The destroyer would not have to pass over the sub before attacking, the way it would with depth charges.

An urgent message came from the radio room. Three other British destroyers were stalking a U-boat; they had made several depth-charge attacks in the past four hours. They had the sub trapped against the Mediterranean coast, near Haifa, but had not been able to sink it. Could Thornton help?

He certainly could.

He had lived for this chance, keeping his men on constant alert for U-boats. At times, his judgment was overwhelmed by his passion for the hunt. He would climb to the crow's nest, and Ulysses-like, strap himself to the mast, awaiting the siren call of a submarine.

The remaining workmen were hustled off, and the *Petard* was soon under way. Even at full speed, it would take eight hours to join the action.

Aboard U-559, men were grimly silent. They had known the perils when they joined the elite submarine service. But, for many, this was their first taste of the terrors of depth charges—the haunting fear that, at any instant, their vessel might be crushed into a steel coffin. Every time the sub tried to break out toward open water, it was rocked with depth charges. The last were very close indeed; two of the younger men cried out in panic. Several small leaks appeared in the overhead piping; the slow drip, drip mingled with the sweat and stress on the captain's face. The captain ordered oil and debris ejected from the aft tubes. He hoped the attackers were bored, would chalk up a victory when they saw the oil slick, and go away. He directed his sub, dead slow, back toward the coast and let it settle gently toward the bottom. The leaks were under control.

The pings from the destroyers' sonar shattered the silence, but the attackers could not distinguish the sub from the surrounding rocks. The waiting game had begun.

It was a grim contest, favoring the destroyers. They could breath. The sub would have to come up for air within 14 hours. The word was quietly sent around. They would wait until 02:00—the time when the enemy above would be least alert—and make a dash. Every man knew: this time would be the final throw of the dice. They would press on, either to the safety of the open sea or to their destruction.

At 21:10, the hydrophone operator had an urgent report. He detected a fourth ship; another destroyer sent to block their escape? The fourth ship was still far away. But its propellers were thrashing; it was approaching fast.

The captain's reaction was immediate. No time to waste; they couldn't wait until 02:00. He ordered full speed southward, along the coast, and then westward toward deeper waters.

A destroyer's signal lamp flashed, informing *Petard:* the sub is headed south. Block our southern flank.

As they closed, Thornton was grateful for his new gadget; the sub was turning and diving, obviously expecting an attack. Thornton ordered the hedgehog fired, and a pattern of grenades flew forward. He counted the seconds; the sea erupted in front of his ship. That should mean a hit. Unlike a depth charge, the grenades were designed to explode only on contact. But once one went off, the concussion would set off the rest.

He wanted to give the sub as little chance as possible. As they passed over the roiling sea, depth charges rolled off the stern. He ordered a hard turn to starboard, returning for a second attack.

Before the *Petard's* turn was completed, moonlight glinted off the snout of the U-559 as it broke the surface. Its hatches opened and the crew began to take to dinghies. The destroyer drew up, preparing to take on survivors as its searchlight illuminated the sub.

A shout came from the bridge: Boarding crew! Boarding crew! A young officer and two ratings stripped. The mission had been drilled into them: they must get code equipment off the sub! Drilled, and practiced. On one training exercise, Thornton had ordered the boarding party to jump into a treacherous, stormy sea and swim around the ship; they were saved from downing only by the presence of a senior officer, who persuaded Thornton to withdraw his order.

The officer leading the boarding party was about to leap into the sea, when he felt a hand restraining his arm.

"Not you, mate. You're married." Lieut. Anthony Fasson was speaking. He too, was stripped to his skivvies. Fasson and the two other men dove into the Mediterranean.

By now, the U-boat crew were climbing rope ladders to the deck of the destroyer. Swimming vigorously in the opposite direction, the three British figures soon reached the sub. Fasson and Able Seaman Grazier were quickly down the hatch, while the third man, as ordered, stood on the conning tower.

The two men found the wireless room—or more precisely, the wireless cubbyhole. Fasson handed rotors and codebooks to Grazier, ordering him to take them to the conning tower and return as quickly as possible. He began to disconnect what apparently was a coding machine. The water was rising around his ankles, adding urgency to his task.

Meanwhile, four other men set out for the sub, using one of the German dinghies. As they approached, the nose of the sub settled lower the water.

Suddenly, it was gone. As the dinghy arrived, it found only one survivor, treading water and holding a codebook and round discs above his head.

For their heroism, Fasson and Grazier were posthumously awarded the George Cross.

The new material was quickly sent to Bletchley Park. With it, and with the new machines coming on line, Hut 8 finally succeeded in breaking Shark.

When they did, they were in for a shock. *B-Dienst* had been reading the Admiralty's messages to convoys. Not only had the Allies been unaware of the position of U-boats; the U-boats had known where to look.

With the roles reversed, the hunters now became the hunted.

15 May, 1943. 10:00 hrs. Kriegsmarine Headquarters.

Admiral Dönitz sat sullenly staring at the large scorekeeping charts on his wall. The first showed U-boat sinkings of Allied ships, revealing a sharp decline in April. This was not surprising. The British had changed their naval code; the Admiral could no longer guide his submarines to their prey.

It was the second chart that alarmed him. During the previous week, no fewer than thirteen submarines had been sent to the bottom. How could that be? Was it possible that the enemy had scored a double success, not only denying him access to their messages but also reading the Kriegsmarine's traffic?

He had asked this question before and received soothing answers. The Enigma simply could not be broken. The wheel settings were changed every 24 hours. Even if the enemy captured one of the new four-wheeled machines, they would need years to figure out a single setting. The submarines would rust away before they could be sunk.

But the question nagged. The fortunes of the undersea raiders had shifted so suddenly. He asked his aide to contact Oberst (Col.) Jurg Lindemann at *B-Dienst* on the secure land line.

"Lindemann? I want another urgent review of Enigma. Our submarine losses have become unbearable, 23 in the past two weeks. Can the enemy be reading our signals?"

"Very unlikely, sir. We're overwhelmed here, trying to crack the new British naval code, but I could spare a few people for another look. Could you tell me something about our losses — perhaps going back over the past few weeks? Anything specific to suggest the enemy is listening?"

"The six lost in the Bay of Biscay certainly do — sunk before they even reached open waters. Before, we've never lost more than one or two per month in that area. Seems the enemy planes know where to look."

"Hmmm. Sounds as though another review is in order. I'll put several of my best people on it."

Lindemann looked over at the small sign framed on his wall: 500 billion billion. He wondered.

Dönitz concluded: "I'll send Capt. Hauser to help. He'll have details on our losses."

15 May, 1943. 15:00 hrs. *B-Dienst* Headquarters.

When Hauser arrived, the meeting on Enigma security was already in progress; he was ushered in immediately. Lindemann invited him to report on recent U-boat losses.

"Unfortunately, since you spoke to Admiral Dönitz this morning, we've lost another sub — the 24th in the past two weeks.

"Nine were sunk when they located a convoy and began to radio other subs, calling them to form a wolf pack. Their transmissions ended abruptly, indicating they were under attack.

"Seven were sunk in the Bay of Biscay, before they reached the Atlantic.

"We have no information on the other eight; they simply vanished. Five failed to report after they had been on the surface at night, charging their batteries."

Hauser paused to let the numbers sink in.

Wilhelm Stumpff had been working on the Enigma for six years; he was responsible for the introduction of the fourth wheel. He exuded supreme confidence in his creation.

"I don't think Enigma can be broken. But, for the sake of argument, let's suppose it could. We still wouldn't have any explanation for the nine subs lost while sending messages. U-boats are given areas to patrol, not precise locations. Even if the enemy could read Enigma traffic, they wouldn't know exactly where to look. And, even if they did know exactly where to look, *why* would so many U-boats be attacked right in the middle of their radio messages? There's only *one* possible explanation. *The enemy must have some new technology.* They've found some way to locate U-boats by their radio transmissions."

"We've considered that," responded Hauser. "But even if they've developed much more powerful receivers in Iceland and Britain, it would be impossible to triangulate precisely and quickly enough for an attack."

"Impossible? Perhaps, sir," responded Stumpff. "But that's the thing about new technology. We *don't know* what it will do."

"Exactly," Hauser countered. "And that argument cuts both ways. You say it's impossible for the enemy to break Enigma. Perhaps they've developed new technology to do just that."

Stumpff ignored the jab and continued his argument. "Consider next the five lost on the surface at night. We *already* know what might be responsible. Recall our intercept two months ago — long-range bombers being equipped with radar and powerful searchlights. Unfortunately, it seems that this weapon is effective. The poor devils on the U-boats," he added, showing empathy for the naval officers in the room. "I don't know which would be worse — to be depth charged, or to be on deck at midnight when a blinding searchlight suddenly flashes on."

Hauser was scarcely mollified. "Granted, they may have much better radar. But the American planes apparently knew where to look. Furthermore, think of what happened early last year. We introduced the fourth wheel; then we sank many more ships. What does that suggest? The enemy had been listening in, but were stopped by the new four-wheel Enigma. If they could read the old three-wheeled machine, isn't it possible that they've now broken the new four-wheeled version?"

"Not necessarily," Stumpff countered. "There's a simpler explanation for our successes early last year. That's when *we* broke the British naval code.

"But I also grant a point," he continued. "The Bay of Biscay losses are hard to explain. But which is more likely: a breaking of Enigma, or some new enemy gadget? Bombers with the new radar might be the culprit, or some other new technology. For example, they may be locating U-boats with airborne infrared detectors. For reasons we've been over repeatedly, such technology is much more plausible than a breaking of Enigma."

Within a week, the group presented a preliminary report, preliminary only because Hauser insisted on further study. Once more, the report reassured Dönitz. Enigma could not be broken. The sudden change in fortunes was most likely the result of new enemy technology. But *B-Dienst* would keep an open mind; they would continue to look for weaknesses in Enigma.

Admiral Dönitz could not wait. At the end of May, with U-boat losses averaging two per day, he ordered his wolf packs withdrawn from the Atlantic. The Allies had won the second battle of the Atlantic.

There would be no third round. By early June, a prototype American bombe was running. An early problem—rotors overheating and warping because they were spinning at 2,000 rpm—had been solved. But the machine ran so fast that the rotors could not be stopped immediately when a decryption was registered. To deal with this problem, the machine had a novel and ingenious feature: it automatically rolled the rotors back to the decryption setting.

Enigma would never again be secure; there would be no more happy hunting for U-boats in the Atlantic.

19
The Last, Fleeting Hope

In anguish we uplift
A new unhallowed song:
The race is to the swift;
The battle to the strong.
  John   Davidson   (1857-
  1909)
  War Song

22 June, 1942. With the British Eight Army,
West of Alexandria, Egypt.

Kaz and Jan had become hardened to bad news: the fall of Poland; the collapse of France; the rapid advance of Hitler's legions into the vast expanses of the Soviet Union.

But they were unprepared for the gloom when they arrived in North Africa. After a siege of scarcely one week, the heavily-fortified port of Tobruk had just surrendered to Rommel's army.

"Defeat is one thing; disgrace is another," was Churchill's depressed and caustic comment.

The Desert Fox, who had been struggling with extended supply lines, now possessed not only the port but also huge quantities of British materiel. His panzers were moving inexorably east toward El Alamein, only sixty miles from the Nile River. Mussolini had already flown to North Africa, strutting and preening in preparation for a triumphant entry into Cairo.

The British were hurriedly fortifying and mining a defensive line near El Alamein—the best hope of preventing Rommel's troops from reaching the Nile. To the north of the line lay the Mediterranean; to the south the impenetrable Qattara Depression. If the Germans broke through, their tanks would fan out across the desert, threatening the whole allied position in Egypt.

Alarmed, Churchill visited Cairo. The main result: Gen. Bernard Montgomery was given command. The stage was set for a desert showdown. To bolster Montgomery, his American allies agreed to send several hundred of their new Sherman tanks by the only safe route—around the Cape of Good Hope and through the Suez Canal.

Kaz and Jan were part of the Polish advanced party, preparing for the main force. As more Poles arrived, they would be quickly organized into a reserve unit, to be committed in case of a threatened German breakthrough.

But there was none. In a final push, Rommel lost 50 tanks, most victims to dense minefields. He then withdrew to defensive positions, laying equally dense minefields of his own. Gradually, as new equipment arrived, the balance of power tilted toward Montgomery. But he had no intention of blundering unprepared into the German minefields; the Qattara Depression blocked any classic flanking move by his tanks, just as it had blocked Rommel. His army began a period of intense training and preparation for a fall offensive.

As the dangers of a renewed German assault faded, Kaz and Jan received new orders. They were to report to the Polish authorities in London.

The Polish Government-in-exile was housed in three adjacent large townhouses. The dull October drizzle made them seem even more drab and nondescript than usual. Two nearby buildings were gutted; they had been hit during the Blitz. But now, as Allied power grew by the day, air-raid sirens had become a rare event. Nevertheless, the signs of war were everywhere. Traffic consisted of olive-drab military vehicles. Almost all the men, and a goodly proportion of the women, were in uniform.

When Kaz and Jan arrived, they went directly to the personnel office. The time had come, they thought, to resume their real identities. Kaz also wanted his rightful rank.

"I'm Captain Kazimierz Jankowski, reporting for duty from the Eight Army in Egypt." Kaz half expected the Sergeant at the personnel office to object; Kaz was still wearing the uniform of a lieutenant. But there was no need for concern.

On the contrary, the Sergeant's response was a pleasant surprise. "Yes sir, we've been expecting you. I'm pleased to inform you, sir, that it's Major Jankowski. You've been promoted on the recommendation of Gen. Sikorski himself."

Jan snapped a mock salute to Kaz, asking if he would be able to see him except by appointment.

"And you, sir, are...?"

"Lt. Janusz Tomczak."

"Good news for you, too.... Capt. Tomczak."

It was now Kaz's turn to mock his friend. The Polish army must be desperate for midlevel officers.

"There's a reason," interjected the Sergeant, deadpan. It was scarcely his place to explain the promotions, but he mindlessly continued. "You'll be dealing with British and American officers. You get more respect with a higher rank."

"We are," thought Kaz, "about to become military politicians."

Kaz and Jan would be working with Brigadier Pawel Piotrowski, who in turn reported to Gen. Sikorski. Jan would expedite supplies going to the Polish Army; Kaz would work on strategy. Sikorski must have been impressed with the two men, particularly Kaz, during their encounter in Moscow.

The Polish Government was struggling with its role in the Allied coalition. Relations with the Soviets had gone from bad to worse. The families of Anders' soldiers—left behind in the Soviet Union—were having trouble getting out. The Soviets were harassing the Polish Embassy in Moscow in countless ways, both petty and provocative. For the hundredth time, Kaz wondered why God hated the Poles so, to sandwich them between Germans and Russians—worse still, between the two great tyrannies of the 20th century: National Socialism and Communism.

Kaz's first meeting with Gen. Sikorski and Brig. Piotrowski came after a few weeks. Only four men were present in the small conference room—the General, the Brigadier, Kaz, and one Maj. Radek Korbonski, who, like Kaz, had fought in Poland. He had escaped through Romania, thus avoiding both German and Soviet prison camps. Sikorski opened the conversation:

"Well, Piotrowski, where are we on the Home Army?"

The Home Army — or AK *(Armia Krajowa)* — had been established at the time of the Polish defeat, as a way to harass the Germans and prepare for an uprising.

"The British are still dragging their feet, sir. Even if we set aside the tricky question — how weapons could actually be delivered to the Army — it's not clear the British really want to. I've been nagging Col. Copplestone over at the Joint Chiefs, but he keeps fobbing me off."

"Keep trying," Sikorski urged. "Remind them of Churchill's threat, that he'd 'set Europe aflame' — arming the resistance and making the occupied countries ungovernable."

"If I could, sir, I've always been skeptical of Churchill's statement." Piotrowski was speaking. "He was most enthusiastic right after the fall of France. The British were desperate. Grasping at anything they could — anything that held the faintest hope of defeating the Boche."

"Churchill didn't really mean it?"

"He may have at the time, sir. But he's less desperate now. He can afford to be more realistic, recognizing what the resistance can and cannot do. He's settled on a limited role for them — collect intelligence and be ready to attack when the Huns are already vulnerable. For example, when the allies invade Poland or France."

"You may be right. But keep pushing for weapons, to build up the Army's strength. And we still face the really tough question — *when* should we commit the army?"

Sikorski turned toward Kaz and Korbonski. "We've been struggling with this question for months. I'd like new, independent opinions. Be prepared to give me your views the next time we meet."

"Yes, sir," the two majors replied in unison.

King George would be decorating Polish pilots. After the ceremony at Buckingham Palace, the fliers would be honored at the Polish Embassy.

It was a welcome break from the dreary routine of wartime London.

Sikorski appeared in a dashing dress uniform. He mingled easily with the crowd; he seemed to know almost everyone's name. Even when he didn't, he had a remarkable knack for pretending that he did.

"Flying Officer mumblemumble, this is Major mumblemumble."

"Sorry, I didn't quite get your name," said the Flying Officer.

"Starzenski," replied Major mumblemumble.

An officer in a Flight Lieutenant's uniform approached. He was limping slightly. Kaz stepped back to let him join the group.

"I'd like you all to meet Flight Lt. Stanislav Ryk" said Sikorski, drawing him into the group. "He's been with the RAF for two years. Shot down nine German planes."

"And was shot down twice myself," said Ryk with a wry smile.

Sikorski went around the small group, telling Ryk everyone's name. This time, as he had heard Major Starzenski's name, he pronounced it clearly. But the Flying Officer was still mumblemumble. Again, Sikorski carried it off so smoothly that the listeners wondered if they should have their hearing checked.

When the introductions ended, Kaz congratulated Ryk on his Distinguished Flying Cross. "We all admire your courage. Certainly gives us a sympathetic hearing with the British."

As the rest of the group drifted off, the two were left alone, comparing notes on the number one topic of the evening: how had they escaped from Poland? Kaz skipped the prison camps, and simply recounted his exit from the Soviet Union to Egypt. Ryk had managed to fly out in an old World War I contraption.

"Ryk? Ryk? We haven't met back in Poland, have we?"

"Not that I recall. Ryk is a common name where I come from."

"And that is?"

"Fifty kilometers west of Warsaw."

"Oh, that explains it. My wife grew up in that area."

There was a pause.

"Lost track of her when the war started," said Kaz sadly. "Can only pray she'll be there when I get back."

Ryk wrestled with his conscience. But only for a moment. His conscience lost. Why should I tell him? For that matter, why should I tell Anna?

Sikorski and the three other officers met again at the end of the week. He turned to Kaz and Korbonski, picking up where the previous meeting left off. How and when should the Home Army be used? To clarify his thinking, Sikorski wanted the two to express their disagreements. Jankowski should begin. Korbonski could act as devil's advocate, raising objections as Kaz went along.

"Even when I agree with Maj. Jankowski, sir?

"For the moment, only when you disagree. We'll get back to other objections later."

Kaz shifted uncomfortably in his chair. His relations with Korbonski were correct, but he couldn't describe them as warm or relaxed. The two were natural rivals for a senior position. Kaz didn't want to create additional stresses by engaging in debate; he was going to have to work with this man. But he could scarcely object to Sikorski's instructions. Perhaps they had something to do with the Byzantine struggles between Sikorski and the Polish President. Korbonski reported directly to the President. His views — expressed in the heat of debate — might give Sikorski a better fix on the President's tough views toward the Soviet Union.

It might also be Sikorski's way of dealing with the curse of leadership. His officers were eager to tell him exactly what he wanted to hear — or, more precisely, what they thought he wanted to hear. By the grapevine, Kaz had learned, with more than a touch of pride, that Sikorski considered him a rare jewel. When Kaz was asked his opinion, he actually gave it. Politely, but directly and without varnish.

Kaz took a deep breath.

"If it were just a matter of fighting Germans, the problem wouldn't be too difficult. We should strike as the Red Army approaches Warsaw, when the Germans are most vulnerable.... But it's more complicated, sir. Our interests differ sharply from the Russians. We all want to defeat Hitler. But they want a Communist regime in postwar Poland. We don't."

"Jankowski put his finger on the problem," interjected Brig. Piotrowski. "But there's one more actor — the Polish Communists.

They're gaining strength." Piotrowski had guts, too. That would scarcely come as good news to Sikorski.

Sikorski turned back to Kaz, who picked up his story.

"The Polish Communists may try to get the Home Army to revolt too soon, in the hope that they'll be wiped out. The Commies may taunt the Home Army — what good are they if they won't fight?"

"Exactly," said Sikorski.

Kaz continued: "But even suppose that the Home Army picks precisely the right time — they attack the Germans in the rear as Russians approach the Vistula River and Warsaw. Things may still turn out very, very badly."

"Why?" Sikorski asked. Kaz suspected that the General already knew, and simply wanted an independent opinion.

"Let's look at it from Stalin's viewpoint. Why shouldn't he simply hold up on the east side of the river, and let the Germans crush the Home Army? Seems ruthless, but he's already shown — with the massacres at Katyn and elsewhere — that he wants our leadership exterminated. And he did *that* when he was losing. Why should he have scruples once he starts winning? After all, he's the one who had his generals shot — and the prewar leadership of the Polish Communist Party, too — for reasons I still can't fathom."

"So I shouldn't have consented to the pleas of your General Anders?" asked Sikorski. "You should have been left in Russia, to advance with the Red Army. Then you could have come to the aid of the Home Army at a critical time."

"In my opinion, sir, the decision to leave the Soviet Union was correct."

Korbonski spoke up. "That's where I disagree."

"Ah, but perhaps that's because you were already in Britain. *You* weren't trapped in Russia."

"That's really unworthy of you, Jankowski. I think..."

Sikorski cut him off. "It's too late to undo the decision. But why was it correct, Jankowski?"

Kaz swallowed hard. "You're familiar with the arguments that General Anders made in Moscow, sir. The impossible position of any

Polish army fighting alongside the Russians—waking up every morning, wondering which way they'd have to point their guns.

"I see only one way out of our difficulties with Russia. That's if Churchill persuades the Americans to attack into the Balkans, through Crete and Greece—what he quaintly calls the 'soft underbelly of Europe.'

"I think the fighting would be tough," Kaz continued. "But it might solve our problem. If the Allies do thrust up into Central Europe, they can help reestablish a non-communist government in Poland. Having our army in Egypt increases the chances of such an attack. We would go into the Balkans with the British."

"I doubt the Americans would stand for such a strategy," interjected Piotrowski.

"Let's dream a bit," suggested Sikorski, glancing at his watch. "But not right now. When we meet on Monday, I want us to talk about a British-American invasion through the Balkans."

The meeting was over.

Kaz went to Jan for a favor. Jan kept in close contact with Brig. Piotrowski; they were working on plans to deliver weapons to the Home Army—the AK—if the British could ever be persuaded to supply them.

"You have contacts with the AK?" Kaz wanted to know.

"Not directly. But I know somebody who does."

"I've got to find out about Anna. Would the AK be able to get information—find out if she's OK?"

"You're sure you want to do that?"

"Of course. Not knowing, it's torture. What's the problem?"

"There's a risk someone from the AK will be picked up by the Germans. If they find out the AK is looking for Anna, they may think she's important and arrest her."

"Hadn't thought of that.... I'm really torn."

Jan pondered for a few minutes and added, "Why don't I check with the people here? Get their view, whether the AK can be safely asked about Anna. She was working with the Air Force Meteorological Project at Poznan?"

"Yeah. But let me think it over. I don't want to endanger her."

Kaz struggled for several days and then got back to Jan. If they could make a low-priority, inconspicuous request about Anna, would they please try? But nothing that would endanger her.

Jan didn't quite know how to handle his friend's request. There was no zero-risk way to find out about Anna.

He did, however, get back to Kaz several months later. Members of the AK had helped a number of people at the Meteorology Project escape to Romania. But Anna wasn't among them. They had absolutely no information on her. She simply vanished at the beginning of the war.

"Damn," thought Kaz. "She wasn't at Poznan when the war began, but at home. I should have asked them to check there."

He would have to give this more thought. A second request might be even more risky than the first.

When Sikorski reconvened the meeting, the group had been expanded. Starzenski—Major Mumblemumble—was also present. Kaz vaguely wondered why; only a few days ago, Sikorski obviously didn't know who Starzenski was. Perhaps he was a protégé of Brig. Piotrowski or the President.

Sikorski got right to the point. "We were going to dream a bit. What are the chances of getting our ideal outcome—an Anglo-American attack through the Balkans?

"Perhaps we might break this down into two questions," continued Sikorski. "First, what are the chances of an invasion across the Mediterranean? Second, if there is such an invasion, what are the chances it will be in Crete and then Greece?"

Korbonski obviously didn't want to play second fiddle again. He launched in.

"The British will push hard for a landing somewhere on the Northern side of the Mediterranean next year. They need to do something to reduce pressure from the Russians to attack across the Channel into France. They won't be ready for a cross-channel invasion. Premature action might lead to a catastrophe. The fiasco at Dieppe showed that.

"Now that the Americans have landed in Algeria," Korbonski added, "we're in a good position to drive the Jerries out of North Africa. I think Churchill has won this round. Next year, the invasion will be across the Mediterranean, not across the Channel."

Sikorski looked at Starzenski. "I agree," said Mumblemumble.

Kaz nodded.

"Well, that was easy," observed Sikorski. "General agreement. So let's look at the three Mediterranean options.

"One is Sardinia and then Corsica, followed by a landing in Southern France. Second is Sicily and then the Italian mainland. Third is our dream — Crete and then Greece. Let's start in the west: Sardinia-Corsica. For the moment, let's confine ourselves to military considerations; we can get back to the politics later."

Kaz took the opportunity. "The Sardinia/Corsica route has a big advantage, sir. We might get into France quickly. And France is the gateway to Germany. We might even avoid an invasion across the channel, with its horrible risks. It would create defensive nightmares for the Boche. Once we take Corsica, we would threaten a huge stretch of the coast of mainland Europe — all the way from the Spanish border to Rome."

"What about the disadvantages?" Sikorski was looking at Korbonski.

"There's a big one, sir. Our invading forces would be subject to attack from several sides — not only from the islands themselves, but also from France and Italy."

Kaz slipped in a final word. "The Sardinia-Corsica route became more feasible recently. The French scuttled their fleet at Toulon, to prevent it from falling into Nazi hands."

"O.K. What about Sicily/Italy?" Sikorski was addressing Mumblemumble.

"It also has attractions, sir. When we get to the mainland, we might once more avoid the risks of a big cross-channel invasion. But I doubt it. If we're trying to get at Germany, going through Sicily and Italy is a long, hard way 'round.

"To start, there's the invasion of Sicily itself. Germany's been using Sicily as its base for supplying North Africa; enemy forces there are much stronger than in Sardinia or Crete."

As Mumblemumble paused, Sikorski looked at Korbonski.

"The fight up through Italy might be very tough, sir—a narrow front in mountainous country. A moderate-sized enemy force might pin down a large Allied army."

"How about the third option—Crete and then Greece?" This time, Sikorski was addressing nobody in particular.

Korbonski jumped in with enthusiasm. "It has a huge advantage, sir. Once the Allies become established in Greece, they'll be able to launch air attacks on the Romanian oil fields. And, once they get to Romania, they'll completely cut off Hitler's oil. Without oil, his tanks and planes can't move. And the eastern Mediterranean is a backwater; Crete isn't nearly as heavily fortified as Sicily."

"The disadvantages?" asked Sikorski.

Neither Korbonski nor Mumblemumble seemed eager to answer.

Kaz picked up the challenge. "Most important, sir, is the problem of supplies. The lines to the eastern Mediterranean would be long. They'd also be vulnerable to attack from planes operating out of Sicily. It might be a real mess, unless we use the route around Africa and through the Suez Canal."

Sikorski sat thinking, then asked. "What's the bottom line?"

"Crete-Greece is most likely, sir," Korbonski replied quickly. "The Romanian oil fields are critically important for the Nazis. And, if we push the Americans and Brits, I think we can increase the chances."

"I agree," mumbled Mumblemumble.

"A tough call," said Kaz. "Big military advantages and disadvantages to each. My guess: The three options are about equal. One third chance for each." He paused. "If I *had* to pick one, I'd go with Sardinia-Corsica. The least risky way into France. But I'm looking at it from the Anglo-American perspective, putting aside the advantages we see in Greece."

Sikorski looked toward Piotrowski. "It seems, Brigadier, that we can no longer avoid politics."

Piotrowski responded. "Churchill's enthusiastic about the Balkans. He's said that, if an army is sent up through the Balkans, 'we can crush the retreating right flank of German armies and save middle Europe from the Russians.' But Stalin would be apoplectic. For exactly the same reason it appeals to Churchill and to us — it would a way to check postwar Russian power in central Europe."

"And the Americans?" Sikorski wanted to know.

"They don't want to alienate Stalin, sir," replied Piotrowski. "They don't want a repeat of the First World War. The Soviets made a separate peace; the Germans then concentrated their full fury on the Western Allies.

"In sum," concluded Piotrowski, "the chances of an invasion somewhere in the Mediterranean are high. The chances of it being Crete and Greece: not good."

"Jankowski?" Sikorski asked.

"I agree about the Russians; they'll be dead set against it. But the Americans, I'm not sure. You've been to America, sir, and have a much better understanding than any of us. The Yanks are presumably just as committed as the Brits to a non-communist Poland. Not to speak of all those Polish voters in Chicago."

"Korbonski?"

Korbonski paused; apparently he didn't know quite how to answer. He had complained to Kaz, how difficult it was to figure Americans out. They were, well, so *non-European;* they didn't seem interested in power politics. At least, not the down-in-the-gutter version practiced in Europe.

Finally he responded, again encouraging his superiors to support the eastern invasion. "I think the Americans can be brought along. And if the Americans and Brits are in favor, that's good enough. They don't need Russian approval; it will be their show. In other words, I think we have a more-than-sporting chance to get the Crete-Greece option — particularly if we push our case with the Americans."

Once more, Sikorski looked back toward Piotrowski.

"I reiterate. The Americans will back the Russians on this one. You don't need to be reminded, sir, that you've repeatedly asked Roosevelt for support in dealing with Stalin. Each time he puts you off—says he's 'evaluating the situation.'"

"Greece is still our best hope," said Korbonski quickly. "We might even be impertinent enough to remind the British why they went to war in the first place—to defend Poland's independence."

Sikorski paused thoughtfully before summing up. "We'll encourage the British to invade through Crete and Greece. But in a low-keyed way. We won't press the Americans unless they specifically ask our opinion. Anything we say may simply draw attention to the way our interests differ from those of the Soviets.

"And, oh, yes. Jankowski, Korbonski, Starzenski. You will leave discussions with the British and Americans to Brig. Piotrowski and me. If any American or Brit asks you about these matters, you will simply say it's above your pay grade. No comment—impertinent or otherwise."

"No, sir," replied Korbonski.

"Yes, sir," said Kaz at exactly the same time.

They looked at one another and chuckled. It broke the tension. They meant precisely the same thing: they understood Gen. Sikorski's instructions perfectly.

Unfortunately for the Poles, the Balkan option went nowhere. The target of the invasion was agreed: Sicily. Thus faded the last, fleeting hope for a non-communist Poland.

20
The Cruelest Month

A pril is supposed to be the cruelest month. For Anna, it was March. March 1943, to be precise.

She thought she had become hardened to her routine: reading grim stories in the newspaper over breakfast; then reading the even grimmer details when she got to work and skimmed the intercepts. But she was not prepared for March 1943.

Early in the month, she noticed a small piece in the *Times:* Jews in the Warsaw ghetto had taken up arms against their Nazi tormentors. But, from the Enigma intercepts, she already knew that, regardless of its heroism, the uprising was doomed. The Jews had acted in desperation, in response to ever-tightening harassment and murder at the hands of the Nazi tyrants. They were woefully under-equipped for a fight with the German army, with its machine guns, artillery and tanks.

She did not have information from Gestapo messages; the Gestapo version of Enigma still stubbornly resisted all efforts of the codebreakers. But she did have intercepts of messages from the SS divisions in Poland, and from these, she could deduce the sad truth: Himmler had ordered the "liquidation" of the ghetto.

Anna thought sadly of her Jewish friends at the University, particularly a young couple—Shimon and Sarah Persky—who were members of the mathematics club. She remembered how they had enjoyed working on puzzles together, how she had laughed at Shimon's understated humor. She recalled how the three young mathematicians had stayed up into the wee hours of the morning, trying to trisect an angle geometrically. They thought they had succeeded, but then, in the cool rationality of the morning, they detected the flaw: they, too, had failed. Anna realized how few Jewish people she had met until she got to the University.

As she was lost in thought, she casually glanced at an intercept of German traffic at the top of her inbox. It immediately brought the war home to her.

> TOP SECRET. IMMEDIATE AND URGENT.
> 6 MARCH, 1943.
> FROM: 112 INFANTRY DIVISION, SMOLENSK
> TO: GEN. KARL SPEIDEL, GENERAL STAFF, BERLIN.
> SUBJECT: MASSACRE IN KATYN FOREST
> ACTING ON INFORMATION PROVIDED BY CAPTURED ENEMY SOLDIERS, WE HAVE BEGUN A LIMITED EXCAVATION OF A MASS GRAVE IN THE KATYN FOREST, EAST OF SMOLENSK. WE HAVE DISCOVERED BODIES OF POLISH OFFICERS DRESSED IN WINTER UNIFORMS. THE STATE OF THE BODIES, AND ACCOMPANYING SCRAPS OF NEWSPAPER, INDICATE THAT THEY WERE KILLED BETWEEN JANUARY AND APRIL OF 1940. ACCORDINGLY, IT APPEARS THAT THE EXECUTIONS WERE CARRIED OUT BY SOVIET FORCES.
> HOWEVER, WE URGENTLY WARN THAT BULLETS FOUND IN THE BODIES ARE GERMAN, SPECIFICALLY FROM THE WALTHER 2. INSTRUCTIONS REQUESTED. SHOULD WE PROCEED WITH THE EXCAVATION, OR REBURY THE BODIES WE HAVE ALREADY DISINTERRED?
> VON WAGENHEIM.

The next page provided the decoded reply:

> TOP SECRET.
> 7 MARCH, 1943.
> FROM: GEN. KARL SPEIDEL, GENERAL STAFF
> TO: GEN. EMIL VON WAGENHEIM, 112 INFANTRY DIVISION, SMOLENSK.
> PRELIMINARY INQUIRIES INDICATE THAT GERMAN FORCES WERE NOT INVOLVED IN ANY MASSACRE IN THAT AREA. WE ARE PUZZLED THAT THE BULLETS ARE

FROM A WALTHER. ARE YOU CERTAIN THAT THEY
WERE NOT FROM A SIMILAR SOVIET MODEL?
RECOMMENDED ACTION: LIMITED EXCAVATION,
INVOLVING AS FEW TROOPS AS POSSIBLE. REPEAT. AS
FEW TROOPS AS POSSIBLE. TERMINATE EXCAVATION
WHEN YOU HAVE A GENERAL ESTIMATE OF THE
NUMBER OF BODIES. SAFEGUARD ANY EVIDENCE THAT
CONFIRMS AN EXECUTION DATE OF EARLY 1940.
THE EXCAVATION SHOULD NOT BE CONSIDERED A
PRIORITY AS LONG AS THE GROUND REMAINS FROZEN.
BUT IT SHOULD BE CARRIED OUT, AS SPECIFIED ABOVE,
AFTER THE SPRING THAW.

Anna sat silently reading and rereading the messages. A tear
trickled down her cheek; then others. She buried her head in her
hands.

"Oh, Kaz, Kaz. Why did it have to end this way?"

She reread the intercepts. Was there any hope for Kaz? Not really.
That was the camp where he had been held. She had already checked
and rechecked with the British Eighth Army, to see if he was among
the Polish soldiers who had left Russia for North Africa with Gen.
Anders. He was not.

Through the next two weeks, Anna felt as though she were
sleepwalking through the day. She couldn't contribute at work; she
thought of taking time off. But wartime travel was difficult, and she
didn't want to spend her days curled up at home nursing a bottle of
gin.

Yvonne began to sense that something was terribly wrong; she
came to Anna's office to chat. As tears ran down Anna's cheeks, she
told Yvonne about the Katyn massacre. Kaz was dead.

She felt weak and helpless. Many of her friends were losing loved
ones without coming apart. Gradually, the pain began to ease. One
weekend, while watching a mindless war movie at the local cinema,
she decided that her life had to go on. The next day, she dropped a
short note in the mail.

Ryk had now been in combat almost three years, with only one extended break. The time had come to be rotated to less hazardous duty; he was reassigned to a reconnaissance squadron. Three times a week, he would fly along the Norwegian coast, taking pictures of the fjords to make sure that the *Tirpitz* and other heavy German ships were still holed up. The navy wanted to know where they were; it didn't want them to surprise one of the convoys making the long, dangerous voyage around Northern Norway to Murmansk, carrying supplies to the Russian allies. Bomber Command was working up another plan to attack the *Tirpitz*, hoping to put it out of action and, with luck, sink it.

The bombers' job would be hazardous. For any real hope of striking their target, they would have to come in low, facing intense flak from antiaircraft batteries on the cliffs rising sharply out of the fjords. To aim the bombs accurately, they would have to fly straight and level for several minutes, making them even fatter targets. Ryk's job, in contrast, was simple; he could fly his Spitfire at 18,000 feet. The ack-ack would undoubtedly open up, but mainly for practice. At that height, there was little danger he would be hit.

The flight from Scotland and back was relatively safe. German fighters were urgently needed back home, to protect cities of the Third Reich from devastating air raids. To ease the boredom, Ryk played word games. Today, he was working on one of his childhood poems, translating it into English verse—that is, it had to rhyme in English, and have a similar meter to the original Polish. This was every bit as hard as it sounds. But he enjoyed the challenge. When he got a line right, he would jot it down on the pad attached to his right leg.

He got over the first fjord, and there it was, the *Tirpitz*. His plane was carving unpredictable curves to avoid antiaircraft fire. The batteries below were throwing up flack, but did not even come close. Ryk abruptly ended one of his curves, and flew straight and level for twenty seconds to get a good set of pictures. A piece of cake. Now on to the next fjord, where he repeated the process.

There was an off-chance that, warned by radar, the Germans would send up fighters to intercept him, particularly by the time he got to the second or third objective. His erratic, curving path would make it hard for them to catch him, but he nevertheless followed the survivor's habit—keeping his head on a swivel, surveying the sky to avoid nasty surprises. He also wanted to keep in practice; he would be returning to his fighter squadron within a month or two.

He therefore continued to scan the sky even as he flew back out over the North Sea, headed home to Scotland. When he got an inspiration with his poetry translation, he would look briefly down at his pad, but otherwise his eyes rotated from his instruments, to the right, behind, left, up, and down. About 100 miles out over the water, he spied a target of opportunity—a large four-engine German Condor patrol plane, prowling for Allied convoys. Ryk flipped a switch on his control panel; he would now be able to fire his guns. He banked to the right and down; within a minute, he was directly behind the Condor. It seemed almost unsporting, to attack a large aircraft with no tail gunner, but he had long since given up the idea that air combat was chivalrous.

With no worries about return fire, he closed slowly on the Condor, not opening fire until he was at short range directly behind the German aircraft. One quick burst from his machine guns; then a longer one. With the second burst, the whole tail section of the Condor began to disintegrate, spewing parts in all directions. Ryk suddenly realized his danger; he pulled the stick sharply backward to rise above the disintegrating plane. But too late. He could feel the impact as a chunk of the German tailplane struck his right wing.

The wing dropped sharply; Ryk panicked. The Spitfire—normally such a docile aircraft—had one deadly vice: it was difficult to pull out of a spin. He instinctively pushed the stick hard forward, applying full left rudder. Within a few seconds, he had regained control, and gradually pulled back until he was once again level. He gingerly banked leftward, turning his nose toward Scotland and home. He was vaguely aware of the Condor plunging toward the cold sea.

Because of the damage to his wing, he had to keep the stick off center, to the left, to maintain his heading. He checked his instruments; his air speed was slower than normal with his throttle setting, but that was presumably the result of damage to the wing. Even with the extra fuel consumption, he should have no trouble reaching his base. He just hoped that he would be able to control the Spit as he was slowing, coming in for a landing. Perhaps he should gingerly try to lower his flaps a few degrees, to see how it affected his control of the plane, and see if the flaps were damaged, too. On second thought, that could wait. He would try his experiments when he got over Scotland. If anything went wrong, he could parachute to earth rather than into the frigid North Sea.

Then he noticed that the engine was running roughly and beginning to overheat. Why? Perhaps some of the chaff from the Condor's tail was blocking the air intake. To compensate, he began to thin the fuel mixture. That helped; the engine was now running less roughly and the temperature rising less rapidly.

But it was still going up. He thinned the mixture even further — as far as his control would allow. Now the temperature stabilized, but he was beginning to lose altitude. More power. Now he held his altitude, but the temperature started rising again.

This was beginning to look serious. No matter how he tinkered with power and mixture settings, he couldn't maintain his height without the engine getting hotter. He even tried lowering his flaps slightly, in the hope that the added lift would help him maintain altitude. That didn't work, either.

After another ten minutes, he realized he wasn't going to make it; the engine heat had already edged into the red zone. He radioed a brief report: the *Tirpitz, Scharnhorst,* and *Prinz Eugen* were in their fjords, as expected. He had intercepted a Condor and shot it down. But he was going down about 50 miles Northeast of Scotland. Mayday, mayday. He continued to send the distress signal, giving the homing stations a fix on his position.

As he slipped below 3,000 feet, the time had come. The water was much too choppy to ditch his plane. Unfortunate, because March is not the time for a dip in the North Sea. He reached behind his seat for the inflatable raft. He was wearing a life vest, but the raft would give him a chance to survive; he would, he hoped, be able to climb out of the icy water. He slid the canopy back. If the right wing wanted to dip so much, he would let it — all the way over until the plane was on its back. He released his seat and shoulder belts with a quick jerk of the pin, and found himself falling through the air.

When Anna got to the office on Tuesday, she found a note: she was to see the security officer, Maj. Phipps, at once. When she entered his office, he invited her to sit down, and expressed condolences at the loss of her husband. He wondered if she would like some time off. She said no; she found that work was good for her morale. Well, he replied, if you change your mind, please let me know.

Then he got to the point. He slid a handwritten letter across the desk. It was her note to Ryk. She had written to say that she would look forward to hearing from him. Kaz was dead.

"I understand your distress," Phipps began. Anna doubted that he really did. "But you know the importance of secrecy."

Anna didn't see the point. Clearing his throat, Phipps continued:

"You sent a letter without clearing it through the censor's office — a breach of security in itself. More important, the note contains information that might be of use to the Germans."

This is ridiculous, thought Anna. A typical, paranoid security officer. "I can't see how. They can scarcely know who Kaz was. Even if they did, I can't see how his death would mean anything to them."

"Ah, but the point is, how did you find out? Through an intercept. It's of course unlikely that they would tie his death to the Katyn intercept. But it's just possible; they may be trying to put together a list of those killed at Katyn, to use against the Russians.

"We can't rule out the chance that Ryk might be shot down and fall into enemy hands. The Germans like to start their interrogations with chitchat, then move to personal stuff, to put the prisoner at ease. Ryk would have no idea that he shouldn't mention Kaz's death; he would have no idea that it was based on secret sources."

Phipps looked her straight in the eye. "At least, I trust he wouldn't."

"No, *no*. I never talk about my work outside Blechley Park — I mean BP." Anna was flustered.

"Because of your contributions, we'll let it go this time. But in the not too distant future, we'll be invading France. You know how important it is to keep our work secret, how many thousands of lives are at stake. "

"Of course."

"That means it's important to guard against even a minuscule risk that the Jerries will find out about BP. *Nobody* here is indispensable, not even Turing. You're aware, how hard we had to finagle to get a Pole on our team, even if you do have an English mother. If you break security—unless you do so intentionally—you won't be shot; we just said that at the beginning to get your attention. But if we do let you go, we won't just let you wander out onto the street. Remember Nigel Winston?"

Anna nodded. She had talked to him once or twice before he suddenly disappeared.

"He got careless. Not treasonous, just careless. He's now working as a supervisor, building a road through Alberta and the Yukon to Alaska. If you violate security rules again, I'm sure we can find a job in the Yukon for you, too."

"Yes, sir." Anna was surprised how meek her voice was.

Phipps' tone softened. He again expressed his condolences; she should come to him if he could be helpful in any way. He had to step out to check on something; would she please wait a few moments?

As he went through the outer office, he nodded to Yvonne, who had been waiting. She went into his inner office and closed the door.

"Well, I see you survived. Hope he wasn't too tough on you."

"Let's just say I've had more pleasant conversations.... But how come you're here? You're not going to give me the third degree, too?"

Yvonne looked uncomfortable. Anna thought: she really has come to reinforce Phipps' message. This *is* laying it on. Then Yvonne responded:

"There's a quotation from Shakespeare, something like, 'when sorrows come, they come not single spies, but in battalions.' I think it's from Macbeth."

"Julius Caesar was the only Shakespeare I read."

"That was just a cowardly way to introduce my message. I'm sorry, but there's more bad news. I'm afraid Ryk's missing. Went down over the North Sea. But there's hope. He got off a mayday and almost certainly had a chance to bail out or ditch."

Anna could see Ryk bobbing in the freezing waters. Her eyes again filled with tears. Yvonne squeezed her hand. They sat silently for a while, then hugged and parted.

When Phipps got back to his office, Anna had left. There was a message for him to call Squadron Leader Lester Bernard at Fighter Command.

"Hello, Bunkie. Hope you have news about Ryk."

"Yes, Phil, and it's good. It was too late to send out a plane to search last night. But a Catalina took off half an hour before first light — they wanted to get an early start. They flew straight down the heading of his last transmission and found him just as dawn was breaking. He sent up a lovely red flare. They landed on the water without any difficulty; it was calm this morning. Anyhow, he's now in hospital up in Scotland. The night was harrowing. He got dunked before he got up on his raft, and he's suffering from severe exposure.

"But he'll be OK. In fact, he'll be ready to resume flying within a fortnight."

They rang off.

Phipps sat thinking for some time, sporadically drumming his fingers on his desk. He then asked his secretary to get Bernard back.

"When Ryk gets back to flying, you'll keep him up there in Scotland?"

"Not very long. Pilots are rotated back to combat duty within a few months."

"You couldn't keep him up there indefinitely?"

"We could. But it might be difficult. He was already getting itchy after a few weeks up here. If he's kept indefinitely, he'll want to know why. I don't suppose you could give me any hint — what the problem is?"

"Not really. But it's important he's not captured. He may have very sensitive information. The problem is, he doesn't *know* it's sensitive; he won't be on his guard. And we can't tell him what it is."

"If it's that important, the Norway run may not be the job for him, either. It's not very likely, but some day, one of our Spits may be shot down. Particularly if the Jerries want to get the *Tirpitz* out to sea, they might commit fighters to attack one of our planes."

"Ummm...."

"Perhaps there's a way out. We could send him to Winnipeg—a tour of duty as an instructor in the advanced fighter training program. His English is more than adequate. He'd be a natural... so much combat experience."

"Sounds great. How soon could he be off?"

"As soon as he's healthy. We have a plane leaving Scotland once or twice a week. They fly pilots back to Gander, where they pick up more bombers to ferry back across the Atlantic."

"Let me know when he's gone."

Phipps picked up the phone to call Anna, but then decided he had better think about it. After a moment, he replaced the phone in its cradle.

It was times like this he didn't much like his job.

Yvonne wished she could do more for her friend, who was in obvious pain. She asked Anna to drop by her office to chat; they would have more privacy in her room than in Hut 6.

When Anna arrived, Yvonne was out; apparently she had been called away on some urgent matter. A note, in Yvonne's distinctive scrawl, was stuck to the door: Anna was to go in and wait. As she stepped into her old office, memories came flooding back—particularly that musty smell from the ancient carpet. But Yvonne had made some changes. Papers were stacked even higher on the desk, and a second desk was snuggled into the corner; it too was piled high with neat stacks of papers. Anna began to wander around the room, looking at the pictures on the wall. Most showed Yvonne's family during the happy days before the war. Several men in uniform gazed calmly down from their frames. They all seemed so young!

The door to Denniston's office was slightly ajar, and, as Anna walked by, she was about to close it. She stopped short when she heard a heated discussion in the next room.

"... completely out of the question. They spent several years in Vichy France."

"But this is idiotic. Rejewski has a marvelously original mind. He figured out the internal wiring of Enigma rotors. And he developed the first code-cracking machine back in prewar Poland. Zygalski provided us with a wealth of information just before the war started."

"The answer is no. When they left Poland, they chose France, not Britain."

"Not true. Not true." Denniston's voice was rising. "They went straight to the British embassy in Romania; they offered us their services. The boneheads in the embassy turned them away, asking them to come back later. The French treated them like royalty. What were they supposed to do? Let the police chase them all over Romania while the nincompoops at the Foreign Office shuffled papers?"

"Sorry. MI5 won't give them clearance."

"Don't those idiots realize how much the Poles went out of their way to help us?" Denniston's visitor was apparently from MI5; Denniston was so angry that he apparently didn't care if he was insulting his guest. "Even after they went to France, they met with Turing to help with the design of his machine. Rejewski would be invaluable in developing new machines. They're urgently needed."

"Sorry, but there's a blanket rule: *no* top security clearances for anyone who voluntarily stayed in Vichy France. MI5 has already assigned them to work on codebreaking."

"What? What? They can work on codebreaking? You mean they can come here, even without clearances?" Denniston was confused.

"No. No. That's not what I said. They'll be working on lower-level ciphers, not the Enigma. They're attached to the Polish Army, and won't be anywhere near Bletchley Park."

"Low-level ciphers? This is crazy. You're putting brain surgeons to work dissecting frogs."

"Sorry. The answer is no. The decision's final." Alastair's visitor showed no signs of anger; he was cool but firm.

"I can't accept that."

"Too bad. You'll have to. And don't don't think you can run around MI5 to the PM. We'll block you. Before you do anything, think about it.... Do you really want to go to war with us?" As the visitor ended the conversation, there was a threatening edge in his voice.

Anna jumped; she was startled by Yvonne entering the room. Anna pretended that she was still doing the rounds, looking at pictures. Yvonne pretended not to notice. But she filed one more thing away in her mental "to do" file. When the occasion arose, she would repeat the warning to Anna: she was not to contact Poles, even in Britain, without checking first with security.

"We haven't had much chance to talk lately. You've had a tough time," Yvonne said softly.

"Sorry; I guess I've been moping. But two men in one month. It's just too much. Kaz was the real blow. We hardly had any marriage at all—only six weeks. I really don't know how I felt about Ryk. When we were together, Kaz was always between us. But now.... "

"I wouldn't give up on Ryk. Lots of pilots are picked up from the sea."

"But after ten days? The North Sea's not exactly a swimming pool. Even if he ditched and got into a raft without getting soaked, he wouldn't be able to survive this long." Her tears began to well up, as she thought of Ryk's slow death in the frigid waters. Maybe he had been lucky enough to be killed outright when his plane crashed.

"He may already have been picked up, and Phipps not informed. You know how sloppy things can get."

"Yeah, but not that sloppy.... Maybe I should run around Phipps to Fighter Command, to see if I can get any information directly."

"I wouldn't. Phipps would undoubtedly find out. You know how he is about contacts with the outside world. Particularly after your little love-note."

Yvonne wished she hadn't said that; it wasn't very kind. After a few moments of frosty silence, an odd half-smile crossed her face. She walked toward her desk, closing Alastair's door as casually as she could manage. Puzzled, Anna looked at her friend and waited. Yvonne took a deep breath, then spoke in hushed tones.

"I'm not supposed to tell you, but Ryk was picked up the morning after he was shot down."

"What? And Phipps knew?" Anna couldn't believe it.

"Yes. Found out the same day."

"Oh!... And how long have *you* known?" There was an accusing edge in Anna's voice.

"Only two days. But I was ordered not to tell you."

"Why the hell not, if I might ask?"

"They wanted to get Ryk out of Britain before they told you. They didn't want you to contact him. He left on a plane for Canada this morning. When Phipps gets back from London tomorrow, I'm sure he'll tell you first thing."

"That bastard!"

"Do me a favor. When he tells you, be sure to act surprised." Yvonne paused. "I don't want to end up in Siberia with you."

"The Yukon, you mean."

"Sorry. Shouldn't joke about such things with someone from Eastern Europe."

They sat there without saying anything for a few minutes. Anna was taking stock.

"You know," she finally said, "I wonder if I've done everything I can to find out about Kaz—to find out if anybody really knows if he's dead or alive."

"I'm not sure how you'd do that. We can't exactly send a message to the Kremlin, asking them if they murdered Kaz."

"I meant"—there was a touch of exasperation in Anna's voice—"I haven't turned over all the stones here in Britain."

"But you were with me when we got Pickersgill to check—and recheck—the Eighth Army's list of Poles who got out with Anders."

"But that's not the only way people got out.... Me, for example."

"So what we need to do is check, not just with the British Army, but with someone who might keep track of all the Poles who got out—and maybe even Poles who escaped captivity but are still in Poland. Sounds like the government in exile."

"Exactly. But Phipps will go round the bend if I call the Polish government. We'll have to do it through channels."

"Let's do it right away. With Phipps still in London, we can go to Pickersgill. He's more likely to be cooperative."

Pickersgill was. As soon as the two women had explained what they wanted, he picked up the phone and had his secretary put through a call to Col. Mikolaj at the Polish government offices in London.

"Hello, Col. Mikolaj, this is Commander Hew Pickersgill, with British Intelligence. I'd like to get some information. Would you like me to leave my number, so you can check and call me back?"

"Depends on what the information is. Try me." Pickersgill was the only one to hear the reply; the two women had to guess what was going on from just one side of the conversation.

"Could you see if you have any information on a Kazimierz Jankowski? At the beginning of the war, I believe he was a Lieutenant" — he glanced over to Anna, who nodded. "In the seventh cavalry" — Anna nodded again.

"Might I ask the reason for this request?"

"Very simple. His wife works with me, and she's trying to find out what happened to him. Do you think you could track down information on him?"

"Yes, it might be possible." Mikolaj paused for dramatic effect. "In fact, he works with us. On the second floor of this building. Shall I try to get hold of him, and call you right back?"

"That would be splendid." Pickersgill gave him the number and hung up.

He wondered if he should tell Anna. But why spoil the surprise? He said simply, "Col. Mikolaj thinks that he might be able to find some record. If he does, he'll call back."

Pickersgill didn't want to miss the moment; he decided to keep the two women in his office for half an hour or more, if necessary. "Perhaps I might be more helpful to Mikolaj if we had details — when you last had contact with your husband, and what you've done to try to locate him. Of course, I recall the contacts with the Eighth Army."

There was little additional information that Anna could add; she talked about his interests, what sort of people he might contact if he escaped.

Mikolaj sent down a message for Kaz to come up to see him. Right away. The answer came back, he can't. He's in a meeting with Sikorsky; John Winant, the U.S. Ambassador to the United Kingdom;

and Averell Harriman, Roosevelt's special envoy to Moscow. Too bad, replied Mikolaj; I need him right now. And I mean, *at once.*

"This had better be important," said Kaz, arriving out of breath. Apparently he had come up the stairs two at a time.

"It is. Someone wants to talk to you." Mikolaj picked up the phone and asked his secretary to return Pickersgill's call.

"On the phone? You interrupted me for *that*? Who the hell is it? Winston Churchill?"

"Somebody more important," said Mikolaj with an enigmatic smile. "Much more important."

"Hello? Commander Pickersgill? This is Mikolaj returning your call. Major Jankowski is here. Would you please put your party on?" He handed Kaz the phone.

"This is Jankowski," said Kaz, somewhat irritably in spite of himself.

"Kaz? Oh Kaz, darling."

Kaz turned his back. He didn't want Mikolaj to see his tears.

First thing next morning, Phipps was walking down the hall toward his office as he arrived back at work. He met Anna.

"I've got great news. Ryk was picked up. He's alive and well. He..."

"That's nice," Anna interrupted, smiled slightly, stepped around Phipps and went on down the hall.

Phipps looked after her. I *never* will understand women.

He soon had an explanation. When he got to his office, Pickersgill came across the hall to give him the news: Anna's husband was alive. In London. He had arranged two weeks leave, and Pickersgill had given her the two weeks off, too. She would be out of the office, starting at noon.

"Two weeks? Without checking with me? That's a bit nervy," thought Phipps, and began to scowl. Then, in spite of himself, he broke into a smile.

21
A Regiment of Troops

One good spy is worth a regiment of troops.
Sun-tzu, Chinese general and strategist, fourth century B.C.

Before leaving for her two-week vacation, Anna spent the last morning working on her cover story, the story she would tell Kaz. She would be seeing him regularly—whenever he could get away from the army—and Phipps insisted that she keep her work secret from him. Phipps wanted to know what she would tell him.

It had to be good. She was unnerved by Phipps' reaction to her note to Ryk, even though she was trying to forget that she had ever written it. Yvonne came to her aid once more.

Yvonne was in a similar situation. Her new husband, Harry, was a Lieutenant in the Navy, but did manage to get back home from time to time. Luckily, her elderly parents were living in the nearby village of Milton Keynes, about five miles north of Bletchley Park, approximately half way between BP and an RAF communications center. Yvonne had an obvious pretext to live in the village: she was there in case her parents needed help. And—so her story went—she was working at the RAF station.

The security officer at the station was in on the plot, or at least the part he needed to know. Harry was given his telephone number. If Harry called, the security officer would say she was busy. The officer would then call Phipps, who would have Yvonne get in touch with Harry. Other than saying that she worked at the RAF station, Yvonne was to be vague. Her work was classified, and Harry was not the sort to pry.

Yvonne suggested that Anna share her flat; lodgings were exceedingly scarce. She could also share the cover story. It would fit nicely with her earlier work for the "Air Force Meteorology Project." Yvonne would be happy to move out—back to her parents' home—for the next two weeks. In fact, she said with a smile, she would move out whenever Kaz could arrange a leave. When Harry arrived—well, they'd have time to talk about that later.

Kaz would meet Anna at the one and only village pub for dinner at six o'clock, scarcely time for her to get her things moved into Yvonne's flat and make it look as though she had been living there for some time. She got to the pub and took a place at a table in a dark corner, facing the door. It will, she thought, be interesting to watch his expression as he glances around the pub, looking for me.

Nothing of the sort happened. A jeep drove up. Kaz jumped out and briefly spoke to the driver. Anna felt herself drawn toward the door; by the time Kaz entered, she was in the small lobby to greet him. They threw their arms around each other.

She heard someone clearing his throat; they were blocking the doorway. She opened her eyes.

"Oh, hello, Sir Andrew." She shuffled sideways to let him and his companion pass, but held her lover's arms to prevent him from snapping to attention. "Nice to see you again."

"And you, too, Anna.... Even though I'm not wearing my dress uniform."

Anna closed her eyes; her lips again met Kaz.

"Your place, or here?" Kaz asked as they broke for air. Then he realized she might not have much to eat in her flat.

"Here, if it's OK with you." She, too, realized there wasn't much to eat at her new home. "There's so much I'm dying to hear—how you got out, what you're doing in Britain. Besides, the evening will have added spice—anticipation."

"And who was that?" asked Kaz as they sat down.

"Just an old lover."

Kaz looked crushed.

"Sorry, darling. I shouldn't joke. Particularly not now.... It was Admiral Cunningham." They were holding hands across the table; she squeezed first one, then the other.

In response, Kaz squeezed her hands back. He was getting over the shock.

"And what was that bit about his uniform?"

She improvised quickly. "He visited our base, to see if we could improve our weather forecasting for the Arctic convoys to Russia." She then recounted the story of the newly-whitewashed wall. For the umpteenth time, Kaz suspected he was not getting the whole truth—maybe not even half. He wondered how three young women working on weather forecasting would meet an admiral—even more, how they could get away with backing him into a whitewashed wall. And how could he know her well enough to remember her name? It was best not to ask; whatever the charade, he would willingly participate. They had better things to talk about.

They started at the beginning; Anna wanted to know about the battle near Warsaw. Kaz took her up to the time of his first capture by the Russians. She wondered how he had managed to escape from Katyn. Without elaboration, Kaz told her, deleting the deaths of the two prisoners on the hillside. He also deleted the meeting with Stalin in Moscow; Anna was not the only one who had secrets to keep. He talked about their training in Russia and their exodus to Egypt, where they joined the British Eighth Army.

"The Eighth Army?" Anna was astonished. And more than a bit put out. She had tried to find out if he were with the Poles who got out to North Africa. But the Eighth Army told her—repeatedly—that he was not.

Kaz explained. He and Jan were using false identities, initially to avoid trouble with the Russians, and later because they were worn down by the tone-deaf administrative officers of the Eighth Army.

Then he wanted her story. How, he asked, did she get out of Poland? She recounted her adventure. A childhood friend who owned an old triplane. Their deadly game of hide and seek, darting among clouds as the unwelcome rays of daylight brightened the eastern sky, betraying them to the Luftwaffe.

Kaz suddenly had an uncomfortable premonition, where the conversation was headed. I've got to have time to think. He had already drained his half and half. Would she please excuse him? He needed to find the loo.

He splashed water on his face and glowered at the mirror. I bet it was that sonofabitch. He stole eight months of my life—what could have been the best eight months. Why couldn't he tell me when we met at Sikorski's reception? The answer was all too obvious.

Kaz splashed more water on his face and started to swear. Then he got hold of himself. Ryk was a cad. But marriage was built on trust. He had no reason to doubt Anna, and certainly no reason to be angry at her. He wouldn't mention the meeting at Sikorski's reception. With a faint smile, he thought how noble he was.

He had been away too long. As he walked unsteadily back toward the table, he could see that Anna was worried.

"Sorry. I suddenly felt lightheaded. Nothing to worry about. Guess I haven't been getting enough sleep. I'm afraid I left you up in the air, trying to get away from Göring's goons." He suppressed the question he was eager to ask: "who was her childhood friend, the pilot?"

She described their search for a landing field, how they risked touching down on an unknown island, and how, luckily, they found that the island was Danish. She spoke warmly of the prefect of police. She guessed what the police officer had said in his phone conversation, switching back and forth from mock Scandinavian to a mock German accent.

"Allo?"

"Zees isst yur friendlich Geshtapo offitziert."

"Yah?"

"Ich vant zee plane und zee kriminalz zat landet."

"Plane? Vhot plane?

"Floon by zee kriminalz von Polandt."

"No kriminalz haf flooohn in."

Kaz smirked as Anna stretched out "flooohn." She got back to the main story.

"We got out to Sweden on a boat that left within a few hours. I only hope our policeman friend didn't get into trouble. Especially after the

Germans occupied Denmark. Too bad we didn't make it all the way to Sweden in the Red Baron.

"Anyhow, I had no difficulty getting out of Sweden—my English mother and the fact that I'm a civilian."

"Working for the Air Force," Kaz added.

"Oh dear, I must have forgotten to tell them about that," she responded with a twinkle in her eye. "The one I was worried about was Ryk. He might be interned as a Polish Air Force officer, Poland being one of the belligerents and all. But he chiseled and wheedled his way out. I met him again at a party about a year ago."

"So did I."

"Stanislaw Ryk?"

"Yes. At a reception. He had just been given the DFC by the King himself."

"I know...." There was an extended silence, with just a hint of electricity in the air. "But how did you guess that it was him, when I only said 'Ryk'?"

"A Polish Air Force officer. Named Ryk. Flew out of Poland in an ancient plane. Grew up in your part of the country. Kind of narrows things down."

"My part of the country? How did you know that?"

"He told me he came from an area just west of Warsaw."

Anna knew there was something missing. "And?"

Kaz paused. "And I told him that was where my wife came from."

Again, it was Anna's turn to pause. "You were introduced to him by name?"

"Yes."

Then she asked, very slowly, "He didn't ask if your wife's name was Anna?"

"No."

So much for noble intentions.

Later, when Ryk finished his year-long tour of duty in Winnipeg and came back to Britain, Anna coldly refused to see him again. Even after Kaz was sent to France. Particularly after Kaz was sent to France. And even though Ryk invited her to accompany him to Buckingham Palace, where he was to receive another decoration. In fact, when he mentioned the Palace, she got in just one quick request before hanging up: send the button back.

He never did.

10 April 1943. Prime Minister Sikorski's Conference room, London.

Kaz had been summoned to an emergency meeting with Gen. Sikorski. This time, Jan had been invited, too. Something was up.

When the small group met, it now consisted of Sikorski, Brig. Piotrowski, Maj. Korbonski, Kaz, and Jan; Maj. Mumblemumble Starzenski was on a trip to North Africa. Sikorski said that the Nazi's "Reichsminister for Public Enlightenment," Joseph Goebbels, had just made an announcement over Radio Berlin. He read from a sheet of paper:

> A mass grave has been discovered in the Katyn Forest, near Smolensk in the Soviet Union. The victims were officers of the Polish Army. They were each killed by a single shot to the back of the head. Many had their hands tied behind their backs. It is known that the Soviet Union had a Prisoner-of-War camp near Smolensk, where Polish officers captured in the 1939 campaign were detained. The evidence is clear. The Soviets have shot prisoners. The barbarism of the Bolsheviks is once more on display for the world to see.

Now Jan knew why he had been invited.

Sikorski continued. "We're already getting inquiries from the British press. They want to know: Can we confirm or deny the German account?"

Sikorski looked at Kaz.

"I recommend we confirm it, sir. We can scarcely deny it. I know it's true. Jan knows it's true. The truth has got to come out sooner or later. Why not now?"

"Perhaps this is worth thinking about, sir." Piotrowski was speaking. "There are several complications. First is the evidence. Jankowski and Tomczak escaped from what, to us, is clearly an execution. But how will we deal with skeptics in the press? Doubters will point out that Jankowski and Tomczak never actually saw anybody shot. The domestic Communists and the Russians will create a hullabaloo: the Polish prisoners were simply being moved, and it was the Germans themselves who did the dastardly deed.

"Even more important: we have to worry about our touchy relations with Moscow. As you know, sir, the Soviets have not only been harassing members of our embassy in Moscow. They have also arrested some of them, in violation of diplomatic norms. If we confirm the German charges now, it will put unbearable strains on our relations.

"We certainly can't contradict Radio Berlin," Piotrowski concluded. "But there may be a third option: to say that the evidence needs to be studied."

"Tomczak?" Sikorski wanted Jan's opinion. Jan's answer astonished Kaz.

"Sir, what happened at Katyn was an atrocity; I want to weep every time I think of all those fine young men — our friends — who are now dead. However, Brig. Piotrowski's argument has force. We must think of the living, not the dead. We need to think: what's good for the future of Poland?"

Jan paused for a moment, then added: "Frankly, sir, I'm not anxious to come forward as a witness. Particularly when there is no chance that the murderers will be punished. I'm concerned about my relatives in Poland. We're going to win the war. But, in the process, the Red Army will invade and capture Poland. I don't trust them. They've murdered our friends. They're perfectly capable of killing my relatives still in Poland."

Sikorski looked back toward Kaz. Kaz was silent; he'd have to think this through. Sikorski turned again to Piotrowski: "More specifically, what do you recommend, Brigadier?"

"Sir, we need some independent, credible group to evaluate the evidence. Perhaps the International Red Cross."

A sergeant entered the room and handed Sikorski a note. He read the unsurprising news aloud. Radio Moscow categorically denied Goebbels' charges. If there were mass graves, the Nazis themselves were guilty. It was part of their extermination policy as their Panzer divisions swept eastward during the dark early days of the war.

Sikorski invited any final comments from his colleagues; there was none. He wound up the meeting by saying he wanted to consult the President. They would be informed of the decision in due course.

12 April 1943, 14:00 hrs. The Library. Polish Government Offices, London

"I shall," said Brig. Piotrowski, "begin by reading a very brief statement and then take questions."

> The criminal Government of Nazi Germany has announced that they have uncovered a mass grave of Polish officers. They allege that the officers were murdered by the Soviet Union. The Soviet Government has charged the Nazis with the crime.
>
> The Polish Government believes that an impartial institution should investigate the death of our officers, to determine who is responsible. We recommend that the International Red Cross be asked to undertake this difficult and unpleasant task.

"You will notice," Piotrowski concluded, "that the statement is for release at 14:00 hrs. today; you may use it immediately."

It was scarcely necessary to read the announcement, as copies had already been placed on the seats before the reporters came in. But it did give the reporters from the *BBC, The Times, The Manchester Guardian,* and *CBS* a chance to frame their questions.

Question 1: "Sir, were you aware of a mass grave of Polish officers?"

"We are aware that thousands of our men are missing. In wartime, it is often impossible to get information on missing personnel."

Question 2: "So you didn't know they had been murdered?"

"As I said, it is difficult to get reliable information. That's why we're asking for a Red Cross investigation."

Question 3: "Radio Moscow says that 'If there are bodies, the Germans did it.' The Russians seem to be suggesting they don't really know whether killings took place or not. If this is the case, how can they possibly know the Germans did it?"

"You would have to go to the Soviet embassy for an answer to that question. One possible explanation is that the Soviets don't doubt the existence of a mass grave. There are mass graves dotted all over the

Western part of the Soviet Union. If the Soviets didn't kill our soldiers, that would indicate that the Germans did, wouldn't it?"

There were another dozen questions, but they essentially repeated the first three, with Piotrowski repeating his answers.

Two hours later, Jan burst breathlessly into Kaz's office.

"We've got trouble. Big trouble."

Kaz looked up. Jan continued:

"Just before two—less than five minutes before Piotrowski began his statement to the press, Goebbels came on Radio Berlin. He made exactly the same proposal—that the massacre be investigated by the International Red Cross."

That couldn't be a coincidence. How the hell did the Nazis know that the Poles were going to appeal to the Red Cross?

Good question.

Whatever the answer, the Germans were obviously trying to cause trouble between the Soviets and the Polish Government in London.

They succeeded.

The Soviet Commissariat for Foreign Affairs summoned the Polish ambassador in Moscow and handed him a note:

> The Polish government in London and Nazi gangsters have made the same, simultaneous request for a Red Cross investigation. They are clearly conspiring to defame the Soviet Union. Accordingly, the Soviet Union no longer recognizes the London clique as the legitimate government of Poland.

14 April 1943. Prime Minister Sikorski's Office, London

"That bastard Goebbels knew about our statement before we released it. There must be a German agent in this building. Your job is to find him—or her. Quickly."

Sikorski was talking to Cyn and Rowecki, the chief security officers in the Polish government's London offices. Cyn, the senior officer, responded.

"Perhaps, sir, we might begin by making a list of those who knew about our appeal to the Red Cross."

Sikorski responded, identifying the five people present when the topic was discussed. He could vouch for Brig. Piotrowski. The investigation should focus on the three junior officers—Korbonski, Jankowski, and Tomczak. Perhaps, on second thought, they ought to include Piotrowski.

Cyn and Rowecki glanced at one another.

"There was no one else in the room, sir?" Cyn asked.

"No. Oh, wait a minute. Sgt. Szostak came in briefly. But I don't think he could have heard our decision. Come to think of it, we didn't make a final decision at the time. Just a tentative decision to appeal to the Red Cross."

"Did any of the three officers *definitely* know of the decision, sir?"

"Yes, Korbonski. He worked with Piotrowski on the press release."

"So others could have known—the clerks who typed the release, and anyone else who handled it."

"I'm not sure; you might check on that."

Within two hours, Cyn came back to Sikorski. He had questioned Korbonski, who pointed out that the clerks could not be responsible. Of course, they knew that there would be a press conference and when it would occur. They had informed the media. A whole lot of people knew about the timing of the press conference—including lots of people in the press. But very few knew about the Red Cross. The clerks did not get the statement to type until 20 minutes before the press conference; he and Piotrowski had been working on the wording until that time.

Cyn suggested a plan of action, and left.

Sikorski had his secretary summon Korbonski.

"I've been talking to a senior member of the British government, major, and they've agreed to drop weapons to the Home Army tomorrow night, at point Cmk-137." The map of Poland had been divided with a very detailed grid; the Home Army would be able to identify the location precisely. "I'd like you to send a message to the Home Army, informing them of the drop. As usual, you can go to Cyn to handle communications with Poland. The message should be sent at once.

"And, oh, yes. As I said, I've arranged this directly at a senior level. Your contacts in the British Army are unlikely to know about the drop.

Don't mention it to them. Or to anyone else except Communications, of course."

Sikorski then called in Jan. His instructions were similar to those of Korbonski, with one exception. The location of the drop was different. Jan wondered why he would be handling the drop, but said nothing. Orders were orders.

Sikorski was interrupted by a call from the British Foreign Office, which distracted him almost an hour. Finally, he got a chance to complete Cyn's plan. He called in Kaz, and gave him similar instructions, again with a different drop location.

Two days later, Cyn was back.

"We have our culprit. Of course, I didn't tell the Home Army to expect a drop. As planned, I only asked them to look out for any unusual sign of German patrols in the specified areas. And to be careful. One area was crawling with Jerries last night—Hla-318. Jan Tomczak's our traitor."

Sikorski sighed. "He seemed like such a good officer. But I don't suppose a good spy snarls at people or flits around in a trench coat. There's one consolation. Apparently Jankowski's not in it with him. They've been so close for so long, I was afraid they might both be involved."

Cyn's brow furrowed; he was deep in thought. Sikorski paused for almost a minute to let him think through whatever it was that was bothering him.

"Are we sure, sir? If the two of them were in it together, Tomczak may have informed Jankowski. An hour later, when Jankowski got a similar instruction—with a different location—they would realize it was a setup. It might already have been too late for Tomczak to protect himself; he might already have gotten in touch with his German contact. But Jankowski would know about the setup; he wouldn't pass information along to the Germans."

Sikorski wondered. Cyn's theory didn't make sense. Suppose Tomczak could contact the Germans so quickly, within an hour—which seemed implausible. Then he also would have been able to get back to them and cancel the patrols, once he talked to Jankowski and discovered it was a setup. Sikorski would have to give this some thought.

He ordered Tomczak arrested and held in a makeshift cell in the basement. For the moment, there would be no court martial and no execution. Cyn was to work out a trap for Jankowski, to find out if he were also a traitor. But Cyn should not set the plan in motion without Sikorski's approval.

Major Leslie "Mike" Tate, U.S. Army Intelligence, didn't quite know what to make of his instructions. But however the Germans were getting information, it was important to plug the leak. He called Major Cyn at the Polish government and asked if they could get together. Cyn made various excuses, but Tate insisted. Finally Cyn agreed. They could get together as soon as Tate wanted — that very evening, if the American wished. Tate did.

As he hung up the phone, Tate was trying to remember the precise details of their earlier encounter. Had he been sufficiently casual and subtle, trying to coax information out of the Pole?

The evening was unusually warm for May, almost balmy. The smell of lilac was in the air. Tate, Cyn and Rowecki escaped to the small, walled back garden of the Polish offices. Cyn had asked Kaz and Korbonski to be on call, in case they were needed. They both agreed. You don't say no to Security. Especially now, with the spy scare.

The three sat at a round wooden table — hemlock green, but not recently painted. Chips revealed its previous color, a bilious yellow. It really was too large. The three had to lean forward, their elbows on their knees, to be sure their conversation would not be overheard. But it was the only table available.

Tate began in a noncommittal manner, designed not to tip his hand. "Quite a coincidence — Goebbels and Piotrowski's announcements."

"Not exactly a coincidence, Major. But we caught the spy. One Captain Jan Tomczak." Cyn gave a brief summary of Tomczak's background. "Unclear what his motives were."

Tate was interested in how they caught Jan. Cyn obliged, explaining the phony instructions to the Home Army to expect a weapons drop.

"Exactly who knew about the Red Cross request ahead of time?"

Rowecki was irked; why was Tate asking for a repeat? How could anyone rise to the rank of major in U.S. Intelligence without the intelligence to remember a few names? Trying hard not to show his exasperation, he slowly went back over Cyn's list — "Sikorski, who was beyond suspicion; Piotrowski, Korbonski, Jankowski, and Tomczak."

"You laid a trap only for the last three? What about Piotrowski?"

Cyn and Rowecki exchanged glances. Tate noticed.

"Sikorski told us to focus on the other three," responded Cyn.

"We got our man," added Rowecki. "So that closes the case."

"Please humor me." Tate was looking directly at Rowecki in the dimming sunlight. "We're interested in how spies are trapped. Want to make sure there are no loose ends. As you probably know, we work closely with the British on security matters. You're sure nobody else knew about the Red Cross request?"

"Actually, I also knew ahead of time," Cyn said slowly. Then, after a lengthy pause: "So did the President. No surprise there."

"That's all?"

No answer. Cyn looked intently at Rowecki.

Rowecki nervously pulled at his earlobe, then dropped his hand back below the table.

"OK. Let's go back a bit," said Tate. "How did you find out, Major? You weren't at the original meeting with Sikorski and the others?"

"No."

"And you found out...?"

Cyn clearly didn't want to answer, but saw no alternative. "As chief of security, I'm privy to a lot of very confidential information. In this case, I was in the room when Prime Minister Sikorski got the President's approval to ask for a Red Cross investigation."

"Anyone else in the room?"

"I was at that meeting," said Rowecki, rather too quickly.

"Why didn't you say so, when I asked if anyone else knew, and Cyn said that he and the President did?"

Rowecki answered smoothly, "Because I didn't know. I had just had a beer and two cups of tea over lunch and had to go to the loo. That must have been when the Red Cross issue was discussed. It didn't happen when I was there."

"So it was a long meeting, with a number of subjects discussed?"

"That's right," replied Cyn.

Tate thought he was going to go cross-eyed, trying to keep his eyes on both Poles at once. Cyn was staring hard at Rowecki. Cyn opened his mouth and was about to say something.

There was a loud shot—a 9 mm pistol—followed immediately by the sound of four globs of putty being hurled against a cement wall: thp, thp, thp, thp.

Tate was on his feet at once. In his hand was a pistol, with silencer. It was pointed directly at Cyn's heart.

Cyn shouted in pain as he fell sideways off his chair. Rowecki was ashen and sank slowly forward. As his head hit the table, it bounced slightly, and his body gradually slumped leftward. As he fell to the ground, Tate saw a pistol in his hand. Just below his ribs were four closely spaced shots. Blood was flowing freely through the holes in his shirt. He was dead.

Tate was keeping his pistol aimed at Cyn. He bent over the fallen Pole, who had a bullet wound to his thigh, probably not too serious. And not much blood. At least, not much external bleeding. Tate patted him down. No weapon.

Tate unscrewed the silencer and returned his pistol to its holster. "Suppose," he said, "you tell me what you know."

Kaz was delighted that Jan was released, but had no idea why until the flight to Gibraltar. He knew that there had been a commotion in the yard that balmy May evening, and that the two Polish security officers had disappeared. But it wasn't until the last hour of the flight that Sikorski looked up from his papers and began to chat with his junior colleague.

"We let Jan go—with apologies—when we discovered the real traitor: Rowecki. To throw suspicion away from himself, he had to frame somebody—somebody who knew about the Red Cross proposal. That wasn't a problem. As Cyn's colleague in Security, he had access to messages being sent to the Home Army. He looked at the three messages and guessed that a trap was being set. He simply gave the Germans one of the three locations. Their patrols showed up on cue.

"As far as we can tell, he picked Jan at random. Just think. You could have drawn the short straw. If we'd acted hastily, you'd have been shot."

Somehow, Sikorski wasn't inspiring much confidence. One chance in three. Perhaps that wasn't so bad. Not compared to what he'd been through in the past few years. But Kaz didn't relish the idea: Anna being told that he was shot as a spy. It might also have messed up her career. Kaz wondered what she really was doing.

Sikorski continued. "Rowecki was pressured into treason when the Germans threatened to kill his older brother. Understandable, I suppose; he idolized his brother. The Yanks saved us from a mess. Tate, of U.S. Army Intelligence, had already suspected Rowecki for some time, and was unsure about Cyn. Tate shot Rowecki that memorable May evening. He really had no choice. Rowecki started the shooting, firing at Cyn. It's not clear why; perhaps he knew that Cyn suspected him. At any rate, Tate killed him before he could get off a second shot."

"So Cyn was killed, too?"

"No. Just a superficial hip wound. He recovered quickly. But we couldn't keep him around; he was chief of security, and had missed a traitor right under is nose. He said he had no suspicion about Rowecki until the day before the fateful evening, when he got a call from Tate. Cyn put two and two together, partly by thinking back to a puzzling conversation he had had with Tate a month earlier. Cyn guessed, correctly, that the Americans suspected there was a German mole in our security section. To Cyn, that probably meant Rowecki. But he wasn't sure.

"Anyhow, as far as we're concerned, Cyn is a non-person. He wasn't very cooperative with Tate; he tried to put him off; he didn't seem very eager to find the truth. He was given a new name and assigned to the American marines in the Pacific. They're pretending he came from Chicago.

"There's also something else you need to know for our meetings in North Africa. We were right: there will be an invasion across the Mediterranean. In the not-too-distant future. Unfortunately, we were also right on another score: it won't be Crete."

Kaz was obviously disappointed.

"I'm afraid, when push came to shove, we simply didn't carry much weight. Roosevelt made patronizing comments, that he didn't want to bargain with Poland or other small states. The big powers would settle things. And we couldn't even count on Churchill, not when it risked offending the Russians. When his colleagues tried to raise the Katyn massacre with him, he abruptly cut them off. He simply didn't want to hear about it."

As the wheels touched down, Kaz was left to wonder: Sicily or Sardinia? He knew enough not to ask.

They were planning a short refueling stop in Gibraltar before proceeding to Tunisia. There was a delay, however, as some high-priority communications equipment—for the coming invasion?—was loaded into the Liberator bomber. Then Kaz got the news: the plane was already over its safe weight, and he was being bumped. If he could catch a ride to Tunisia within the next 24 hours, he should do so; otherwise, he was to stay in Gibraltar. Sikorski would pick him up on the way back.

The pilot was in a hurry to take off. He had skimped on fuel, and wanted to get off while the engines were still warm; he didn't want to waste fuel on a preflight runup.

The Liberator swung out to the end of the concrete and immediately began its takeoff run. It used the full runway, finally rising slowly over the rocks.

Then disaster struck. The outboard right engine began to miss; the plane sank from view. A flash of fire rose from the rocks below.

Five days later, American and British amphibious forces splashed ashore in Sicily. Their assault on the Continent of Europe had begun.

Kaz was now back in Britain. With the new Prime Minister, he felt out of the loop; he was no longer invited to high-level meetings where grand strategy was discussed. More than ever, he lived for the weekends and visits with Anna.

As the months rolled by, he became increasingly bored. Finally, he was transferred to the southeastern corner of England, part of a small Polish group that was to be attached to the new, powerful American First Army under Gen. George Patton. They would act as liaison, preparing to integrate the Polish Armored Division into the First Army. Patton's aggressive reputation in Sicily made his army the obvious spearhead; he would lead a thrust into the heart of the continent. Kaz was excited; he would be in on the action. But he also felt ambivalent. The time of the invasion was approaching. Once he joined Patton, the security curtain would close behind him; he would no longer be able to visit Anna.

He was bitterly disappointed. He had been told that Patton was assembling a full 45 divisions. In fact, Patton had none. It was a hollow army, an imaginary army with only one purpose: to convince the Germans that the invasion would come directly across the narrowest part of the Channel, to the sand beaches of the Pas de Calais. Actually, sand and cement. Rommel had injected a new urgency in the German army. The defenses must be built up. The marauders must be stopped at the water's edge. If Patton ever got loose in France....

"The phantom first" or "our grand paper army," the junior officers called it. More accurately, it could have been called the rubber army — thousands of inflatable dummy tanks, all neatly lined up across the fields of Kent, just waiting to be photographed by the next Focke-Wulf pilot who dared a quick, five-minute dash across the Channel.

Everyone was frustrated, but Kaz was not prepared for Patton's sulfurous temper. "Why don't they let me at those sons of bitches? I was born for this moment, I can feel it. The great throw of the dice. To determine the history of the next hundred years. What am I doing here, playing kiddies' games with toy soldiers?"

"Calm down, Georgie. Calm down." It was a one-star general speaking. "You're being tested. If you can just manage to control your temper, you'll get another crack at Rommel."

Kaz was astonished. It was the first—but not the last—time he heard a junior officer (though still a general!) call Patton "Georgie."

That sort of thing would never, ever happen in the Polish Army. And could you imagine Rommel calling Hitler, "Dolphie?"

22
Normandie

Our landings... have failed.... The troops, the air and the navy did all that bravery and devotion to duty could do. If any blame or fault attaches to the attempt it is mine alone.

Draft statement of Dwight D. Eisenhower, to be released if the invasion failed.

6 June 1944. 01:50 hrs. With Patton's Phantom Army
35 miles south-southeast of London.

Kaz stirred fitfully; the banging on his door wouldn't stop. He had counted on a good night's sleep at last, after the break in the weather; the forecasters had promised at least a temporary interruption of the howling gusts of wind and driving rain that drummed on the thin tin top of the hut. But they must have gotten it wrong. The banging on the door was even worse than during the storms of the previous two nights. Perhaps he should jam a towel in the door to keep it quiet.

As he stirred from the fog of sleep, he realized it wasn't the wind; it was a fist thumping on the door. He swung his feet out of bed onto the chilly floor, and shouted for his tormentor to come in. A British Warrant Officer appeared in the doorway. Kaz didn't remember having seen him around camp before. In the dim light, he could see the WO's neatly clipped mustache. Kaz thought there was a slight reddish tinge to the mustache and fair hair. Perhaps one of the new men brought in from the Northern Irish regiment.

"Sorry to wake you, sir, but the General has ordered a staff meeting in the briefing room at 02:00 hours, in just ten minutes. Not exactly come as you are, but casual, in light of the short notice." Kaz was already pulling his pants over his pajamas. "Something seems to be up. My guess is, this may be the big day."

As Kaz shuffled, half awake, into the quonset hut, he joined a bleary-eyed, unshaven, most unmilitary-looking group. But they did manage to stumble to their feet—and a few of the lieutenants could even be said to snap to attention—as the general entered, stage left.

Incongruously, Patton was in full uniform, wearing a polished steel helmet and an open holster with an ivory-handled revolver.

"Gentlemen. At this moment, allied paratroops are dropping into France. Within a few hours, a flotilla will appear off the coast of France. The assault on Fortress Europe is about to begin."

"For obvious reasons, I won't tell you exactly where the invasion will occur; you will all know soon enough. Let me simply say that it is to the west of the Pas de Calais.

"Our reconnaissance aircraft report that our little ruse has been successful in keeping the Germans focused on the Calais area. The Boche have some of their best infantry and Panzer divisions along the Calais coast, supported by heavy guns.

"I know that most of you will be eager to transfer back to combat units, but our job here is not done." Kaz thought he detected a wistful wince in the general's otherwise enthusiastic face; he could not hide his pain in being shunted aside during the historic D-Day attack. "Our intelligence indicates that Hitler firmly expects our main attack to be across the narrowest part of the channel towards Calais. Our job is to reinforce this belief, to play to the Führer's preconceptions, and thus to keep an extra dozen German divisions east of the Seine. Off the backs of our boys in Normandy."

Kaz glanced to the officers on his left. Apparently no one else noticed Patton's slip, mentioning the location of the invasion. But it didn't matter, now that allied battleships were about to open fire on the coast of Normandy.

"Our job is to convince Hitler and his gang that the attack in the west is just a large-scale feint, that the main attack will come within the next week or ten days right across the channel to Calais.

"To achieve this goal, we will immediately step up our fictitious radio traffic. This will be a big task; after all, I'm supposed to be in charge of an Army Group here, with 45 divisions and thousands of tanks." With a wry smile, Patton glanced around a room that suddenly seemed very small indeed. "Major Edwards will give you details. Oh, by the way, if you do want to ask for a transfer back to your combat units, Major Edwards will be handling the paper work. I should warn you, however, that the major will be overwhelmed with work in the next two weeks, and will not even have a chance to look at your applications until that time." Patton smiled slightly.

"As before, you are forbidden to have any communication with the outside world except through the mails—which will still be closely censored—or through channels which Edwards specifically authorizes and arranges. Major Edwards." With that, Patton took his seat to the left of the lectern.

Edwards was much more casually dressed than the General. The stresses of recent weeks were beginning to show. He looked exhausted.

"Over the next 72 hours, we will simulate the move of a large army from our present camps towards ports of embarkation in the southeast. We will gradually move the source of our radio transmissions toward these ports. The German direction finders are so good now that they can triangulate to within a mile—or maybe even a few hundred yards—so that it is important for our messages to come from the right locations. Simulated traffic jams should be in towns, please, not in pastures.

"We will want considerable low-level traffic sent in the clear—tank commanders chewing at others over traffic foul-ups, occasional requests for help with mechanical breakdowns, and so on. One of your jobs will be to provide plausibility to these messages. But don't overdo it. Let's not have all the imaginary tanks break down at once.

"Oh, by the way. Lt. Pitcairn will be handling arrangements to move our inflatable tanks along with the radio transmissions, just in case a Jerry pilot buzzes over and snaps our picture. It goes without saying that, during daylight hours, the inflatable tanks should be kept right side up. Four men underneath should have no trouble carrying a tank along without tipping it over.

"Finally, to add color, we've decided to make the Poles into an undisciplined lot. Sorry about that, Jankowski, but we might as well play on German preconceptions. You Poles may include messages of a personal nature in your communications. You might even include some bitching from junior officers about incompetent generals, just to titillate the Boche." Edwards began turning toward Patton, but caught himself. The general forced a half-smile as many in the audience smirked. "Would you see me about the details of your assignment right after the briefing, Maj. Jankowski."

Kaz threw himself into the deception. But, like almost all the others, he applied for a transfer. He was one of the lucky ones; his transfer back to his Polish division came through within two weeks. He would become a real soldier again, and, as the need for security lessened, he hoped that he would occasionally be able to get away to see Anna.

The time with Patton was well spent. Hitler clung to the whisperings of his soothsayer and to his intuition that the main allied thrust would be at the Pas de Calais. For six critical weeks after D-Day, he kept 15 sorely needed divisions east of the Seine, poised to repel Patton's cross-channel assault that never came.

In the time Kaz had been away, the First Polish Armored Division had been beefed up. It now had four times as many Sherman tanks—a full complement. Kaz was given command of about three dozen, and focused on the final stages of training. His main task was to get his tanks to attack in a coordinated way, particularly when the black team—the simulated Nazi panzers—succeeded in "disabling" several of his tanks in the mock battles. Kaz was worried. Because of the lack of space, maneuvers had to be confined to no more than 30 or 40 tanks. If he had so much trouble coordinating just a few tanks, what would happen if they were thrown into large-scale tank battles, with the Germans shooting back?

As the days went by, news from Normandy led Kaz and his comrades alternatively to elation and depression. The Allied forces accomplished an enormous feat by establishing a foothold, and they clearly held the initiative. But the going was excruciatingly slow. In the east, the grueling battle for Caen ground on week after week. Caen was one of the early objectives of the British—they hoped to capture it on D-Day, and, in fact, allied forces penetrated to within 3 miles of its outskirts by nightfall on that first day. But it did not fall into allied hands until July 9, five arduous weeks after the invasion.

The struggle by American armies to the west was equally frustrating. The bocage country of Western Normandy was marked by woody, marshy areas, interspersed with farmlands broken down into tiny fields separated by hedgerows—mounds of earth six, eight, or more feet in height, generally topped with heavy vegetation. To get across the hedgerows, tanks would have to climb sharply up the embankments, exposing their vulnerable underbellies to enemy fire. Furthermore, in this exposed position, their guns were aimed skyward, making it impossible for them to shoot back.

After weeks of bloody and frustrating fighting, it was a noncommissioned officer—Sergeant Culin—who came up with a simple but brilliant solution: welding steel rails to the front of a Sherman tank, allowing it to cut through the hedgerows while maintaining its level position and firing as it went. Often, chunks of the hedgerows were carried forward on the rails, providing camouflage and protection. The sergeant's contraption, appropriately nicknamed "Rhinoceros" by grateful armored troops, was widely adopted. The Germans had accommodatingly—but unwittingly—provided the rails in building their Fortress Europe, scattering "Rommel's asparagus"—steel obstacles—profusely along the landing beaches.

The exhausting, grinding battle wore on. The Allies urgently needed to get out of the Normandy pocket into the open, tank-friendly fields where the Germans could be overwhelmed by numbers. But now, six weeks after the invasion, the Allies had still not advanced beyond the line they expected to hold just five days after D-Day.

They had, however, landed over a million men, with fresh troops flowing in daily. A new addition was to be the First Polish Armored Division, which would be attached to the Canadians. To prepare for their arrival, Kaz, Jan, and a dozen other Polish officers and men were dispatched to the eastern end of the front, near Caen.

17 July 1944. With the Fourth Canadian Armored Division east of Caen.

When Kaz and his compatriots arrived, they expected to participate almost immediately in action against the enemy. The Canadians, however, had other ideas. They and the British were on the eve of an armored attack, and it was too late to integrate Poles into the action. A young officer, Lt. Bud Swann, was assigned to them, and invited Kaz and Jan to a half-demolished farmhouse that was serving as a makeshift officers' club. In anticipation of the next day's offensive, it was almost deserted. After a few pleasantries, Swann got down to business.

"At last, we've gotten through that Caen mess; we're now to the edge of open fields where tanks can maneuver. This may be our best chance so far to break through the German lines. Apart from the landings themselves, tomorrow may be the most decisive battle thus far in Normandy."

Rather stiffly, Kaz responded that he wished them luck. In spite of his years in Britain, he still didn't feel his English was up to the sort of banter that lightened the worries of soldiers.

Swann continued. "We're going to need all the help we can get. We're up against two of the best panzer divisions—Panzer Lehr and the Hitlerjungend SS."

Kaz had heard horror stories about these two elite divisions, but he wanted to hear about them directly from someone with firsthand experience. He encouraged Swann to go on. "The Panzer Lehr?"

"Yeah," replied Swann. "They're tough. The best battle-tested veterans, brought together in a demonstration division. Originally used to train other panzers. Not a surprising name—'Lehrer' is the German word for teacher.

"The Hitlerjungend may be even worse," continued Swann. "Perhaps the worst of the SS storm troopers. A bunch of fanatics. A gang of teenage thugs with heavy weapons. Leaders in the Hitler Youth back in Germany. Don't take many prisoners. When they do, they shoot 'em."

Jan was about to say something, but held back.

Swann began sipping his third beer. "Of course," he glanced around the empty room, "we don't take many of them prisoner, either."

Kaz didn't know how to interpret that; he felt a real culture gap. He decided not to say anything. Swann apparently noticed his hesitation, and added:

"They're too fanatic to surrender. Just like the Japs."

Kaz thought back to his early contact with Germans in the Polish churchyard. He wondered: Was Swann simply preventing a nasty misinterpretation, or was he putting a gloss on a horrible story? Bloody-mindedness seemed strangely out of keeping with his boyish face and floppy blond hair. Kaz's thoughts were interrupted as Swann got back to his main topic.

"We have a big problem: how do you press an attack against hardened defenses? We expect German tanks to come out and meet us in the fields. But behind them are dug-in 88 field guns. If you get within a mile of one of them, you're dead. They can hit a small, moving target. They were originally designed as an antiaircraft gun, but proved their effectiveness against tanks in North Africa.

"I'm not sure we've really cracked the fundamental puzzle. We want to follow standard tank tactics, pushing rapidly forward to exploit any enemy weakness; we want to get our tanks behind his lines and create havoc. But we have to guard against the tactic Rommel used so effectively in North Africa—having his tanks appear to be defeated and retreat, drawing the British tanks towards his deadly 88s."

Kaz couldn't help but notice the disturbing trend in Swann's tone as he worked through his three beers—starting with an optimistic statement about a decisive breakthrough, but now talking about how dangerous it would be to exploit any advantage. Worse was to come.

"I'm afraid that the last six weeks have taken a toll on our morale. In some ways, the Sherman tanks are great—fast, rugged, and easy to repair. They've introduced a whole new stage into armored warfare. Now, we don't have to worry that we'll lose more tanks to breakdowns than to enemy fire. And we don't have to nag our tankers endlessly about maintenance.

"But we were told that Shermans were the best tank in the world, and they're not. In one-on-one engagements, their 75 mm guns are simply no match for the new Tigers with their high-velocity 88s, or even the Panthers. And some idiot designed the Sherman with a gas rather than diesel engine. When they're hit, there's likely to be a flash fire and explosion. Some of the guys call them cigarette lighters."

Jan was looking increasingly uncomfortable. Swann continued:

"I should know. I made the bad mistake of tangling with a Tiger two days ago. I was the only one to get out alive. Fortunately, the Boche don't have very many." His voice tailed off.

They sat there, not knowing what to say—perhaps two or three minutes. Finally, Kaz broke the silence.

"So what will we be doing tomorrow?"

"I haven't got a new tank or crew yet, so I'll be sitting out the big one. It'll be a British, not Canadian, show anyway. I've picked a spot near the top of a hill, where we can get a view for several miles over the fields. If you have any questions, now's the time to ask. It may be too noisy tomorrow, with the artillery firing over our heads."

They spent a leisurely hour talking about tank warfare. Then they retired early, hoping for a good night's sleep before they were awakened at 5 a.m. by the artillery barrage and aerial bombardment. The attacking force even had help from the single monstrous turret of the ancient *HMS Roberts*. It was a symbol of how little progress had been made in the six grueling weeks since D-Day, that the enemy was still within range of naval guns.

As the air attack ended and the British tanks began to roll forward, Kaz noticed that they were clustered in three narrow columns. He was puzzled; this made them vulnerable to enemy artillery. Deafened by the British guns, he mouthed his question to Swann, who fumbled for a piece of paper and scribbled the answer. Only three corridors had been cleared through the minefield laid by the British as protection against a German attack.

Somebody had, however, slipped up; not every mine had been cleared. Kaz was appalled to see explosions under the treads of several tanks. By the time the procession was beginning to form up abreast on the other side of the minefield, they had left four of their tanks behind, victims of the mines.

As the tanks were proceeding through the minefield, the artillery bombardment had slackened. Now, as the tanks began their advance, the artillery recommenced with full fury, this time firing much shorter. The gunners were laying down a rolling barrage that crept forward several hundred yards in front of the advancing tanks. The tactic was successful. As far as Kaz could tell, there was little or no incoming fire from the Germans. Survivors were too busy keeping their heads down.

As the attack moved off into the distance, it began to disappear into the haze, smoke, and dust of battle. The show was over. Swann nudged Kaz gently on the shoulder, signaling him to follow. Soon they were in the communications hut, where they could hear sounds of battle over the radios.

Unfortunately, the reception was full of static, and eight or ten channels were being received at the same time, in a language still unfamiliar to Kaz. He couldn't tell what was going on. But soon, from the grim faces, he realized that the attackers were running into trouble. He gradually figured out the problem. As tanks proceeded beyond their supporting artillery, they began to meet stiff resistance. The rolling, apparently tank-friendly countryside was dotted with villages, which the Germans were defending tenaciously. Then, as a group of British tanks moved through a large grove of fruit trees—without infantry protection—they were attacked in their vulnerable flank by surviving 88s.

So ended *Operation Goodwood,* at best a partial victory. The British had moved their lines forward, and accomplished one of their goals: to keep the pressure on, and thus encourage the Germans to transfer reserves away from the western end of the front where they were blocking an American breakout. But they had not achieved a breakout themselves. And they could ill afford a war of attrition. British manpower was being stretched to its limits. Montgomery could no longer count on reinforcements, or even full replacements for his casualties. He would now command a dwindling number of troops.

Nor was it clear that Canadians were in much better shape. To Kaz's astonishment, Swann explained the inflamed debate within

Canada: whether "zombies" — draftees who had been training for years for home defense — would be sent to Europe against their wishes. If not, the Canadian Army would have to depend on raw, half-trained new volunteers to replace their casualties.

It was becoming increasingly obvious that the Poles would have a much greater role than he had anticipated.

He looked forward to the prospect with mixed emotions.

It was only later that, courtesy of German prisoners, Kaz learned details of British tank losses in the orchard. The tanks had been passing a hidden group of antiaircraft 88s when an aggressive German Colonel, Hans von Luck, arrived from furlough in Paris. As befitting his name, he had the good fortune to miss the bombing, and appeared on the scene at a critical moment. The Colonel ordered the crews to lower their barrels, which were still pointed skyward, and to fire at the tanks. Not my department, replied the battery commander; my job is to shoot down enemy planes. Von Luck thereupon drew his Luger and suggested that the commander might prefer to be a live hero rather than a dead coward. The 88s were soon in action.

Once again, over beers, Kaz, Jan, and Swann tackled the tough problems of breaking through, particularly those posed by Tiger tanks. They could be destroyed and even turned over by bombing, in spite of their 60-ton mass. They were also vulnerable to a direct hit from artillery. But if the allied tanks couldn't deal with them face-to-face, it was going to be a grim business. How, they wondered, could they beat the Tigers on the ground?

Jan: "They must be vulnerable *somewhere*. What about trying to hit them in the joint, where the turret meets the rest of the tank?"

Swann: "Not very practical. It's an awfully small target. When they're shooting back, it will seem even smaller — minuscule."

Kaz: "Treads are a bigger target. The best way to attack them may be from the side."

Jan: "Or better yet, get around behind, where the armor is thinner."

Swann: "Easier said than done. While we're sneaking around the back, Jerry will presumably be turning his tank, or at least his turret. That means that, unless we get lucky and come upon a Tiger from the side or behind, it won't work."

Kaz: "In other words, if you come upon a Tiger, watch out for its claws. The best thing to do is run. Sounds like the jungle." He paused. "Doesn't seem like a very promising way to keep an offensive going."

Jan: "You need at least two Shermans—coming from different directions—to even dream of attacking a single Tiger. But how would you coordinate them?

Swann: They wouldn't have to approach from completely different directions. If they were spread out—proceeding in a line....

Jan: "But what would stop the Tiger, with its much longer range, from picking off the whole line, one by one?"

Swann: "We might do it if we have something to hide behind."

Kaz: "In other words, what we really want is something like an orchard, to help you maneuver and sneak up on a Tiger."

Jan: "So we should send the word to Jerry: Keep all your tanks in the woods. Not near the edge of the woods, where they can fire at us. In the center, where we can sneak up on them. I suppose we should say, 'please.'"

Swann: "That may not be so impossible. The bombing encourages the Germans to keep their Tigers hidden in the woods."

Kaz: "So how many Shermans do we need? Are two enough?"

Swann: "Five would be ideal. You want the Tiger surrounded. But not so many that we start knocking one another off. Circular firing squads aren't such a great idea."

Kaz: "So what we want is five tanks—say, in the 1 o'clock, 4, 6, 8 and 11 positions—with six o'clock representing the position directly in front of the Tiger."

Swann: "Sounds promising. Spread out like that, in a starburst formation, we might kill a Tiger. The real trouble is, how do you get into position without the Tiger knocking off our tanks as they try to circle around to the back? Let's sleep on it, and decide tomorrow whether it's worth trying."

20 July 1944. Headquarters, Army Group West.

Kurt Dietrich—now Oberst (Colonel) Dietrich—still felt nagging pain from his many injuries, particularly his stomach, arm, and hip wounds from the Russian campaign. His facial wound, received in Poland on that first day of the war, had long since ceased to hurt, but he was still self-conscious, occasionally rubbing the nasty, slashing scar across his left cheek.

With the demands of battle, he could no longer be spared. Pressed back into active duty, he reported for his new assignment as chief of staff to Field Marshal Günther von Kluge, commander of all the German armies in France. Von Kluge had specifically asked for him; he had served with distinction under von Kluge in Russia. In spite of the grim military situation, Dietrich was looking forward to being in the middle of things.

When he reported for service, about noon, his new boss was out at the front. The scene in the headquarters was tense; generals were debating whether to move two armored divisions eastward, to face the new British threat near Caen. Rommel had recently ordered these two Panzer divisions into reserve in the west, fearing a major American attack. But now, Rommel was gone from the scene. Just three days earlier, a low-flying Typhoon had strafed his staff car, wounding him in the head so severely that he was not expected to live through the night.

In the absence of von Kluge, Dietrich decided to remain in the background as a relatively junior officer. The scene quickly reminded him of his last days in Russia — generals desperately trying to patch together a defense in the face of overwhelming enemy power. Under the pressures, they began to snap at one another. Dietrich wondered why they could not put off the decision, leaving it to their commander, von Kluge. But Dietrich soon sensed that his new boss inspired little confidence in his generals; they considered him a conniver who would go whichever way the wind blew strongest. The two sides were competing to see who could create the stronger wind.

"Der kluge Hans," observed one of the generals sourly — "the clever Hans." Dietrich winced at the play on von Kluge's name; der kluge Hans was a bumbler in German folklore. But, after an exhausting debate, the generals could not reach agreement. The decision would in fact have to be left up to von Kluge.

At 16:30, the generals broke for air. Gen. Kurt Student, commander of the First Airborne Army, motioned to Dietrich to join him in an adjacent room. Dietrich suspected that, in the light of his close position with von Kluge, Student would try to enlist him as an ally in the debate over the two armored divisions. But Student was just trying to be helpful; he wanted to fill Dietrich in on the battles that had been grinding down the German army.

"We know our duty as soldiers: to fight to the best of our ability. But the situation has been getting worse by the day. Our men are exhausted and we're running out of tanks. The British didn't break through with their recent offensive, but it was a mighty close thing. It may only be a matter of time."

"But," replied Dietrich, trying to be optimistic, "we have the two reserve Panzer divisions. Give me a few of our tanks and I'll pulverize some of those Shermans."

"I admire your spirit, particularly after what you've been through. But let me give you a bit of unsolicited advice, my boy." As a colonel, Dietrich was not used to being called a boy, but he realized how young, at 28, he must seem to the generals. Student continued.

"It's not good to be too enthusiastic. Your boss came here with great optimism, but his reports to the Führer have become much more guarded. Even pessimistic."

Deitrich's expression conveyed some skepticism. Student became more blunt. Perhaps the pressures of the campaign had made all the generals less cautious.

"Yes, my boy" — there it was, again — "when your boss assumed command several weeks ago, he, uh...." Student paused for the right words. "Hitler believed that gutless generals were responsible for the problems in Normandy. Or, perhaps I should say, irresolute field marshals. Your boss was determined to put some spine into us."

Deitrich decided the time had come to keep his mouth shut. Student went on:

"Ja. When he first met Rommel, there was quite a scene. He started right off by suggesting that Rommel had not shown sufficient enthusiasm in following the Führer's orders. To drive home the point, he added: 'Now you, too, Field Marshal, will have to get used to taking orders.'

"Well, of course, Rommel wouldn't take that insult, not even from his new commander. He bluntly suggested that von Kluge might wish to visit the front before making snap judgments. When von Kluge did, he was shaken. Every time he comes back, he looks more grim. I shudder to think of what will happen when he gets back in a few hours."

At that point, there was a knock on the door. A corporal in the signals corps entered, saluted smartly, and handed Student a message. Student turned pale, rose abruptly, and left the room without saying a word.

Dietrich waited five minutes or so, thinking that Student might return, and then went back to the main room. Officers were huddled in small groups of four or five, talking intensely. Enlisted men were scurrying to and fro in great agitation. Deitrich picked a group that included several middle-level officers—majors and colonels—and wandered over.

Their faces were ashen. At once, Dietrich found out why. Hitler was dead.

Soon, rumors began to circulate: Hitler had been assassinated by a group of generals. Abruptly, officers began to say very little. In his mind, Dietrich went back over conversations among generals that he had heard in recent months. Was any of them, he wondered, involved in the assassination? And who would be in charge now?

A teen-aged corporal tapped Dietrich on the shoulder and saluted, somewhat casually. He was wearing combat fatigues, and, to judge from his grimy appearance, had just returned from the front. "The Field Marshal has returned and wants to see you. Please follow me."

He was taken to von Kluge's quarters, where the Field Marshal was getting into a clean uniform. He greeted Dietrich warmly; they had not seen one another for over a year. Then von Kluge began a rambling report of his day at the front, and the difficulties he and his driver had faced moving from one command to another. The constant threat of attack from the air had clearly been a strain. As von Kluge rambled on, Dietrich was astonished: was it possible that von Kluge had not yet heard about Hitler? Finally, his curiosity got the better of him:

"Have you heard the news from Germany, sir?"

"What news?"

Dietrich was even more surprised. "Hitler is dead."

"It's not quite so clear. There was a message, in code, about an hour ago, saying that he is dead. But just a few minutes ago, German radio announced that the Führer is very much alive, and will address the nation tonight. I have a call in to Keitel to confirm this. I want to be sure before we have dinner tonight with von Stülpnagel."

Dietrich's thoughts came in a jumble: Why does he need to know before dinner? Is General Heinrich von Stülpnagel—the Military Governor of France—in on the plot? And how about von Kluge? If he knows that Stülpnagel is involved, doesn't that mean he's in it, too? Dietrich had never thought of von Kluge as someone to take unnecessary risks, but he had gotten some idea of the desperate military situation during the afternoon's debate over the depleted Panzer reserves. The time has come, thought Dietrich, to be very careful. His caution was heightened when von Kluge added:

"Let's not forget our time in Russia. I'm counting on your loyalty, my boy."

Ach, thought Dietrich, this "boy" business is a disease. Maybe it's because these guys have been away from their sons and grandsons for so long. A deeper thought nagged his subconscious: loyalty could be a dangerous virtue.

The phone rang. Keitel was on the line. The radio report had been correct. Hitler was alive and only slightly wounded. He had met that afternoon with Mussolini, as planned. In Hitler's mind, his escape was one more confirmation that he had a destiny to fulfill.

There was a knock on the door. Stülpnagel and his chief of staff, Lt. Col. Hofacker, were downstairs, and urgently wanted to see von Kluge before the other guests arrived.

Von Kluge and Dietrich went quickly down to a drawing room where Stülpnagel and Hofacker were nervously waiting. After quick introductions, Stülpnagel got down to business:

"Now we've gotten rid of that old bastard, it's important that we move quickly to consolidate our position."

"I should inform you, general, that the Führer survived the assassination attempt," von Kluge replied in even tones.

Stülpnagel was thunderstruck. "Then we're all in mortal danger. We must act at once."

Von Kluge said nothing.

"It's absolutely essential," Stülpnagel's agitation was visibly increasing, "that we arrest the SS generals and anyone else who can block the coup."

The pause was painful. Then von Kluge calmly responded:

"What do you mean, we? This was your plot, not mine."

Hofacker was now turning red and was apparently about to explode, but he was interrupted by a knock on the door. The other guests had arrived. Before Hofacker could say anything, von Kluge had already left for the dining room.

When the guests were seated, von Kluge expressed a few lukewarm words of welcome, and the diners fell into a stony silence. It was a macabre scene—lit by candlelight, with only the sound of knives and forks occasionally clicking on the fine bone china settings. It seemed that the house had been visited by the Angel of Death. Perhaps it had. As Dietrich would find out later, several of the other conspirators were also present.

After dinner, Stülpnagel and Hofacker tarried as the other guests left. When they were gone, Stülpnagel, in an agitated tone, insisted that they must talk. Von Kluge glanced uneasily at the servants, then led the other three back into the drawing room, closing the door.

"I'm not sure that we have anything more to add. As I said before, it was not my plot." Von Kluge's tone was flat, expressionless.

"What do you mean, not your plot?" Hofacker was obviously having trouble controlling himself. "As the Field Marshal might be so good as to remember, he met with us last year in Russia. He committed himself to being a part of the conspiracy."

"Ah," said von Kluge, maintaining his unperturbed air, "but that was on the condition that the pig was already dead."

"You bastard," retorted Stülpnagel. "You can't slip out of it that easily. You're already committed. I've issued orders to have all the Gestapo and SS men in Paris arrested."

It was now von Kluge's turn to explode. "You've done *what*? Well you had bloody well better unarrest them. And, as soon as you reverse your order, I'm relieving you of your command." At that point, von Kluge's tone abruptly softened. "In light of our old friendship, Heinrich, I would advise you to disappear. You might not have to hide so very long before you're safe."

My God, thought Dietrich, headquarters duty may be just as dangerous as being at the front. But at least I won't have to go through another of those ghastly Russian winters.

And, oh, yes, von Kluge did decide to move the two Panzer divisions from the west to face the British threat. He guessed wrong. Rommel had been right: the western sections of the German lines were in peril.

Just four days later, after the Panzers had been transferred eastward toward Caen, Dietrich received a puzzling message from the western end of the front, near St. Lô. Elements of the American army were beginning to withdraw, even though the German army was applying no pressure. "Im Westen, Nichts neues," thought Dietrich: "All Quiet on the Western Front."

He would not be puzzled for long. The next morning, the quiet was shattered. Wave after wave of Allied aircraft—almost 3,000 in total— began laying a carpet of bombs on the German army facing St. Lô. The purpose of the American tactical withdrawal now became clear: to prevent a repeat of the accidents of preceding days, when a combination of bad weather and poor navigation had led American planes to bomb their own troops. The new attack devastated the German defenses. Every tank in the forward area was destroyed, many being tossed through the air as if they were Patton's inflatable decoys. Through the gap, American tanks began their rush.

Von Kluge's staff meeting was tense. How quickly should they make their stand, and where? Following the Führer's standing orders, von Kluge sent a curt message to the front: No one is to retreat. Dietrich was appalled by the reply:

> Every one is holding out. Not a single man is leaving his post! Not one! Because they're all dead. Dead! You may report to the Field Marshal that the Panzer Lehr division has been annihilated.

Even though Dietrich had served in Russia with von Kluge, he decided that it was wise to keep this reply in his pocket. He reported only that the division was being overrun and was in imminent danger of disintegrating.

The Führer's order to stand firm was irrelevant. Within a few days, American tanks advanced 25 miles to Avranches, a seaside town at the base of the Normandy Peninsula. In the vanguard was Patton, who had left his phantom army in England and was now in charge of flesh-and-blood troops and real steel. Ignoring orders to post a strong defense on his left flank, he pushed two infantry and two armored divisions across a single bridge within 24 hours—about 80,000 men—with three more divisions following within the next two days. They fanned out into the open countryside, moving westward into the Brittany Peninsula with its ports, southward toward the heart of France, and eastward towards Paris. They thereby cut off German access to the whole of the northwestern quadrant of France.

After weeks of grinding struggle, the battle of Normandy was coming to a sudden end. The battle for central France was opening—and beyond that, the battle for the Third Reich itself.

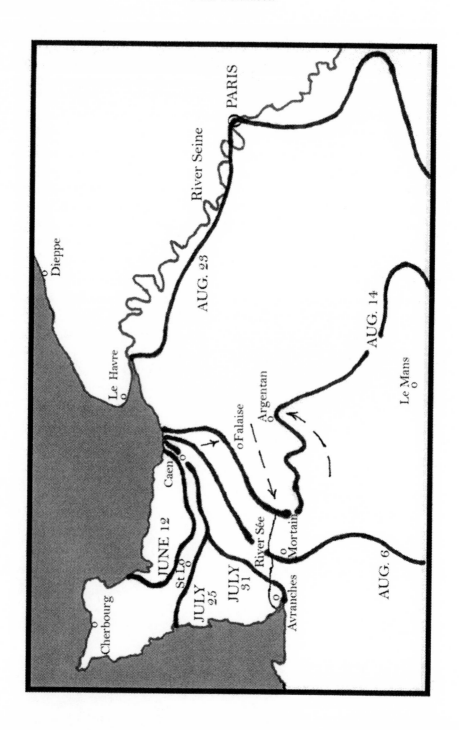

23

Headlong Into the Trap

There is only one extremist and that is Hitler himself.

> German aristocrat Ewald von Kleist-Schmenzin, attempting to disabuse the British Foreign Office of their illusion, in the weeks before Munich (1938), that Hitler was a passive leader being egged on by "extremists."

At Headquarters, Army Group West, panic was setting in. Von Kluge was increasingly depressed by his quarreling generals, and took solace in one-on-one conversations with Dietrich. Von Kluge faced an urgent question: where could he make a stand? But his defensive plans were brushed aside when the Führer, from the isolated depths of his *Wolfsschanze* (Wolf's Lair) in East Prussia, saw an opportunity where others saw only peril. He ordered his forces to attack westward toward Avranches, to cut the narrow corridor through which Patton's tanks were rushing. "We must strike like lightning," he urged von Kluge. There must be a "bold and unhesitating thrust" to the sea. Hitler emphasized the stakes in the coming attack: "On its success depends the fate of the battle of France."

With Hitler's orders came an unwelcome guest: a senior member of the German General Staff, to "observe" von Kluge. Was this just an indication of the Führer's waning confidence in his Field Marshall? Or was it a hint that von Kluge was now suspected of treason, of complicity in the plot against Hitler's life? As Dietrich was already well aware of von Kluge's contacts with the conspirators, von Kluge had little to lose by being frank with his subordinate.

"How can we possibly follow this order? If we do, we'll be delivering ourselves into our enemy's hands. We'll be rushing headlong into the American trap. They'll swing north, behind us, and link up with the British."

"But, sir, with our new 'guest,' we can't use the most obvious ruse. We can't pretend we didn't get the order. With all the people at headquarters, we wouldn't get away with it, anyhow."

"Then what are my alternatives? I could ignore Hitler's command and attempt an orderly withdrawal."

"There's a powerful case to do that, sir. It's a fundamental of blitzkrieg: if we rush at our enemy, with insufficient forces to protect our flanks, we'll be blundering into a trap; we'll be surrounded. For the sake of our men, we should be setting up a tenable defense. But I should point out, sir, that I can't advise you to defy the Führer's direct order." By now, Dietrich was becoming accustomed to the desperation around headquarters and added, "Of course, I'm not sure that I know what it's like to be a field marshal."

"Ah, so field marshals are entitled to defy orders?" Von Kluge was trying to salvage a bit of humor from the gloomy outlook.

"Not exactly, sir." Dietrich still did not feel comfortable enough to banter with his boss. "But field marshals do have some leeway in interpreting orders in light of the situation at the front."

"Not in this case. Not with our new little guest. He's here to have me removed if I waver. I don't see how I have any alternative; it wouldn't make any difference. If I don't order the attack, they'll get somebody who will. But if we're going to attack, the sooner, the better. The fewer Americans we'll have at our backs."

Dietrich took this as a decision; he said nothing. Von Kluge summed up.

"It's incredible: blissfully planning an attack while Patton is rushing along our southern flank, eagerly forming a noose to strangle us."

The German plan was to drive down the valley of the River Sée toward the ocean, spearheaded by the 1st SS Panzers—the heretofore invincible Adolph Hitler Division. The plan was not entirely without hope of success. Patton had skimped on the defenses on his flank. His situation was less precarious than it seemed, however, because

Eisenhower had assured him that his army could be temporarily resupplied by air if it were cut off.

The stripped American defenses proved surprisingly resilient. On high ground overlooking the Sée Valley, American infantry were dug in, supported by assault guns. On the second morning of the German attack, the U.S. Second Armored Division launched a counterattack after materializing, according to a contemporary account, "out of thin air" — the thin air being supplied by top-secret Enigma intercepts. To compound their woes, Nazi tanks were repeatedly stung by hornets from the sky: American Thunderbolts and British Typhoons hurling their rockets earthward.

Having stopped von Kluge's thrust, Bradley and Patton saw the chance of which they had dreamt, and which had given von Kluge and Dietrich nightmares. Aware of Hitler's orders committing his Panzers to a full-scale westward assault, Patton reinforced his armor racing eastward along the German left flank. His tanks then swung north toward Falaise in a classic armored maneuver: a great hooking move to encircle the German armies.

As a precaution, Dietrich had approached an old friend from the Russian front — Lt. Jurg Bock, a communications expert. Through him, he arranged backdoor communications to other old comrades from the Russian front who were now serving in Hitler's command post in East Prussia. "Little Sir Echo," he called Lt. Bock, borrowing from a song he had been taught many years ago by an English nanny. Bock sadly reported the Führer's reaction: a cold fury that the German counterattack had failed because von Kluge *wanted* it to fail.

6 August 1944. With Canadian/Polish forces south of Caen.

Kaz and Swann dropped by the operations office early in the afternoon to see the most recent aerial reconnaissance pictures, hoping to find a place where their "starburst" tactic might be tested. After flipping through hundreds of pictures, Swann whistled softly and handed a photograph to Kaz. He could not have invented a better location. There was nothing special about the road running through the middle of the picture, a typical French country lane with straight stretches of several hundred yards interrupted by mild curves.

Rather, it was what lay on the sides of the road that made for an ideal location. For 100 yards on either side was a young pine forest — trees of approximately the same age and height, perhaps the result of a reforestation program, perhaps natural growth when farmers abandoned the cultivation of infertile land. As far as Kaz could tell, most of the trees were about 20 feet high, quite adequate to hide a Sherman, but small enough that they could easily be pushed over without impeding the progress of a tank.

Swann delicately raised the question of who would go where in the formation. It was Swann's squadron, but Kaz held the senior rank. Any awkwardness was avoided, however, when Kaz informed him of the explicit understanding when he had asked to maneuver with the Canadians: the Canadian officers, regardless of their rank, were to be in command; he was there simply as a guest to observe current battlefield tactics. This made sense to Kaz, and he had readily agreed. He knew the importance of esprit de corps. He didn't want, as an outsider, to be giving orders to resentful tankers in a language that was not his mother tongue.

As the squadron leader, Swann would take the command position at the base of the star, at 6 o'clock. He offered Kaz the 11 o'clock position — one of the two best locations to get a killing shot at any adversary they might meet. Kaz also noticed that Swann was taking the most exposed position, where he was most likely to be knocked out by a Tiger. The other four positions were filled out by the rest of Swann's squadron.

They did not begin their foray until 16:00; they wanted to go over details with their whole squadron. As they started out, they would stay quite close together, so that they could communicate with hand signals and maintain radio silence. They would either keep in line, when they were in a confined area, or spread out closely side by side, where the terrain permitted. Two jeeps — eight soldiers with assorted bazookas, machine guns, and rifles — would follow closely behind.

When they got to their target area at the beginning of the pines, they spread out side by side, with Kaz and Windsor to the left of the road. Shonberg stayed on the road, slightly behind and to the right of Swann, with Martyn off to the right.

They proceeded slowly, at about 10 m.p.h., without event for about half an hour. Kaz wasn't sure whether he was disappointed or relieved by the absence of an enemy. Then suddenly, as they rounded a bend, Swann was terrified by the picture 200 yards ahead. From its huge size and massive turret, he recognized a Tiger. Fortunately, the German's turret was pointed to the side, and only slowly began to swing towards Swann. Swann got off one quick shot, which ricocheted harmlessly off the side of the Tiger's turret with a low, whistling sound. Swann ducked down into the tank and slammed the hatch—just in time, as machine-gun bullets raked his turret. His terrified driver headed for the ditch on the left. Swann couldn't believe his luck. The ditch was deep enough to hide his tank from the German's line of fire, but he could still see the action from his periscope.

Shonberg headed for the ditch on the other side, as did the two jeeps. But Shonberg was not quite so lucky. Before he got completely down into the protection of the ditch, the Tiger fired. The shell hit a glancing blow, not penetrating the tank. Shonberg was almost immediately on the radio:

"Just a flesh wound, chaps. We're OK, but there's so much ringing in our ears we can't hear a thing. We'll stay off the air until we get our hearing back. Once Jerry rotates his turret in another direction, we'll head for our assigned 4 o'clock position."

Apparently Shonberg was by now also in a protected position where he could observe the German from his periscope without presenting a target.

But the German was bearing down on Swann and Shonberg. Not very fast—he had slowed to 5 m.p.h.—but inexorably. Swann was sweating profusely. He would soon be exposed to the German fire, and he was trapped in a place where he couldn't move.

"We need help. Quick. Can anybody get off a shot to distract the Tiger?"

"Coming up, cap'n." Martyn was by now about even with the Tiger. There was a thinning in the woods that gave him a clear view of the German. He fired a round, which again deflected harmlessly off the Tiger's turret. He recognized his mistake—his next shot would be lower and to the left, where the side armor ended and the wheels and treads were exposed and vulnerable.

The German commander apparently realized his peril; he began to back up along the road. His turret was turning to the left, towards his tormentor. Martyn decided that he had better get out of the German's sight. Quickly. Rather than take a second shot, he moved forward, to a much heavier section of pines. But he was not safe. The German could see the tops of the pines bend as Martyn proceeded, and knew his approximate position. There was a sharp report as the German's 88 fired. The shell sheared off one of the pines neatly, just to the rear of the Sherman. Martyn ordered his driver to stop, to avoid giving the German any better idea of where he was. The next 88 shell passed about 15 feet in front of his tank. It was now Martyn's turn to shout over the radio for help.

Kaz had meanwhile found a trail, made by trucks or tractors, through the pines, about 75 yards to the left of the road and parallel to it. He accelerated rapidly down this path, without fear of giving away his position. By the time he heard Martyn's shout for help, he figured that he was beyond the German tank. He swung his Sherman sharply to the right and headed for the road.

As he came to a sparse section of trees, he could scarcely believe his eyes. There, only thirty yards in front of him, was the fattest target he had ever seen — the rear of the Tiger. He did not have to give his gunner an order; he had already pressed "fire."

The shell struck home. But there was none of the smoke and fire that Kaz expected from the Tiger's engine. Kaz's crew was already reloading; the German's turret was turning away from Martyn and toward him. It was then that Kaz discovered, to his great relief, one of the few defects of the Tiger: its turret was severely underpowered and could be rotated only with excruciatingly slow motion.

The Sherman fired again, this time achieving the desired result. Wisps of smoke began to appear from the Tiger's engine, and the rotating turret slowed to a halt. Over the radio, Kaz could hear cheers from several of the other tanks. But he wanted to make sure.

"Fire!"

With the third shot, greasy smoke billowed from the Tiger's engine. The hatches swung open, and the crew began to bail out. As their feet hit the ground, a rapid series of rifle shots rang out, and the German crew collapsed to the ground. In the middle of the tank action, the infantrymen had moved through the edge of the woods, where they had pointblank shots at the Germans.

Kaz wanted to make sure that there would be nothing left of the Tiger for the Germans to salvage from no-man's land. He ordered his gunner to fire again.

With the next shot, the smoke thickened and began to billow out of the main hatch. Kaz raised his hatch for a better look at the dying Tiger. Suddenly, there was an explosion. One of the shells inside the Tiger had gone off. A round black puff belched from the hatch. It rose slowly in a tight circle, reminding Kaz of the smoke rings that his grandfather, rocking contentedly by the stove with his pipe, used to demonstrate for his awed young grandson.

It was followed, in quick succession, by four or five more puffs. Then came a major explosion, blowing off the turret. They wouldn't have to worry about the Germans salvaging that Tiger.

Swann ordered the tanks to resume their formation, and proceeded cautiously down the road about a mile in search of additional victims. But it would soon be dusk.

"The Tiger hunt is over," Swan announced over the radio, indicating that the time had come to return to their base.

On the way back, Kaz thought back over the action. He mused on the peculiar rules of war. When a warship is sunk, the crews, having taken to lifeboats, are simply not to be attacked; they are out of combat, and, if the perils of the moment permit, they are to be picked up rather than left to perish slowly in the cruel sea. Armored land warfare is quite different: crews bailing out of tanks are fair game. Perhaps the difference is the speed with which a tank crew can be equipped with a new tank and once again become a mortal enemy. Perhaps it is because naval warfare is fought at greater distances. Combatants rarely see their adversaries face to face; they are not attacking flesh-and-blood enemies, but the steel of a destroyer, cruiser, or battleship. The conflict is less personal and less hate-filled.

Battleship crews are taught gunnery, the skills needed to hit a dimly seen target ten or even twenty miles away. Infantry, in contrast, begin their training with running charges, shouting "kill" as they plunge their bayonets into limp dummies.

Then, thought Kaz, there is the nasty business of fighter pilots. In the officers' mess back in England, he had heard stories of pilots who had bailed out, being machine gunned as they floated helplessly down. It was a barbaric act, but it was done. Not very frequently — German air crews were too busy trying to survive — but just often enough that pilots had begun to fall freely and not pull the ripcord until they were a thousand feet off the ground. At that height, they wouldn't have much choice of a landing spot, but it was better than the alternative.

That evening, they were told to get a good night's sleep, even sleep in past noon if they wanted. There would be a briefing the next day at 15:00 hrs. on an upcoming operation the following night.

When Kaz arrived for the briefing, a group of officers clustered around Swann, warmly congratulating him on the action of the previous day. Still feeling like an outsider, Kaz held off to the side, but his discomfort was quickly ended when the briefing officer entered the room and they took their seats.

"Before I outline tonight's action," Col. O'Brien began, "I want to congratulate Capt. Swann and his associates, particularly Major Jankowski." The briefing officer was conspicuously looking down at his notes; he seemed unable to remember Polish names. "In fact, Swann's tactics were brilliant. I will give him the floor to explain what they did. Some of you may have the opportunity to repeat his success in tonight's action. But first, I want to let you in on something even Swann doesn't know yet. Intelligence has just discovered that, in their tank battle, they killed none other than Hauptsturmführer Michael Wittmann — the scourge of the Russian front, who personally destroyed more than 100 Soviet tanks. Also, as some of you may have heard, he inflicted some nastiness on the Scots shortly after D-Day. Col. McGonagle has already called to congratulate us for settling scores with Wittmann."

Nastiness, indeed, thought Kaz. Just a week after D-Day, Wittmann had been in his Tiger in a forest alongside a road when he observed a number of Scottish Cromwell tanks approaching. He held fire as they moved closer, then dispatched the lead Cromwell with a single shell, blocking the road. Disdainful of the ability of the Cromwells' guns to pierce his armor, he then emerged from his hiding place and proceeded methodically down the line of Scottish tanks, knocking them out one by one with his 88 shells while his machine guns chewed up the accompanying infantrymen.

Swann then gave his account of the previous day's action, in an appropriate offhand, low-key way. He was most generous to single out Kaz, both for his development of the tactic and his part in knocking out Wittmann. He then turned the floor back to the briefing officer.

"The time has come," said Col. O'Brien, "for a major drive southward from our end of the front. As you know, we have had trouble attacking the German positions, particularly because of their 88s.

"We propose to use the cover of darkness to close on the enemy. We will proceed in several columns along a narrow front. Each of the tanks and other vehicles will leave their low running lights on at the back. Each vehicle will stay close to the vehicle ahead, following its lights. Your job will be to proceed four or five miles down the road, and spread out as day breaks. The purpose will be to create as much havoc as possible in the enemy rear, to rip the enemy's line open.

"At this point, those of you who are in the infantry may be alarmed—as you advance, won't you be at risk from hidden dangers in the dark? Quite apart from the Boche, won't you be in danger of being run over by our own tanks? To deal with this problem, we've invented the 'defrocked priest.' We've removed the guns from some of our older self-propelled artillery, to provide armored carriers for the infantry.

"In addition," the Col. proceeded, "the German positions will be bombed heavily. If this operation succeeds—and I have every confidence that it will—we will be able to join up with the Americans and trap much of the German army, opening the way for an attack directly eastward to Germany. That's why we're calling our operation *Totalize."*

"Jeez," thought Kaz. "The Limeys and Canucks don't have much imagination. Goodwood. Totalize." In contrast, "Cobra" was the American offensive that unleashed tanks from St. Lô towards Avranches two weeks earlier.

Nevertheless, thought Kaz, it will allow the Polish tanks to get into action.

As they started to line up at dusk, American bombers began to fly over. Unfortunately, communications were not as good as promised; some of the bombs fell short, inflicting casualties and creating confusion at the front of the columns. Not an auspicious beginning. But Kaz took some consolation as he heard the heavy explosions ahead; bombs were falling much more heavily on the German defenders.

Kaz and a group of 40 Polish tanks were on the left flank of the attack. In line with their plans, they proceeded forward, following the lights of the vehicle ahead. It was a rough ride, advancing over land so recently torn up by bombs. As dawn began to lighten the eastern sky, Kaz and a dozen other Polish tanks could make out the battlefield, and began to fire at targets of opportunity. It was only then that Kaz realized that only half of his tanks were with him; the rest had apparently lost their way during the night.

If the purpose was to create confusion, it succeeded brilliantly. Thousands of allied soldiers were milling around, exchanging fire with Germans in an area only two miles by four. Casualties were heavy on both sides, and by the late afternoon the allied advance ground to a halt. Fortunately, the casualties among the infantry were less than might have been expected; the defrocked priests—the first armored personnel carriers to be used in battle—were a notable success.

The attack did not, however, succeed in breaking through the enemy lines. But for the Germans, it was a mighty close thing. As their lines stabilized, they nervously took inventory. They had just 35 operational tanks left in the sector—only one for every 20 on the allied side. The next stand might be their last.

14 August. Headquarters, Army Group West.

With his defenses crumbling, von Kluge now faced the outcome he dreaded — his forces were in danger of being encircled. How to escape? He had to withdraw. But the Führer, standing before the map in his East Prussian fantasyland, was maneuvering divisions that no longer existed; he was insisting on preparations for a new attack toward Avranches and the sea. What the Führer was demanding, in short, was a repeat of Dunkirk four years before, when the Wehrmacht was approaching the peak of its power. Von Kluge came to Dietrich in desperation.

"I owe it to my men to withdraw, consequences be damned. I no longer put much value in my own life."

"I doubt that you can get away with this, sir, even for a brief period. I'm sure you haven't forgotten about our little guest from the General Staff."

"Of course not. But perhaps he could have an accident."

"If I might, sir, I don't think that will work."

Von Kluge's eyes narrowed, piercing his subordinate.

"You've been running around my back, Dietrich, communicating directly with people around Hitler.... 'Little Sir Echo,' I believe you call him," von Kluge added, to prove that his accusation was not just a lucky guess. "You have something to tell me?"

"If I might, sir, I was only trying to find out what was going on, so I could be of more help to you."

"And?"

Dietrich paused, but saw no alternative to an honest, if somewhat stilted, answer. "Your doubts about your position are well founded."

It was now von Kluge's turn to pause. Then he asked slowly, "Do they think I was involved in the plot against Hitler?"

"I have no information on that, sir. But I do know that the Führer has come to doubt your loyalty. After the failure of the attack to the west," Dietrich saw no point in softening the blow, "he fell into a rage, accusing you of failing because you wanted to fail. You sabotaged his plan by attacking too soon. He wants the new attack to be well prepared."

Von Kluge laughed bitterly. "Well prepared? In this chaos? Of course, we'll draw up a complete order of battle. Do dead men count?"

"If I might, sir, I would like to make a suggestion."

"Be my guest. And while we're alone, cut out this 'sir' business."

"As you wish, si—" Dietrich caught himself before he finished "sir." Habits were hard to break—which of course was precisely the point of military training. He then answered. "You might be able to hide behind the SS generals whose loyalty to Hitler is utterly beyond question....

"As you know," he continued, "a couple of them have already recommended that the drive westward be aborted, that the forces be used to shore up our crumbling southern flank. You might forward these recommendations to the Führer."

Von Kluge did. He also added a postscript: "I associate myself with their recommendations."

How sad, thought Dietrich. Not even his field marshal's baton gives him the confidence to express his unvarnished views to the Führer. He has to pass them off as the ideas of his Nazi subordinates.

Hitler appeared to accept these recommendations; he authorized a withdrawal of the most westerly units. But then came a new order. This was only a tactical withdrawal; forces were to be regrouped for a new, powerful thrust to the sea. The attack must not be launched until fully prepared. Hitler himself would give the final order.

"This is utter madness. Madness. The great corporal is floating off into never-never land." Von Kluge was again alone with Dietrich. He went on:

"Have we got down to the end game, where we have no option but to defy the Führer?"

Dietrich was not going to respond to that one.

"Dietrich.... Dietrich.... You wouldn't be Sepp's son, by any chance?"

"No sir," Kurt replied briskly. SS General Sepp Dietrich, one of Hitler's favorites, was then in charge the Panzer army guarding von Kluge's southern flank. He also was Kurt's uncle. Because of his Nazi enthusiasms, he had been shunned by Kurt's side of the family during the mid 1930s, particularly after Sepp oversaw the Night of the Long

Knives, when Röhm and others were executed. Kurt's immediate family considered themselves professional soldiers, not politicians; not Nazis and certainly not cold-blooded killers. They didn't quite know how to react when Sepp Dietrich parlayed a job as Hitler's chauffeur into the command of an SS Division.

How old von Kluge suddenly looked! Just a few days ago, he had seemed indignant, almost defiant. Now his shoulders were stooped, and a tick twitched at the side of his face. To all appearances, he was a beaten man, almost reconciled to his fate. Perhaps Kurt was motivated by pity. Without knowing quite why, he added:

"He's not my father. He's my uncle."

"Then you may be our last hope."

"How?" Dietrich sensed that his single word was hanging, naked. He almost added "sir" out of habit.

"I want you to go to your uncle. Ask him to make the case directly to Hitler for an orderly withdrawal."

"But I'm not close to him. I scarcely know him. After my uncle joined the Nazi Party, my father refused to speak to him. Well, actually, he tried to make up a couple of years ago. He thought it might be good life insurance. But by then it was too late. His overtures went unanswered."

"Nevertheless, you're the best chance we've got."

Kurt saw absolutely no chance of success. "I'd really rather not."

"And I'd really rather you volunteer."

Kurt realized that was an order. In good military tradition, he had just been "volunteered."

"What should I say to him?"

"Ask him to tell Hitler the truth. If we don't withdraw at once, we'll be encircled. It will be another Stalingrad.... On second thought, you'd better leave that out. It's bad salesmanship to mention Stalingrad to the Führer. Just keep it simple.... But you might add one thing, in case Hitler is having trouble counting. The Americans and Canadians are less than 30 kilometers apart. Once they link up, we're doomed."

24
Falaise

Cry "Havoc!" and let slip
the dogs of war.
                    Shakespeare, *Julius Caesar*

The next morning, Dietrich headed off to see his uncle on the southeastern flank. Von Kluge was on his way to view his crumbling defenses in the rapidly shrinking pocket. To keep contact with his command, he was accompanied by a van crammed with radio and coding equipment.

As Dietrich's staff car approached his uncle's headquarters, Kurt was concerned that he might not even be able to get in to see his uncle. A message had been sent from von Kluge's headquarters, but, in the midst of the chaotic battle, he couldn't be sure it was actually received. Should he emphasize that he was bringing a message from von Kluge? Or should he use the family angle — stress that he was Sepp Dietrich's nephew? He chose a middle course, and instructed his driver. As the driver stopped at the checkpoint, he spoke to the guard.

"Col. Dietrich, with a message for Gen. Dietrich from Field Marshal von Kluge." The driver said the name "Dietrich" slowly each time, to make sure the guard got the point.

Kurt had removed his hat to make the family resemblance more obvious. He raised his finger to cover the scar on his left cheek. The guard glanced into the back of the car and saluted. "The message, please." He held out his hand.

"It's an oral message, to be given only to Gen. Dietrich directly," replied the driver.

The guard retreated several paces to a field telephone, and after a brief conversation, waved the car on.

Kurt was kept waiting about 20 minutes, nervously rehearsing several possible opening statements, depending on his uncle's mood.

When he was called in, he was astonished by his uncle's warmth. The past slights of the father were not held against the son. In fact, the General seemed to be apologizing for neglecting his nephew for so long. It was Kurt who had to bring the conversation back to the point.

"My actual message is quite short, sir. Field Marshal von Kluge sends his regards. He asks that you communicate the desperation of our situation directly to the Führer, who holds you in such high regard. Specifically, we must have permission to withdraw or we will be surrounded."

"My response is just as short. Of course, *I* know that we're about to be encircled. You're asking me to tell the painful truth to the Führer, to destroy his illusions. No thanks. If I want to get shot, that's the way to do it." And the General was gone.

While Gen. Dietrich was unwilling to put his neck on the block to prevent a catastrophe, he was not about to get caught himself. He detected a loophole in Hitler's earlier order permitting a temporary withdrawal, and his tanks were rushing eastward to escape the closing jaws of the pocket near Falaise.

While Kurt Dietrich was returning cautiously to headquarters — mindful of Rommel's fate, and continuously scanning the skies for enemy fighters — Field Marshal von Kluge's inspection party was picking its way along the back roads with equal caution. As they were approaching a narrow bridge, they were particularly vulnerable, and all eyes — except those of the drivers, but including those of the Field Marshal — were on the skies. Just as their communications van got to the middle of the bridge, it exploded. A Thunderbolt roared over, only 50 feet above the ground; it had approached out of the sun. Although unhurt, the driver of von Kluge's staff car took to the ditch. Von Kluge was thrown from the car, and the driver rushed towards a clump of woods. Von Kluge was after him, shouting for him to stop — the plane had already disappeared. But then, out of the corner of his eye, he saw a second Thunderbolt. As he dove to the ground, he could see machine-gun bullets kicking up dust and sod, proceeding rapidly towards the staff car. Suddenly, it, too, was in flames.

When Dietrich got back to von Kluge's headquarters in mid afternoon, the Field Marshal had not yet returned. Dietrich headed for communications, to Lt. Bock. He needed to find out if there were any movement in the Führer's position, if they were being given an opportunity to withdraw.

The answer was no. In fact, Hitler was in a rage. He couldn't communicate with von Kluge; the Field Marshall had disappeared. But where? The Führer suspected treason. He suspected that von Kluge had contacted the Allies; German intelligence had intercepted an American radio message asking where von Kluge was. The Führer feared that von Kluge was about to lead the whole Western Army into capitulation. Himmler had been whispering in Hitler's ear of von Kluge's treachery; the Field Marshall was involved in the July 20 bomb plot. The Gestapo were collecting evidence. "This," moaned the Führer, "is the worst day of my life."

"The bomb plot, perhaps," thought Dietrich. "But this sort of treachery? Unthinkable for a Prussian officer. But then," he caught himself as he wondered: "capitulation in France might not be such a bad idea. We can't win this war. Further bloodshed is senseless. Wouldn't it be better to let the Western allies occupy Germany, rather than leave ourselves to the tender mercies of the Russians?" He reflected briefly on the three-year slaughter on the Eastern Front, and on the white rage with which Stalin would deal with postwar Germany.

About midnight, von Kluge appeared in a battered kübelwagen. He had spent most of the day skulking in ditches, dodging American planes. He didn't want to talk about it, but he did want a report from Dietrich. No hope from his uncle, was all the younger Dietrich had to say.

Von Kluge was about to retire in exhaustion when a message was delivered. He had been relieved of command and was to fly back to Germany.

"The time has come," he whispered as he reached into his desk and drew out a bottle and two glasses.

The two men sat glumly sipping cognac. The older man reminisced about his early days in the army, when he was being promoted rapidly and was so full of hope. Dietrich wondered, should he tell the Field Marshal of Hitler's fury? What was the point? The point was obvious: von Kluge should have no illusions about his reception back in Berlin. To his horror, Dietrich had learned that a number of the July 20 plotters had been strangled, hanged by piano wire from meat hooks. The Gestapo made a motion picture of the grisly scene for the Führer's entertainment.

"My backdoor source from the *Wolfsschanze.*" Dietrich was throwing out a hint that he had information of interest to his boss.

The Field Marshal said nothing. Dietrich had lost track of how much they both had had to drink. He continued.

"Hitler's in a panic. He had all sorts of hallucinations about what you might be doing today. He couldn't contact you."

"Of course not. My communications van was blown up."

Dietrich decided to skip the bit about surrendering the army. Instead, he took a deep breath and got to the main point:

"According to Little Sir Echo, Himmler told the Führer that you were in on the bomb plot."

So now he had done it. Von Kluge could be under no illusions. The Gestapo would likely constitute his welcoming party in Berlin.

They sat in silence for perhaps 45 minutes. The Field Marshal then sighed and indicated he would like to retire. As they walked unsteadily toward the door, von Kluge made a most unmilitary gesture: he put his arm around the younger man and squeezed him.

"Try to survive, my boy. Try to survive. The war won't last forever."

First thing the next day, von Kluge issued new orders: All forces were to escape the Falaise Pocket without delay. The Führer be damned. Ironically, Hitler gave the same order later in the day, after von Kluge left for Germany; a withdrawal was finally permitted.

As von Kluge's plane approached the military airport near Berlin, his batman shook the Field Marshal to stir him from a deep sleep. He felt a chill on the Field Marshal's face. Von Kluge was dead. He had slipped a vial of poison into his mouth during the flight.

In the previous few days, Dietrich had given up any hope of surviving. In spite of what von Kluge said, death was simply a matter of time. As there was an acute shortage of officers, he volunteered (truly, this time) to fill in as a tank commander. Somewhat to his distaste, he was asked to fill a spot in an SS division, the fanatic Hitlerjungend. His task would be simple, but perhaps hopeless: to lead a group of tanks through the tightening noose.

16 August 1944. Patton's 3rd Army Headquarters near Alençon.

Almost, but not quite, thought Patton. We must close the trap before the Huns slip out. His men were still pushing forward, but they needed more help from the north. He put in a call to Bradley, the overall commander of American ground forces. After a few pleasantries, he got down to business:

"We need help from the Brits, and we need it now. If we don't get it, we'll miss a once-in-a-lifetime chance."

Patton was silent for a moment, listening to Bradley's response. He then continued, his voice rising into the squeaky range in his agitation:

"But Montgomery may dilly-dally, Brad. He doesn't like to attack unless he has overwhelming odds. He already has odds; the Germans are beaten. We've got to trap them now, not let them slip away to fight another day."

Another silence, then Patton exploded:

"Well you can tell Montgomery that if he doesn't get off his ass, I'll push forward. When I cut off the Germans, I'll keep right on going. I'll drive him back into the sea. It'll be another Dunkirk."

Patton hung up.

Montgomery didn't need prodding. He had already ordered the Canadian army—with the Polish Armored Division attached—to attack toward Falaise.

17 August 1944. With Canadian and Polish forces northwest of Falaise.

By the time they received the order from Montgomery, the Canadians and Poles had regrouped and were ready. But they still faced the same problem: how to close on the deadly 88s before the Germans could see them coming. This time, they would not wait for dark. Their initial cover would be a smokescreen laid by B-25s; it would be supplemented by the dust thrown up by the vehicles, and by additional smoke if needed. They had now advanced to the relatively open countryside, and their attack would be along a much broader front of several miles. In order to avoid the straggling and chaos of the earlier attack, when one wrong turn led a whole group of tanks astray, they were given very simple instructions: proceed through the smoke, toward the sun, until they met the enemy.

This time, the tactic worked. They pushed through the weakened German defenses and were soon in Falaise.

The Poles were now ordered to move southeastward from Falaise, along the Dives River, to block the German escape. They were an obvious choice, even though they had arrived in France only recently and were the least experienced of all the divisions under Montgomery's command. They longed for an opportunity to smash the Nazi legions in their moment of peril, to avenge the humiliations of 1939. They met their order to attack with cheers.

Because of the length of his experience in Normandy — a whole month with the Canadian armored division! — Kaz was chosen to lead the column that would aim for the further of the two bridges that the Germans were using as escape routes. His task was to reach this bridge, at Chambois, as soon as possible; to take the high ground above the bridge; and to use this position to deny the bridge to the enemy. "As soon as possible" meant exactly what it said; he was to avoid unnecessary contact with the enemy until he reached his objective. Because they would be confronting enemy tanks at Chambois, they were provided with six of the new "Fireflies" — Sherman tanks equipped with high-velocity, armor-piercing guns.

The initial advance was much less eventful than Kaz had expected. There was only sporadic contact with the enemy, who faded away when they were fired upon by his powerful column. The Poles encountered fierce action just once, and then only as spectators. As they rounded a curve on a hill, they observed a column of a dozen German tanks interspersed with a large number of trucks, horse-drawn artillery, and lighter vehicles on the narrow road below. It was an inviting target, but his orders permitted no delay. Perhaps the orders could be stretched? Fortunately, the temptation was suddenly removed. Three Typhoons came sweeping in, firing rockets at the lead tank, setting it ablaze and blocking the road. Several more Typhoons quickly followed, attacking the rear vehicle and trapping the hapless column. The Typhoons, now accompanied by Spitfires, began to proceed methodically down the line, setting one vehicle after another ablaze with rocket, cannon, and machine-gun fire.

Kaz had already instructed his radio operator to get on the air — quickly — to inform the British pilots of their location, to avoid a terrible mistake. He wished he had time to watch the aircraft complete their deadly task, but he ordered his column to press on, to reach his target as soon as possible.

After several more hours, the French guide announced that they had reached their goal; Chambois lay immediately ahead. Kaz was puzzled. He thought that the bridge was on the near side of Chambois, yet a bridge was nowhere to be seen. Nor could he see the commanding heights that he was to occupy. He sent out several runners, on foot, to find out where they were. The runners were back in a few minutes. They were not at Chambois, but Champeaux; apparently the French guide had misunderstood the heavily accented words of the Poles. There was nothing for it but to patiently — and this time carefully — communicate their objective to the guide.

Soon they were on their way, this time towards the real Chambois. On either side were rolling hills of what apparently was wheat, but was now beaten down by the weather, never having been harvested. Much of it was chewed up by the tracks of tanks and other heavy vehicles. They then moved into more hilly country, mostly covered with trees. The trees, too, showed the effects of war; many had been knocked over, and the forest was pockmarked with shells.

Going over a rise in the road, Kaz, in the lead tank, saw a German column directly ahead, passing through an intersection in the center of a small village. He was about to give the order to fire when the traffic controller halted the German column and waved for Kaz's tanks to pass through. Kaz was astonished; didn't the soldier recognize the Shermans? He quickly gave the order: hold your fire. Commanders, keep your heads up out of the hatches, as usual. Do not rotate your guns in a threatening way. But be ready to fire, aiming at the armored vehicles first, if anyone starts shooting.

As they got to the intersection, Kaz looked straight ahead, avoiding eye contact with the German controller. He crossed his fingers as his trucks began to pass through the intersection. But soon the whole column—thirty tanks plus fifteen trucks and other miscellaneous vehicles—was through without event.

Now Kaz could think back to his earlier question: is it possible that the traffic controller didn't recognize the Sherman tanks? Or the American-made trucks? No, very unlikely. He had to admire the German's quick thinking. One cool corporal. He didn't relish a pointblank encounter with Shermans. Perhaps others in the German column also recognized the Poles, but decided they wanted to live. Kaz found himself thinking: I hope he survives the next few hours, to become our prisoner. Some day, I'd like to talk to him.

Later, that evening, one of his officers raised a question with Kaz: why hadn't he attacked the Germans, who were no match for the Polish tanks? Kaz's answer was brief: True, but they would have created a shambles in the village, and been delayed at least an hour. If the Germans had gotten off a couple of lucky shots and knocked out one or two Shermans, the Polish advance would have been blocked; the delay would have been much longer. Their job was to get to Chambois, and quickly. Their mission was to trap Germans, not kill them. At least, not this time.

Nevertheless, their trip was not entirely uneventful. About three miles further along, beside the road, Kaz saw an old castle. He stopped briefly: it was an ideal spot for a German ambush. To attack the castle made no sense: they would expend valuable ammunition, and they couldn't really demolish it, anyhow. Should he play it safe, and make a detour, or chance it, passing close to the castle? Once more, the decision was made for him. A white flag began to wave from the castle's tower, and soon a group of forty German soldiers began to file out, their hands in the air. Kaz decided he didn't want to be encumbered with prisoners. He left eight infantrymen, who herded their prisoners back into the castle.

Once again he was puzzled: Why hadn't the Germans used their fortified position to fire on his tanks? One of his men, who spoke German, came back with the answer:

"They heard the Poles were coming. They didn't want to start a fight. If they made us mad, they weren't sure we'd take prisoners."

Only a few miles further, they took more prisoners. As they reached the top of a hill, they found their progress blocked by a group of vehicles, apparently the remnants of a Panzer regiment: ten or eleven tanks, two with their treads off, and the others looking decidedly shopworn. They were surrounded by a scattering of other vehicles and men, many of whom were lying down, either exhausted, wounded, or both. Kaz gave a hand signal for five other Shermans to come up alongside him.

He noticed that none of the German tanks had its gun pointed in his direction. He sent a message to the other tanks: Regardless of what I do, hold you fire unless the Germans swing their turrets in our direction, or unless we get other incoming fire.

He then took aim at the treads of what, to him, looked like the least damaged of the German tanks. He fired a single shot. The tread clanged as it was blown off the wheels. Kaz waited. Soon, white flags began to appear.

Again, it was up to the infantry to take and guard the prisoners. Kaz now had a difficult decision. He was encumbered with prisoners; if he proceeded, he would have little or no infantry protection. Worse, he was running low on food and fuel; the diversion to Champeaux had been costly. He decided to leave his main force behind and concentrate all his extra fuel for a minimum force of ten tanks.

As the fuel drums were being brought together, an excited lieutenant reported that they had just captured the remnants of the 2nd Panzer division. His men had been looking through the pay books of the prisoners, and found familiar names: Wysoka and Naprawa. These were the sites where, five years earlier, the 2nd Panzers had chewed up the light tanks of the Polish armored brigades.

A young sergeant had found something even more interesting: an undamaged communications truck crammed with radios and other equipment. Kaz jumped up into the back of the truck and slid into the operator's chair, in front of a complicated-looking typewriter. It had an extra set of letters above the keyboard, and at the bottom was a tangle of wires plugged into a board. "Looks like coding equipment," he thought. "And complex. I wonder how it works?" Just as he was about to start playing with it, Captain Pulaski came up to inform him that the ten Polish tanks were ready to leave.

Kaz spoke briefly to Pulaski, who would be in command of the twenty tanks and infantry that would be left behind. Because of the shortage of fuel, they should take up defensive positions on a nearby hill; their task would be to block any Germans attempting to escape eastward along the roads at the base of the hill. Before moving to the hilltop, they should blow up the German tanks, but the communications truck must be saved for Intelligence; it looked too important to destroy. "I wonder," mused Kaz, "if it is some sort of secret newfangled coding equipment."

He also gave Pulaski a blunt warning. It was all very well to capture veterans of the early Polish campaign. But he wanted to make sure that things didn't get out of hand. He wanted to find all the prisoners alive when he got back.

19 August 1944. 10:00 hrs. With Polish armor near Chambois.

As they reached the heights at Chambois, Kaz ordered his ten tanks into an extended arc commanding the river below. Through the haze and greasy smoke of battle, they gazed down at the grim panorama of war. To the right, the road was cluttered with burned-out tanks, smashed assault guns, and broken carts dragged by terrified horses, straining to break loose from their harness.

The sides of the road were littered with the detritus of war: disabled trucks, staff cars, and ammunition carts that had been rudely shoved off the road. A jumble of small arms and nondescript fragments of equipment cluttered the ditches, interspersed with corpses, both men and horses, some whole, some dismembered. As the wind shifted, Kaz was overwhelmed by the oppressive, sickening stench of death.

Through the shambles, a dozen German tanks were picking their way toward the narrow bridge. One tank was already across, and quickly accelerating towards the escape route to the east. Kaz gave the order: his men were to fire at will at the other tanks as they looped around the bend and came to the bridge, presenting ideal targets. Within a few seconds, a German tank was disabled in the middle of the bridge, its near-side tread blown off. The crew scrambled from the hatches, slipping down behind their tank and thence into the river below to protect themselves from the machine guns and heavy fire from above.

A second tank moved up behind, its treads skidding on the damp bridge as it strained to push the lead tank out of the way, off the bridge and into the river. Its uncertain efforts came to an abrupt end when several direct hits set it on fire. Only one trooper emerged, but, as he got half way out of the hatch, he slowly came to a stop. After a second's pause, he slid back into the tank, his battle suit in flames. A few moments later, the tank exploded, blowing the heavy turret ten feet into the air.

It was at this point that Kaz received a shouted message from his radio operator: the main Polish column, proceeding on their left parallel to the river, had just made contact with Patton's Third Army advancing from the south. The Falaise Pocket was at last closed; the main lines of German escape were cut.

Kaz had little time to reflect. The blazing hulk blocked a German escape across the bridge; most of the crews were abandoning their tanks and fleeing on foot towards the river. But two of the German crews were intent on escape, edging their tanks along the bank of the river toward a strip of white water that marked a shallows. For Kaz and the others on the hilltop, they were now out of range.

Kaz glanced to his right; another German tank was approaching in the distance. Apparently, its crew had been warned of the dangers ahead. They had left the road, and were slowly proceeding on a parallel path toward the shallows, safely out of range of the Poles on the hilltop.

Kaz had to make a decision: would he attempt to block the escape route across the shallows, or count on the main Polish force and the Americans to stop the Germans further east? It was too late to stop the first two German tanks, but their was still time for the third, and, perhaps later, a fourth, fifth and sixth. To take up a blocking position on the far bank, Kaz would have to cross the river. This would be no problem; there was a second shallows almost directly below the hill, where he could cross under the protection of his tanks remaining on the bluff. But he would then have to cross the road and proceed along an open, flat lowland edged by woods. It presented a considerable risk. He had left his infantry behind, and thus would be vulnerable to enemy soldiers who might be lurking in the woods with their *Panzerfausten*—the snub-nosed, single-shot, hand-held antitank weapon. But once they reached the treeless bank opposite the white water, they would be in an ideal position to block approaching German tanks. There was a ridge behind which they could take cover, overlooking the shallows.

His reflection was over; he would stop the German. His orders were to block the escape route. And he had waited too long to avenge the losses on that crisp September morning almost five years before. Leaving Jan with eight tanks to maintain their commanding position on the hill, he signaled Ciezki to accompany him. The two Polish tanks picked their way down the steep slope, then crossed the shallows and the road to the caked, cracked clay of the river flats beyond. He and Ciezki pulled up and waited behind the ridge. With little more than their turrets vulnerable, they would have the Panzer at a disadvantage. And they had their new tanks with high-velocity guns.

Kaz wanted to improve the odds even more. He sent a message to Ciezki: hold your fire until the German tank is in the middle of the river and unable to maneuver.

They waited. The German approached cautiously, pausing briefly on the far bank before moving slowly into the river. Kaz and Ciezki rotated their turrets, waiting for a pointblank shot.

Suddenly there was an explosion. Ciezki's tank rocked sharply and erupted in flame. With his head out the hatch, Kaz could feel the sudden burst of heat on the side of his face; he held his hand up for protection as he ducked down and slammed the hatch.

Kaz had been focusing so intently on the tank crossing the river that he hadn't seen a second German tank approaching from the left, along the far bank of the river. Because of the angle, it had a clear shot at Ciezki.

Now, it presented an immediate peril to Kaz and his crew. They swung their turret away from the tank in the river, and opened fire at the newcomer. The German's side was exposed as it moved along the bank; the Poles' first shot hit home, passing between the wheels and into the interior. Smoke began to belch from its hatch.

Kaz quickly turned his attention back to the enemy in the river. The German was struggling with unsteady footing on the slippery stones of the riverbed, and he was completely exposed. Both tanks fired at the same time; each hit its target. The Panzer slipped sideways, its gun pointed at an odd angle, in the general direction of the bridge. It had lost power; its turret no longer moved.

But Kaz likewise faced a crisis; smoke was filling one side of his tank. He pulled himself out of the hatch and staggered several dozen yards, collapsing near a clump of bushes. He became of aware of blood trickling over his goggles.

In the river, a haze of smoke and steam enveloped the German tank. Kaz could discern one tanker escaping from the hatch and throwing himself into the water. His head bobbed up and down as he swept past. His war was over; the current would take him downward toward the main Canadian force. A second man was by now out of the tank. Rather than take his chances with the river, he was struggling toward the bank, less than thirty yards from Kaz.

Perhaps to help him fight the current, he had thrown off his helmet. As he pulled himself up the bank, he was, in spite of his bedraggled appearance, the picture of a Prussian officer — firm chin, broad forehead, and blond, Aryan hair. Like Kaz, he had blood trickling down his face. The blow to his head had apparently been severe; as he rose uncertainly to his feet, he seemed disoriented. He began making his way unsteadily up the beach, limping noticeably.

There was something more than his Teutonic appearance that caught Kaz's attention, something more than the lengthy scar on his left cheek. Kaz had seen that face before. He wondered where. Then he recalled the face in the rifle scope five years before, on that first tragic day of war. Kaz fumbled inside his jumpsuit for his Luger, a trophy from one of Wittmann's men. Staggering closer, the German noticed the Pole, who was by now supporting himself on one elbow. The

German blinked. His face hardened into an arrogant sneer. He turned his back on his adversary, and began to limp unsteadily across the dried mud toward the safety of the trees.

Kaz found that he was unable to get to his feet; he was aware of a numbness in his back. He carefully aimed the Luger until it pointed directly between the German's shoulder blades. Now that the Allies had blocked the lines of escape, the German was almost certainly headed toward captivity. Kaz let the Luger sag. Then he thought back to that day five years before, his comrades holding white clothing as they were machine gunned....

But he also thought back to his military college days, with its instilled code of chivalry.

After five years of war, what remained of that code?

POSTSCRIPT

The Battle of the Falaise Pocket was one of the great Allied victories of the Second World War, ranking close to Stalingrad. At Stalingrad, an estimated 275,000 German and Romanian soldiers were encircled when the Red Army closed the trap on Nov. 22, 1942. During the remaining ten weeks of the battle, about 25,000 wounded were flown out of the pocket, leaving about a quarter of a million men to face death or capture. Stalingrad marked the great turning point of the war in Europe; thereafter, Germans were everywhere on the defensive.

The toll on the Germans in the Falaise pocket is less easily quantified, in part because there is no simple starting point for the count, comparable to the time when the trap was sealed west of Stalingrad. The Falaise pocket was closed only slowly, allowing German columns to move eastward through the gap during the second and third weeks of August 1944, particularly under the cover of darkness.

If one picks the American thrust southward from St. Lô towards Avranches as the beginning of the Falaise battle, total German losses approached those at Stalingrad—200,000 men, of whom a fifth were killed. If, on the other hand, one considers only the German casualties after the trap was more-or-less closed, the total was less than half as large. But, by any estimate, the Germans suffered heavy losses.

One can, however, only speculate on the lost opportunities, on what might have been. There were recriminations among the Allies — Americans and British each accusing the other of insufficient vigor in closing and sealing the neck of the pocket, allowing perhaps as many as 300,000 German soldiers to escape. Many would face the Allies again, defending the channel ports. In those fortified positions, they slowed the Allied advance into Northern Germany.

The lost opportunities may be traced in part to the difficulties of coordination when two allied armies attempt to join head-on. Bradley was worried that Patton's vigorous advances would lead to accidental attacks on British, Canadian, or Polish troops. He became so concerned at one point that he ordered Patton to withdraw one of his northward thrusts toward Falaise. In fact, there was a minor — but harmless — skirmish between Polish and American forces when they finally did meet; it ended quickly when an American officer raised a white flag, signaling a request for parley.

At a critical time — August 14 — Bradley became so frustrated by British inaction that he thought to himself, "If Montgomery wants help in closing the gap, then let him ask for it." Bradley thereupon ordered a major spearhead, under Gen. Haislip, eastward toward the Seine, diverting troops that otherwise might have been used to seal the gap. Soon, he did receive a request from Montgomery to advance north to meet the Poles at Chambois, but Haislip was already on his way to the Seine.

For the Germans, Falaise was a catastrophe. But it could have been more. If the trap had been sprung more quickly — and more firmly — the whole German position in the west might have collapsed, leading to an end of the war by late 1944. Perhaps the partial, bittersweet nature of the victory explains a puzzle. Why does the Falaise encirclement command so little attention compared to the two other great events in the west in 1944: the D-Day landing — on whose success depended all that followed — and the Battle of the Bulge, when the dying Third Reich turned fiercely one last time on its western tormentors?

For the Poles, the battle of the Falaise gap reinforced their pride. Although many were untested in battle, they were chosen to lead the final thrust from the north, to link up with American forces. During one critical battle on the "Mace" — a ridge near Chambois — they were surrounded by Germans slipping through gaps in the allied lines. Raining fire on their enemies below, they stood firm. But then, they had little choice; they did not have the fuel to attempt a breakout. Later, when Royal Canadian Engineers passed over this ridge, they found it dotted with fresh graves. To honor their fallen comrades, the Engineers erected a simple sign: A Polish Battlefield.

But for the Poles, the Second World War was a tragedy. Invaded from the West by the Germans and from the East by the Soviets during the first month of the war, they faced continuous turmoil. First one, then the other, of their historical enemies launched devastating offensives across their land.

The Home Army ended in disaster. Predictably, the Soviets incited them to revolt. "People of Warsaw! To arms! Attack the Germans!" urged Moscow radio as the Red Army reached the Vistula River, across from Warsaw. The Home Army leadership was split: should they act? They were woefully ill-equipped after the recent German discoveries of their weapons caches. But their time had come; they revolted on the first day of August. Thereupon, the Red Army paused and marked time on the eastern side of the River.

This should scarcely have come as a surprise; the objective of the Polish uprising was to preempt a Communist takeover. Stalin wanted the noncommunist leadership eliminated, to clear the way for his puppet regime.

Why not let Hitler do his dirty work?

Hitler obliged. In seven weeks of heavy fighting, his troops crushed the uprising, killing 10,000 members of the Home Army and perhaps as many as 200,000 civilians. Week after week, Stalin refused to let British planes drop arms to the Home Army and then land at Soviet bases. He relented only after the sixth week of the uprising, when the outcome was no longer in doubt.

At the end, the proximate objective of the Second World War — a free Poland — remained unfulfilled.

That goal had to wait forty long years, for the peaceful revolutions of the 1980s. Then, the famous names would no longer belong to the aristocracy—names like Sikorski, Komorowski, or Raczynski—but rather to men of humble beginnings: a shipyard electrician turned labor leader, Lech Walesa, and a man who started his career as an obscure seminarian: Karol Wojtyla, Bishop of Rome. The Soviet leader, Gorbachev, also played a central role. In 1987, as part of his policy of *glasnost* (openness), he decided to shine light into one of the more gruesome corners of Soviet history. He appointed a joint Soviet-Polish board to investigate the Katyn Forest massacres, foreshadowing an end to the already-shaky legitimacy the Communist regime in Poland. It was the beginning of the final chapter of Soviet domination of Eastern Europe.

Field Marshal Günther Von Kluge was buried in a quiet military ceremony, unlike his erstwhile subordinate, Field Marshal Erwin Rommel. Hitler's most celebrated General was given a state funeral with full military honors, after he, too, was linked to the bomb plot and committed suicide. In each case, the official cause of death was the same: cerebral hemorrhage.

25

Epilogue
History, Fiction, and Lies

> ... mostly a true book, with some stretchers.
>
> Huckleberry Finn, describing Mr. Twain's earlier work, The Adventures of Tom Sawyer

The classical Greek word *plasma* means fiction. It also means forgery or "lies." We may cringe at the word "lies." But there is no denying: much of this book is not exactly true. Five of the main characters—Kaz, Anna, Ryk, Yvonne, and Jan—are fictional; they never existed.

Nevertheless, the main story is historically accurate. World War II was precipitated by Hitler's invasion of Poland, and by the decision of Britain and France to honor their commitment to Poland by declaring war on Germany. Yet Poland was beyond salvation, caught between Hitler's Germany and Stalin's Soviet Union.

In addition, the fictional five participated in many real, historical events—the defense of Warsaw, the massacre in Katyn Forest, the exodus of the Polish army to North Africa, the significant role of Poles in the Battle of Britain, and, most of all, the early and indispensable Polish contributions to codebreaking.

A whole list of characters were real people, from the Polish codebreakers Marian Rejewski, Henryk Zygalski and Jerzy Rozycki to the main British characters at Bletchley Park—Alan Turing, Alastair Denniston, Alan Welchman, Harry Hinsley—to most of the German protagonists in France: von Kluge, Sepp Dietrich, von Stülpnagel, and

Hofacker. They did approximately what they are reported to have done in this novel.

"Approximately." There's the snag. How is the reader to know what is fact, and what is fiction? Interested readers may find footnote information at www.lastgoodwar.com. For the more casual reader, this epilogue will provide some guidance, some help in separating history from "lies."

First, the flesh-and-blood *dramatis personae* should be identified, in addition to those listed above. Among the Poles, only Sikorski should be added to the real historical figures; the rest are fictional, although some of Anna's relatives are *very* loosely based on Polish diplomats of the 1930s. Bertrand, Lemoine, and Schmidt are real historical figures; they did meet in Verviers, Belgium, where Schmidt gave Enigma secrets to Bertrand.

At Bletchley Park, Yvonne joins Anna as a fictional character, but Mavis Lever was very real indeed. She did notice the strange absence of the letter L in an early Italian naval message; the result was the breaking of the Italian code and the British triumph off Cape Matapan. Admiral Sir Andrew Cunningham was indeed the victor in that naval engagement. When he came to BP to offer his thanks, he was backed into a newly whitewashed wall by Mavis and other vivacious, mischievous young women.

The two Americans at Bletchley Park, Bill Bundy and Lewis Powell, were also real people, although their role has been fictionalized. In later life, Bundy went on to become a senior official of the State Department, while Powell was elevated to the U.S. Supreme Court.

In the Battle of Britain, the characters are fictional, with the notable exception of Sgt. Josef Frantisek. He was a Czech ace, who, in the words of Len Deighton *(Fighter)* "had flying and air-fighting skills in abundance but he lacked any kind of air discipline. Once in the air, he simply chased Germans. More than once this conduct endangered the men who flew with him. He was repeatedly reprimanded until finally the Poles decided to let him be a 'guest of the squadron.'" He did decline to fly with his fellow Czechs, and he was credited with shooting down seventeen German aircraft before flying off, never to be seen again. His seventeen victims put Frantisek at the head of the list of allied aces at the time of his death, and the Polish 303 Squadron did shoot down more than twice as many German planes as the average RAF fighter squadron.

Among the Germans, most of the characters—apart from those mentioned above and well known individuals such as Hitler, Göring, Rommel, Himmler, and Dönitz—are fictional. Thus, Kurt Dietrich did not exist, even though his uncle, Sepp Dietrich, was indeed the commander of the Fifth Panzer Army and a favorite of Hitler. He did in fact stretch his orders to escape the Falaise pocket in spite of his closeness to the Führer; or perhaps *because of* his closeness to Hitler, which may have given him an extra degree of freedom. Nevertheless, when senior officers asked him to inform Hitler of the desperate situation in the Falaise Pocket, he did retort that such rashness was a good way to get himself shot. Likewise, Jeschonnek really was the Luftwaffe Chief of Staff, whose concern over a relative on the *Bismarck* betrayed the battleship to the codebreakers of Bletchley Park. Incidentally, Anna's wish—that Jeschonnek never find out that his message had betrayed the *Bismarck*—came true, although not, perhaps, in the way she might have hoped. Under the crushing strain of allied air raids, he committed suicide on the night the allies bombed the rocket development station at Peёnemunde.

People are not the only problem, but also events. In this book, real people do fictional things, and fictional people do real things. For example:

— The characters in the Warsaw Post Office are fictional, but their activities are real: the Poles did intercept and open a package with the Enigma machine.

— Churchill really was First Lord of the Admiralty during the First World War, and then again before he became Prime Minister in 1940. He could hardly have intervened in Anna's security clearance, however, as she is a fictional character.

— In this novel, Kaz plays a key role in the demise of German tank commander Wittmann. This is obviously untrue, since Kaz is a fictitious character. The Polish Armored Division was, however, attached to the Canadian Army, and the Poles played an important role in closing the Falaise gap. But they were not present at Wittmann's final, fatal encounter; he was trapped by five Canadian Sherman tanks.

—Anna's role in codebreaking is exaggerated, which is scarcely surprising, as she didn't exist and therefore played no role whatsoever. To fit the story, the work on Enigma has been greatly simplified. For example, the steckerboard was introduced at a much earlier date than this novel suggests, although the Germans did begin to use it much more heavily in 1938-39, and in this sense, the account in Chapter 6 is *very* loosely consistent with the facts.

In spite of the liberties taken to simplify the Enigma story, an attempt has been made to retain the flavor of how codebreaking actually worked: the meticulous, painstaking building of one small block upon another—interspersed with flashes of insight that unlocked parts of the code, and with windfalls from German misuse of the machine or from captured equipment or codebooks

Of course, real people also do real things in this novel. For example, Marian Rejewski did figure out the internal wiring of Enigma wheels in a brief period of several months in late 1932, aided by information provided by Schmidt and passed by French Intelligence officer Bertrand. Rejewski did repeat his feat by reconstructing the wiring of the fourth and fifth wheels in a more difficult setting, an achievement that Gordon Welchman "found hard to believe." And Welchman himself was a mathematician.

The codebreakers did live with the nagging worry that the enemy would suspect that their messages were being deciphered. Observation planes were sent out, with the objective of being observed. But there were lapses. At one point, late in the war, the Allies used decryptions to sink two tenders that were scheduled to meet U-boats at obscure locations in the Indian Ocean. The Germans came to the conclusion that Allies must have known about the rendezvous points, either from a breaking of Enigma or from a traitor. Dönitz issued an emergency order. Rather than setting the rotors from their codebooks, U-boats were to use the initials of their radio operators. Unfortunately for Dönitz, this provided little protection. By then—March 1944—allied machines were so powerful and so numerous that they continued to break Shark.

The tales of the First World War are factual: the Zimmerman Telegram, which is described in fascinating detail in Barbara Tuchman's book with that title, and the story of the drunken German commander in the Middle East who sent out season's greetings in a number of different ciphers. The term "snookered santa" is, however, invented. Other codebreaking terms, such as "kisses," are not.

The story of the real Polish codebreakers after the outbreak of the war is also factual. Rejewski, Zygalski, and Rozycki did flee to Romania, where they offered their services to the British embassy, only to be rebuffed; they could come back in several days. The Poles thereupon went to the French embassy, where they were cordially welcomed. When the Germans occupied Vichy, Rejewski and Zygalski escaped to Britain—Rozycki having lost his life when his boat went down between Algeria and Vichy France, perhaps as a result of a mine. In Britain, the talents of the two survivors were in fact wasted; they were given low-level decryption tasks.

Their sad history did not end there. At the end of the war, Rejewski and Zygalski were finally promoted to the elevated rank of Lieutenant. Rejewski joined the trickle of Poles returning from Britain to Communist Poland, where he searched without success for a position teaching mathematics at a high school. Having lived in England, he was considered untrustworthy. For decades he was ignored until, in a tardy act of contrition, a Polish University offered him an honorary degree in 1978. By then, just two years before his death, he was not interested. Zygalski's story had a happier ending: he stayed in England and became a college teacher in London.

The hopeless situation of the Polish people, trapped between Hitler and Stalin, was one of the great tragedies of the war. The barbarism of Hitler is well known, particularly the horrors of his extermination camps. Perhaps less well known is the ruthlessness of Stalin. The murders at Katyn Forest may have made some sort of perverted sense, as they helped clear the way for a Communist regime in postwar Poland. But Stalin was equally ruthless with fellow Communists. As mentioned in the novel, most of the leaders of the Polish Communist Party were shot during the purges of 1938.

Wladyslaw Gomulka was a notable exception; he had the good fortune to reside in a Polish prison, thus escaping Stalin's purges. When he was released in the early months of the war, he moved from the Soviet-occupied sector of Poland to the German one. Why, is not clear. Perhaps he wanted to build a Communist resistance to Hitler; perhaps he preferred to take his chances with Hitler's storm troopers rather than his treacherous Soviet "comrade." It was only later that he came to an uneasy, unstable truce with Stalin—a truce that was scarcely reinforced by Gomulka's sad postwar observation: "The masses do not regard us as Polish Communists at all, but just as the most despicable agents of the NKVD" (an earlier incarnation of the KGB). From the Soviet viewpoint, he had misplaced loyalties; he looked on Polish Communism as a shield against Soviet imperialism. He went on, after Stalin's death in 1953, to head the Government of Poland. Soon, it was threatened by a Soviet invasion. In a tense confrontation, Gomulka stared down Nikita Khrushchev.

The list of enigma seizures by the British Navy is accurate, although not exhaustive. Some details have been embroidered. *HMS Gleaner*, under the command of Lt. Cmdr. Price, did sink the U-33, but the rest of the yarn is fictional, particularly Price's interview of the U-boat captain. Liberties have also been taken with the encounter between *HMS Petard* and U-559 in the eastern Mediterranean, although in this case, the story is closer to the truth. Three British naval men did swim to the foundering U-boat, and two of them—Fasson and Grazier—died as the submarine slipped below the waves. They were awarded the George Cross for their heroism. The Honours and Awards Committee judged that their "gallantry was up to the Victoria Cross standards," but they were not granted that highest of British awards because their heroic acts were not, as required, "in the face of the Enemy."

The stories of the bizarre characters at Bletchley Park are based on fact, except when they are interacting with fictional characters like Anna. Josh Cooper did jump up and say "Heil Hitler," returning the salute of a German pilot. Turing was an eccentric genius who wore a gas mask as protection against asthma, he did bury silver bars as a hedge against inflation, and he was said to have chained his coffee cup to a radiator. Frankly, there is reason to doubt that last story. A teacup, perhaps, but it is hard to believe that anyone would cherish a cup from which he would drink the horrid British coffee of that era.

Lt. Commander Ian Fleming did propose to ditch a captured plane near a German rescue ship in order to seize Enigma codebooks. The plan — *Operation Ruthless* — was taken seriously, in spite of Anna's skepticism, and an airworthy German plane was procured. But Anna's reservations soon turned out to be correct; after a month of preparation, the navy concluded that *Operation Ruthless* was impractical. The fictitious Anna was also right on another score. With Fleming's overcharged imagination, he had missed his calling; his talent lay in spy novels. He went on to invent 007 — James Bond.

Strangely enough, Yvonne's note — about the plan to blind submarines by training seagulls to poop on periscopes — is based on fact; the British did consider such a scheme during WWI. Wartime spawns a strange eagerness to pursue crackpot ideas, and not just for comic relief. In his book, *Roosevelt's Secret War*, Joseph Persico reports one of the "madcap schemes" of Wild Bill Donovan, the head of the Office of Strategic Services (OSS, the predecessor of the CIA). He hatched a plot to put female hormones in Hitler's food to raise his voice, make his mustache fall out, and enlarge his breasts. Quite apart from the medical implausibility — female hormones in an adult male would not cause a higher voice or the shedding of facial hair — the scheme does raise an obvious question. If you have access to the Führer's food, why not just poison him? But, according to Persico, this cockeyed caper "did not offend, but seemed to excite the President's own imagination."

Then there are parts of the story where the historical record is unclear. In the early chapters, the Poles have an Enigma machine bought on the commercial market, prior to the German adoption of the machine for their military services. This account is true, according to most of the recent sources. According to others, the Poles stole German machines just before the Second World War. This lack of agreement runs throughout the Enigma story because so much of the original record was destroyed, both accidentally and intentionally, and participants were forbidden to write about their experiences for decades, until their memories had been subjected to the tricks of time.

Likewise, it is uncertain whether the Polish Government in exile definitely knew of the massacre at Katyn forest at an early stage, although they certainly had strong suspicions. Relatives of prisoners stopped getting letters after April 1940. The Poles did raise the question of the missing officers with Stalin in December of 1941 and got the ludicrous response, that the missing men had run off to Manchuria. But there was no Kaz and no Jan; as far as I know, the government in exile had no first-hand information. There apparently was a single escapee from the massacre, but his whereabouts thereafter are vague.

By the time the thread is picked up, in April 1943, the government-in-exile undoubtedly knew what happened at Katyn. This part of the story is accurate: the Polish request for a Red Cross investigation; the simultaneous request by the Germans; and the Soviet breaking of diplomatic relations.

The simultaneous request by the Germans indicates that they somehow got information from the government-in-exile, and therefore, that somebody in the Polish offices was a spy for some country. But there is no readily available record on this point; the story of the spy is invented.

Most of the story of the Normandy invasion is accurate, with the exception of incidents involving the fictional characters, notably Kaz and Kurt Dietrich. The Poles did lead the spearhead that closed the Falaise Pocket from the North. One of their columns did get lost at a critical time because their guide misunderstood their heavily accented French, delivering them to Champeaux rather than Chambois. A Polish column was waved through a German checkpoint, apparently by a quick-thinking German soldier who decided he wanted to live. And Germans in a castle did surrender, unwilling to provoke a possibly-vindictive Polish force.

Likewise, the story of the temporary American withdrawal near St. Lô is accurate; the American Air Force constantly worried that it might bomb friendly troops. Though cautious, the American forces were not cautious enough. In spite of the withdrawal, bombs still fell on advanced units, killing over a hundred American servicemen, including Lt. Gen. Leslie J. McNair, the highest ranking American officer killed in battle during the Second World War. Unfortunately, casualties from "friendly fire" were far from uncommon. The 30th U.S. Division suffered so many losses that their commander adopted a simple rule. Whenever he was given an order to attack, he flatly refused the support of heavy bombers. And the brilliant colors on the wings of allied aircraft on D-Day — broad, bright blue stripes alternating with wide white stripes — were the opposite of camouflage. Their purpose was to announce the presence of allied aircraft, to prevent a repeat of the Sicilian invasion when numerous aircraft fell to friendly fire from the ground.

In contrast to the military operations, almost all of the messages have been made up, even where they are based closely on historical events. There are two exceptions. The report to von Kluge from the division facing St. Lô — "Not a single man is leaving his post! Not one! Because they're all dead. Dead!" — is an abbreviation of a real report. And the intercepted order to deliver Röhm "dead or alive" is the actual message. The Poles had advance warning of the Night of the Long Knives, an early demonstration of Nazi barbarism.

Likewise, almost all the dialogue is fiction. Again, there are several exceptions, where conversations might reasonably escape classification as *plasma*. Stalin's curt responses to Sikorski's queries about the prisoners at Katyn — "They have run away," and "Well, to Manchuria" — were reported in Dmitri Volkogonov's *Autopsy for an Empire*. According to Bradley, in *A Soldier's Story*, Patton did threaten to close the Falaise gap and "drive the British back into the sea for another Dunkirk."

In addition, the interchange among von Kluge, von Stülpnagel, and their associates on the evening of the attempt on the Führer's life is quite close to what actually happened that surrealistic and haunting night; it is based largely on the account by Samuel Mitcham in *Hitler's Field Marshals*. Incidentally, Graf von Stülpnagel was a patrician supporter of Hitler even before the Nazi leader came to power, but he soured on the Führer by 1944.

In light of the success of the codebreakers of Bletchley Park, an interesting puzzle arises. How did the Germans take the Allies so completely by surprise in the final December of the war, in the Battle of the Bulge?

One reason lies in the radio silence observed by German forces prior to the attack. There is also a second, less reassuring explanation. It is one thing to intercept information; it is quite another to use it. Decrypted messages pointed toward a major German counterattack in the Ardennes. Jim Rose and Alan Pryce-Jones—military advisers from Bletchley Park—flew to the Supreme Headquarters of Allied Forces in Paris in November to brief British General Kenneth Strong, Eisenhower's chief of intelligence. Rose recalled their frustrating encounter:

> Strong said, "This is the way we read it. The Germans are losing a division a day and this can't be maintained. They're bound to crack." Alan Pryce-Jones was just a major. He just sort of sat on the corner of the desk and said to Strong: "My dear sir, if you believe that you'll believe anything."

Three weeks later, the Germans launched their Ardennes offensive.

Almost without exception, I have relied on secondary sources in this novel; it is not a serious historical work. It is, however, perhaps worth noting that I did not make up the story of Patton's generals calling him "Georgie," or the tendency of his already-high voice, on occasion, to rise into the "squeaky" range. I got these anecdotes from the widow of one of Patton's generals. Sorry, Hollywood. Sorry, George C. Scott. But I did like your movie.

The accidental bombing of London by a single German plane on the night of Aug. 24-25, 1940, which led to the retaliatory attack on Berlin the next night and then to the Blitz, is based on the accounts by Sir John Keegan *(The Second World War)* and Len Deighton *(Fighter)*. One important detail has been changed. The German plane was not attacked by a Spitfire, but was simply lost. There is, however, an even more fundamental problem with this story. Respected historians do not universally agree; according to another account, the August 24 raid was by a large number of German planes, and was no accident.

This is a matter of some significance in attributing blame for one of the more ghastly practices of the Second World War—namely, the indiscriminate bombing of civilian populations—although Germany had obviously committed the first offense by attacking cities in Poland, Holland, and other countries that were in no position to return the insult. (Even earlier, German bombers had practiced their techniques on defenseless cities during the Spanish Civil War, Mussolini had bombed Ethiopia, and Japan had bombed Chinese cities.) I am inclined to go with Keegan's account, not only because I am swayed by his remarkable writing style, but because of his reputation for accuracy. Furthermore, circumstantial evidence supports the lost aircraft version. The bombing of London did not begin in earnest until Sept. 7. If Hitler had really intended to demolish London, it would have been out of character for him to wait two weeks between the initial attack of Aug. 24 and the full-scale blitz.

Bombing is a sobering illustration of how quickly the veneer of civilization can chip and crack in wartime; truth is not the only casualty. During the first months of the war, Bomber Command attacked German naval ships, including those in harbor, but avoided civilian populations. British planes flew over the heart of Germany only to drop leaflets, urging the German people to overthrow their tyrannical Führer. At least, that apparently is what the leaflets said. The facts are not altogether clear, as Harold Nicolson, a noted writer and Member of Parliament, reported in his diary. When the American correspondent, John Gunther, asked the "duds" at the Ministry of Information for the text of a leaflet, the request was refused.

> He asked why. The answer was, "We are not allowed to disclose information which might be of value to the enemy." When Gunther pointed out that two million of these leaflets had been dropped over Germany, the man blinked and said, "Yes, something must be wrong there."

In spite of their bombing of cities in Poland and Holland in 1939 and 1940, Germans also showed restraint in the initial stages of combat with Britain. On occasion, German bomber crews returned to base with their bombs if they were unable to identify a military target, and at least one German pilot was reprimanded for attacking an "unmilitary" target—a train. On the British side, Air Minister Sir Kingsley Wood was shocked by a proposal to set German forests on fire with incendiary bombs. "Are you aware," he said in disbelief, "that they are private property? Why, you will be asking me to bomb Essen next."

Then came the Blitz of London, the bombing of Coventry, and the thousand-bomber allied raids on the cities of the Ruhr—including Essen. By the final months of the war, allied bombs were raining on the beautiful, historic city of Dresden, long after it could possibly play any significant military role.

There is no good war.

And yet.... Hitler had to be stopped.

Perhaps, then, after all—and in spite of it all—it *was* a good war.

Hero's Lament

They went away, so proud before,
The sons of sorrow, off to war,
To save their honor, evermore.
    But their mothers wept

Their honor, though, could not stand true
when battle stresses seared them through.
Their honor slipp'd, when swords they drew.
    And their mothers wept.

It ended thus, the battle's roar.
The promise of the days of yore
was lost in tattered, shattered lore.
    And the mothers wept.

CPSIA information can be obtained at www.ICGtesting.com
Printed in the USA
BVOW021120150412

287719BV00004B/18/A